About the

Mark Bowsher was the last child to be born in Gravesend Hospital in 1983. The journalist there at the time was only interested in the first baby born in 1984 (where is he now, eh?). He has since moved to London to earn a few pennies making films professionally. His first three shorts won Best Short awards at festivals in the UK and the US and gained praise from the *Huffington Post* and the BFI. He's previously written for *Den of Geek*, *Cult TV Times* and Lionsgate's *Fright Club* ezine. *The Boy Who Stole Time* is his first novel but he's threatening to write more.

He is not married and does not live in Surrey but did once climb a mountain dressed as Peter Pan.

@MarkBowsherFilm

THE BOY WHO STOLE TIME

THE BOY WHO STOLE TIME

MARK BOWSHER

Dear Tiffany,

'Mγ∂hali! The Sands
of Time!'

Hope you enjoy iLL
thanks for the wondrous
'Dark Skies'—

Mark Bowsher
17/4/20
Ladywell, London

Unbound Digital

This edition first published in 2018

Unbound

6th Floor Mutual House, 70 Conduit Street, London W1S 2GF

www.unbound.com

ISBN (eBook): 978-1-912618-65-1
ISBN (Paperback): 978-1-912618-64-4

Cover design by Lyall McCarthy,
with additional work by Mecob

Printed and bound in Great Britain by Clays Ltd, Elcograf S.p.A.

MIX
Paper from
responsible sources
FSC® C018072

For Nan and Grandpa
Most people have two parents
We had more
Thank you for everything

And for Jackie Turley and Jane Bowers
Who've written more of my own
words than I ever will

Dear Reader,

The book you are holding came about in a rather different way to most others. It was funded directly by readers through a new website: Unbound.

Unbound is the creation of three writers. We started the company because we believed there had to be a better deal for both writers and readers. On the Unbound website, authors share the ideas for the books they want to write directly with readers. If enough of you support the book by pledging for it in advance, we produce a beautifully bound special subscribers' edition and distribute a regular edition and e-book wherever books are sold, in shops and online.

This new way of publishing is actually a very old idea (Samuel Johnson funded his dictionary this way). We're just using the internet to build each writer a network of patrons. Here, at the back of this book, you'll find the names of all the people who made it happen.

Publishing in this way means readers are no longer just passive consumers of the books they buy, and authors are free to write the books they really want. They get a much fairer return too – half the profits their books generate, rather than a tiny percentage of the cover price.

If you're not yet a subscriber, we hope that you'll want to join our publishing revolution and have your name listed in one of our books in the future. To get you started, here is a £5 discount on your first pledge. Just visit unbound.com, make your pledge and type KRISH18 in the promo code box when you check out.

Thank you for your support,

Dan, Justin and John
Founders, Unbound

Super Patrons

Caspar Addyman
James Agha
Ben Allen
Eli Allison
Georgiana Anstruther
Allison Bennett
Rebecca Benson
Ian Betts
Dan Bindschedler
Judy & Monte Blue
Irene Botten
Bill & Peg Botten
Jack Bowsher
Alex Bowsher
Neil Bowsher
Jenny Braham
Emma Brand
David Breheny
Peter Burns
Andy Bush
Tim Cashmore
Rebecca Claire Jackson
Rik Clarke
Gary Clarke
Mathew Clayton
Philip Connor
Tuula Costelloe
Mark Cousins
Robert Cox
Hugh David
Kelly Davies
Ben Debnam

Joe Dreier
Kirsty Fox
John Fricker
Junko Fujihara
Wayne Garvie
Erika Gerhart
Josie Healy
Emunah Herzog
Elise Histed
David Howe
Jessica Hudson
Kerensa Jennings
Alice Jolly
Dan Kieran
Nigel Knighton
Jacqui Knighton
Daniel Kutcher
David Lars Chamberlain
Charlotte Louise Murray
Patrick MacPherson
Dr Julie Magnus
Sarah Maguire
Gautam Malkani
Jake Martin
Jessica Martin
Lyall McCarthy
Aidan McQuade
Sam Melling
Adam Merten
John Mitchinson
Samantha M. P. P. Neill-Paton
Sam Nelson
Helen Nias
Georgia Odd
Kwaku Osei-Afrifa
Joelle Owusu

Scott Pack
Lev Parikian
Sheila Parry
Nasrin Parvaz
Nicola Pearcey
Sarah Pennell
Sullivan & Julius Petersen
Justin Pollard
David Puckridge
Gayle Richardson
Lucy Rowena Bradshaw
Dean Scott
Carla Sinclair
MTA Smith
David Thomas
Brian Thompson
Keith Tutt
Mark Vent
Daniel & Veronica
Patricia Walls
Julie Warren
Naomi White
Nicholas White

A note on pronunciation

If you're not sure how to pronounce any of the names or words uttered in the magical worlds in the story, there's a handy guide at the back of the book. Or just pronounce them however you like.

– MB

As the seconds, the hours,
The years, the ages march on,
Neglect not the dust left at Its feet.
Myrthali! The Sands of Time!
Take It! they say,
And reclaim that which is lost.

CHAPTER 1

THE STOLEN HOUR

It was a cold, crisp March morning, the gentle sun from the tail end of winter setting the curtains aglow, when the hour was stolen from Krish.

But of course, you can't 'steal' time. You can't borrow some from your wristwatch and give it to your alarm clock to get another half-hour in bed. Not in Krish's world anyway. A painfully ordinary world with twenty-four long, boring hours in its day, full of plenty of dull activities such as maths lessons, homework and waiting for buses. A world where the walls didn't breathe, mountains were firmly planted on the ground and magnificent birds were not born in storms of fire in the sky above. And shadows certainly didn't get up and go for a walk. At least, not until today they didn't.

Krish was awake and he was not happy about it. He was still trying to detangle his dreams from his memories of the night before. He'd gone to bed pretty late, after a boring black and white film about the kidnap of a general in Crete during the Second World War. His Dad said he should watch it to the end so he would 'learn something'. He learned that black and white films about kidnapping generals were long. He slipped off to bed while his Mum and Dad had stayed up chatting. At some point, as he lay in bed, drifting off to sleep, he'd heard his Dad downstairs starting to sound very concerned. His Mum had brushed off everything he'd said. Was this part of the dream by now? Had it been a dream at all? He'd heard Uncle Ravi's voice in the early hours and several times there'd been the sound of a car approaching then leaving the house and the front door opening and closing. His family didn't make a habit of inviting relatives over in the middle of the night or of going out joyriding in the early hours so it couldn't have been real. A rather dull sort of dream, though.

Krish yawned widely and quickly forgot about the oddly uneventful dream. He looked at his alarm clock: 7.27am. Almost an hour until he had to get up. He saw his phone next to the alarm. He often awoke early and wasted some time on the internet before he got out of bed. He stretched a tired arm out to pick up his phone. As the screen lit up he took in the time at the top: 8.27.

In a panic, Krish jumped out of bed and threw on his hockey kit. How could he forget? The clocks had gone forward overnight. His phone was attached to the internet, so it had updated itself automatically, but his alarm clock was still stuck in the past.

How dare they? thought Krish. *How dare they steal an hour from me!*

He threw open the curtains. Not a soul on the street. The sun was low but bright, the air was clear. A world of golden light, frost on the pavement, cold shadows huddled in corners. All was unnervingly still. The kind of day where curious things hide in plain sight.

Krish shivered and headed for the bathroom.

He splashed some water on his face (something he'd seen his Dad do to wake himself up when he'd overslept and was late for work). He stared at himself in the mirror. He hated seeing his own stupid face. His Aunt Nisha said he had 'puppy-dog eyes' but he thought they were blank and boring. In fact, he thought he was rather boring all over. He wasn't short, he wasn't tall. He wasn't fat, he wasn't thin. He had a little muscle from playing hockey, but not too much. His hair was short at the sides and longer on top, where he tended to use a little wax to make it stick up a bit. His Mum always said he had 'classic features', which he knew was just a slightly politer way to say 'boring'. That was who Krish was really; the polite, boring kid who people liked, but never loved (if they noticed him at all), who rarely had much to say outside of his own head.

Krish dried his face with a towel, returned to his bedroom, grabbed his hockey kit bag and headed for the kitchen. He almost ran into his Dad as he reached the bottom of the stairs.

'Dad!' he cried out. 'Why didn't you get me up? You *knew* the clocks were going forward!'

His Dad didn't seem the least bit apologetic. But he *did* seem concerned. Krish wondered what was wrong with him. His face looked heavy. He could see all the lines on his forehead more clearly than usual. He looked much older somehow.

'Krishna…' He hated it when his Dad used his full name. 'Erm…'

In the pause Krish noticed the breakfast table in the kitchen. There was Dad's bowl of cereal – which he'd usually polished off by now – sitting there, the cornflakes all soggy, and his mug of coffee full but no steam was coming off the top. Krish's cereal was in a bowl with the bottle of milk next to it, ready to be poured, and some thick white buttered toast plus a portion of blueberries and raspberries on a plate for his older sister, Joshi. There was no breakfast set out for anyone else.

'Where's Mum?' Krish demanded.

At this time of morning on the weekend she was usually bustling about the kitchen, coating lamb in salt and lemon juice or marinading chicken in yogurt, garlic, ginger, cardamom, cumin and chilli; teasing her family with all the wonderful aromas of dinner half a day too early.

'Oi! You'd better not forget the naans!' she'd call out to his Dad with a wry smile. 'You made the milk too hot last time, killed the yeast! Came out tough as old tyres!'

'Oh, well I guess *you'd* better do the naans, I'll do the chicken!' his Dad would reply with a chuckle.

Then his Mum would stare at his Dad in mock-seriousness. 'Don't threaten me with your cooking, Bhasker!' They'd both laugh. They loved going through this routine every weekend; same old jokes, same old smiles.

Right now his Dad didn't look like he'd ever smile again.

'Your mother isn't very well, Krishna.' His forehead suddenly looked even heavier somehow. 'She had to go to the hospital again in the night. Uncle Ravi came and stayed here to look after you and Joshi. He's gone now. We didn't want to wake you.'

For a moment Krish didn't know if he felt more concerned for his Mum or more annoyed that hockey would be starting in twenty minutes and he still hadn't had his cornflakes.

'What? Mum's ill again?' Krish asked. 'I thought she was getting better?'

'We all thought that, but no. She's still not very well. Not very well at all.'

The corridors of the hospital went on for ever. Turn after turn after turn. Trolley beds in the corridors, waiting rooms, vending machines, patients wandering about lost, doctors and nurses marching purposefully past them. Did this hospital never end? Every ward he peeped into he wondered for a second if he'd see his Mum's face.

And then, at last, the nurse accompanying Krish, Joshi and their Dad led them into a small room on its own at the end of a corridor. Nobody else was there. Just a woman who looked very much like his mother but less lively, lying motionless in the bed, ignoring the view of the car park through the window. Joshi's eyes widened and Krish's mouth fell open in shock at the sight of this woman who was usually so full of energy. They both tried to mask their reactions when their Mum turned to see them. She sat up. The nurse smiled politely and departed. Krish's Mum smiled too. But it took effort. Krish had never realised how hard it could be for someone to smile. It was as if there was some incredible weight on his Mum's lips.

'God! Smells worse than a dentist's in here, doesn't it?' his Mum said. She let out a small noise that was almost a laugh. There was an awful silence for a moment or two.

His parents spoke for a while but Krish didn't hear a word. He just stared at his Mum. She didn't look right in a hospital bed.

'Well you'd better be better for your birthday!' Krish said once his parents had ceased nattering. 'Seriously, you've no idea how much pocket money I've saved up to buy your present.'

His Mum attempted another smile and just about succeeded. The corners of her mouth creased upwards into a faintly warm expression. 'Pocket money *I* gave you!' she said in a weak, tired voice. It was as if she was clinging to that smile for dear life. 'I can't wait to open it. Maybe I could be very naughty and open it early! Just in case I don't have enough time. You just never have enough time, do you?'

Krish looked at his feet. The grey-white linoleum flooring, covered in scratches left by hospital beds being wheeled around, was not a pretty sight, but anything had to look better than that smile. Was the smile her attempt to distract him from the sadness in her eyes? He could swear that smile was hurting her. Holding her lips in a poor imitation of an expression that normally came to her so naturally.

Krish was staring at his trainers. His mind wandered back six months to when he first took them out of the box. A time when life for his family was so different from now...

CHAPTER 2

LAUGHTER IN BATTLE

Some six months previously, life had been rather different for Krish and his family. The rain had come and gone and people were quietly optimistic for the October half-term. After the last few weeks of torrential downpours people seemed contented with the prospect of an overcast week. But before the joys of a week off from school, pupils at Krish's school first had to contend with the horrors of parents' evening.

Krish was standing at the edge of the assembly hall with his Mum. Over the years she'd gained a few extra pounds to the top half of her body but her short legs were surprisingly slim. Her clothes were simple, graceful and usually dark with hints of colours. Her outfits often featured shimmering vine-like patterns; dark greens, purples or reds.

Her face told a story of its own. Somewhere between an owl and an eagle, his father had once said. Her hair was straight, shoulder-length and black, combed backwards allowing her no fringe. Her lips thin, her nose small and sharp. Her eyes were also small, as well as being dark and, at times, unreadable. When narrowed they could be piercing, intimidating, but she could move seamlessly from such an expression to one of loving, caring, admiring. Her face was weathered a little with age (she and her husband had decided to have children a little later in life than many, not that she always acted as old as she was). Krish's Mum had a certain majestic air about her. As if she could stand with a gale blowing in her face without blinking. Although she was rarely serious, when she was, she was not to be trifled with.

Most of the plastic chairs in the hall had been piled up into unsteady-looking towers and shoved into one corner to make way for twenty or so table-and-chair combinations where teachers passed judgement on tense pupils. Krish and his Mum were waiting for his next appointment, while watching his father deep in conversation with his maths teacher Miss Leek (his Dad had to brush off accusations of 'fancying her' from his Mum every parents' evening). Krish was worrying about his GCSE subject choices.

'You have plenty of time to decide!' his Mum said. 'You don't have to worry about that until next year!'

'But what if I choose the wrong subjects?' he said. 'All the teachers said the same thing. Like they had a script or something! *He's doing fine, blah, blah, just needs to put in a bit more effort, blah, blah!* They don't think I'm any good at anything!'

'No, Krishna, they think you're *good* at everything. So you have a choice. Pick something and work hard at that and you'll go from being good at it to being brilliant. What's your favourite subject? You love sports; what about PE?'

'Yeah but Dad said I can't be a professional hockey player; it's not realistic.'

'Your father's an accountant. Don't take careers advice from him.'

'But what if I make the wrong choice? What am I going to do with my life?'

His Mum laughed heartily and put her arm round him. 'My son is having a mid-life crisis at *exactly* the same time as my husband! Wonderful! I should be so proud!'

'What *is* a mid-life crisis?'

His Mum pointed to his Dad, who was still chatting to Miss Leek. Like his son, Krish's Dad was neither tall nor short. He had a skirt of greying black hair around his head and was bald on top (save a few wavy hairs that stuck up in the middle). His belly protruded somewhat but nothing that couldn't be hidden by keeping his shirts a little baggy. Today his Dad was wearing a horrific combination of his racing-green corduroys and a short-sleeved beige flannel shirt with a Daffy Duck tie.

'*That* is a mid-life crisis!' his Mum said. She gave Krish a warm little closed-mouth smile. 'Stop worrying! Have some faith in yourself, for God's sake! Anyway, you have plenty of time to pick your subjects. Plenty of time.'

After a brief but hopeful assessment from Mr Ilson, his geography teacher, Krish was released from the terrors of parents' evening.

'Are you all packed?' his Dad said when they got home. On Saturday morning they were off for a week's holiday in a caravan, which was essentially like being imprisoned in a small box on wheels with your family for seven days. 'And don't forget your trainers!'

'Dad, I'm not going to…' Krish started but then he noticed that his parents were smiling. They were up to something. 'What?!'

His father opened the cupboard with the ironing board and washing basket in it (somewhere Krish never looked) and produced a shoebox.

'For doing well at parents' evening,' his Dad said.

Krish opened the box eagerly. They might have been dark brown, a typically practical choice by his parents, but they were certainly better than his mud-stained white trainers that were full of holes.

'Wow, er, thanks,' he said.

'So you bought them before you even knew how well he'd done?' Joshi had just strolled into the kitchen and was being her usual sceptical self. Since going to 'uni' she'd started questioning everything, from how many carrier bags they had in the house to why they didn't have more paintings on the walls.

His parents responded to Joshi at exactly the same time.

'We knew he'd do well,' said his Mum.

'We kept the receipt,' said his Dad.

'And I hope you're packed as well, young lady!' added his Mum.

In an impressive display of multitasking, Joshi grunted in annoyance at her parents' nagging, rolled her eyes, shrugged briefly and exited the room all at once. Krish's sister was tall and slim, a little gangly. She used to spend ages straightening her hair, which was so long it reached her hips. Only on the hottest days of summer would she tie it up. Since going to university she'd decided to let it grow long and curl slightly in places. She said it felt more 'natural' and 'authentic' (the family weren't really sure what 'authentic' meant when talking about hair).

The next morning they were up at a time Krish considered horrifically early and his Dad moaned was ridiculously late.

'Come on!' said his Dad. 'Let's go to Battle!'

Battle was not an actual battle where people poked each other with swords and spears until enough people had died to decide who was in charge. Battle was a place where there had been a battle almost a thousand years ago. The Normans had decided that they should be in charge of England and the English disagreed. Many people were killed in a great battle before the Normans won and plonked their own leader on the throne. The battlefield was just around the corner from the caravan park they visited almost every half-term.

The car moved slowly with a caravan strapped to the back and what made the journey feel even slower was his father's insistence on telling him and Joshi the whole history of the battle every time they went camping.

'And do you know how King Harold died?' his Dad said to his less-than-captivated audience as they were stuck in a traffic jam.

'Er, dunno,' said Krish. 'Was he bored to death by his Dad?'

'Krishna!' his Mum said warningly. 'Come on, you might learn something!'

Krish sighed. 'I already know it! He tells us every half-term! He died with an arrow in his eye!'

'Ah!' said Joshi. 'Actually I Googled it and they actually don't know how he died. It's actually a misconception caused by the Bayeux Tapestry.' Joshi was studying the History of Art and had already banged on several times about some massive old tea towel (or that's what Krish thought it looked like) that told the story of the battle.

'Well, who cares how some stupid old king died anyway!' said their Mum. 'The point is, were *the people* happier with their new king?'

'I dunno,' said Krish. 'Were they?'

Blank looks between their parents.

'No idea,' said their Dad. 'Let's put the radio on.'

'NO!' Krish and Joshi cried out in unison. Krish's Dad twiddled the control on the radio and the words 'BBC RADIO 2' flashed up on the display. Radio 2 was the worst thing ever. It played all the dullest songs from periods of ancient history like the 1970s or the 1980s. Krish had always guessed that the music was so boring on purpose, to make sure that all the old people who listened to it would struggle to dance to it. This probably stopped lots of people having to have hip replacements and stuff.

Krish and Joshi pulled out their phones and headphones to drown out the radio with their own music.

'No!' said their Mum. 'Come on! Let's not be a divided family before we even get to the campsite!'

'Just killing time before we arrive, Mum!' said Krish.

'Let's not *kill* time,' his Mum said. 'Let's use it instead.' She produced a pack of cards. Their Mum always had a pack of cards on her. She often found an excuse for a quick game of Rummy while waiting at doctors' surgeries, airports or even bus stations. Attempting a game in the car was a new one though.

'We can't play cards in the car!' protested Krish. 'The cards'll go everywhere!'

'It'll be fine!' his Mum said, starting to deal cards to her children. Krish and Joshi just about managed not to drop their cards when the car suddenly accelerated as the traffic jam ended. 'Look, the deck can go in the cup-holder!' Their Mum placed the deck in the circular groove behind the handbrake, one end sticking up, the underside of the deck clearly visible.

'Mum!' said Joshi. 'I can see the card at the bottom of the deck!'

'Don't worry about that!' their Mum said. 'I'll have won way before you need to worry about that card!'

'But I *need* that card!' said Krish.

'Good!' their Mum said. 'Then you definitely won't win! But never mind. You're young! Plenty of time to learn to beat your old Mum!'

This was typical of his Mum. She'd start the conversation saying that people should never 'waste time' or complaining that she never had 'enough time' and then she'd finish the conversation saying everyone should 'relax' because they all had 'plenty of time'! He wished she'd make her mind up; did she have oodles of time or not a second to waste?

Whatever she really thought about time she certainly wasn't wasting any of it showing him and Joshi any mercy at cards. She spent the rest of the car journey reminding her children that she was and always would be the undefeatable champion of Rummy. Krish claimed that he kept losing because the cards he wanted had all fallen under Dad's seat.

They arrived at the campsite two hours later than his father's estimate. His Dad started to moan that if they'd left at six o'clock as *he'd* suggested then—

'Bhasker!' his Mum interjected. 'How much time did you schedule for complaining about not being up early enough to beat the traffic? Three minutes? Good! Your time started two minutes and fifty-five seconds ago.'

'But—'

'Time's up! Now let's get parked and get the bloody awning fiasco out of the way.'

They drove into Normanhurst Court campsite in Battle. They were greeted, as always, with a feast of green dotted with caravans and camper vans of all shapes and sizes. The spacious pitches sat on neatly trimmed lawns backing on to an unbroken wall of trees and shrubs that hid the site from the rest of the world. The road wound round the site, passing pitches, shower blocks, play areas and open parkland where kids played football, swing ball or catch with pink and green Velcro pads. Other kids were darting off towards the wild woods that bordered the parkland.

Once they were parked and had the caravan supports rolled down, the aforementioned 'awning fiasco' began. The awning was a sort of large tent they attached to the side of the caravan, where tables and chairs and all manner of bits and bobs that had been stored in the caravan when they were on the road were kept. Krish and Joshi took up their normal posts holding on to the metal poles used to support the far side of the awning while their Dad dished out orders. Their Mum got impatient fast.

'Stop talking about it and get the hell on with it, Bhasker! Krishna!'

'What?!' said Krish. 'I haven't done anything!'

'I know! So go and play. You're relieved from duty.'

'Erm,' said Joshi, looking up from the phone she'd been toying with in her spare hand, 'what about me?'

'You've been on your phone the whole time!' their Mum said. 'You can't go and play yet!'

'Mum,' said Joshi, 'I'm not six! I don't "go and play", and, er, neither does Krish.'

'*Er*, I can fight my own battles, *Josh*!' cut in Krish.

'*Errr*, don't call me *Josh*!' said Joshi. 'And no you can't.'

'My brave little man can stand up for himself!' said their Mum.

'*Mum!*' said Krish through gritted teeth, deeply embarrassed. 'I *could* stand up for myself if someone gave me half the chance!'

'Excuse me!' His Dad, as the self-elected commander-in-chief of awning construction, was not taking kindly to being ignored. 'Are we going to put up this awning or not?'

'A good point!' his Mum said. 'Let's not bother. Life's too short. If it rains we'll bung everything in the boot of the car. Awning class dismissed!'

Before their father could utter a single syllable of protest, the awning poles clattered to the ground as Krish and Joshi abandoned their posts.

Joshi slunk into a camping chair. She would usually stay there for the day, chatting to friends on her phone or researching an artist for her course. At school her parents were always nagging her to get her homework done but since she'd been at university she actually seemed to enjoy doing work. She couldn't get enough of it. She was always reading up on weird artists who chopped off their own ears or cut cows in two.

Krish, on the other hand, loved running off and joining in random games of football or rounders with other kids. At school he was quiet and nervous and was never good at approaching people his age he didn't already know, but at the campsite it was different. He might never see these kids again so he felt less self-conscious. And when he wasn't playing football he was joining other kids on adventures into the woods. Krish wasn't normally one for storybooks but here was different. When you really were running through forests, leaping from stepping stone to stepping stone across a brook or climbing trees, adventures were far easier to imagine.

Krish even found himself taking command of groups of kids on the campsite. Children he'd never met before followed him as he led them to 'the rocket ship'. This was a gigantic tree that had been knocked over in a great storm over thirty years ago. It lay on its side, its roots exposed, looking, Krish thought, like the fire that blasted out of the end of a rocket. They'd climb up the roots and onto the broad trunk of the mighty tree. Then they'd climb across the trunk, one foot in front of the other, and dodge imaginary meteors speeding towards them. Somehow, being out in the countryside was one of the few times Krish was really able to fire up his normally rather limited imagination.

Although Krish still took some young kids to the rocket ship, he was now feeling a little old for these games. Just after dropping the awning pole, he'd rushed over to a caravan a few pitches away where three brothers, Josh, Nathan and Zack, were playing football. He played with them for hours until his Dad re-emerged from their caravan and called out:

'Come on, Krish! Dinner!'

'Two minutes, Dad!' replied Krish. 'It's two all! One more goal and we're done!'

'You said two minutes ten minutes ago!'

'Two minutes!'

'Don't make me send for back-up!'

Krish chuckled. 'Ha! You cannot be serious!'

'I am!' his Dad said. 'I'm calling for back-up!'

'Come on, Dad!' Krish laughed. 'Not again! Not—'

'I'm coming, I'm coming!' His Mum appeared from the caravan and ran barefoot towards the game Krish was playing with the brothers, a cheeky smile on her face.

'Oh God!' said Joshi, mortified. 'Please! This is so embarrassing!'

'Back-up is here!' Their Mum invited herself to join the game. 'Look at me! I'm David Beckham!'

Krish and the three brothers burst out laughing. Zack tried to tackle Krish's Mum but she picked up the ball.

'Oh my God, Mum!' Krish managed through his laughter. 'You can't pick up the ball!'

'Yes I can!' she answered. 'I can do what I want! I'm the greatest player in the world! The only one clever enough to think of picking up the ball!' Everyone laughed hysterically at Krish's Mum as she played the silliest game of football ever seen. Everyone was laughing too much to stop her. She scored a goal and ran up to her son.

'See!' she said. 'That's how you play football!'

This was Krish's Mum all over; life was just too short to be taken too seriously.

Krish's face ached from smiling. His Mum approached, ruffled his hair affectionately and smiled in return; wider and brighter to see her son amused, almost proud of how wonderfully silly his mother could be.

⁎⁎

Right now, some six months later, sitting up in bed in the clinical surroundings of the hospital, her smile was not coming so easily. And it was not a smile of happiness. It was a valiant attempt at reassurance. Krish just didn't know what to think. How could this be the same woman? Usually so full of life and energy and humour and now here she was. A living woman with all the life drained out of her.

Krish turned back to the floor in despair. And then something caught his eye. For a moment he caught sight of a strange shape that bewildered him. Did he just see...? No. Can't have been. He blinked. Everything was normal. He was just looking at the underneath of a hospital bed. A white, scratched floor partially coated in shadow and the underside of a mattress held up by white metal slats above. Nothing unusual. It was just, for a second, he could swear he'd seen one of the shadows under the bed get up and walk away.

Outside, the gentle warmth of spring in the sun, still winter in the shade. The shadows, Krish swore, were gathering round.

As he climbed into his Dad's car with Joshi – cold, tired and sadder than he'd ever felt – he had an odd sensation that he was being watched. There was something. Something near. A dark, terrible something that was nowhere to be seen and everywhere to be felt. Cold. Not on the outside. Cold under his skin. Like ice spreading slowly, soundlessly through his veins. As if his heart would stop dead; every artery, every capillary clogged with frosted blood. Silent terror infecting every corner of his body and—

There!

His head darted to one side. The large blue wheelie bin, overflowing with burger wrappers and carrier bags. There had been a cruel smile. Somewhere in the darkness a small patch of yellowy light had appeared. A crescent shape. Like mean, rancid teeth framed by unseen lips, cracking into a mocking grin. But that smile, that malevolent expression was not attached to any body he could see. It just hung there in the...

... shadow...

No. There was no shadow. He couldn't have seen the shadow the smile hid within. Because it wasn't there. He must have imagined it. There was no shadow.

CHAPTER 3

THE SHADOW TALKS

There was no house. No shop. No pub, no block of flats, no lamppost, no chimneys. Not a plane, not a bird, not a wisp of cloud in the sky. So what was it between the sun and the corner by the big, blue bin that had cast that shadow?

A blink and it had gone. The sky was clear, the sun was low. There was nowhere to hide. Where had it gone? That crouched patch of darkness. Crouched? Yes, it had been crouching. The thing that could not have been there.

Nobody said a word in the car on the way back from the hospital. He could see it in both his father's and his sister's expressions – they too had that image of his Mum looking so ill, so out of place in a hospital bed, burned into their minds. She just didn't look right and they were all praying that they would get to see her anywhere else soon. Krish stared out of the window at the blur of the streets as they whizzed by, counting shadows.

Krish was experiencing guilt for feeling it but he was just so irritated that he'd missed hockey. He lived for hockey. He'd waited all week and now he'd missed it. He'd have to wait a whole week until he could play again! Was he a terrible person for becoming cross with his Mum for being ill and making him miss playing his favourite sport?

The irritation he felt at missing hockey managed to keep the other things floating around his mind at bay. For a time at least. He couldn't have imagined it. The shadow. He *couldn't* have. He had no imagination. Or at least that's what his friends always said.

Most of his friends at school were geeks. He wasn't the most confident of boys so he'd ended up hanging around with the quiet, nerdy kids like Jess, who was always found with her nose in a book. She didn't understand the excitement, the rush you got from playing

17

sports. And the people he knew who *did* understand the thrill of hockey were the players on his team, who only ever talked about TV shows (usually soaps he didn't watch, with some 'well fit' girl in them). No wonder Krish was described by most teachers, aunts, uncles and everybody who knew him as 'quiet' and 'shy'. He just didn't know what to say to anybody and rarely had much to say anyway.

Krish was at that awkward age when he didn't know what interested him in life outside of sports, and all his geeky mates cared about were stories. Stories of adventure, mainly. Stories of jungles and stories of deserts and oceans and of submarines and knights and dragons and spies and pirates and all sorts. Stories in films, on TV and in books. None of it was real; what was the point?

'You just have no imagination!' Jess would say, after going on about the latest chapter of the book she had been reading for the whole of morning break.

'I *do* have an imagination!' he'd reply, trying to imagine what an imagination actually was. 'I just don't care about some stupid wizard or something!'

'She's *not* a wizard! She's-an-orphan-in-Vienna-living-in-the-library-because-she-accidentally-burned-down-the-orphanage-when-she-tried-to-steal-a-candle-to-read-her-favourite-book-and-all-the-other-orphans-hate-her-for-burning-down-their-home-so-now-she-pretends-to-be-an-adult-because-also-they-always-bul-lied-her-for-looking-older-than-she-was-and-she's-found-a-book-full-of-pictures-of-master-criminals-and-she's-trying-to-stop-a-witch-from-stealing-it-because-they're-the-only-pictures-of-these-particular-master-criminals-which-the-witch-is-going-to-use-to-bring-them-back-to-life-because-there's-a-plot—'

'God! Do your sentences ever end?' said Krish at last.

'No. But this book does. Which is a shame. Because I love it! You should read it.'

'But you're not an orphan! And you don't live, like, whenever they had candles. *And* you don't live in a library! You don't even live in Venice.'

'Vienna! Wouldn't it be great to live in a library in Vienna?'

Krish sighed. *Stories.* Why should he care? Exciting things only ever happened to exciting people.

'Well now!' his Dad said that evening, clapping his hands together and forcing a big smile onto his face. 'How about we just get takeaway, eh? Chinese! Better than my cooking, eh?'

'Dad,' chipped in Joshi, laughing along with their Dad, 'you'd burn breakfast cereal! Aaah! Can I get lemon chicken?'

'You know Mum's still in the hospital?' His Dad and Joshi turned to him.

'There's not much we can do right now, Krishna.' His Dad's tone was grave again.

'Dad's just trying to cheer us up, Krish!' added Joshi.

Krish knew she was right but he just couldn't stand it. He hated them acting as if nothing was going on and he hated thinking about what was happening to his Mum even more. He stormed out of the house. Unfortunately all the sad thoughts that had been infesting his brain for the last few hours came with him. And there was something else that accompanied him. Something he saw but did not want to see. A patch of dark. Nothing but a space where light should be.

✹

Time.

That's what his Mum had said in the hospital: *You just never have enough time.* Krish had always thought he *did* have plenty of time. Long Christmas and Easter breaks. Half-terms. Long summer afternoons playing football with his friends on the green by Dawson's house after school, using their jumpers for goalposts. And the summer holidays themselves, which stretched on for six whole, glorious weeks.

Now all of a sudden he'd lost an hour, missed hockey and he had no idea whether his Mum had months, weeks or days left to live. He'd never thought she'd live for ever, but he hadn't thought about her dying either. Not anytime soon, anyway. And he could just see the next week being full of school, trips to the hospital, Uncle Ravi and Aunt Nisha popping round every other day to see if they were all okay, Joshi telling him to concentrate on his homework to distract him and trying to talk to him about his subject choices for next year, and suddenly he saw his week getting swallowed up with no time to see his friends or play hockey, and what if he *did* make the wrong choices for his subjects and then he'd study the wrong thing at university as well and end up as an accountant in a flannel shirt with a Daffy Duck tie and his mind was going at a hundred miles an hour and why was he wasting time trying to match three fruit on some stupid game on his phone when he should be doing something, *anything?*

Krish threw his phone down. He was sitting on the ground in the alley between the old swimming pool and the long wall that led to the park full of rusty old swings and slides. He'd been sitting there for the best part of an hour, thinking over the events of the day, ignoring texts from his Dad and his sister saying that he'd better be back soon or the takeaway would beat him home. He wished so much that he could give his Mum more time somehow. He didn't know what she'd do with it (go to lots of National Trust houses and read more books, he supposed), but she wasn't an old woman; surely she was too young to run out of time right now. He needed more time so badly.

'Oh, how happy those delicious words of yers makes I feel, little 'un!'

The words slithered out of nowhere. A croaky, oily voice that came from no lips he could see anywhere around him.

'I... didn't say anything...' said Krish.

'*Time... time... Wish I had more time!* Tha's what yer said, didn't yer, boy?' That foul voice again. 'Yer don't need to open up those pretty lips of yers for what yer thinkin' to be clear f'rall to hear, do yer?'

It was coming from the grubby grey-blue wall opposite. The bricks were covered in scratches, flecks of paint and scribbles upon scribbles of graffiti. There was a large patch of black. Like damp. Like... a shadow. Like *the* shadow. A huge, hunched creature staring over at him from the expanse of darkness on the wall. Its yellowy smile... those teeth. Ice began to spread through his veins once more.

Splodges of yellow spray paint were its cruel eyes, the scratches on the wall were marks on its bent-over body. The creature looked like it was entirely composed of jagged, burnt wood. Lumps of charcoal all glued together. It wore a long, tattered robe the same colour as its skin, slashed and stained, great tears all over it. Round its neck was a long chain of faded gold; a heavy-looking gold vessel encrusted with rubies hung from it, only just visible between the rips in its robe. The gold vessel was the only thing anywhere near clean on the creature's person.

Those eyes chilled him to the bone, not least because this enormous creature seemed to know his every thought.

'Yer want to know how yer can get more time?' A feast of grim, rancid teeth, almost all of them broken or misshapen. They were either murky green, dirty yellow or black in colour. 'I'll tell yer a tale if yer wanna listen?'

Krish looked away from the hideous thing. It wasn't there. It couldn't be real.

'I's still here…' came that oily voice after a moment or two, and suddenly Krish was aware that the creature was not a huge beast over by the wall but a much smaller being, crouching very close to him indeed. He shuddered and felt himself shift away from the disgusting thing before him. He could see all the grooves in its charcoal-like skin.

'Don't wanna talk to I?' it said.

Krish stood and turned away from the creature.

'No,' he said, remaining calm because why shouldn't he. He was in an alley, all alone apart from his tired mind.

'Why don't yer wanna talk to I?' said the thing that was not there.

Krish stood there for a moment, unmoving, wondering how mad he must look talking out loud to himself.

'Because I don't talk to figments of my imagination,' he said, accidentally glancing over his shoulder and catching a glimpse of the creature he didn't believe was there.

'If I's a figment of yer imagination what's the harm in talking to I?'

Krish watched his feet not moving. He had thought about time all day and he couldn't deny that the idea of having more of it was tempting. But still… what was this thing? What business was it of this creature? He'd done it again. He'd glanced at it over his shoulder.

'Maybe you're a part of my imagination I don't wanna talk to!' Krish spat out.

'Well if *you're* talkin' to yerself then *I*'s gonna talk to I-self too!' It dragged towards itself an empty fruit box that had been left next to the bins and sat on top of it. 'Hello, imagination! How is you today? I is fine, thank you very much for askin', m'dear!'

How did it move that box? If it didn't exist, how did that box... he had turned. He wasn't glancing over his shoulder any more. He'd physically turned round to look at it, hardly able to hide his interest in this strange being. Why was he so fascinated by it? It was barely human; how could it exist? It wasn't real, but there it was and he couldn't take his eyes off it.

'Yer wants to know, don't yer...?' it said, looking up at him with fierce old eyes and hungry lips.

'No,' Krish said. 'I... I really don't—'

It put a knobbly finger to its cracked, swollen lips. 'Hush yer silly mouth! I hears yer mind doin' the talkin'!'

It was in his mind. Crawling around, seeing, hearing, feeling his thoughts. He had never felt more trapped than in that moment, knowing that even if he left that horrid creature would still be there; prowling amongst his deepest, darkest thoughts. It knew he wanted to listen to every word it said. Besides, he knew you mustn't judge anybody (or anything, for that matter) by their appearance.

'Yer know that there's a thing, a real thing that is time?'

'What?!'

'Time! Is a real thing!'

'Well of course it's real!' Krish let out a little chuckle infused with sarcasm. 'I mean, I get that time's a thing! In clocks and stuff and—'

The creature shook his head. 'No, no, no! Not just a thing yer *knows*. A thing yer can touch! Yer can feel! Yer can hold in yer hand!'

Krish couldn't picture what this repulsive being was talking about.

'A thing yer can own!' it continued. 'A thing out there to be found... Yer wants more time? Time for you? Time for yer precious mumma? It's out there!'

Krish was struggling to hide his intrigue. He said nothing. He tried to maintain his stubborn expression and not allow the creature to detect just how interested he was becoming.

'Yes… yeeesss! Time is real! Yer feels yer don't have enough time? Well now yer knows it – there's plenty more out there to be had!'

Krish shook his head. 'This is the most ridiculous thing I've ever—'

'Yer mind says somethin' different to yer words, boy! Yer wants to know more! Time! It's real and it has a name…'

Krish was listening.

'Myrthali! The Sands of Time! The dust the ages leave in their wake!'

'Oh, really!' Krish gave sarcasm another go. 'So it's what? Like some kind of time energy bar thing?'

The creature laughed slowly, a true menace in its cackles.

'Not bad, boy! Not bad! Myrthali truly is a substance. Believe I! Is a powder yer take. Boil a little up on a teaspoon with milk and liquorice and yer'll be livin' for another four years! And some's got a lot more than a teaspoonful, I can tell yer…'

Krish shook his head. 'That's not true. Time isn't some powder, some medicine! They would have mentioned it in science at school or something!' He knew it was a stupid thing to say before he'd even finished saying it.

With a brief growl the creature stuck out its tongue and made a small gesture as if it was swatting a fly in front of its face. 'Them teachers don't know nuffin!'

'They know that "I don't know nothing" really means "I *do* know something".'

'Yes! And I knows somethin'! It is true time is not a medicine but it is a real thing. A real thing in short supply. Let me tell yer…'

Krish couldn't lie, there was no point. He couldn't say he didn't want to hear because he did. So badly. So he listened to the creature's tale.

CHAPTER 4

THE HARVEST OF TIME

This is the story the creature told and soon Krish, even with his distinct lack of imagination, would have good reason to believe that every word of it was true:

Somewhere out there, there were other worlds. Worlds full of people and animals and skies and rivers and mountains; full of hopes and fears, hates and desires, cities and streams and queens and kings and beasts and all sorts. Worlds just like ours but at the same time altogether different.

In one world was the city of Bahrtakrit. Bahrtakrit was at the edge of a mighty desert, halfway down a canyon, suspended by ropes and canvases tied to the opposing rock faces. The people lived simple contented lives in the warm sunshine until the reign of the Empress Benhu'in.

The Empress Benhu'in was a beautiful woman of silky smooth olive skin, with long cascading curls of pitch-black hair reaching all the way down to her hips. But she was a cruel woman. She treated her children harshly, was unforgiving of any mistakes committed by her handmaids and was spiteful towards the pretty young noblewomen milling about her court.

The Empress feared nothing more than growing old and grey, so she forced all of the most skilled physicians and magicians of Bahrtakrit to come up with a solution to keep her looking youthful forevermore. And so they did. They coated a fragment of helmstone, a jewel of deepest purple, in crushed leaves from an evergreen tree that grew in the eastern valleys mixed together with the blood of a newborn child, and hung it above the Empress's bed.

The helmstone channelled the youth of the people into the Empress. For 999 years babies were born old and shrivelled, their first hairs grey, and they stayed old and decrepit throughout their miserable lives while the Empress remained young and beautiful, the helmstone glowing over her bed of silken sheets. She saw all the gorgeous noblewomen she had once envied grow old and withered and die. Even her own children were now no more than dust. She cared not. She would outlive the stars themselves and be twice as beautiful.

But as the light of the sun ebbed over the land on the dawn of the first day of the thousandth year, the people of Bahrtakrit awoke to find themselves restored to their proper ages. No more children were born old and wrinkled. No one alive at that time had ever seen young skin before, except on the Empress Benhu'in, who now found she had a single grey hair among the black and one wrinkle on her soft olive skin.

With a furious scream she smashed her mirror and demanded that all others in the palace be destroyed as well. The physicians and magicians were locked in a room for nineteen days with nothing more than a hunk of stale bread and a goblet of sour wine (which the Empress had spat out in disgust at a banquet three nights before) until they found another solution.

The physicians and magicians realised that they couldn't keep her young for ever unless they somehow gave her more time. They hatched a plan to harvest time itself, grind it up and turn it into a draught which the Empress could swallow in one gulp.

The physicians and magicians knocked on the door and the Empress let them out and within hours the harvest began.

Time, of course, was not really a crop (like the ones the people of Bahrtakrit grew in woven baskets hanging over the sides of the city) so the physicians and magicians proposed to rid the city of time altogether by gathering up all time-keeping devices and grinding them into a powder.

A battalion of the Empress Benhu'in's most loyal guards tore through the city, seizing every clock, sundial, hourglass and egg timer they could lay their hands on. Each device was then ground into a fine powder and a quantity of the powder was left to boil in a large vat of milk and liquorice for seven whole days.

The potion was prepared and the Empress took her finest golden goblet and drank a generous draught. Immediately after, a streak of grey ran down a second hair and the physicians and magicians found themselves locked up again, this time with only a crust of mouldy bread and a thimbleful of steam. They knew something was missing from their time potion. But what? Kalrika Mavalrh, the oldest of the physicians, spoke of a herb she knew of that only grew in the shadow of a large sundial at the highest point of the north side of the canyon.

The physicians and magicians rapped on the door, the Empress let them out and they sped past her to the north canyon. The herb, oorarka (meaning 'the shadow plant'), had barely survived in the unseasonably hot summer but one single specimen was left. The ancient Kalrika Mavalrh picked the herb, ran down into the city, crushed it with her bare hands, mixed it into the dust of time and dropped a quantity of the dust into a bubbling pot of milk and liquorice.

The concoction was brewed again, this time for fourteen days, while the Empress paced her room impatiently.

Finally, it was ready.

The Empress Benhu'in took the potion and waited. She felt no different. And then she watched as the grey hairs faded to black, and she rubbed that accursed wrinkle for a few moments until her skin was silky smooth once more.

The Empress Benhu'in was overjoyed, but her happiness would not last long. She immediately threw the physicians and magicians to their deaths at the bottom of the canyon (all except Mavalrh, whom she kept alive against her will, forcing the potion of time she made her brew down the ancient physician's throat), and she cut out the tongues of any soul who breathed a word of the secret recipe so only she and Mavalrh knew it.

But somehow there were people who knew about her concoction. Thieves appeared almost on a daily basis to try and steal the powdered time which she kept in her bedchamber at the centre of her palace. Some looked like no kind of person she or indeed anyone in Bahrtakrit had ever encountered before, with clothes and skin colours no one had seen anywhere in the whole world.

But their 'world' was not our world. It was a different world and there are many more worlds out there other than the Empress Benhu'in's and ours.

The Harvest of Time was a unique event in all of existence and this caused holes to be ripped between worlds. People were coming from many different worlds to steal what the Empress called her 'Myrthali' (meaning 'The Sands of Time' in ancient Bahrtakri) and these 'time thieves' had gathered an army to force their way into the Empress's palace.

The Empress's guards encircled the palace and were instructed never to lower their swords morning, noon or night. For decades the Empress and her household were trapped within the palace. Eventually the Empress grew sick of living in hiding and came out onto the battlements to goad the time thieves. The time thieves who had not been slain or died of old age grew restless and rushed towards the guards. Most were slaughtered within seconds but a handful evaded the guards and made their way into the palace.

There was only one time thief, Evia, who had fought her way through a hundred thousand worlds to reach Bahrtakrit, who made it into the Empress's bedchamber alive. Evia found the Empress clutching the final sack of her Myrthali. She threatened the Empress with her blade but she would not let go. Evia tore the sack from the Empress's grasp and disappeared, never to be seen again. As for the Empress, the moment the sack left her grip she fell to the floor and breathed no more.

In the chaos that ensued the palace was set on fire and burned to the ground. The body of the Empress was dragged from the flames by her most loyal handmaid, Viona, who had always respected her mistress, despite her cruel, spiteful nature.

The corpse of the Empress was displayed in a glass case on a raised dais at the centre of the city of Bahrtakrit. Some saw it as a mark of respect to the city's longest-serving ruler, others as a warning to all not to meddle with time.

Only a handful of people in Bahrtakrit had information on the current whereabouts of the final sack of Myrthali. They called themselves 'the Council of the Few' and met in secret once a month, each remaining hooded throughout their discussions. The rips which had first led to their world had healed themselves but there were tales of others. Evia, it was believed, no longer had the Myrthali, which had been split and distributed to the highest bidders and transported to a multitude of worlds. The gateways between these worlds were now more complex, more difficult to locate. But still there were tales, rumours of where quantities of the Myrthali now resided, or so the leader of the Council of the Few stated. Their leader was a young woman who claimed to be the heir to the Empress's throne and who vowed to search a thousand million worlds to claim what was rightfully hers. And soon the Council of the Few gave her enough information to start her quest. Shortly afterwards she left Bahrtakrit, never to return, and, so the tale goes, is still searching for the Empress's Myrthali.

As for the Empress herself, she got her wish. To this day her body lies in the glass case at the centre of the city, remaining young and beautiful for all time.

CHAPTER 5

THE DEVIL'S PROPOSAL

'I don't believe it,' said Krish.

'But yer listened to it,' said the creature. 'Start to finish.'

'Yeah, well…' Krish struggled to explain why he hadn't just got up and walked away. He wasn't sure himself. He didn't believe it. Of course he didn't. But he couldn't deny that he *wanted* to believe it. 'It's just…' He was trying to think of a nice, big, juicy word that would make him sound smart. 'Implausible!'

The creature turned up one side of its upper lip in semi-disgusted puzzlement. 'What?!'

'Your story. It's *utterly implausible!*' 'Utterly' was a fairly sizeable word as well, thought Krish. He was feeling rather pleased with himself. 'Completely ridiculous! "On the dawn of the thousandth day" and all that rubbish! Really?! On *exactly* the thousandth day? And, and Evia going to like a thousand million billion worlds! It's not possible! And the oo…whatever – that herb, plant, thing… it was the last one there? Just *happened* to be the *only* one left?'

The creature squinted at Krish with one eye, trying to figure something out about the boy. 'Magic worlds and Myrthali you is fine with… but it's the silly little details that yer don't believe…?'

'Oh! I don't believe a single thing you've said! But it's the little details that just prove it's absolute rubbish! It's just all too convenient.'

'Stories, boy! Stories! Little details aren't important. The big things, the important things – them happened! The Harvest o' Time and the big stuff I told yer all happened. Don't matter how. Stories is stories. I can't prove nuffin'. But yer can see for yerself…'

Those nasty yellow eyes pierced him with their eagerness, their hunger. The look of a starving person outlining where the two of them might find a feast to fill their bellies to bursting point.

'I hears yer,' the creature tapped the side of its head and Krish was surprised that lumps of charred, blackened wood didn't fall off of its moistureless skin. 'Up here! Yer can't deny it. Yer listened. Yer stayed and listened. Yer remembered the names...'

If the creature before Krish wasn't crawling through his subconscious anyway, he realised that he had indeed already given himself away. He'd mentioned Evia's name, so he'd clearly listened to the story closely.

'Well, it's not even a complete story!' Krish spat out. 'What happened to Evia and Viola?' He deliberately got Viona's name wrong. 'And – and what about the heir? The story doesn't even give any hint about who...'

Krish stared at the creature. That hunched bag of bones in its tattered robe. It watched, waiting for the precise moment when the realisation hit Krish. When it did, the creature nodded.

'You?' said Krish. 'You're the heir to the Empress's throne?'

The creature smiled. It took a little bow.

'So, you must have found *some* Myrthali?' asked Krish.

The creature nodded. 'Some. Not all.'

Krish gave up pretending not to care. His head was swimming with too many questions to keep them in any more. 'But why did the Empress leave it to you? And why did you leave if you were going to be Empress? And what happened to—?'

'Thought yer weren't interested in stories, boy? Didn't believe 'em?'

Krish ignored the creature's question; something else was confusing him. Another detail about the heir returned to him from the story 'You are... a woman?'

'Not all girls is pretty dresses and flowers and such, young 'un.'

The creature looked different now. It was still stooped, gnarled and haggard, but suddenly Krish could recognise something in those yellowy eyes set into its charcoal-like skin. It wasn't that it looked more like a man but rather that it didn't really look much like a human being at all. He could see her eyes clearly now. Eyes that hid something familiar.

'I is what I is but they once called me "she" and "her" but I is nuffin' to nobody now.'

'Which means you're something to somebody.'

She winced for a moment and then hissed at him, 'Does I look like anybody has cared or loved I in a thousand years?'

'I don't know what a thousand years feels like.'

'But yer wants to, don't yer?'

Krish pondered the notion. It scared him. The idea of being that old. Old like her. The devil before his eyes. How could he trust that creature? That disgusting thing? He shouldn't judge by appearances – but those eyes. Those horrible, rotten yellow eyes. The devil repulsed him. Yes. She was a devil. Not '*The* Devil'. The one with the horns and the fiery red skin you saw in films and cartoons. But something like that. Something hateful and cruel beyond belief.

'You are wise to judge I for I is a devil.' She was in his mind again. 'But I is mendin' my ways. I *am* hateful, but not cruel. Cruel I would be not to offer this gift to you. Time can be yours. Yours and whoever yer shares it with. I promises yer.'

Krish did want it. Not all of it. He wouldn't know what to do with all that time. But he could have some. Just a little. Just to try. And the rest his Mum could have. What she'd do with it he had no idea. He didn't care. She could spend as much time reading and gardening and visiting old houses in the country as she wanted. Surely it would be better than hardly having any time at all. And his friends. Jess and Dawson would certainly find uses for a little more time. Maybe. Just a little. He wouldn't allow them too much. Maybe too much time would make them lazy. Yes. Dawson (named after his Mum's favourite TV show, apparently) would just waste it playing on his PlayStation anyway. *It would make me lazy too*, he thought. Maybe he could stay young and play hockey for the rest of his life but then… would he become sick of that? What *would* he do with all that time? He'd have time to think about what he wanted to do. All the time he could want.

'You is burning time dreaming of what yer'd do with more of it!' said the devil.

Krish thought of something that unsettled him.

'Why me? Why don't you go and steal it yourself?'

The devil hesitated. 'I would.' She scratched her bare, scarred head, flakes of skin flying off in the process. 'But I haven't the strength. I is too old now. A thousand years ago maybe… But I've settled here now. Won't be journeyin' to other worlds again.'

'You've *actually* lived over a thousand years?'

She spat and made that dismissive gesture with her hand again. '*Over a thousand years?!* Much older! *Much!* I fell asleep for three thousand years once! Is nuffin'!'

'Maybe you've had too much time.' There was a little quiver in his voice as the last of these words left his lips but the beast did not appear perturbed. For a moment he thought her silence suggested that she agreed (to an extent) but then she shook her head. Krish was hesitant to say another word but he felt more uncomfortable not speaking with that thing in his head. Hearing her hoarse, croaky voice saying what was on his mind made him shiver all over.

'So…' Krish felt he was clawing around in his own head, trying to stitch a few words together, words that made sense of the bizarre situation he found himself in. 'You know how to get into these other worlds? Where the Myrthali is?'

She nodded with a gleeful grin.

'And you just…' He didn't want to sound stupid. 'Step into these worlds…?'

The devil let out a rasping groan, waving her hands about in disgust. 'Yer not listenin' to I! It were too easy las' time! Is like all the worlds knows it weren't right! It weren't right jus' walkin' into a new world to steal time itself! No! This time they is hidden. Secret places with secret rituals to let yer through.'

Krish was imagining some weird scene he'd seen in an old film his Dad had watched once, which he'd seen through the partially open door, while he sat at the bottom of the stairs when he was much younger. Silently – trying not to breathe, his parents thinking he was tucked up in bed fast asleep – he had watched fifteen minutes of that film and had seen a man get chained up by another man and have his beating heart pulled out while deranged worshippers all around chanted as if they were possessed.

'Gah!' interrupted the devil. 'Nuffin' like that! Stupidy stupid boy! Just simple things. But unusual things. Combinations o' stuff that peoples never does unless they is told to. I has lived long. I has searched. I has experimented. I knows. But I is too old now. Someone else must go.'

Suddenly it struck Krish. What this was all about.

'You want me to go instead of you! To bring back Myrthali for you!'

The devil jumped about with joy, giggling madly.

'Yes! Yes! Yes! Course! Wha's yer thinkin' I be askin'? Is a bargain, see? Half for you, half not for you. For I!'

'But my Mum—'

'Yer shares yer half with her. *Your* half becomes *your* quarter and her quarter. Tha's deal.' A few more giggles escaped her mouth.

He wasn't sure he really wanted any Myrthali for himself any more. Or not much anyway.

'What yer does with it's your choice,' the devil answered. 'But yer'll try some. Believe me. Yer won't let yerself *not* try some.'

'You...' Krish began, cautiously, 'have a map...?'

A full-bellied laugh. The devil rolled back and forth, clutching her stomach. 'Yer plots to steal it from I! H-ha! No such luck!' She rolled back onto her feet and scurried up to Krish, shoving her face in his, closer than she'd ever been to him before. 'Yer wants map? Take it!' Her breath was as foul as milk left out in a hot room for days. 'Here's map!' She was poking her own forehead. 'Take it! Take it away! Jus' yer try!' She resumed her little routine of rolling about and laughing.

Krish had had enough. What was he doing here? Why was he listening to this thing? It can't be real. It can't be! He ran. He couldn't see the devil now. It was... it *had* been behind him. But it wasn't there. He was sure that if he looked back now it wouldn't be there. The laughing must be the other kids in the playground.

'Yer wants map?! Yer can have it! I shares it with yer! And I shares the Myrthali with yer! Half for you, half for I!'

Those kids say the weirdest things, thought Krish, not looking back.

CHAPTER 6

BETWEEN THE SUN & THE MOON

The thing with the devil, it didn't happen.

Krish thought about the thing that didn't happen every day from then on. He thought about it at school, when he saw the face of the devil he'd definitely never met in the corner of the whiteboard. When he was playing hockey, its eye in the ball as he hit it as hard as he could. And over his Mum's bed in hospital. That crooked, sinister smile; grinning with so much vile vigour over his mother's weak, tired lips that struggled to curve upwards.

No. It *didn't* happen. And he definitely hadn't searched 'weird devil real' and found lots of quite disturbing websites that would have made his Mum raise an eyebrow if she'd caught him looking at them. Absolutely not. The devil did not exist. She had never been here. He'd never spoken to her in the alley by the swimming pool and those were not her foul, yellow eyes staring at him from the shadows under his bed.

For a day he managed to rid his head of all of thoughts of devils and Myrthali.

His Dad dropped him at his friend Dawson's house before driving straight back to the hospital. Krish didn't mention his Mum to Dawson and Dawson was too preoccupied with talking about a new PlayStation game his older brother had where you stole cars and got into fights. Dawson's Dad had said Dawson was too young to play it. Dawson was probably Krish's best friend (and perhaps the only one who didn't really care much about books and films and TV shows).

They sat in silence almost the whole time as they played a Formula One racing game. They usually said very little, just a few whoops, gasps and cheers as they sped round corners of the race track on the TV, but today it was only Dawson who whooped, gasped and cheered. And he spent too much time staring over at his Dad, waiting for him to disappear for an hour and do the shopping so they could play the stealing and fighting game, but he never left so Dawson didn't really notice how quiet his friend was. Krish just sat there feeling he was wasting time as his car made last place again.

Later he visited Jess, who spent ages talking about the book she'd started two days ago and had already finished. She insisted Krish borrow it. He took the book reluctantly and asked if it was going to be made into a film. Jess said that not all books get made into films and that it could never be as good as the book anyway so he gave up being part of the conversation and let her talk.

'You're quiet,' said Jess. At least she's noticed, thought Krish.

'Am I?' he answered.

'Yeah.' Then she remembered another book by the same author and got excited because she'd seen it on the bookcase at Krish's house. Krish said he hadn't noticed it; they were his parents' books.

'Oh. Cool,' said Jess. 'Don't suppose your parents would, like, lend it to me or something…? I wouldn't let it get damaged or anything.'

'It's Mum's…' Krish couldn't find the words for a moment. 'I'll ask her.'

Krish wanted to tell Jess about his Mum. He had wanted to tell Dawson too. He just didn't know what to say. He didn't even really understand what was happening to his Mum, but he just knew he wanted to talk to somebody. He wanted to talk about the devil as well, but he knew nobody would ever believe him. He hardly believed it himself.

In the end all he said to Jess was that he had to go.

'Pop by later if you want,' said Jess. 'Mum can't be bothered to cook tonight so she's getting pizza. There's always too much. She gets tons of sides so there'll be, like, loads.'

Krish said he would if he had time.

All of a sudden, it had been a week. Where had the time gone? He had burned it. He realised he was using the devil's words. Yes, he'd burned time. Time was a physical thing to the devil. Not just an idea that somebody someday long ago had thought up and poured into watches and alarm clocks and the timer on his cooker. Time was something he could touch, something he could hold. Something he could boil up with milk and liquorice or whatever it was the devil had said.

"Tha's right,' her sly, oily voice came to him at the dinner table as he stared into space while Dad did the washing up. 'Milk and liquorice! Yummy yumsk! Yer gotta taste it! Yer wanna taste it...?'

He couldn't lie to it. To her.

'Yes,' he whispered. His Dad didn't hear. A smile appeared in the shadows between the fridge and the washing machine in the corner of the kitchen.

'Yer *gonna* taste it...?'

'Yes.'

'Yer gonna see her live? She her smile properly again?'

'Yes.'

The devil tiptoed forward. Her lean body, like lumps of burnt, blackened wood all clumped together under her tattered robe, came briefly into the light then quickly skipped back into the safety of the darkness in the hallway. 'Come with I...'

Krish followed.

The devil moved soundlessly into Krish's bedroom, not bothering to turn on the light. A streetlight outside the window provided just enough illumination for them to navigate the room. The radiator under the window was on and drying his socks and T-shirt from the other day when he'd got caught in the rain. The world outside was hidden from view by condensation. The devil rubbed the glass with her hand to create a clear, moisture-strewn patch in the misty pane. She jabbed at the patch in the glass, her charred wood-like fingertips at the end of her bony fingers making no marks on the glass.

'There! Theeeere!' came the devil's hoarse whisper.

Krish could barely see a thing through the glare of the streetlight. A few rooftops, a couple of bent old TV aerials and there, faintly in the distance, a dark bump on the landscape.

'Brandhurst Hill...?' said Krish.

The devil nodded. 'That be it. That be where yer goin'.'

'So,' said Krish with a sigh. 'What do I wear? What do I take? What do I even do when I get... wherever I'm going...?'

'Can't take nuffin' but yer wits!' Krish wondered how much use they would be. 'Anythin' other than the clothes yer wear'll turn to dust! Can't bring nuffin' back neither. 'Cept the Myrthali.'

'Nothing?'

The devil grumbled something to herself, turning her face away from Krish for a moment.

'What did you say?' said Krish, getting impatient.

'Nuffin'!' spat out the devil. 'Can't bring nuffin' back! 'Tis a pity, though.'

'Well how do I dress?'

The devil pondered this. 'It be hot but none of them little trousies. Yer'll not look right. Long sleevies, long trousies, thin jacket. Yer'll look right and not be too warm.'

'And when I—?'

'When yer get there yer find yer way to the palace of the King. He got Myrthali.'

'And how am I meant to get the Myrthali off him?'

The devil struggled to find the words. 'I... I... Yer'll find a way.'

'That's it?! I'll find a way?'

'Many has tried. Yer gotta be cunning! Take yer time. Make friends, comrades. Hatch a plan to steal the Myrthali. Yer'll find a way. Yes, yer'll find a way.'

'That's not massively helpful.'

'Well that's all yer'll get! Yer wanna save Mumsy? Now, set yer alarm thinger. Yer go jus' before dawn. Tha's when the gateway opens.'

'And do I need to do anything when the, er, gateway opens?'

The devil's cruel smile returned to her vile lips but there was more humour than cunning behind her grin.

'Yer stand on hill, crushin' gooseberries in one hand, blackberries in the other, yer look into yer sun for a second, then look at moon for a second, back to sun, at moon, at sun, keep goin' singin' "hi-li-li-far-doohm, weee-shlalalalam" while standin' on one leg.'

For the first time in days, a laugh burst out of Krish's mouth.

'I'm sorry... what...?!' he said.

'I knows yer heard I!' the devil spat out.

'Yeah, but that's the stupidest thing I've ever heard *ever!*'

'Course is stupid! Very, very stupid! If it were sensible and easy to do, even by accident, people'll be goin' other worlds and whizzin' back and forth all the time, wouldn't they?'

Krish let out another sigh. 'Okay. I'll try it. But how do I get back?'

The devil wandered over to Krish's bed and examined one of the wooden bed knobs at the foot. She toyed for a moment with a splinter on the bed knob and proceeded to pull the fragment of wood free. Then she opened the gold vessel around her neck and delicately extracted a single grain of what looked like sand. She closed the vessel. She held the splinter and the grain in the palm of her hand and passed her other hand over them. The speck of wood and the minuscule grain glowed violet then emerald green and finally the blue of the deepest ocean all in an instant.

'Place under yer tongue.'

Cautiously Krish took the splinter and the grain. He thought he could taste the devil's skin from where his finger had brushed her palm; dry, leathery. A taste like the smell of mould on a window in a damp old room where nobody goes.

'Put yer tongue to roof o' yer mouth.'

Krish did so.

'It gone?'

Krish wiggled his tongue to try and find the splinter and the grain but to no avail.

'It gone. Next time yer touch a grain of Myrthali, yer'll find yerself home again. Standin' by this very bed knob. Myrthali'll come back with yer. All of it. Time will pass for yer there, none will have passed here. Tha's all yer gotta do. Touch it.'

Krish nodded. His eyes widened, looking at the golden vessel.

'You've got some...' he said. 'In there! You've—'

The devil's eyes narrowed and she clutched the vessel close to her chest. 'Not enough,' she said. 'Enough for a few weeks, a few months perhaps, but then...' She shook her head slowly, her eyes still narrowed. Those rotten, yellow slits on her face bored into him and goosebumps rose on his skin. 'There's one simple rule,' she said. 'Yer get Myrthali by stealin', outwittin' and such, however yer please, but no bargains! Yer make a bargain to share Myrthali and it not all be returnin' with yer and maybe cause other troubles too! Yer don't risk it! Too dangerous! Understand?'

Krish said he did.

He went to go and get dressed, wondering if he was really going to go through with this (as well as wondering whether the twenty-four-hour supermarket around the corner sold gooseberries), when something else struck him.

'What happened to the other time thieves?' he asked.

'Them 'as gone.'

'Gone?'

'Not there no more. Not nowhere.'

'They died?'

'If tha's what yer call it when people ain't nowhere to be found no more.'

'How?'

The devil shrugged, toying with the vessel around her neck. 'Ran out o' time.'

⁑

Krish stood on the hill waiting for dawn. A crack of light was spreading across the horizon as the start of a new day was dimly beginning to illuminate the sleeping world around him. Minutes before, he had been staring at the shadowy wilderness surrounding Brandhurst Hill. A grey-black mire of vague shapes that were now just about recognisable as houses and corner shops and petrol stations and florists and off-licences. Every one of them would remain as quiet as a grave until the sun rose fully in an hour or so, lighting the way for the half-asleep children and adults to trudge wearily to school or to work or to who-knows-where.

He was glad no one was awake. No one was there to see him make a fool of himself as he lifted one leg in the air and began to crush the gooseberries in his left hand and blackberries in his right. He cautiously opened his mouth...

'Hi-li-li—'

He stopped there. What was he doing? This was ridiculous. He knew it and he couldn't bear to go through all this nonsense. There wasn't another soul in sight. No one to spy the strange kid chanting bizarre incantations on the hillside. No one to see the weirdo on one leg with fruit juice trickling out of his sticky, clenched fists. But still it felt stupid. All his brain could do was list various places that could be the nearest to wash his hands of the juice from the berries that he had started to crush.

Krish turned to go but one footstep seemed to tire him out. He'd put all his energy into getting to the hill, preparing for adventure and excitement. Adventure and excitement? He hated adventure and excitement. Playing sports and watching telly were all he really cared about. And hanging around with his mates. Dragons and castles and wizards (most of all wizards) were stupid and boring ideas to him.

But here he was. *If I don't try I've wasted my time. Got out of bed –* (a jaw-achingly big yawn) – *for nothing.* He knew deep in his heart as he looked through the fizz of the weak light of morning to see the waking town taking shape around him, all those familiar sites – Bob's Store, the bakery on Singlewell Road, the bus shelter by St Mary's where Todd Harding had kicked Simon Penton in the face when he was tying his shoelaces – that all this was not going to disappear as he was transported to a faraway world. And if he was wrong, then he could find the Myrthali (somehow) and save his Mum. So what did he have to lose?

Back towards his house, a wall of grey clouds was spreading. In minutes, if not moments, the sun would be blotted out. Krish turned around, faced the glimmer of the sun peeking over the horizon, lifted his right leg up, began to clench his fists and spoke those stupid, *stupid* words.

'Hi-li-li-fardoohm, weee-shlalalalam. Hi-li-li-fardoohm, weee-shlalalalam.'

He looked from the rising sun to the fading moon.

'Hi-li-li-fardoohm, weee-shlalalalam.'

From the sun to the moon, the sun to the moon, the sun to the moon, over and over, feeling the strain in his neck.

'Hi-li-li-fardoohm, weee-shlalalalam.'

Sun to the moon, sun to the moon, sun to the moon, sun to the moon, sun to the sun...

He stopped. The moon had gone. His eyes narrowed. They stung and he blinked at the glare of the sun high in the clear blue sky. But this was not his sky.

CHAPTER 7

THE POCKET WORLD

Krish's world hadn't melted away around him to reveal a whole new unfamiliar landscape. It hadn't faded or transformed. He couldn't even get his head around the idea that it had vanished. This new world was simply there. As if it had always been there. As if he had always stood part the way up a mountain, looking down over the dry, barren landscape of dusty yellow cracked earth.

Krish turned and took in the mountain itself. He was on a ledge near the summit, which appeared to be more of a lumpy plateau of brittle, sandy-coloured rock than the pointy, snow-covered tip he might have expected. The 'lumps' of rock which made up the mountain put him in mind of hooded figures dried out by the sun. On closer inspection the rocks weren't smooth but covered in holes, almost resembling coral. He cupped his hand around one of them. Many small spikes indented his skin. The rock crumbled a little in places. He brushed the fragments away and stared at the dust and indentations left on the skin in the palm of his hand. This was no dream, no strange vision; he had felt this place. It had marked his skin. All of a sudden this world was unnervingly real.

This strange new place was eerily close to silent. Krish thought it had been the constant looking back and forth that had led him to build up a sweat but now he realised it was the mighty sun overhead, slowly baking him alive. And this sun was monstrously big. It must be almost twice the size of the sun he was familiar with back home. He swore, as he glanced at the gigantic star for a fraction of a second before looking away, dots of yellow and purple clouding his vision, that he could make out a vague patchwork of orange and yellow. Wisps of flame whipping soundlessly into the sky. As if he could feel the rage of this world's local star.

He looked around the scorched landscape. All appeared dead. Yellowy wastelands dotted with dead-looking white trees, the terrain scarred with what was once maybe an entire network of streams.

The horizon was curved. Very obviously curved.

'Small world,' the devil had said. 'Tiny world! Pocket world! World go round sun whizzy quick! Days short.'

The devil had been right about that. He didn't know how long he had been taking in this strange new place but he observed that the tree slightly to his right was now casting its shadow across his arm whereas some minutes ago it had been parallel to his arm, pointing directly behind him.

Had it been minutes ago? Krish suddenly realised that he had no idea how long he had been standing there just staring. The sun was definitely a little lower in the sky now. If night was coming he'd better find shelter or a settlement of some kind quick.

Krish wandered along a roughly hewn path. Nothing. More empty world stretched out before him. He walked a little further along the precipice but his view of the never-ending wilderness was not obscured by rock or tree or anything. He could walk for miles along this side of the mountain and not get any better a vantage point on the dead land below.

Krish stopped.

There was nothing.

That dreadful silence crept over his skin like some paralysing disease. Not a sound, not a bird, not the tiny disturbance of a pin dropping in a hundred miles. The occasional gust of wind only made the faintest noise as it brushed invisibly past his ears.

Krish stifled a feeling as his brain fought to keep logic in charge of his train of thought. A feeling of being helpless and alone so far from anything he'd ever thought of as home. He considered for a few moments. Much of the view was obscured by the mountain. Would it take long to reach the top? He didn't want to start heading down and realise that he'd missed some grand civilisation. He turned and looked behind him. A ridge of coarse yellow rock ran between two peaks, maybe ten, twenty metres up from where he was standing.

He climbed up, his hands struggling to grip the dusty rock, and found himself looking over the ridge. The sun was behind him now, just peeking over the ridge and casting long shadows on tiny shapes that littered the land below. Caught in the low light of the sinking sun were a number of sandy-coloured huts that blended into the landscape and ahead of them a cluster of khaki canopies, a flurry of activity in front of them, dust rising up into the air, way above the ramshackle town he was apparently observing. He squinted to make out tiny figures and there, on the edge of the collection of minuscule structures, he saw a mighty palace of pointed black turrets. Its long shadow was almost pointing straight up at him. There must be some incredible heat coming off the palace as he was certain it shimmered slightly. As if it was not entirely solid.

Far beyond the palace Krish was certain he could make out the silhouette of a tree. The fading light must be playing tricks with his eyes; how could a tree be so big that he could make out branches and even leaves from so far away? And it looked like there was some other gigantic object protruding from one of the branches.

He blinked unbelievingly and looked from side to side. Here and there were patches of green springing out of the landscape, chasing rivers which snaked through otherwise dead lands. Looking behind him, away from the sun, there were slim mountains that looked more like ginormous darts, reaching so far up that they overlapped with the curve of star-dotted darkness that was the spreading blanket of night. Shadows no bigger than grains of sand drifted across the land below. People? Creatures? Whatever they were, they were dwarfed by this world, tiny though he was assured it was.

Krish stared back towards the palace and the town. If he was looking for a king, a palace was the obvious choice. He began to head in that direction.

The sun was an enormous ball of an orange so deep in hue (yet somehow not quite red) that Krish was convinced he was seeing a colour he had never seen before. It was heading towards the horizon with such furious speed that he feared it would crash into the ground and crack this tiny world in two.

As night wrapped itself around the land he was glad of the cooling air. The coolness fought the heat rising from the rocks that had been baked by the sun all day as he completed his descent, but soon the heat died away altogether and Krish found he was freezing and thirsty.

He stumbled on, terrified of falling into one of the ravines he hadn't observed from on top of the mountain. But the night was far from entirely dark. The sun had vanished to reveal a dome of shining stars twinkling in the night sky. And where the land around him was mostly flat, 'dome' really was the right word. He had never seen stars so vivid. He was so used to looking up to see them that he'd never thought of them being in front of him or behind him and on either side. Everywhere he looked there were pinpricks of starlight glistening in the dark to show him the way forward. Moonlight joined the sea of illumination overhead. This moon too was bigger than his own world's, scratched and scarred and dotted with craters. But that was not all. Four more moons circled the mother moon; tiny and beautiful they danced around their parent as they journeyed towards dawn. The night had never seemed so bright and he felt at last that he could achieve what he set out to do. He *would* find the Myrthali. He *would* return home. He *would* see his Mum smile properly again.

There was firelight in the distance and the smell of strange food. Smoked meat and a musky, almost spicy aroma.

A few more hours of treading carefully in the relative darkness, his dry tongue sticking to the roof of his mouth, and the gigantic sun had risen again after the short night to warm his tired frame. The glistening black palace ahead of him was playing tricks with his mind once more. It appeared to be shimmering in the heat but nothing else around it was moving. His brain seemed dedicated to convincing him that he was heading towards a living, breathing structure.

Krish came to a slight groove in the ground. Water flowed with a delicate, burbling sound through veins in the rock. Excitement took him over and he fell to his knees and slurped greedily at the water. The refreshment it provided was an indescribable ecstasy to his dry lips and parched throat.

Then he became aware of sounds. The scratching of wood scraping against rock. Shapes appeared. Tumbleweed-like objects rolled towards him. But these tumbleweeds were as big as cars. Collections of dusty-white, wiry branches. He backed away in fear. Although they showed no signs of life as the wind appeared to hurl them in his direction, it felt as if they were fighting. Brittle branches cracked and dropped to the ground again and again as the tumbleweeds rammed into one another. One reached the groove first. The mighty tumbleweed stopped exactly where it was the second it made contact with the water, which it instantly began to soak up. Within moments the water had vanished from the groove.

In minutes the gigantic tumbleweed creaked into the shape of a lean, silvery tree, luminous in this barren world. As he watched, hundreds of purple flowers blossomed all over the tree, grew dry, shrivelled, detached and flew off with the breeze. The tree creaked back into a ball and rolled off into the distance with its companions. Krish shook his head unbelievingly.

His shadow and those of the wire-like white branches of the dead-looking trees (all firmly planted in the ground and looking unlikely to roll off anywhere) stretched across the ground in front of him. There were a few small tents dotted about on the outskirts of the settlement. There were pens – pale branches tightly tied together with dried vines – holding animals that were both strange and familiar. Some looked like sheep but their legs were much shorter, their bodies longer and their wool short and matted. They really weren't that much like sheep at all but his mind seemed to want to call them 'sheep'. The same for the 'cows', which were darker and leaner than the cows he knew, as if someone had stretched them.

He heard the heavy rustle of canvas to his right. He saw a man emerge groggily from one of the tents and walk over to a series of shallow trenches cut in perfectly straight lines across the land. The man wore simple, practical clothes, sandy-coloured, just like everything else. He paid no attention to Krish. He supposed this man had no reason to think anything of him. His clothes might be different but now they were so caked in dust he would probably look just like everyone else.

Krish then realised that there was a woman at the far end of another trench already at work. There were several more women working silently beside the shallow trenches as well. Then he noticed that they all seemed to have lanterns of some kind (all extinguished now) on the ground next to them. They looked tired but in a different way to the man he'd just seen come out of the tent. As if they were winding down. He guessed that maybe, with the days being so short, some people simply worked all night.

The man Krish had been observing stopped at the end of one of the trenches, pulled a trowel-like implement from the ground, where it had been partially embedded, sat down, his feet in the trench, and started digging, quite clumsily. He pulled out a knobbly purple root vegetable, dropped it by his side and kept digging. Once he'd found a couple more he rolled out a small rectangle of canvas, produced a knife, peeled the purple knobbly thing, chucked the peelings away from the trench and within minutes he had three pale indigo vegetable sticks lined up on the canvas. He bashed his left hand against his trousers to get the dirt off it and proceeded to munch down the little stick of root vegetable.

'Malka! Babu!' the man barked through a mouthful of vegetable in the vague direction of his tent.

Panic spread through Krish's mind; he would have no idea what anybody was saying. How would he understand the language of the people here? The thought vanished seconds later and was hastily replaced with curiosity.

'Malka! Babu! Come here! Breakfast!'

He understood. He understood exactly what the man had just said. Malka and Babu were clearly names and their owners were just emerging from their tent. A woman and a small child, similarly attired to the man. They sat beside him and ate their vegetables. A few words were exchanged, a little bit of *You sleep well?* and *Plenty to harvest today, plenty,* and when they had finished eating, which took a minute more, maybe less, they spread out along the trench, got on their knees and started digging without another word. The child must have been only four or five but he worked as hard as his parents.

Krish watched for roughly half an hour, fascinated by this curious new land and its people. He saw them dig up only three or four vegetables between the three of them. The three the man had dug up must be part of some stash left over from the previous day for him and his family to eat.

Others now joined them while those with lanterns had mainly gone to sleep in their own tents. The night workers had wisely pitched their tents in the shade of some of the bigger trees to stay out of the daylight as much as possible although the wiry trees hardly sheltered them from the glare of the sun.

Krish looked back at the interior of Malka, Babu and the man's tent. It was no bigger than the one-man tent he'd used during his brief spell in the Scouts last year. A hammock hung quite low in the tent and there was a small space underneath with a blanket and pillow in one corner and tools, water bottles and few packages spread out across the rest of the floor.

He imagined the tired child sleeping under the blanket in the corner with hardly any space to breathe between the tools and packages scattered about him while his parents slept above. He decided never to complain about having a smaller bedroom than his sister Joshi ever again.

Krish looked on to the town in the distance and saw a whirl of dust and heard the sounds of chaos. If he was going to complete his mission (and not die of hunger and tiredness in the process) he'd better get a move on, he thought.

The settlement was a flurry of activity. As the sun climbed higher in the sky there was a human traffic jam in the street. Men, women and children in their torn old clothes, battered by the desert winds, hurried from one place to another, battling to get past other people selling all manner of goods from bags at their sides.

'Take this one!'

'Good craftsmanship!'

'The King himself uses these to sharpen his knives!'

How could he understand all of this? The devil must have done something to allow him to make sense of everything that was being said. Occasionally words didn't seem to translate and he'd just hear some word he didn't know, but often an object or animals or whatever that looked very similar to something from his own world would go by the same name even though it wasn't quite accurate.

Most of the townspeople were preoccupied with the market under the khaki canopies in the centre of the town, where even more sellers tried to convince them to part with money for strange beasts or unusual fruit. Some goaded their beasts into a fury with sticks and rocks to demonstrate the strength of the creature for sale. Others were selling dead animals for meat, smoking the flesh and offering samples to prospective customers. Some offered hot fruit they had boiling in aromatic concoctions bubbling away in vast cauldrons over open fires. He saw one old man sitting on a box holding a magnifying glass over a square of wood no bigger than a coaster, using the sunlight to burn a remarkably detailed image of the palace onto the wood.

Krish tried some dried meat on a stick, which tasted to him like burnt chicken with a sweet aftertaste, like a salty version of maple syrup. This barely sated his hunger but gave him the strength to persist. He was sure he must look unusual to the people of this world but none stared too long; as if they were used to strange faces cropping up in their town every so often.

He headed on towards the black palace but struggled to get past a large crowd at the edge of the market who were watching what appeared to be magicians performing on wooden boxes. Some conjured up beasts which ran around the circle of people surrounding them to a chorus of impressed noises. Others seemed to be predicting the future, which was met with a mixture of shrieks and applause. He could barely breathe as he squeezed his way through the sweaty crowd.

He saw a smaller circle not far from the exit to the street and made his way towards it. A very young magician stood on a particularly small box. She must have only been a few years older than him. Her creased robe was of midnight blue and she wore a pointy hat like a wizard. Well, it would have been pointy if it hadn't been bent just above the brim, the peak drooping down at the side. She had a staff made of particularly knobbly wood. Her dark hair was braided and dotted with coloured beads. Her long necklace and leather bracelets were similarly beaded.

'And now, ladies and gents!' said the magician. 'Prepare to be amazed as I turn this rabbit–' (it wasn't actually a rabbit but it was so close to one in appearance that Krish's mind translated it as 'rabbit') '–into an 'at!'

A hat did indeed appear. A very small one. But the crowd didn't really get to see it as it was so small that the rabbit (which was very much still there and not a hat) had a very good view and decided that the hat looked like a rather delicious snack. Before the meagre collection of people around the magician could focus on the tiny item of headgear it was gone. The rabbit looked up at the magician.

'Oh no, yer don't!' the magician replied to the hopeful-looking bunny. 'Yer've 'ad enough 'at today!'

The crowd didn't look impressed and half of them left. The magician looked momentarily disappointed and then promised that her next trick – turning the rabbit into a qualified tax advisor – would be far more exciting. It wasn't. The rabbit appeared particularly disillusioned by the not-so-tasty-looking miniature abacus that had just appeared next to him. The only real advantage for Krish was that it gave him a moment to slip away quietly while the magician was distracted.

Krish reached the edge of the town and saw the palace now looming directly in front of him. Something about it sent shivers down
his spine (and he apparently sent shivers down *its* spine, as the whole
structure before him seemed to shake slightly). A line of guards
dressed in black armour, blending into the palace somewhat, was
stretched out in front of the great structure. All held long pikes, one
hand on their sheathed swords. There were gaps in the ranks but
the pikes were long enough to stop any unwanted visitor getting
through.

He ground to a halt. It all struck him at once. That feeling he'd tried to
stifle on the mountain. What was he doing? Why was he here? How could
this all be real? He'd not really taken it all in. He'd got dressed that morning, awash with tiredness, scarcely a bone in his body that was fully awake
and not a corner of his brain that was totally aware of what he was actually
doing. And now here he was. Wherever 'here' was.

Krish felt lost, alone and scared. He had wandered as if in a day-
dream for so long – hunger and exhaustion just about driving him on
– that he had forgotten that he had absolutely no idea how far away
from home he really was.

He remembered driving to see Aunt Nisha in Glasgow and how it
had taken two days. And when they had flown to America they had
changed planes in Houston, Texas. Uncle Ravi had said that the state
of Texas was bigger than the whole of Britain and there were forty-
nine other states. How could the world be that big? And there were
bigger planets than Earth in the Solar System, *much* bigger, and there
were billions of planets and stars, and at this point Krish stopped trying to comprehend how big all existence was and how far away from
home he was when he didn't even know where he was right now.

Krish was frozen to the spot, dust from the heels of the townspeople passing him by gradually coating his clothes, without any comprehension of
what he should do or feel. He looked about at the streets full of strange
faces and strange clothes. The devil had said he needed to find a group of
thieves or similar and work with them, but now he was here he didn't feel
he could approach a single one of them. What would he do? What would
he say? How would he convince them to leave him the Myrthali? The devil
had said *no bargains*. The King must have riches they'd want, surely. All he

knew was that he felt like he was losing time he could be spending with his Mum, although he knew he'd lose no time and return at the moment he'd left. But he couldn't help but feel the urgency of his situation. He had to get back. He *had* to bring her more time.

After some indeterminate length of time, all his thoughts of cunning, of ingenious plans to steal the Myrthali, evaporated. He decided he was only capable of one course of action. He would blag his way into the palace, demand an audience with the King and beg for a quantity of the Myrthali. Maybe just convince them to let him look at it. All he had to do was touch a single grain and all the Myrthali in this world would be transported back with him.

That was the problem with being a quiet, well-spoken kid who people just don't notice most of the time; there were times when you had no confidence at all and times when you would gather all that unused confidence together and blunder recklessly into some pretty insane situation without any real plan. Krish was also very hungry and had thought that maybe he could touch the Myrthali pretty soon, be sent back to his own world and run to the shop and get a chocolate bar.

Have some faith in yourself, for God's sake!

With his Mum's words echoing in his head, Krish turned and marched in the direction of the palace. He crossed a large wooden bridge over a deep trench which wound around the palace, appearing to be a dried-up riverbed. As he looked up at the shimmering black palace he felt as if a thousand eyes were watching him approach. And, as he soon found out, he wasn't wrong.

CHAPTER 8

THE BREATHING PALACE

'I demand to see the King!' Krish could sound impressively arrogant when he was hungry.

'Oh, demand, eh?' answered one of the guards. 'You'll get far in life, boy!'

Krish had realised before the words had even left his mouth that this was unlikely to work but he was too tired to come up with any kind of logical strategy. His mind raced to think of something but the second guard gave a little chortle and turned to him with an encouraging smile.

'He's pulling yer leg, mate,' the second guard said. 'Come on, kid. Let's go.'

And somehow he found himself being ushered towards the entrance. Krish really wasn't sure how this had worked. They approached the door. But instead of swinging open like a normal wooden door, it appeared to wriggle aside to let Krish and the guard through. As he entered, he realised why the palace shimmered and shook. Why something about it seemed alive. It was because it was alive.

The smell of stale sweat filled his nostrils and the sounds of laboured breathing crept around him. The palace was not built of wood or stone or bricks and mortar. It was made of living people. A sea of dark, glistening skins, poor souls wearing little more than a few pieces of cloth, made up the walls, the ceiling, the columns, the doorways. They hung there, clinging to each other, hundreds of vaguely curious eyes following him down the wide corridor to the throne room.

All of sudden, a sickening thought shot through his body. What was he walking on? His eyes darted to the ground and he breathed a sigh of relief to see dusty yellow earth beneath his feet.

'You've never set foot in the palace before, have yer, boy?' asked the guard. 'You're from across The Scar, aren't yer?'

Krish decided it was best to nod.

'The King likes most people to see it at some point. We used to have a prison but it cost too much to maintain that and a palace as well so His Royal Highness came up with this! Ingenious, eh? Not that His Majesty ever has enough criminals to keep the place together! Has to keep coming up with new laws. Like never placing coins with the King's head face down. Many an untalented pickpocket has made a pretty penny tipping off us palace guards about some coin he or she's turned. Pig-pokin's the new crime, I hear.'

Krish became aware of the occasional figure climbing down while another climbed up to take his or her spot.

'Yeah,' said the guard. 'They get a few hours off. In fact, we have to enforce it. Or else the whole palace'd fall down!' Krish really didn't want to be about to see that.

Krish also noticed that there were no staircases but occasionally he saw the ceiling open up and the bodies (which appeared to be wearing tiles on their fronts so people in the upper levels didn't have to walk on slippery flesh) would pass down some expensively robed advisor who proceeded to march off without a word of thanks to the obliging prisoners.

Then ahead of him he saw a long line of anxious-looking citizens. They all held boxes or packages made up to look as fancy as the holders could present them, but none seemed all that impressive. And from the way they all shuffled nervously on their feet he wasn't sure they were that convinced of their gifts' worth either.

'Hope yer brought a good 'un, kid,' said the guard. ''E's not in the best of moods.'

Krish had no idea what he was going to do. He had no gift. He hadn't been able to bring anything with him at all. The devil had said it would disintegrate.

'Just a quick briefing first, kid,' the guard said as he stepped aside rather abruptly. Another subject holding a gift suddenly landed on the spot where the guard had been moments before and Krish found himself hoisted into the air and up to the first floor before he knew what was happening.

'Next!' The command was infused with boredom. The speaker came into view as Krish was hurled into the room, the floor which had delivered him closing up underneath him. A grey-haired lady in a black robe and cap peered over small round glasses at a book on a lectern consisting of one exhausted-looking prisoner holding up a slab of wood at a forty-five-degree angle for the woman's papers to rest on.

'No grovelling, no foot-kissing, no persistent bowing, no averting your gaze in awe and anyone uttering that tiresome line about "not being worthy of His Majesty's divine excellence" or words to that effect will immediately be sentenced to ten years in the south-facing wall of the royal lavatory, no questions asked. Is that understood?'

'Erm…'

'Good. What's your gift, boy?'

'I, er…'

'Well, you'd better have one! A few more no-hopers today and we'll have to consider an extension of the north wing and do you have any idea how much paperwork that would involve?'

'I…' He was distracted by the fact that he could feel the floor tile beneath him breathing gently.

'No. Didn't think you would. Arms up please.'

A stern-faced and equally bored-looking wizard had entered the room. Krish put his arms up, the wizard pointed his outstretched arms at him and he found himself engulfed in a cloud of purple smoke.

'He's clean,' said the wizard before departing.

'Good,' said the woman in the black cap. 'You're not an assassin. We don't get many. Shame really. Tends to get a bit exciting. Oh, well. I suppose you're a fool then. Enjoy your new career as a fixture and/or fitting.' She was ushering him away before he could say another word and he soon found himself lowered back into the main corridor again.

Krish joined the queue and tried desperately to think of something he could offer as a gift but his mind wasn't a lot of help.

'Excuse me?' Krish tried asking the tiny, starved-looking man in front of him. 'What are these gifts... for?'

The man was a little confused that Krish didn't seem to know already but answered anyway. 'For a few square metres of farmland, a few more scraps of food, a pardon for a loved one perhaps, if you're bold, or whatever little thing you can beg for. Without actually begging of course. They say he *hates* begging.'

Krish realised he didn't have much hope for a quantity of Myrthali in return for anything, let alone nothing.

The queue seemed to be moving quite fast and in half an hour or so he found himself at the front, just a few shaking citizens ahead of him. He was becoming dizzy with hunger, swaying a tad on his unsteady legs. He killed the time by mentally listing all the foods he'd eat when he got home – Mars Bars, thick slices of Hawaiian pizza, mashed potato smothered in barbecue sauce...

His gluttonous fantasies were interrupted by the occasional muffled cry of disdain or mocking laughter from the adjacent chamber.

'His Majesty!' called out a guard by the entrance to the throne room. 'King Obsendei!'

CHAPTER 9

THE KING & THE LADY OF THE NORTH

The wall of entwined bodies ahead of him opened up and he stepped into a gigantic chamber. The enormous, echoing room was twice the length of any cathedral he'd ever visited during all those boring visits to France and Belgium with his family, and twenty times as high at least. The roof of the chamber formed a narrow spire that was so tall that he couldn't see the top. From the darkness hung a line of prisoners that culminated in a chandelier of inmates hanging upside down, each holding a candle. He had vertigo just thinking of what it must be like being at the top of the spire.

'Noooo!' The word brought Krish crashing back down to Earth (or wherever he was) and his eyes were drawn to a man wearing a long, simple robe and a large, extravagant, bejewelled wooden crown, a shining convex oval of silver as its centrepiece. The King had grey eyes above a large, sharp nose and a short, frayed beard of iron grey streaked with white. Just seeing those eyes immediately sent a stab of fear through his already suitably intimidated soul. Surrounding the King were various advisors, noblewomen and noblemen.

To one side of them was a circle of guards and in the circle were about a dozen men and women, all dressed in ludicrously colourful gowns of garishly bright colours, many of them loose-fitting and rather revealing. They lounged about on beds of pillows being fanned by servants, eating fruit and drinking from goblets, and several were bathing in jewel-encrusted golden bathtubs. All of them had the most beautiful clear skin and they all had completely shaved heads, the men no beards or moustaches, which he guessed must be some kind of fashion for the ultra-rich in this land. Each of them seemed too preoccupied with preening themselves to pay much attention to the goings-on in the rest of chamber. Each of them wore a wooden ring on a necklace.

The King hadn't yet seen Krish as he was preoccupied with throwing a music box to the ground, a few notes escaping from the chimes within the box before it shattered into a pile of tiny, silent pieces.

'I could order a *hundred* orchestras to play me that tune all at once if I desired! You really think that your pathetic little music box would amuse me?' The King's voice was old, hoarse and deep. The voice of a man who had issued a thousand orders of execution and the odd merciful pardon, when it amused him. 'And as for these...' A repulsed expression as he held out in front of him some of the purple root vegetables – cleaner and less knobbly than the ones Krish had seen earlier – as far away from his upturned nose as possible. 'Hardly worth tossing in the direction of the condemned for an afternoon snack.' He threw them to the ground and a wall tensed, trying to stifle its appetite. The King let out a large sigh. 'But I suppose it's quicker than summoning a maid.' He waved a hand vaguely in the direction of the guards.

'Grub's up, boys and girls!' grunted a guard and a nearby wall collapsed and scurried in the dirt, fighting furiously to get a bite of the dust-coated vegetables. The commotion was over in seconds and the prisoners were ushered back into position.

'Put her in the north wall!' cried the King.

The shaking subject kneeling before the King was dragged away, her face streaked with tears.

Krish didn't know whether he was glad there were three people still in front of him or whether he'd rather get it all over with sooner rather than later. He decided that he was glad of the three ahead of him... who all seemed to wear similar, plain black robes. And they all appeared to be glancing at each other occasionally, as if they were waiting for a cue. A second later, they received their prompt.

'Next!' bellowed the King.

'Your Majesty!' The first of the robed figures had a rich, lyrical voice. One that was accustomed to addressing a crowd. All three figures stood up straight and threw aside their robes in perfect unison, revealing brightly coloured costumes of red, yellow and blue beneath.

'We are the most magnificent!' said the first.

'The most stupendous!' said the next.

'The most magical—'

'No you're not,' said the King, turning away from them and rolling his eyes.

'Wait...' The voice came all the way from the far side of the chamber. A low, flat, quiet voice, but still everyone paid attention. An old woman in a simple grey robe, like a faded version of the robe worn by the magician at the market but made of finer material. This woman, who must have been a magician as well or maybe even a wizard, had clearly worn her garment for decades but kept it in better condition than the magician from the market. Unlike most of the court her skin was pale as porcelain with a hint of grey, unlike her straight hair, hanging down just below her shoulders, which was deep orange with the odd streak of blue. Her eyes were ancient, calculating and, unless Krish was very much mistaken, rather bored of court life. She was as tall and as straight as a post. In one hand she held a staff which appeared to be made of the roots of a tree. At the top a misty, rectangular crystal was entangled in the roots.

The wizard moved across the chamber in a perfectly straight line, her attentive old eyes never leaving the lapel on one of the performers' outfits.

'What is that?' The court watched in silence as the wizard's staff moved a millimetre or so towards the performer's lapel. Krish saw that there was a pinprick of light at the centre of the crystal and it became brighter the nearer it got to the performer.

'That...?' said the quivering performer. 'Er... erm... my brooch is not magical... it's just—'

'Not the brooch... *that*.' She was pointing at a dark blue patch on the performer's sleeve.

The performer's eyes widened for a moment before she looked away, clearly not wanting the wizard to know she was on to something.

'It's... I couldn't get it to match...' said the performer. 'The other uniform. The market had sold out of blue dye so I treated the yellow—'

'How?' the wizard asked so simply, so quietly, but the whole court could hear and was hanging on her every word. The performer's mouth hung open but not a sound escaped.

'What's your name?' asked the wizard.

'Marteese. Marteese Shek, Madam Eshter,' answered the performer.

'You ran out of dye, didn't you, Marteese Shek?' said Madam Eshter.

'Yes,' said Shek.

'So you used a spell to turn the yellow dye blue?'

'I-I-I-I did not use any magic in the court!'

'You defiled His Most Noble Majesty's court with a magically enhanced garment.' Eshter's eyes seemed too tired to ever blink. 'You know the punishment for performing magic in the court of the King?'

'I-I... Please! I didn't perform magic *here*! I—'

'I am just stating facts.' Eshter turned to face the King. 'It is His Majesty's choice.'

The King sat on his throne, slouching, a hand holding up his weary head. He considered for a moment.

'The south wall,' he said simply.

'He's going soft in his old age,' a new voice from across the chamber muttered as the performers were dragged away.

'What did you say?!' the King spat out across the chamber.

'Nothing, Your Grace.' The voice was warm and beautiful, just like its owner, who stepped away from the group of nobles to stare at the King with the kind of smile that encourages people to shower her with gifts. Her straight dark hair and red and gold dress were immaculate. Her large brown eyes were stunning in their calmness but the cunningness behind them was clear for all to see. There was a fire in them waiting to erupt.

'Vira, Lady of the North!' cried the King. 'You have no authority to question how *I* punish *my* citizens!'

'I am only thinking of you, My King.' Her smile was unwavering. Her rich, low voice washed over the crowd, who seemed enchanted by her beauty. 'I want only for you to reign supreme. For all your people to respect you. Fear breeds respect, Your Eminence. There was almost a revolt after the Four-Year Famine. If you had listened to my advice, O Fortunate King, perh—'

'I did not lose their respect,' interrupted the King. 'They did not revolt. Your war was unnecessary.'

'Of course, My Lord. You are always right. I was merely suggesting that, with a stock of arms rusting in your stores, we could find an opposition, incite war, sell them arms through a third party at a premium, pay a small band of mercenaries to skew the final battle in our favour and exit the conflict with our pockets lined.'

The King was slouching on his throne again. His expression suggested that his brain was throwing all Vira's words around in his head, having no insight as to which order they had just arrived in.

'War sounds exhausting,' he said. 'If coffers empty I will raise taxes.'

'If they revolt—'

'Are you a wife of mine?' shouted the King. 'Are you a husband of mine?' He clutched at his necklace and Krish noticed that from it hung a dozen wooden rings and he realised that the bald beauties in the circle of guards must be the King's spouses. It was clearly okay for a king to have many wives as well as many husbands in this land. 'No! You will know your place, Vira, Lady of the North! You are not in a council meeting now.'

Vira's eyes remained calm as they locked with the King's. A coy smile lingered on her lips as she took a step back.

'Of course, Your Noble Magnificence,' said Vira. 'I will save my thoughts on these matters for a meeting of the council. I forget of course that His Illustrious Majesty has reigned over us gracefully for such a time that he no longer has an appetite for war. And the noble Eshter has served you for many of those years.' Eshter winced a little, her hand gripping her staff tightly. 'And long may your reign continue. I have no doubt that the vicious rumours that Your Most Magnanimous Majesty is too old and lazy to do anything more than spend the people's money and allow his kingdom to rot, will die out long before His Masterful, Much-Revered Majesty *ever* does.' The bow that followed from Vira could well have lasted a whole year.

The King groaned. 'We will make this meeting of the council brief. R'ghir! Lord of the East! Report to me on the state of affairs in that scrap of *my* kingdom you preside over.'

One of the nobles stepped forward. He did not look quite as comfortable addressing the King as Vira did. Krish observed that both R'ghir and Vira wore golden, quarter-circle necklaces.

'Things are going smoothly, Your Grace,' said R'ghir. 'The citizens of Terl are an affluent people, as you know, living high in the Lean Mountains, and they grumble little about your new altitude tax as they can afford to pay it. The money is simply rolling in.'

'And what of your district, Hesh, Lord of the South?' said the King to another noble.

'Oh, all is well, My Liege,' said Hesh. 'The harvest in Melkur was plentiful this year. The people are happy; their bellies are full.' Hesh also wore a necklace. Krish noticed that each corresponded to a point of the compass.

'And you, Elwynt, Lord of the West,' said the King to yet another noble. 'What news of the Undertowns?'

Elwynt was a large, pale man, more hesitant even than R'ghir and Hesh as he stepped forward. 'Er, My Lord, My Most Noble Majesty...' he began. 'The, er, peoples of the Undertowns are wise in the ways of the tax loophole. Many, although loyal, *most* loyal, of course, to Their Beloved Majesty... many argue that as the law states that His Majesty's kingdom encompasses every corner of the land that the light falls upon, that they, with a sky of rock over their heads, should be exempt from—'

'They have shafts! They see sunlight!' interjected the King.

'Oh, yes, Your Majesty,' continued Elwynt. 'And they greatly appreciate that, My Lord, but some feel... *reluctant* to pay taxes and are not easily persuaded.'

The King inhaled slowly. He looked from Vira to the Lords R'ghir, Hesh and Elwynt and then back to Vira.

'So,' said the King. 'My kingdom is... profitable overall. R'ghir, Lord of the East, you will raise the altitude tax by five per cent. Hesh, Lord of the South, well done. Elwynt, Lord of the West, in future you may find swords more persuasive in extracting taxes. Vira, Lady of the North, speak of war again in this chamber and I will reward you with a necklace from which will hang a jar containing your tongue. This meeting is adjourned.'

The King glowered at the grinning Vira as she and the three lords took their places once more. He now turned his attentions to Krish for the first time.

'And what have we got here?' The King's eyes bored into Krish for a moment as he scanned him from head to toe.

'Your Majesty...' All eyes were on him. The echoes in the chamber seemed much louder than the tiny words he had uttered. There was a prickle in the air. Krish looked about and felt exactly what that disturbance in the air was. Sweat. The perspiration of thousands, maybe millions of prisoners, each with their eyes upon him. Each breathing in and out cautiously, filling every moment of comparative quiet in that dreadful palace with the sounds of the undercurrent. The sound of breathing. Slowly, calmly, in and out. Droplets of sweat falling from their near-naked bodies into the furnace-like atmosphere and evaporating into the formidable sense of dread hanging in the air of the colossal chamber. That prickle of heat. That sense of millions as tense as anyone could possibly be trickling down through the very air. The tension from the million eyes that stared at him from above.

The King sat on his throne, toying with his beard and eyeing him curiously.

'Your... Most Exalted—' He'd heard that word used in a film, but before he could be impressed with himself he was interrupted.

'You'd better make with the gift, boy!' one of the advisors jeered at him.

The King raised his hand to silence the calls of assent that mumbled around the room as he kept his gaze on Krish.

'You have only been before me for a few seconds, child,' began the King. 'But it is clear to all that there is no gift in your hands. I would advise you to produce one or an explanation with haste, young man.' The King was still furious from his confrontation with Vira but the distraction Krish was providing seemed to have subdued his rage somewhat.

The sea of eyes from the advisors, the nobles, from the very walls, the chandelier, the ceiling and more than anything from the King himself burned into Krish. Eshter glanced at her staff, which was no longer glowing, and then back to Krish.

'That is because...' Krish was trying desperately to think. 'That's because... my gift is... a story.'

He wasn't entirely sure how interested the King was but at least he wasn't interjecting.

'A story... about a woman. My mother.' Krish tried to build up a good story (without involving the devil), but nothing that eventful had ever happened to her. She was just his mother and he loved her. He focused on how she was so determined, how she always pushed him to be more confident and how much she would be missed. But with every word he just felt more and more pathetic.

The King allowed him to speak for a few minutes but he didn't seem convinced.

'A charming woman, I'm sure,' said the King. 'But the story of her life is hardly entertaining. Put a few jokes in next time. As for your fate: it is hardly a crime to love your matriarch, deluded as it was for you to come here. I find no pleasure in the prospect of punishing you. Get rid of him!'

Guards seized him by each arm.

'No, wait!' cried Krish. 'I have another story!'

'And I have another hundred or so subjects to get through before I'm utterly bored,' said the King, walking back to his throne.

'But-but—'

'Drag him away quicker, please!'

'A story about... Bahrtakrit!'

The King turned briskly and faced him. The motion itself was enough to make the guards stop dead in their tracks. The King thought for a moment and then marched up to him. Enraged, he spoke in hushed tones, clearly hoping that even those restraining Krish might not hear.

'Where have you heard that name, child?'

Eshter approached. She pointed her staff at Krish and ran it through the air in front of his body. The crystal stayed dull. She looked at the King and shook her head.

'You are no great conjuror,' said the King. 'No wizard. You are lying. You know nothing of Bahrtakrit.'

'I know all about it. All about where your Myrthali came from. About the Empress Benhu'in.'

'Died of extreme old age long, long ago, a billion worlds away, child. Or so the story goes.'

'I know how to get more. *Lots* more.'

'Where?'

'I need a sample—'

'OH!' The loudness of his voice and the glee in his grin cut right through Krish. 'I know what your game is now, boy! Don't need much Myrthali to extend your life to twice its length, do you? You're not the first, child!'

'But if I can take a sample—' *Come on! Come on! Just one touch and I can take it all!* '—I'll bring back all the—'

'Why of course you may have some of my Myrthali!' The words trickled sweetly out of the King's mouth, infused with an untrustworthy amount of kindness. 'Have it all.' He circled Krish and stood before a large font of inmates who looked like they hadn't been relieved from their shift for weeks. 'Go on.' The kind, enticing words caressed Krish's ears.

Krish approached the font. Slowly it came into view. He could see it!

'Come on... come on...'

The substance that could save his Mum's life! The reason he had come all this way! No more than a sandcastle bucket's worth of Myrthali, but it was enough. More than enough. Nothing more impressive to look at than particularly fine sand, but when you knew the powers it held...

'Come on...come on, child...'

He just had to extend his arm, reach out his fingers...

'Take every last grain!' The room was tense. The King stepped up to the font. 'Go on!' The King took a handful of the Myrthali, the Sands of Time. 'Go on! Take it!' He was offering Krish the Myrthali as you would offer a puppy a dog biscuit. 'Go on! Help yourself!'

Krish's fingers almost touched the Myrthali. He could almost feel a handful in his grip...

The King seized Krish's extended arm by the wrist and turned his hand over so his palm faced upwards.

'Go on...' the King said in a gentle whisper. It was so quiet Krish wondered if anyone else in the now silent chamber could hear him. He waited for the King to drop the Myrthali into his hand. For him to disappear and to never have to look into those cruel eyes again. He waited for a grain, just *one single* grain to fall from the King's grip, to brush the skin of his fingertips...

The King violently pushed Krish's hand away and clutched the fistful of Myrthali to his chest.

'When you fetch me a pearl from the Night Ocean, bring me the still-flaming feather of a FireHawk and tie a pretty bow around the globe!'

The room roared with laughter and Krish could barely hear the King over the cruel mockery erupting around him. The King chucked the Myrthali back into the font and strolled back to his throne while shouting over his shoulder:

'And take the crumbs from my dinner table and stamp them into the dirt before him so he knows he is not even worth those!'

And as he was dragged from the throne room, somewhere towards the rear of the chamber, Krish swore he could hear the sweet song of a bird echoing in the deep.

CHAPTER 10

THE BROKEN SCYTHE

Krish, lying on his side, his knees grazed, dirt stinging in a cut on his lip, could only just make out the guards walking away through the dust that had been thrown up around him. He had been so close! One touch and he would have been home! He was furious. Absolutely livid. The image of the King's mocking him was running on a loop in his head. Krish was not a violent kid but the idea of running up and punching His Royal Highness hard in the face certainly had a lot of appeal right now. And what was that strange sound he'd heard when he'd been dragged out? Like birdsong. A high, sweet beautiful song echoing from somewhere in the throne room. It just didn't seem to fit in with the whole feel of that dreadful palace.

Maybe the devil was right: he should take his time, get to know this world a little and see who he could find to help him. The idea of spending another minute in this place made him feel sick and he longed for his stupid, boring little world back home. All he wanted to do right now was scoff down the takeaway Dad and Joshi had got the night before, which he'd barely touched, and then collapse into bed. His stupid old bed with the missing slat that he suddenly longed for so much. But lying in the dirt in a heap of self-pity wouldn't save his Mum or get him home.

Krish picked himself up off the ground and looked away from that accursed palace. He'd been hurled into the dry riverbed that circled it He climbed up to the bank. He had no idea what to do or where to go so he headed back into the town.

He eyed the smokeries hungrily. Cones the size of teepees made of wooden slats rising up from the ground, tied together with dried vines at the pinnacle. Smoke billowed out of the gaps in the slats and the mouth-watering, smoky-sweet smells of the cooking meat poured into the air of the market. A market-seller pulled a curly strip of meat – blackened edges, orange-red in the middle – with long metal tweezers from between the slats. Krish's stomach gurgled but he was not sure if could eat right now. And what would he do about money?

As he wandered aimlessly, his empty stomach doing all the thinking, he passed a small gathering and saw the rather bad magician again, this time trying to cast a spell on a little wooden chair.

'Stand back, ladies and gents! Stand back!' the magician was shouting. 'This may look like yer ordinary, run-of-the-mill chair but in a few seconds time it'll be a mighty 'orse and yer'll be saddlin' it up and speedin' off on your way to Alvaris! Behold!'

And in a puff of violet smoke the little chair transformed into... a slightly smaller chair. With a missing leg. The chair then promptly fell over.

'Oh,' said the magician. 'Bugger.'

The crowd laughed and turned to leave, hurling a little loose change at the magician out of sympathy. One little girl even decided to throw the vegetable she was chewing at the magician. It hit the magician on the ear and then Krish swore he saw something fly out of the magician's finger, carefully aimed at the little girl. The tiniest shimmer of green and moments later the shimmer bloated into a ball of orange with black stripes. Muscular legs shot out of the shape, beating across the dusty ground, and finally there appeared a tail at one end and at the other a fearsome face of long, sharp teeth, whiskers and wild eyes. The mighty tiger reared up, opened its mouth wide and growled silently. Krish couldn't hear. Nobody could hear. But the vegetable-throwing girl it was growling at heard and screamed. The crowd turned but the tiger had vanished, disintegrated into a scattering of yellow dust that disappeared into the sands covering the ground of the marketplace before anyone else saw it. The girl was pointing at the place where the tiger wasn't and sobbing uncontrollably. Her parents sighed deeply, shook their heads and dragged her away. Krish turned to the magician and saw her smirk, but seconds later she sighed too and started to pack up her things.

Krish was fascinated by her. When he looked closer he observed that she could only have been a few years older than him. Krish didn't realise how long he'd been watching the magician pack up until she looked up and caught his eye.

'What are you staring at?!' the magician shouted at him. Her eyes large, dark and angry.

'I, er, I'm,' Krish said. 'I'm, I'm just… nothing. Nothing, really.'

She eyed him curiously, her upper lip slightly curled. 'Bloody idiot.' She continued packing up. 'And you look out for them trap markets!'

The magician occupied his mind for quite a bit of his wander across the town. She was clearly secretly rather good, so why pretend to be so awful?

As the stream of people flowing through the streets lessened with the waning sun, Krish realised he'd better find somewhere to sleep pretty soon. And preferably something to eat before he starved to death. He was pushing all thoughts of getting a band of thieves together or finding the Night Ocean or whatever to the back of his mind. *Get something to eat and somewhere to sleep and then worry about every other problem you have in the world,* he told himself.

Krish came across one of the largest buildings in the town. If you could really call it a building. It was made of huge mud bricks (large quantities of straw mixed in with dried mud and sand), precariously balanced together in such a way that it looked like a light breeze might knock it over at any minute. Hanging outside there was a painted sign of a clumsy-looking farmer reaping his field using an implement with a long shaft which had clearly been snapped in two and then badly fastened back together again with a belt. The sign read 'The Broken Scythe' at the top and, farther down, 'Vacancies'. It looked very much like a sign for a pub, but inside it wasn't quite how he expected it to be.

Instead of there being lots of people sitting on chairs at regular tables, everybody sat on the floor at low circular tables. They appeared to be drinking hot tea, much of it minty-smelling with steam flying off the top, but most were talking as jovially as if it were beer in their mugs.

There was no sign of anything like a bartender, but in one corner of the room there was a pile of silver teapots next to a line of black metal fire pits, a teapot or two on each slowly coming to the boil. Whoever was in charge of this place couldn't be far away. Perhaps... yes! If he took a teapot off its fire pit someone would surely say something and maybe that person would be... He didn't know. Maybe this wasn't the best plan, but it was all he had. His tummy gurgled at him again as he headed over to the fire pits but his brain wasn't exactly in gear as he lifted the silver pot off the fire. In a moment he felt it: the red hot metal sent a stab of pain right through him as his skin burned. He dropped the teapot and as he rushed forward to retrieve it from the ground he knocked over the fire pit. The grate fell to one side and ash and hot coals spilled onto the rug. He scrambled around on the floor with more energy than he'd had for hours, trying to get the coals back into the fire pit, but a hubbub had erupted around him. The Scythe's patrons rushed forward and were grabbing the coals with their sleeves and tossing them back into the fire pit and then shaking their burnt fingers cool in the air while gritting their teeth. There was nothing Krish could do and the rug was catching light...

A roaring voice. The patrons jumped away from the fire pit and then large, leathery hands reached to grab the coals and chuck them back into the pit. The hands' owner stamped out a small gathering of flames on the singed rug before throwing the grate back onto the fire pit with a great clang.

Krish collapsed onto his knees, the last of his energy sapped by the past few seconds' misadventure. He had nothing left. As he lost consciousness he looked into the furious eyes of a man with a weather-beaten face...

He awoke. His lips were dry and cracked. He had a splitting headache. From the fall? From the lack of food and water? And... The sight in front him was...

He inhaled quickly through his nose as he sat bolt upright. The sight in front of him was the same as the one he'd been faced with when he'd lost consciousness. The weather-beaten-faced man with the leathery hands. Only the angry eyes were now more stern than furious.

'Well, I hope yer weren't plannin' to go anywhere in an 'urry,' said the man. His face was covered in patches of grey bristles and he had a large, knobbly nose that oddly resembled a ginger root. Krish stared blankly back. 'I don't know what yer thought yer were doing but yer destroyed one of my best rugs and yer'll be workin' 'ere until yer've earned the cost of a new one!' The man sniffed, scratched his nose and sniffed again.

Krish stared dizzily around. He was in a small, round room piled up with dirty plates and teapots and several wooden butts filled with water, many of the plates and teapots soaking in them. Then he remembered everything. The devil, the palace, the King, the magician with the deep, dark eyes that he couldn't look away from, even when they scolded him.

'I said!' The angry man was still talking to him. 'Don't think yer'll be goin' anywhere fast!'

Krish looked at the man. He thought. He spoke: 'What if I keep working? After I've made enough to pay for the rug?' His brain was going full pelt after his impromptu nap. 'I-I mean if that's possible. If you need someone. I could cook and clean and you could give me some food and somewhere to sleep and…'

He stared at the man, who was examining him as if he were a whole new species.

'Yer cheeky little sod!' The man's eyes then landed on Krish's cracked lips. He scratched his nose again. This took some time as there was plenty of it to scratch. He sniffed decisively then picked up a cup made of bone and filled it with water from a butt that contained no plates or teapots. He passed it to Krish and Krish downed it so fast he thought for a second he'd drown himself as the wonderful, refreshingly cool water poured down his parched throat. His lips tingled as he ran his tongue over them to relieve the pain; they felt more like jagged rocks than skin right now.

The man was now using one hand to select lumps of meat and vegetable left on the dishes waiting to be washed up, scratching his nose again with the other. He placed all the scraps on a single plate. He passed the plate to Krish, who ate the cold food so fast that he hardly noticed how different the meat tasted from anything he'd ever had in his own world.

'Yer one of them orphans?' said the man. 'From across The Scar?'

Krish considered this and nodded.

The man thought for a moment and then mirrored Krish's nod. He wandered around the room, lost in thought, scratching every millimetre of his large, ginger-root nose at least twice. Then he picked up a large box and placed it lengthways on the ground. The refreshing smell of dried mint leaves wafted Krish's way from the direction of the box. The man sat on the box. Gruff and old though he was, he now looked almost childlike as the box raised him high enough for his feet to dangle off the ground. One side of his mouth curved up a little in what Krish supposed was a lazy smile.

'Yer know much about 'ygiene?' the man asked.

'Hygiene?!' parroted Krish.

'Yeah. Cleanliness. Means what plates and mugs and stuff are like for a few seconds 'fore all the germs jump aboard.'

'Oh. Right.' Krish knew perfectly well what hygiene and cleanliness meant. He was actually more surprised that anyone who'd ever set foot in this kitchen knew the words' meanings. 'You, er, want me to do the washing up?'

'No,' said the man, scratching his nose again. 'I want you to tell me that if I give you room and board for a bit o' work sweepin' and such that yer'll keep yer trap shut if anyone comes sniffin' around usin' words like "'ygiene" and "cleanliness". Particularly anyone... "inspectory"-lookin'.'

The man nodded at Krish knowingly. Krish nodded back, hoping he looked convincing enough.

'My name's Tol,' said the man. 'I'm in charge 'ere and yer'll do as I say. Yer'll clean 'ere for a couple of weeks and then... then we'll see.'

Krish ended up staying at the Broken Scythe for a quite a few days. The wait was killing him. He quickly settled into a slow pace of life and every now and then he'd remember why he was there and a cold feeling would rush through his body as if he'd just woken from a dream to find himself in a very real nightmare. Krish had decided that the best thing to do was to try and ignore all the worries in his head and get on with exploring the town to see what he could discover.

The first thing he stumbled upon was a trap market; something the magician had warned him about. He saw an entranceway to a souk adorned with purple drapes. Turbaned merchants were offering spices and silver teapots and rugs and all kinds of exotic items to entice him in. He was intrigued and entered a labyrinthine arcade of market stalls set into alcoves, all no larger than a few telephone boxes, each packed with lanterns or spices or furniture or rugs or teapots of all shapes and sizes. A man wearing an eyepatch tried to force a game board, very similar-looking to draughts except with hexagonal spaces, on him. Everyone attempted to persuade him to part with money he didn't have to purchase souvenirs he didn't want. 'Where you from?' they'd ask. He could never quite find a way to explain. He moved faster and faster and journeyed deeper and deeper into the souk until he swore he was encountering the same merchants and the same stalls he'd passed earlier. He even ran into the man with the eyepatch and the hexagonal draughts board again. Krish began to cotton on to what was happening. The whole passageway was slightly curved and he noticed that a long way back along the walkway there were merchants furiously at work packing up their stalls. With one decisive sprint to the right he evaded the merchants and dived under the purple drapes. He emerged onto the street and looked back to see that the souk was only a few hundred feet long. It comprised a series of tents that were being taken down at one end and quickly reconstructed at the other. The tents were pitched in a rough circle so the unfortunate customer became trapped within as the market went on and on and on. The merchants gesticulated and threw spices at him. He never set foot in a trap market again.

During his time at the Broken Scythe he didn't find out much. He discovered that people laughed at him if he mentioned the Night Ocean or FireHawks. He knew it was ludicrous, and clearly a joke that the King had made, but he preferred to have some hope to cling to.

He struggled to adjust to the short days and nights on this world. He tried staying awake for two days and the night in between, sleeping during the second night, but he then found himself sleeping through the night and the next day, only to wake up as the sun was setting. His body was confused and he walked around in a daze through the nights and the days, which were often just as noisy as each other as there were always some people who were still up and about at all times. A nocturnal existence didn't curry much favour with Tol either, who wanted him to be washing up teapots during the day when the Scythe was busiest.

Tol also liked Krish to write out the new menus for him. Tol wasn't the best at spelling. Krish was pretty surprised that he was able to translate not only this world's spoken language but also its written language. This helped him correct errors in Tol's old menu.

'This creature—' he pointed to one item on the menu '—"mined trarker". Do you have to, like, dig it up?'

'What the 'ell yer babblin' on about?' Tol was half laughing, half looking genuinely cross. 'Course yer don't "dig it up"! Yer got trarkers your side of The Scar!' Krish kept forgetting that his cover story for not knowing much about this world was being from the other side of something called The Scar. 'They live out in the wilds! Any kid knows that!'

'Right,' Krish tried to retain his patience. 'So they're not found in mines?'

Tol laughed and shook his head like Krish was stupid. 'No!'

'Well, why does it say "mined trarker" then?'

'It don't say that! It says "*minced* trarker"! Can't you read?'

Krish smiled politely and started correcting the menus. He could read. He just found it easier to understand if all the letters were both present and in the right order.

After a few more days he settled into a pattern of going to bed just before the sun rose, sleeping through the next day and night, and waking just as the sun was coming up on the second day. It began to feel more like a winter's day back home where half the day was dark anyway. As he got used to this routine his mind began to feel more awake. Unfortunately this also meant he was all the more aware of how hopeless his situation was and how little he'd achieved in the week or so since he'd arrived. He set himself a deadline: *three more days and I'll... well, I'll have to come up with another plan. Perhaps one that actually is a plan.*

Krish also discovered the school, which was in the bar at the Broken Scythe.

He came downstairs on the first day, knowing he had an hour or so to kill before he was meant to clean the carpet in the bar, and found thirty or forty children sitting on the floor in front of a teacher who was writing on a blackboard.

'Now,' said the teacher to her class, 'who can tell me the best way to fix a crop-spinner?' A sea of hands appeared in the air above the children. All the questions were similar; questions about crops, about farming or about mining. Nobody learned about science or maths or English or history or anything. The teacher was fairly young and slim, with a round, friendly face and short straight, black hair tied back. Her face might have appeared kindly but she was capable of giving harsh, piercing glares when required.

Krish found out from Tol that the reason the teacher, named Madam Nboosa (you had to say the 'N' from the back of the throat through closed lips), always seemed so tired was that she came straight from the field where she worked during the night. One day by the trenches he saw her giving an impromptu lesson to a number of the children working there, who Tol said couldn't afford to go to school. She would even bring the occasional satchelful of vegetables into the class to share with the children, which seemed to be an incentive for some of the smaller, hungrier-looking children to turn up. (For the better-fed kids who screwed their noses up at the vegetables it appeared to be good motivation to bunk off.) As far as he could tell, Madam Nboosa was an entire school all by herself; a teacher, head-mistress and dinner lady all rolled into one.

'Where's Balthrir today?' Nboosa asked her class. 'She's been off for the last week. If anyone knows and isn't telling me they'll be in detention for a year!'

The children sniggered and said that her parents couldn't afford the fees any more. Another said that she preferred to hang around the market these days. Some minutes later Krish realised exactly who this Balthrir character was.

He had gone upstairs to sweep the landing by the guest rooms. When he opened the broom cupboard, the sight that greeted him took him quite by surprise. In the cupboard were a number of people, all standing around, apparently completely unaware that he was gawping open-mouthed at them. One lady was humming away to herself, as if looking around at some picturesque landscape rather than the side wall of the broom cupboard. One was miming having a shave and another appeared to be fast asleep despite standing bolt upright.

To say that Krish was confused would be an understatement roughly the size of Australia.

'Oi!' came a voice behind him. 'Get off my turf!'

Krish turned around to see the magician, still wearing her bent hat, coming up the stairs holding her staff. She looked furious.

'If yer think yer gonna muscle in on my territory yer got another think coming, matey boy!'

'Sorry, I have no idea—'

The magician turned around and saw a guest coming up the stairs. She threw her hat and staff into the corner and quickly tied a belt around her middle. She suddenly looked much less like a magician. She turned to Krish and thrust a coin into his palm.

'Five Kalrahs. Keep yer trap shut, all right?' She turned to the guest, adopting a smile so wide that it must have hurt. 'My friend! Lookin' for a room?'

'Well, yes, as a matter of fact,' said the guest.

'Step right this way, sir! The manager's out and about at the mo doin' whatever managers do but do you know what? Sneaky bugger always overcharges for the worst rooms. You want something decent-sized for a decent price, right?'

'Well, I suppose.'

'Excellent! Got just the right thing for yer!' The magician led the guest over to the broom cupboard, her hand on his back to guide him. 'Now this room has the best view of the Forgotten Mountains and it's ten Kalrahs off tonight.'

'Oh marvellous!' The guest quickly parted with his money and Krish noticed the magician grab hold of her staff from the corner and, unseen by her customer, wave it over his head. Colour bubbled briefly over the guest's head before she opened up the cupboard door. 'How charming!' he said before the magician slammed the door shut behind him.

The magician spun round to face Krish. 'Temporary delusion spell. Advanced stuff, eh?'

Those big, deep, dark eyes again, staring right at him. He'd better say something smart. 'So...' he began. 'You're a magician?'

'Oi!' The 'magician' produced a rather pointy finger and practically stuck it up Krish's nose in disgust. 'I wasn't the only seventh-grade pupil to get a double-distinction in wizardry to be a flippin' conjuror, boyo!'

Whoever she was she was coarse and rude and determined to annoy him. Krish liked her very much. He spent most of his life being polite and kind and half the time he just wanted to say whatever he felt like without caring who he offended.

'So, what are you?' he asked.

'Cor, you really ain't the sharpest tool in the utility belt, are yer? I'm a bloody wizard!'

'But that thing you did... with the temporary delusion... thing... and the tiger! I saw you... magic up a tiger in the street! But you didn't want anyone to see. I mean, I don't really know anything about magic but... you seem much better than the other mag— wizards, but you were acting like you were... well, a bit rubbish at magic.'

'Ha! Yeah. Not much room for a good wizard round 'ere.'

'Erm, why is it such a bad thing to be a good mag— wizard?'

'Listen, sonny Jim! There are three types of wizard – the cheap conjurors who make a bob or two on the street and –' in hushed tones, looking around – 'ones who run the odd little scam –' then back to her normal volume – 'or the super-uber-awesome wizards who work for kings and queens and nobles and all that.'

'Oh. You must earn a lot of money then, I guess?'

'Enough.' And then little quieter, 'Almost enough.'

'Oh.' Krish detected that he shouldn't really be probing but since she was the first person he'd had a proper conversation with in a long time he risked it. 'Enough for...?'

The wizard stared into nothingness for a moment, looking away from him. She seemed tense, as if she was sucking some great feeling in. All of a sudden she peered over at him, her face lighter, relaxed. She turned her head on its side and pulled an odd expression.

'Sorry,' she said. 'But, why the 'ell are you listenin' to anything I'm sayin'?' She didn't seem cross. In fact she appeared quite amused.

'What?' said Krish.

'I said, why the 'ell are yer listenin' to anything I'm sayin'? In't I clearly a bloody maniac?'

'Er... yeah. I guess.'

'Well, people don't tend to listen to bloody maniacs. Particularly when they're like, well, *me*.'

In a strange way, Krish knew how she felt. 'People don't really listen to me much either.'

The wizard nodded. 'Yer a bit borin'.'

'Sorry.'

'What for?'

'For being boring.'

'I wasn't sayin' there was anything wrong with that. It's interestin'. More interestin' than most people 'round 'ere 'oo pretend to be interestin' when really they're bloody borin' down to the bone!'

'So...' Krish was trying to get his head round what she'd just said. 'You're saying that I'm *so* boring that I can't even be bothered to pretend to be interesting and that's... interesting...?'

'Yeah! At least you're yerself.'

'You're very much yourself too.'

'Well 'oo the 'ell else would I be?'

'Good point. I just meant... you don't pretend to be anything you're not, I guess.'

They stared at each other for quite some time, approvingly Krish thought, until he braved breaking the silence.

'So, you're not a super-uber-awe—'

'Well, I probably am but there's no place for a good wizard on the streets. The rubbish ones don't think it's fair that there are some better than them and yer end up being turfed out of town pretty sharpish. Best to play it for laughs and 'ope for a few sympathy Shellas. The best wizard always ends up in the court of the King and that's old Eshter in this neck of the woods and she's been hangin' around a long time!

It's one good wizard per king. That's the rule. Ain't another crown-wielding fat-cat this side of The Scar!'

'Why don't you cross The Scar?' By now Krish had figured out that 'The Scar' was some kind of river or even ocean.

'I'm scared of water.'

'And you're meant to be in class!' came the voice of Madam Nboosa from below, accompanied by the sound of footsteps.

The wizard muttered a word Krish had heard a lot on Dawson's stealing and fighting game.

'Quick!' she said. 'Cover for me! Just nod yer head a lot. Don't say a word!' The wizard passed her staff over Krish's face and he felt a tingle before she disappeared behind a wooden statue at the far end of the corridor.

'There you are!' said Nboosa to a rather confused Krish. 'Come on, Balthrir! Back to class!' *Balthrir?* Did he look like this Balthrir character?

Krish suddenly realised he was wearing the wizard's clothes. And had her hands as well. He was a bit taller too. More her height. Then he realised.

'Balthrir! Come on! I'm not making the whole class wait for...' Nboosa stopped and examined Krish from a slightly different angle. An amused smile crept across her face. 'Oh, very good! The nose isn't quite right and there's not quite the right level of arrogance in the eyes but a good try! Balthrir! Come out!' She was talking to the rest of the room now.

Balthrir emerged from behind the statue.

'Oooh!' Balthrir's smile was so bright Krish felt he needed sunglasses, and her tone was sickly sweet. 'Madam Nboosa! Fancy seeing you 'ere! Looking for a room? Mr Nboosa kick you out again?'

Madam Nboosa's crossed arms did not look amused.

'If that broom cupboard is full of people under a temporary delusion spell you'll be in serious trouble, young lady!'

'I wouldn't say "full",' said Balthrir under her breath in a tone that suggested she wished she'd crammed in a few more.

'And I suppose you haven't bothered with your homework either,' added Nboosa.

''Omework…?' said Balthrir in the tone of someone trying to remember what they had for breakfast three Tuesdays ago. 'Oh that! Yeah, done that!'

'Really?'

'Uh-huh.'

Nboosa re-crossed her arms a little tighter than before. 'Have you considered maybe progressing from having done your homework to handing it in?'

'Oh, well I would've done, miss, course I would've done, but it was too good. Not one to blow my own trumpet but it was pretty damn awesome. *Too awesome*, in fact, for anyone to read. Didn't want you to 'ave to go through all that "Oh, Balthrir's the best! She's so brilliant! You lot, pack yer bags and get out of here! Balthrir clearly has such an advanced intellect that I'm just going to have to tutor her one-on-one if I'm to have enough energy to match her mental prowess!" Would 'ave been embarrassing for yer, miss. So I burned it.'

Nboosa raised an eyebrow. 'You burned it?'

'Yep. It was *so* good that I 'ad to burn it. Plus I know yer can't burn stuff in the classroom, miss. Wouldn't want yer to get in trouble again. Not after Tol caught you smokin' in there last week.' Balthrir said this last sentence a little more quietly as she took a tentative step towards Madam Nboosa. Nboosa tried to retain her composure but Krish could tell a pang of nerves had just shot through the teacher's body. She uncrossed her arms and spoke to Balthrir in a lighter tone.

'Just empty that broom cupboard and give everyone their money back. And release whoever *that* is.' Nboosa indicated Krish and he felt a tingle as Balthrir returned him to normal. 'It's a good mask spell, Balthrir.'

'One of yours, miss.' Balthrir gave a hopeful smile to her teacher.

Nboosa sighed. 'I'm sorry I couldn't teach you more magic, Balthrir. You know it's very much…' She lowered her voice. 'Of personal interest to me.' Nboosa returned to normal volume. 'But the King demands that the syllabus focuses almost exclusively on mining and agriculture these days.'

'But, miss, I don't want to learn about plants and rocks and all that! They're rubbish!'

'Well, you don't have a choice.'

'But I can't afford all the exams! I mean, *my parents* can't afford 'em,' Balthrir hastily corrected herself. 'Why can't I just sit my wizardry exams?'

'Because wizardry isn't compulsory. Agriculture and mining are. You'll never make a Shella out of magic anyway. No matter how good you are at it. Now get that broom cupboard cleared and if I ever catch you running a scam while you're meant to be in class again I'll take you straight to the authorities. I'm sorry, Balthrir, but I won't have a choice in the matter next time. And you'll have to give me that staff once you're finished with this lot. You can have it back at the end of the lesson.'

Madam Nboosa walked back downstairs.

Balthrir looked crushed. She walked up to the cupboard, let the guests out one by one, gave them their money back and solemnly apologised to them all as Krish swept the room.

'Balthrir!' Madam Nboosa called from below.

Balthrir turned to Krish, removing the belt from her middle and picking up her staff and floppy hat.

'See yer 'round, kid.' And then, rather sheepishly, she added: 'Thanks for listenin'.'

'Krish.' He offered his hand and they shook. Then he said out loud something that had just crept across his mind. 'Your parents don't pay for your lessons, do they?'

Balthrir glanced over her shoulder. 'No. They had to see a man about a dog.' Then in a whisper: 'The man was the Criminal Justice Department. The dog was a prison sentence. If they find out my parents are inmates they'll send me to work in the fields.' Her eyes darted from the window to the stairs and then back to Krish. She put a finger to her lips and then sulked off. Krish stared out of the window and took in the shimmering black towers of the palace once again.

CHAPTER 11

SMASHED GLASS

The next few days were quiet. Or as quiet as a world that never sleeps can be.

Krish was sleeping badly, not just because of the lack of progress he was making but mainly due to sleeping in the Broken Scythe. His tiny room stank of damp, the bed was as comfortable as sleeping on a cold stone floor with a thin layer of cardboard between you and the ground, and the tap in the bathroom spluttered water for just a few seconds before giving up completely. There was no shower either so the best Krish could ever hope for was a small volume of water in his cupped hands to wash his face with. He didn't smell great and his clothes got worn and torn within a few days, but it all seemed to help him fit in.

Tol fed him rice and spiced meat in the mornings and rice with sugar and currants in the evenings. This world (which he'd now discovered was called Ilir) had only two meals a day, both of which he had at the bar with a glass of mint tea. The town by the Black Palace was named Al Kara. Al Kara controlled many of the nearby towns and settlements, with the Lords of the West, East and South (Elwynt, R'ghir and Hesh) and the Lady of the North (Vira) enforcing the King's control over their lands. In return for a share of the harvest (most of it coming from the fertile fields of Melkur), Al Kara unburdened many citizens of the little wealth they possessed. Most were willing to obey, as the alternative was a sword separating your head from the rest of your body or an extended stint as part of the Black Palace. Tol said (in hushed tones) that the King often felt that his citizens were too obedient (many were indeed obedient but only through fear) and that his palace would soon run out of convicts to hold up the walls. So he simply invented new crimes to keep the walls standing. Tol stated, after giving his nose a particularly long scratch, that he'd almost ended up as a wash basin in the royal lavatory for a month because all the mint leaves he placed in the glasses of tea he served were purportedly 'the wrong way up'. This was how people usually talked of the King and his Lords and Lady: quietly and with a shake of the head. If anyone said they liked or respected him they'd state it flatly and without much conviction.

Krish was getting a little sick of the laughter he was met with every time he mentioned the Night Ocean, FireHawks or tying a bow around the world, so he became even quieter than usual. He worried that he was wasting time but the devil had said that time would only move for him; when he returned it would be exactly the same time he left. Somehow this didn't help.

He passed Balthrir in class a few times as well and she looked progressively more miserable with each day that went by. Occasionally she caught his eye and directed an exaggerated yawn at him while Madam Nboosa explained crop rotation, but mainly she just sat there, staring into nothingness, asleep with her eyes open.

One evening Krish was surprised to see Nboosa and Balthrir alone in the classroom together. He sat at the top of the stairs for a while and watched them.

'No, like this!' said Nboosa. A vision of a miniature pink horse shot out of her fingertip and ran across the desk. It was a little faint and hazy.

'What, like this?' Balthrir held up her staff and a full-sized purple horse with yellow spots dashed across the room, clear and solid-looking.

'Well, yes... but...' Nboosa looked embarrassed. 'Well, it's easier with a staff, of course! Look, I'll write to Madam Eshter. If she permits magic to be taught as an extra-curricular activity then, well... maybe we can consider you sitting your wizardry exams.'

Balthrir instantly perked up. For a moment Krish thought she was going to hug Madam Nboosa. On all other occasions he'd seen them together he could have been certain they were sworn enemies. Right now they seemed much more comfortable with each other – they were still wary but there was a certain respect between the two of them. Until Balthrir almost spoilt everything by eyeing up a potential customer lingering outside of the Scythe. Nboosa turned sour.

'I'm serious, Balthrir!' said Nboosa. 'Do you have any idea how much trouble you'll be in if you're caught cramming people into broom cupboards again? *And* how much trouble I'll be in as your teacher for not knowing what you were up to and stopping you? You'll get us both thrown into the walls of the palace!'

Balthrir brushed off her obvious interest in the potential customer outside and the lesson continued.

The next evening, as Krish was tidying the bar area after all the customers had gone home, he heard a familiar voice outside the window.

'Seesi Nboosa!' The voice belonged to Madam Eshter, the court wizard. She strolled up to Madam Nboosa, who was eating a bowl of soup in a doorway with two friends who sat on little stools playing cards. Nboosa looked up. She was shocked at the sudden appearance of Eshter. She quickly put down her bowl and took to her feet.

'Madam Eshter!' said Nboosa. 'It's a real honour—'

'You are Madam Seesi Nboosa?'

Nboosa considered for a moment. 'Yes,' she answered, flatly.

'You've been teaching magic to a pupil, I understand?'

'Well, yes, I... I didn't think it was a crime if it was voluntary and the pupil was keen to learn.'

'You are correct that it is not a crime to teach extra lessons.' Eshter drew herself up to her full height as she spoke, just to emphasise to Nboosa that although the teacher was younger and more beautiful than her, she, Madam Eshter, was at least considerably taller. 'But are you a fully qualified wizard...?'

Nboosa was silent but she refused to look down in shame. Eshter drew close to Nboosa. Krish strained to hear what was being said. He only just made it out.

'It's my job to hunt down and prosecute amateur wizards masquerading as professionals,' whispered Eshter. 'It involves a lot of paperwork. I am not keen on the concept of "paperwork". And you wouldn't want to overburden me with time-consuming paperwork, would you?'

Nboosa shook her head, masking her fury well.

'Good,' said Eshter. 'No more magic lessons, *amateur*.' She narrowed her eyes at Nboosa as she walked off. Nboosa stared in Eshter's direction long after she'd gone, boiling with rage.

Krish spent the rest of his evening sweeping and feeling quite sorry for both Nboosa and Balthrir. He was also aware that it was the most exciting thing that had happened in days. The monotony of working at the Broken Scythe was making him restless. He knew he had to do something soon or he'd never get home.

One day Krish returned from another fruitless jaunt into town to find that both Madam Nboosa and Balthrir were absent from school and a short man with rough and filthy clothes was explaining to the class about the advantages of children – who didn't have the obstacle of extreme height to overcome – working in the mines of Traldaar and that there were plenty of work placements there this summer.

Krish thought little of this scene as he climbed the stairs to sweep the hallway. As he reached the top he found Balthrir pacing up and down the corridor. After a moment she caught his eye.

'Thank Jingaloid!' He didn't have time to stop and ask who or what Jingaloid was as Balthrir marched up to him. 'Listen, Krist – that was yer name, weren't it? – I need yer help! One more scam and I can do m'wizardry exam! That rhymes! Gotta make sense, innit?' Krish half nodded, half mumbled in agreement. 'Nboosa's stopped giving me extra lessons for some reason but she's said I can take the exam… and I can do it soon, she says! Even better, the old bat's away today! It's perfect! Right, listen up – this is the plan—'

'Hang on!' said Krish. 'I haven't agreed to anything yet!'

'What?!' Balthrir looked genuinely confused. 'What d'yer mean? You're the boring one! The boring one that just goes along with whatever the not-boring one (that's me, by the way) says!'

Krish thought fast. 'In return for what?'

Balthrir's head jolted backwards as a half-shocked, half-disgusted expression spread across her face. 'What the 'ell are you talkin' about?'

'W-well,' Krish hadn't quite thought this far ahead. 'You do magic tricks for money! I want something in return for helping you! L-like a trip to the Night Ocean or-or—'

'What?! We only just met and yer want me to take yer on an 'oliday? To the *Night Ocean*?! What are you...?' Balthrir stopped. They heard voices downstairs. It was a new customer speaking to Tol at the bar. They caught a little of what the new customer was saying...

'Just for a night or two...'

'Right!' said Balthrir. 'Whatever you want! But first, this is what yer've got to do...'

A minute or so later they had a plan ready and they heard the new customer (or 'sucker' as Balthrir liked to call them) head up the stairs.

'Right,' said Balthrir under her breath. 'Ready?'

'Yeah,' answered Krish. 'I guess.' He spoke up so that the customer/'sucker' could hear. 'It is indeed a most excellent room, madam, and the view is to die for! But my father says he won't pay a Shella more than forty-five Kalrahs!'

'That is a real shame, sir.' Balthrir was a very good actor and she seemed to have a captive audience in the new customer. 'We reduced the room from sixty-five Kalrahs to fifty-five this morning! Tell yer what, if yer can stretch to fifty I'm sure I can smooth things over with the management.'

'Sorry,' said Krish. 'My father can't go over forty-five. Even for that amazing view!'

'Not to worry, sir,' sighed Balthrir. 'I don't suppose *you're* looking for the best room in the house for a bargain, Mr...?'

As Balthrir turned with a winning smile to face the customer he passed a hand in front of his face and the 'sucker's' whole body rippled as if someone had dropped a pebble into a pond. The form standing before them settled and they were faced with Madam Nboosa's furious gaze.

'Ah,' said Balthrir conclusively.

'*That* is how you do a convincing mask spell, young lady,' said Madam Nboosa, hardly moving her lips from the pursed expression they were participating in.

'Blimey! I've been rumbled!' Balthrir's voice quavered with hysteria.

'I gave you so many chances, Balthrir.' Nboosa shook her head. 'I gave you one last warning and you *completely* ignored me! You and your accomplice are going to pay a visit to the authorities.'

'Ah. Sorry, miss.' She seized her staff from the corner. 'Allergic to the fuzz.'

'Is that so?' Nboosa sighed. 'Come on, Balthrir. Enough of this.'

Balthrir turned to Krish, her eyes as wild with panic as they were with excitement. 'What d'yer reckon, kid? Hand ourselves in?'

Krish answered with a gaping open mouth from which syllables seemed reluctant to escape.

'Y'er right,' Balthrir continued the exchange without him. 'Better jump out the window. Much more sensible.'

And without another word she took his hand, sped past Madam Nboosa, who reached out to apprehend both of them, and Krish found himself experiencing the sting of smashing glass against his body and the crashing sounds of destruction followed by the whooshing of air in his ears. He was in the air just long enough to see three things: firstly, the ground coming up rather quickly. Secondly, Balthrir's staff swooshing across his field of vision accompanied by a burst of colour. And finally, the ground suddenly becoming slightly nearer and considerably more mattress-shaped just before they crashed into it.

Balthrir dragged him to his feet. Krish could only focus on the number of little cuts across his arms and the shouts of Nboosa above.

'Come on!' cried Balthrir. 'Let's get the fudge-monkeys outta here!' Krish didn't know quite what his brain had just translated but judging by the proceeding minutes' activities it definitely involved a lot of running.

CHAPTER 12

A POT OF HALFIRE

'What now?' asked Krish, struggling to keep up with Balthrir.

'What now?!' Balthrir answered. 'What now?! *Now* is time for me to get the 'ell outta here! That's it, mate! No wizardry exams for me! *Nothing!* I'm done for! I'm outta here! Thanks for screwin' things up!'

'I-I-I... I'm sorry! I—'

Balthrir stopped, turned and shoved her face so close to his that she almost poked his eye out with her nose. 'You're the boring one. The boring one shuts up now before 'e gets us into further fughundi do-do!'

Balthrir led them to the edge of town where there was a mule tied to a post. Krish was too out of breath to ask any more questions as Balthrir, without looking at him, produced two large water bottles coated in animal skins from the mule's saddle bags and disappeared round the corner, where there was a handful of merchants' stalls. She returned minutes later with a few items wrapped in brown paper and the water bottles looking a little heavier than before. Then she led the mule towards the end of the road and Krish followed. The dry solid earth turned to hot powdery sand in minutes and the noise of the town soon left his ears.

The sand got everywhere. His mouth, his nostrils, the corners of his eyes. He swore it had even found its way into his underwear. Removing it from his hair was almost impossible. And his shoes filled with the stuff with every footstep. He tried walking barefoot but it was like torture: the sand, having been exposed to harsh sunlight all day long, burned the soles of his feet, but a moment later his feet would sink into the ice-cold grains beneath the surface that the sun had not had time to heat in Ilir's short days. Balthrir kept on marching forward in her beaten-up old sandals without looking back at him, apparently not feeling the sand or letting it hinder her.

The sand appeared to change colour as the sun arched across the sky. A pale, off-white hue in the mornings, light yellow at midday and deep orange as the sun was swallowed by the horizon, becoming almost red in the dying light of the day, minutes before the sky filled with stars and darkness.

Krish was glad when the sand turned to earth once more: a large stretch of light brown ground, baked by the sun and riddled with cracks. This world was so small he swore he could see the curvature of the land on the horizon, just as he had up on the mountain when he'd first arrived. He stared into the distance, the shape of Ilir so clear, so real, tasting the sand in his mouth, feeling the warmth of a sun so far from his own, and wondering how any book, any story Jess or anyone else had ever read could compare to this. Feeling, tasting, smelling another world that appeared, in many respects, so normal. Yet it was so far from normal. The way the breeze meandered around him, the way the sun warmed him to the bone and the flavours of this world's food were so subtly different from anything he had ever experienced he could not begin to describe how much this world looked like his own but *felt* like nothing you could possibly have imagined.

The sand returned. Dunes as high as houses to his left. To his right there was a small ridge in the sand, a natural border stretching for miles. Across the border was a channel of sand and small grey rocks. Beyond this, a valley and hills appearing to consist of more dunes covered in the grey rocks. Ahead of them, clusters of trees and scrub atop small mounds. These must be oases: pockets of water beneath the surface, or perhaps there were even underground rivers here that fed the hardy flora growing in this barren terrain.

Day faded into night once more and they stopped in the shelter of one of the oases. Balthrir enchanted an axe and sent it to work chopping wood from a dead tree. It took her some time to get the spell right. At first the axe was hacking away at the wood with such vigour that splinters were flying off all over the place. The mule decided that it was safest to place Krish between himself and the maniacal axe.

'Bloody thing!' shouted Balthrir as she cast another spell to slow it down. Once she'd got the speed right she started searching the oasis for kindling. Krish tried to gather some kindling himself but when the wizard struck up a fire she politely left his rather pathetic-looking collection of twigs to one side. She then produced a large spiky fruit from the undergrowth, wrapped it tightly in a dark-coloured skin from a bag on the mule (who was munching on shrubs growing at the foot of the tree they were seated under) and placed it just off the centre of the fire to cook.

It was only when Balthrir spoke, as they both stared tiredly into the flames, that Krish realised that they'd scarcely said a word to each other all day.

'So, yer still 'ere, eh?' said the wizard, her voice merry but tired.

'Erm, yeah. I guess,' answered Krish.

They examined each other over the crackling fire, their faces deep orange against the endless black that blocked the rest of the world from sight. The smoke stung their eyes.

'So,' began the wizard. 'Maybe it's time for some proper introductions and all that. Hello, as I said, my name's Balthrir. Well, Balthrira really. Balthrir is a boy's name. My grandfather's. But Balthrira is a rubbish name. Sounds like an ear infection or summink. You ever 'ad an ear infection? They're rubbish. Kriss, innit?'

A second or two after Balthrir had finished speaking Krish realised it was his turn.

'Krish. Er... Krishna. But... yeah, Krish. Krish is best.'

'And yer followin' me because...?'

'I... thought we skipped town.'

A knowing smile and a raised eyebrow from Balthrir invited him to say more.

'And because... I don't know anybody else,' he said.

'Yer don't know me.'

'No. I'm sorry. I don't...' Krish just couldn't find the words.

The young wizard eyed him curiously. For a few seconds she spoke slowly, even bothering to pronounce everything (well, almost everything) correctly. 'Where are you from? You're not from round 'ere. And however weird your story is, I bet I've 'eard weirder. And what's all this stuff about going to the Night Ocean?'

Krish waited for a few more moments, in his mind begging Balthrir to keep talking, before he took a deep breath and told her everything.

About his mother, the devil, his journey to Ilir, meeting the King and the fact he simply had to touch the Myrthali to return home.

Balthrir inflated her cheeks and then exhaled slowly.

'Nah,' she said. ''Eard weirder. I 'eard of a man who once divorced his 'at.'

'You mean he was married to his hat?'

'Course 'e was! What kind of man buys an 'at and doesn't marry it first? It's not decent!'

Things were clearly different in Ilir, thought Krish.

Balthrir prodded the fire with her staff, causing sparks to fly off the blackened logs. 'Far as I'm concerned, I 'ad a good racket goin' and as soon as I got in cahoots with you m'luck runs out and I'm on the run.'

'But...' said Krish. 'I didn't do anything wrong!'

'Not sayin' yer did, mate! Just sayin', was all going well till *you* rocked up! Yer some kinda bad luck charm, eh?' She chuckled briefly, almost bitterly, Krish thought, as she jabbed at a blackened log until it split in two. More sparks went flying. 'Now.' Her toned lightened. She proceeded to chat to herself as she poked the fire. 'Falkesh is swamped with wizards and they only trust grey-bearded wotsits in Calcara. Vra'hool, too close to Al Kara. The authorities are probably sniffin' around there. Might get recognised. So yer've effectively knackered m'short-lived professional career, matey boy.'

Krish looked at the ground. The heat of the fire was burning his forehead and right now he felt so guilty that he wanted the darkness to swallow him up.

'Bloody 'ell, mate!' shouted Balthrir quite suddenly. 'Stand up for yerself!'

Krish fixed her with a stare. 'Wasn't my fault your bloody stupid, your—' he used a word that made Balthrir raise her eyebrows '—stupid scams backfired! You were ripping people off!'

'Better!' said Balthrir. 'Knew there was some fire in there some-where, mate! Now, yer hear stories of time thieves and gateways opening up and all that cobblers, but can't say I've ever seen any real sign of all that stuff. One way to check it's not a load of hornack's tallywackers, of course.' Balthrir removed one of her worn old scandals. 'Toenails are best, they say.' Using a knife Balthrir cut off the end of a toenail, waved her staff around it and the nail was suspended in mid-air in purple glittering light. She breathed a few curious words and it flew over Krish's head and into the night, leaving a trail of purple shards falling to the ground. Balthrir nodded with satisfaction.

'South-west. Perfect. That's where I'm from,' said Balthrir.

'You… sent one of your toenails home…?'

'Don't be daft! That's where I was born! Where m'parents live! Or used to live.'

'And why would you send a toenail clipping to your old house?'

'To prove a point! That spell sends any part of yer body back to where you were born. Now stop asking stupid questions and make with the toenail!' She was brandishing the knife in his direction. Krish did as he was told and Balthrir conjured up some more of the purple glitter around the toenail clipping. Rather quickly it turned from purple to green, then buzzed from side to side, apparently confused about which way to go. The clipping flew around in increasingly violent circles for a few more seconds and then burst into red sparks that turned to blackness as they fell.

Krish looked over at Balthrir expectantly.

'Well…?' he said.

Balthrir pondered for a few more moments before answering. 'Either I got the spell a bit wrong or… it couldn't find where you were from because…' Balthrir looked deep into Krish's eyes before continuing. 'Well… time thief from another world, eh? Very interesting. Very interesting indeed. So, what's yer world called?'

'Earth.'

'Earth?! Yer mean this stuff?' She pointed to the ground, one side of her upper lip arched upwards in mild disgust. Krish nodded. 'Blimey. Bet yer glad it wasn't raining on the day they named your gaff or it would 'ave been called "Mud"! So what's the kingdom yer from called?'

'England. I mean Britain. Or the United Kingdom.'

'The United Kingdom?! Bloody 'ell, they're not all that imaginative with names round your neck of the woods, are they?'

'Yeah.' Krish let out a tired chuckle. 'I guess not. They just call it the UK on the news.'

'"Uk"?!' Balthrir spat out the word out like 'yuck' missing its beloved 'y'. 'Your kingdom's called "uk"? That's a bit rubbish, innit?'

'I… No one calls it that. Actually, I don't think anyone's noticed, to be honest.'

'Not noticed?! It's called "uk"! 'Ow can no one 'ave noticed? 'Ow about moons? 'Ow many o' them yer got? We got five: Mother and Sons. Mother, or Jashir if yer fancy, and 'er four sons 'oo whiz around 'er. There's Jarhi, Sia, Hri and Reb.'

'We just have one.'

'Oh. Borin'. What's she called?'

'The Moon.'

'The Moon?! That's it?! The best yer could come up with! Blimey, your lot sound thicker than a fumbala that needs to go on a diet!'

Krish was surprised at how easily he had laughed after this, despite how tired he was (plus he wasn't sure what a fumbala was, although he could guess). He and Balthrir exchanged warm smiles before she returned to the matter of dinner. Balthrir uttered a spell and the black skin rose out of the fire. As the skin came towards her it wobbled slightly in mid-air. Abruptly it plummeted and Balthrir just about caught it. She threw it from one hand to another very quickly, making sucking noises until she managed to drop the steaming-hot bundle into her lap.

'See,' said Balthrir, 'mask spells, very complicated. Like 'em. Something yer can really get yer teeth into. Simpler spells are too easy. I lose concentration.'

She unwrapped the package and cut the fruit within in half. Krish glimpsed juicy red flesh before steam poured out, engulfing them both in a smell that was like mulled wine and roast beef all rolled into one.

'Halfire,' said Balthrir. 'Delicious stuff.'

Balthrir continued to consider Krish's tale as the fruit cooled, and soon after – picking a moment when both their mouths were full of juicy, rich, almost meaty and surprisingly filling fruit – she spoke.

'Well, guess yer'll be needing some help then.'

CHAPTER 13

THE MOUNTAIN ATOP A TREE

'Lad,' Balthrir laid out her brief explanation in response to Krish's 'Why?' 'I got three choices in life. Carry on being a rubbish wizard for rubbish money and keep runnin' scams where the law *always* catches up with you. And if they appre'end me without a wizarding licence, without even 'aving passed m'wizardry exams, I'll be pretty screwed. Or cross The Scar to get work over there. *Or* impress the King enough to work for him. Right now, can't see me ever crossing The Scar, *but*... if I help you... I'll either have to cross The Scar or accompany you back to the palace with yer pearl from the Night Ocean and yer flamin' feather from a FireHawk, bit o' string round the world and that. Cause you ain't doin' all that without a bit o' magic, are yer?'

'I guess not.' Krish hadn't really thought about it. What he had thought about was Balthrir's parents. 'Your Mum and Dad... you said they're in prison...?'

Balthrir's tone darkened, her brow weighted with grief. She spoke cautiously, even taking time to pronounce her aitches, and at sinisterly low volume. 'Yeah. In the Black Palace. You won't have seen them. They're at the top of the Five-Point Tower. They didn't do anything serious. Late on a couple of tax bills. Not exactly a rich family, mine.'

'And you'd work for the King? Even though he has your parents impris—'

Balthrir shot him a fierce look across the flames.

'Kid, I do not want to talk about it!'

Krish stared at his feet.

Balthrir's gaze was lost somewhere between the fire and the blackness of the night beyond. After a few minutes she pulled out her best smile and her voice was cheery once more.

'So come on then: in't yer got more stupid questions to ask?'

Krish supposed he did. 'So, The Scar…? That's a river…?'

'Ocean. Runs round from Meslahir to Meslahir. Perfect circle cuttin' through the east of the globe. Can't get around the world without crossin' it.'

Then Krish thought of another stupid question.

'Hang on,' he said. 'Can't believe I didn't think of it! You know that… "mask spell" you did in front of Nboosa?'

Balthrir smiled. 'Forget it, mate! I know where yer goin' with that one. Did yer see an old wizard with red and blue 'air and a staff with a crystal in it?'

'Yeah…' Krish racked his brains. 'Er… Eshter?'

'Yep. Madam Eshter. Best wizard in the kingdom. From Baala, one of the Undertowns. Undertons are a learned lot. All that livin' underground for centuries. Not much more to do down there than read books. Lot of wizards are Undertons. You imagine me tryin' to be the court wizard when they got an Underton 'andy? Seriously, yer take a step into that place with a splinter from a magic wand 'er staff'll glow so bright yer'll be seeing spots for years as yer prop up one of the palace walls! Yer not sneakin' in there and stealin' the Myrthali. Trust me.'

Krish remembered how Eshter had reacted to the performer who had magically dyed part of her costume blue.

'Anyhoob,' continued Balthrir. 'Let's sleep for a couple o' days and then we'll get on the road to Old Margary.'

'So, Old Margary's…?' asked Krish.

'Old Margary?' said Balthrir. 'Oh, she's the witch in the tree on top of the mountain atop a much bloody bigger tree, of course.'

Of course, thought Krish. He was too tired to absorb any more information tonight. Devils and kings and wizards and witches in trees on mountains in trees and days and nights as long as a handful of lunch breaks. His eyelids were creeping together and he found himself lying back. As he drifted off he saw Balthrir arranging some thick bandages around him, but he was more interested in the yellow light peeking over the curved horizon.

'Balthrir… it's almost daylight… Is it really the best time for…' The word 'bed' was lost in a yawn. The bandages were now slipping gently underneath him and wrapping themselves into a cocoon, giving him a little space over his head to breathe.

'Baaalfeeearr,' Krish mumbled while the bandages blocked out the sky as sunlight inched across it. 'Waaa if va kin don keee hii... pomise...'

'Do what, mate?'

Krish finished yawning before speaking this time. 'What if the King doesn't keep his promise?'

'Did you hear the song of a bird in the deep...?' came the soft voice of Balthrir in the dawn air.

Krish muttered something along the lines of a yes.

'Then the King'll keep 'is promise...'

⁂

Krish awoke twice during his sleep. Once as more bandages wrapped themselves around his body as the chill of night spread through the air while also opening up over his face to reveal bright stars in the sky above him. The moon and its offspring, the four miniature moons which danced around their parent, arched across the twinkling firmament. Then once more as this was reversed, the bandages retreating with the heat and the dome reappearing to block out the sunlight.

Krish woke again at dawn to find the bandages slithering off him and into one of the satchels hung over the mule. There was no chance of a lie-in here; the ground was rather bobbly with the bandages gone, so he made himself sit up. Balthrir was placing a small wooden tray holding a teapot and two glasses filled with green leaves on the back of the mule.

'Up yer get,' she said. 'Mint tea on the move. Come on. Or we'll never get to Ugethrid before dusk.'

Ugethrid, Krish soon discovered, was the mountain Balthrir had mentioned earlier. The mountain on top of a mighty tree named Oobna. He couldn't quite picture it. Old Margary lived in a treehouse (in another tree, of course) on top of the mountain. The mint tea, although steaming hot, was cooling and refreshing in taste; much better than the stuff he had drank at the Broken Scythe. The tea did an admirable job of combatting the intense heat of the desert. For the whole journey, which took several hours, the enchanted tray managed to stay perfectly balanced on top of the mule. Well, almost perfectly. The tray's infrequent wobbles were enough to make the mule glance at it untrustingly over his shoulder.

The deeper they journeyed into the desert the darker the colour of the sand became. It started off a dull yellow, and reached barely higher than his ankle, broken up by islands of baked earth that looked solid as rock from a distance but crumbled underfoot. Later on there were mighty dunes of deep orange sand, which were at times as tall as multi-storey car parks. But most of the time all they passed through were long, flat stretches of dusty scrubland dotted with rocks and dried weeds that were scarcely managing to stay alive. Krish was fascinated by how well Balthrir knew the route. He was so lost without the map on his phone to tell him where he was and where he should go.

'So this is really your only option?' asked Krish as they trudged through the wastelands. 'If you really can't go back to school and do your wizardry exams.'

'Well...' Balthrir looked about, not that there was anyone in the surrounding wildness who could overhear them. 'I did kinda 'ave a back-up plan. Just in case I cocked up m'big exam or I wasn't allowed to sit it or summink.' She looked around again. 'I invent things.'

'Invent things?'

'Yeah, yer know... master a few spells to bewitch some tools and Budap's yer uncle...' She rummaged in the backpack she'd made Krish carry, one of the ones that didn't fit on the mule, and pulled out a rough faded green sphere covered in interchangeable tiles, each with a number on. Out the top stuck a bent metal aerial. 'How about that, eh?'

Krish wasn't keen to dampen Balthrir's winning smile.

'It's... wow... er... what is it?' he said.

'It's a clock-confuser!'

'Oh... What's that for?'

'Confusin' clocks – what d'yer think?'

'Oh. Right. Is there a lot of call for them round here?'

'I dunno. People buy all sorts of junk. Got a distress stone in there somewhere.' She pulled out a small pointed red rock.

'And that... gets distressed...?'

'Noooo! Sends up a flare, dunnit?'

'Right. That does sound quite handy actually.'

'Yeah. *Booorin'* though.' She tossed the distress stone back into the backpack. 'Got some amazin' itchin' powder but there's no market for the stuff!'

Krish mentally jettisoned his follow-up question on why Balthrir hadn't become an inventor.

Progress was slow. Although the light of the moons, Mother and Sons, was enough to light their way through the cool night, Balthrir stated that there were hidden ravines or the edge of a canyon nearby shrouded by the dark, so they would have to stop and wait for daybreak. For an hour or so in the middle of the day the heat was too intense to walk. They sheltered when they could, the sun burning Krish's skin, the air boiling around them, even in the shade of the Calvir trees of the oases. Krish often begged Balthrir for water to soothe his parched throat and his companion, far more used to desert life than him, would only allow him a meagre swig.

As the sun melted into the shimmering ground behind them they took in the striking image in front of them. Illuminated in the deep orange light of dusk was a mighty tree, bigger and broader than any Krish had ever seen. The monstrously large tree appeared too big for the pocket world on which he stood. Its trunk was thick and bulged like a barrel of gunpowder frozen in mid-explosion. Its stocky branches twisted and turned in all directions and there was a scattering of leaves of yellow and orange, which were as big as houses. A canopy of cloud hung just below some of the higher branches. Seeing Oobna in the haze of the fading daylight made it all the more unreal.

Then Krish caught his first sight of Ugethrid. On top of a clump of earth embedded in a collection of branches was a small but impressive mountain. The snow-dusted peak rose higher than the loftiest of Oobna's branches, its backdrop the deep blue of the dying day fading swiftly into the dark of the star-dotted night sky. Somewhere below the summit, Balthrir reassured him, there was a lone tree in which Old Margary lived.

Balthrir unburdened the mule and allowed him to roam free.

'There's plenty o' grass to munch on 'ere and a stream round the corner that 'e knows 'is way to. 'E'll still be 'ere when we get back.'

The two of them turned their attention to the intimidating form of the mountain atop a humongous tree.

'You sure about this, kid?' said Balthrir. 'I mean... from here on... it gets kinda serious. And I don't mean the climb. I mean Old Margary. Old bat's fiercely loyal to the King but even more devoted to helping old friends. She's His Maj's secret weapon really. Makes all kinds of stuff for the palace but the King tells everyone she's some terrifyin' monster livin' up a tree so most stay away. Used to go up there quite a bit as a kid. Gotta be a pretty poor family to brave a visit to Old Margary but... guess those were desperate times.' There was something she didn't want to say. 'My family were the only ones who give 'er the time o' day, so she'll 'elp us out. She's a witch; they're bound to 'elp out other magical folk and their, er... associates. Long as they're truthful, mind. Just be honest with 'er and everything'll be fine. But just be sure. Yer still wanna do this?'

Krish tried to think of his Mum. Of how happy he'd be to see her every day without fear that each could be her last. But he couldn't think of any positive thoughts regarding her. All he knew was that he had to climb that tree and that mountain.

'Yes. I'm sure,' he said.

As the sun left them for the night, Krish wondered how they were going to reach the top of the tree safely in the dark. Minutes later his question was answered. He saw black shapes, dashed with neon blues and oranges, emerging from holes burrowed into the wood. Balthrir began to chant softly, waving her staff gently in the air, and the creatures arranged themselves roughly into steps. Within minutes the creatures were still.

'Takes a lotta practice to get these guys to do that,' said Balthrir over her shoulder as she approached the tree. 'Old Margary likes it though. Only way that doesn't involve fighting off the woodsnipes, which puts most people off, so she gets a lot of peace and quiet.'

The 'stairs' squelched under Krish's feet and although they were clearly strong they still buckled a little under his weight. The whole way up he had a sinking feeling in his stomach. It was like stepping off a cliff and trusting your weight to a bridge made of jelly. All he could see was the neon marking the way and vague shapes of twisted branches to his right and the gloom of the night, hiding the ground far below, to his left.

They climbed up the outside of the trunk, passing shadow-clad boughs as thick as skyscrapers and branches as big as aeroplanes, twisting through the night.

The neon vanished as Krish found his feet touching solid ground again. Balthrir whispered a few more words and the creatures slithered back into their burrows. Balthrir began to rifle through loose sticks on the ground. There was a pause for a moment as she appeared to have found what she was looking for. She hurled something into the air and it ignited. Flames licked around a tumbleweed-like structure. She walked forward. After a few seconds of intermittent wobbling the tumbleweed hovered above the ground ahead of them, lighting their way as they walked.

So they climbed on through the dawn. With the coming of light Krish could see where they were. A claw-like collection of branches held several stadiums' worth of tightly packed earth, at the centre of which was Ugethrid. They were currently standing in the mighty mountain's shadow. Krish shivered. At this height, the clouds were a short climb above them, and in the shade the day brought little warmth.

They followed a rough path up the mountain until the sun swept across the landscape and Krish looked down at the tiny world below. Ilir looked like a model. He could see the curve of the globe, almost a whole side of the world, and not far below them he could make out a layer of light fading into a band of dark blue, which in turn became black with pinpricks of light. Krish was from a world where you could stand on the tallest mountain and see only the tiniest fraction of the land and seas. Here he could see almost all of it. Its small cluster of mountains to the south, the Black Palace to the west, the tents and hovels of small settlements to the north, and to the east a thick, dark covering, stretched across the land like a black clod of moss. Farther still was what Krish assumed was The Scar, a watery ring around the whole eastern hemisphere of this world.

They took the path through Lal'Fryaill Col, a long, slow ascent along the east side of the mountain. As the path started twisting right and left, Krish's leg muscles began aching as the climb gradually steepened. The sun had returned and although they were still in the shade, Krish was hot and sweaty from their non-stop ascent. After scrambling over a near-vertical ridge covered in loose rock, Balthrir allowed them a brief rest and something to eat.

The wizard told him a little of the history of the mountain. Long ago, before Oobna was big enough to tear the mountain from the earth, some adventurous Undertons had journeyed across the Nahbrin Desert and settled on the Lal'Fryaill plateau, not far from where they were sat now. Used to living underground, the Undertons preferred cooler climes. They renamed many of the cols and passes in their own tongue and were very happy and safe there for centuries. But then Oobna grew strong, lifted the mountain into the air and conditions in the winter became too cold to endure. People believed that the tree would be crushed by the weight of the mountain and that they would feel nothing more than a bump as it fell a short distance, but the tree kept on growing. Some left but many stayed, believing their god Maiylyr would save them. Maiylyr did not materialise and one winter the snows fell like never before. The peoples of the mountain who had stayed all froze to death, it must be presumed. In the spring, morbid spectators gathered round Oobna as the ice melted and was washed down the mountain with the rains of the new year. But no corpses appeared. For a century or so some of Ilir's climbers were obsessed with searching the mountain for signs of the lost people of Lal'Fryaill. They found nothing. A shadow fell over the mountain in the minds of the people of Ilir. Most avoided it. The name Ugethrid, Balthrir informed him, meant 'she keeps her dead'.

As they passed through a particularly deep crevasse, Balthrir's story conjured up images of dead bodies hidden in the very rock surrounding them. Farther down the mountain they'd passed birds of prey in coarse nests of straw and goat-like creatures devouring any dried-up weeds they could locate, but here there was hardly any life at all. Just a stooped, single-eyed, black-feathered bird watching patiently, waiting for them to fall to the ground and move no more. Easier than chasing and attacking in the rarefied air at this altitude. Patches of snow dotted the landscape as they neared the summit. The sun shone strongly but the chill in the air was palpable. With every gust of wind the cold felt as if it were slicing through Krish's body.

From the ground, the peak had looked like a single point where all of the mountain ran out at once when you reached a narrow tip. In reality, you climbed one final ridge, a narrow gap between rock faces, scree dusted with snow, and emerged onto a crumpled white landscape the length of several lorries.

Krish caught his breath. The air was so thin he felt sure they'd run out soon. The sun warmed him in the still air but his feet and knees were sodden thanks to the snow on the final ascent, which had been completed on all fours. The devil might have mentioned scrambling up snow-covered peaks when telling him what clothes to bring. He looked down to a thick layer of cloud crawling over a range of mountains like a sheet of cotton wool. The curvature of Ilir was more apparent than ever. A sky full of stars was sweeping from the west, Mother and a Son were poking over the far horizon, dim in the low, harsh, dying light of day and the sun was sinking in the east, relinquishing control of the heavens for the briefness of the night.

Krish scanned the summit of Ugethrid and saw on the far side a large tree (well, a normal-sized large tree, a tiny tree in comparison to the one the mountain was on top of) with a badly nailed-together collection of wooden planks on top of it. Krish supposed it could be some sort of dwelling. A line of smoke rose from its chimney. As they got closer he realised that it was probably just as big as his own house but the mountain and the tree below it dwarfed everything in sight.

'Oh, and don't expect any kinda in-depth discussions with Old Margary,' said Balthrir. 'She's the last of her kind and has lived waaay too long to have much time for conversation. You know they say 'ow time seems to go faster the older yer get? Well, time flies for this old bird. Heard she blinks and misses a couple o' days sometimes. Didn't speak at all for decades at some point. No one ever knew if she was right narked off or just considered it a natural gap in the conversation. And remember, she's fiercely loyal to the King. Bound to 'elp magical folk but *fiercely loyal* to 'Is Maj. *Don't* forget that! Just be honest and yer'll be fine!'

'Okay, okay! I get it!'

They climbed a rickety ladder and Balthrir rapped on the hatch. To Krish's surprise, Balthrir started to make her way back down the ladder again.

'Probably be a few hours till she answers.'

But within about ten minutes, the hatch swung open.

CHAPTER 14

OLD MARGARY

Krish had a few minutes to take in the face looking down at them. It was as if Old Margary was composed entirely of filthy old starched rags. Her face was a swirl of rough canyons on dry and mottled skin that did not look like it had moved for years. Hidden in her ghostly features were two shallow dark craters which he presumed were her eyes. She looked through him for some time, stiff as a statue, and then slowly turned to Balthrir.

'Baaaaal—' came the elongated croak from the small crease which was Old Margary's mouth.

'Balthrir!' interrupted Balthrir 'Yep, that's me! Been a long time, old girl. Might need a bit of assistance, if yer've got the time…'

Old Margary considered this for roughly twenty minutes, then took five minutes to lower her head and another five for it rise up again to complete her nod. Then, with unexpected swiftness, she re-entered the house. Balthrir climbed the ladder and Krish followed, leaving the cold of the encroaching night behind them.

The house was filled with pages. Books torn apart, the pages suspended from strings, positioned all about the ramshackle abode. Cauldrons, test tubes and mixing bowls were strewn about the worktops and a mattress-lined alcove encircled the whole of Old Margary's home. In fact, much seemed to be replicated around the room, perhaps so the ancient witch – who clearly moved at a pace that would see her being lapped by snails if she were in a race – would always have food and somewhere to rest for night, wherever she was in the room. The bubbling cauldrons and a fire on the eastern side of the room brought warmth and the odour of strange potions and woodsmoke to the dwelling, banishing the chill of night. Stars shone through the gaps in the rafters.

Old Margary stood by a hanging cauldron, flames flickering around the rim.

'Teeeeeaaaaa?'

'Let me help!' butted in Balthrir.

While Old Margary was caught in a bow of thanks for a few minutes, Balthrir leapt forward and picked up a large black sphere resembling a cannonball, filled it with water and placed it at the heart of the roaring fire. Krish was aware of Old Margary's inquisitive gaze washing over him. The skin of her sack-like face was surely about to crack, Krish thought, as the corners of her mouth moved upwards for the first time that he had seen.

'Reeeeelaaaaax.'

Telling someone nervous to relax is about as effective as placing a large, scrumptious-looking cake in front of a hungry child and leaving them alone in a room with it, with the express order not to consider even the tiniest of morsels. Instead, Krish gave all his attention to the process of tea-making. The fire was so intense that steam billowed out of the holes in the top of the cannonball kettle. Balthrir had lowered glass tubes into these holes and all the steam was travelling up them at great speed. The tubes made a right-angled turn, all heading out from the central point at which they met, and the steam passed through porous sachets filled with tea leaves before the tubes dived another ninety degrees to bulbous flasks fastened to their ends. Once they were full, Balthrir removed the flasks and stoppered them tightly before placing them in a sink filled with cold water. Within minutes the steam had condensed into liquid and Balthrir was serving their contents in teacups with a little cold water.

Krish was overjoyed that Old Margary sprang her question moments after sitting down rather than pondering for hours on end.

'Viiiiisssiiiiit?'

Balthrir launched immediately into an explanation (playing down the King's hostile attitude towards her young companion) and Krish enjoyed his smoky-sweet tea, which had a warm, comforting aftertaste of baked apple. Then he turned his attention to something in the room he had not noticed before. On the wall in front of them was a large charcoal-coloured canvas covered in dashes of light grey, some straight, some curved. It was like fog or smoke or a cloud overburdened with rain. They were vague shapes on the canvas somewhere but he couldn't quite make anything out. The painting (if that's what it was – could be some enormous, filthy tea towel hung out to dry for all he knew) perplexed him a little but as Balthrir concluded her tale he lost all interest in the mess of grey on the wall.

'So, Night Ocean for the pearl and the Pale Hunting Grounds for the feather we're fine with, no probs... Well, lots of probs, potentially, but all possible, yer know? But this tyin' a bit o' string round the world malarkey is a bit of a puzzler. And I thought if there's anyone 'oo can 'elp, Old Margary's m'girl!'

Old Margary contemplated this for a while – during which time Krish and Balthrir had a leisurely lunch break of mikan bread and spiced quanta – before she journeyed to the triangular gap in the planks of her home which formed a misshapen window. The light of a fresh, new day was now spreading from the west. The ancient witch produced a number of shoulder-height interconnected wooden stands, each with a small circular mirror the size of a coin at its pinnacle. She placed a large basket on the floor next to the contraption. After several minutes, the bright light of dawn hit the first mirror and bounced onto the next one and then the next and then the next and then the next. The beam of light was mesmerising to watch and after some time it began to change. Its brightness decreased and it appeared to be moving. The thin, dimming sunlight accelerated and became solid. It poured from the final mirror and filled the basket with a silvery twine. Old Margary moved the first of the mirrors away from the light and the stream of sunlight twine ceased. Then she wound the shining wire into a surprisingly compact ball and held it out for Krish.

'Uuuuunnnnnbrrrrreeeeeaaaaak—'

'Unbreakable...?' offered Balthrir. Old Margary gave her a hasty thirty-second nod. 'Great stuff! Except, 'ow we gonna cut the twine it we 'ave too much o' the stuff? Yer know, so we can actually tie it around the world and all that?'

The old sorceress then scanned one of the workbenches for several minutes before producing a long thin grand-looking box of dark wood. Balthrir helped her open the box to save them a half-hour interval. Lying in the blue velvet interior was a rather plain wooden handle, no bigger than a teaspoon, which was less than half the length of the box it sat within. The minutes drew on as Old Margary was busy holding up the handle until the outline of what looked like a short glass knitting needle appeared against the beam of sunlight emanating from the window. Krish swore he heard a crunch from Old Margary's ancient wrist as with unexpected haste she tore through the streak of sunshine, which fell to the ground and fizzed to nothingness, its bright light extinguished in a haze of smoke on the scorched floorboards.

'Blimey!' exclaimed Balthrir. 'A Salvean blade! 'Eard there're only a couple o' these left in existence. We are 'onoured! Only thing that can cut through sunlight. So the only blade that'll cut through that—' she indicated the twine '—I'll bet! No mortal blade'll get through it and...'

Balthrir delicately took the knife from Old Margary's hand – the lines on the old witch's palm seemed as long and as deep as canyons and were probably just as old – and ran the almost invisible blade over her own palm. It left no mark.

'There!' proclaimed Balthrir. 'Not a scratch!'

Krish nodded his head in awe at the tiny knife. Then he noticed Old Margary staring at him, the ball of twine in her hand. He hesitated and then reached out to take the ball. Old Margary's hand was not giving up the twine of sunlight so easily.

'Whhhhhyyyyy?'

Old Margary was a statue once more. Those eyes, darker than the dead of night, still as ice, bored into him.

'Just tell her the truth,' softly and cautiously came Balthrir's plea.

'My mother,' said Krish. 'I... want to give her more time. As much time as I can.'

Old Margary still wouldn't surrender the twine.

'Kiiiiinnnnng?'

'The truth,' came Balthrir's prompt.

Krish thought. He feared this ancient woman with the face of rancid old cloth, her barely visible crease for a mouth and those eyes...

He knew he should tell the truth but Balthrir had said Old Margary

110

was loyal to the King. If he said he wasn't, surely she'd never give him the twine. But what if a lie would make things worse? Couldn't he just politely say he wasn't exactly a fan of the King? Krish couldn't picture that going down well and if he stumbled here his quest would be over in a heartbeat.

He looked into those eyes: old enough to have seen mountains rise up, towering above the land, before the ages weathered them down to gravel. Perhaps her pupils had swallowed the whites and the irises of her eyes in a desperate bid to allow in more light as her sight failed. He was lost and afraid in the chasm of her unseen eyes; darkness beyond darkness. He must find a way out.

'I am loyal to His Majesty,' said Krish.

He could sense Balthrir stifling a sigh behind him.

Old Margary did not move. Some time later she turned away, taking the ball with her.

What had he done? Was this it? Would she throw the ball away? Destroy it? He looked to the window. If she tossed it out there he knew he could find it. What about the fire? Would that consume it? He kept his eye on the fire.

But Old Margary had placed the ball of twine on the worktop. Now she was working at a furious pace (furious for her, at least). She picked up the skull of a small creature, tore it into four or five pieces and one by one crushed the fragments with a pestle and mortar. She hurled the powder into her cauldron and tossed in a number of potions.

The day wore on. Eventually Old Margary completed her work and held out her hand to Krish. Krish didn't know quite what she wanted until he saw that she was eyeing his forearm. He placed his arm in her coarse, dry palm. With astonishing speed she pricked his skin with a needle and then placed the drop of blood she had collected in the concoction. Then she added a drop of her own. He noticed that the bead of red which rose to cover the tiny piercing in the witch's skin was meagre and slow to arrive at the surface; as if her blood itself was old and frail.

The foul potion bubbled away and soon Old Margary produced a ladle, poured the mixture into a cup and offered it to Krish.

'Kiiiiinnnng?'

This draught was clearly meant to make him truthful. And that was what Balthrir had said – *tell the truth*. There was no point in lying now. None whatsoever. Even if he tried this stuff, whatever it was, it would correct him.

He drank. Sickening, curdled milk with a musky aftertaste. He almost gagged. He had to say something. Conflicting thoughts fought for dominance in his mind: what was worse? Lying? Saying he wasn't the biggest fan of the King and would be pretty happy if his head just fell off one day? Why didn't he say something vague? *I have an agreement with the King.* Yes! That was it! Nice, vague and completely truthful. *I have an agreement with the King.* It was only all Balthrir's talk of loyalty that made him think that he had to make it sound like he was a big fan of the old man.

'I am loyal to the King.'

The words had slipped out. He'd panicked. He'd had Balthrir's talk of loyalty on the brain, twinned with a thought – a *stupid, stupid thought!* – that had shot into his head at the last moment: *If the draught will make me truthful then I could risk lying. It'll just correct me! Say I'm loyal – Balthrir said it was important to her! I bet anything it'll correct me! What have I got to lose?* Everything. As he stared from Old Margary to the twine on the worktop he realised that he had everything to lose and he might just have thrown it away by allowing himself to panic.

Old Margary's face was still but he knew she was furious. She snatched the twine from the worktop. Krish was prepared to fight. Could he grab the twine from her rough hands?

He needn't have bothered even considering this. The ball was thrust into his hands, Old Margary turned away and Krish never looked into those haunting eyes again.

Krish was confused. He began to turn to Balthrir but his gaze settled on the painting. He could see it so clearly now. It was not grey. It was black. The colour of a tormented sky in the middle of a storm. A cloud billowing with thunder. And he hadn't seen the red before. Flecks of red set into the heads of cruel beasts. The arched backs of dogs, incandescent and ravenous. Frothing at their spiteful mouths, staring straight at him with their vicious eyes. They were staring right at him. How had he not seen them before? Because they had turned. Yes, they had turned to him while he'd been watching them! He backed away, their growls filling his ears. How could he hear them? Their roaring fury was filling in his ears!

'Balthrir! BALTHRIR! They're after us! We gotta get outta here!'

Balthrir glanced in the direction Krish was looking in and then around the room but she clearly couldn't see a thing.

'What? What are yer talkin' about?' she said.

'The dogs! Look at them! God, we've gotta get outta here!'

Balthrir's eyes settled on the painting. 'Where do yer see 'em? There? In that painting?'

'Yes! Yes! They're coming! Balthrir, we've got to go!'

Krish was desperate to run for it but Balthrir didn't budge. Something was dawning on her.

'A Malshrael…' she said. 'Come on! We should *never* 'ave come 'ere!'

Balthrir headed for the hatch.

Krish followed, the heat of the fire stinging his eyes as he passed it. Then the dogs. The dogs were rushing across the room at him. No. No! They were still in the painting. They… there was one emerging from behind a workbench. Its dull, red eyes, like the glow of charcoal in a dying fire, sliding into view. Bigger and clearer and more fearsome than before. They were there! Right in front… no… NO! They were in the painting! The painting was slightly obscured by the workbench so it created the illusion that they'd escaped… NO! They were bearing down on him! They were here! There was a chair between one and the painting. Their snarling muzzles and shadow-like coats. They were real! They were in the room! Barely any fur, black skin tight over bones. Murderous eyes. Spittle hanging from their mouths. Cruel, sharp teeth. His whole body flinched as the sound of their bloodcurdling snarls shook him. A scream shot from his throat.

'Krish! Open yer eyes!'

Krish opened his eyes. They were gone.

'I… I…' Krish stammered as Balthrir dragged him out. Where had they gone?

'Next time yer blink, remember to open yer eyes again!'

'What?! They weren't shut...' Krish caught one last glance of Old Margary, huddled in the corner, feeling as if her ancient eyes were boring into him through the back of her skull, as they fled via the hatch.

'The fire got in yer eyes,' said Balthrir. 'Yer closed 'em and didn't bother openin' 'em again. For some reason...'

'Those dogs—'

'I told yer to tell the old bat the truth!' cried Balthrir as they rushed down the ladder. 'She weren't gonna deny us anything if yer told her the King was a pompous old plonker! I just meant kind of avoid the subject and be polite! She was doin' us a favour! But she'd still 'ave 'elped. Yer don't lie to Old Margary. You DO! NOT! LIE! T—'

'But what happened?! What... Oh, come on... those dogs—'

'They're not 'ere.' And then more quietly to herself Balthrir added: 'Not yet.' He could see that she was suppressing panic. She hadn't had time to take everything in and the conclusion she was reaching was clearly something she didn't want to think about.

Whatever Krish was about to say was interrupted by a terrifying crash reverberating around the land. They turned to the horizon. Caught in the low, dimming light of the setting sun, its shadow stretching across the land, was the Black Palace. It shook with rage, Krish thought. A shockwave tore through the palace from its base to the tip of the highest turret. It was as if every prisoner who made up the palace had been pushed a tiny distance away from the centre before grabbing hold of their neighbour to make certain the great structure remained intact, stopping themselves plummeting to the ground. This monstrous vision was quickly followed by a brief cacophony of cries. Krish realised that the delay between what he was seeing and the sound reaching them meant that it was most likely to be the furious screams which were shaking the palace. He thought of Balthrir's parents in the walls of the Black Palace, which was now steady once more. Balthrir remained unnervingly calm.

'The King knows,' said Balthrir. Then in what was almost a whisper: 'They're comin'.'

Krish looked over the shadow-laden landscape, waiting for something to appear from the palace. For a hundred thousand knights to burst forth from the main entrance and head towards them. Or those dogs... those terrible, terrible dogs...

But nothing came.

'What's coming?' asked Krish.

Balthrir didn't answer. Her eyes were locked onto the motionless palace. The whole panorama before them was filled with unmoving objects. Not a thing stirred. The silence was deafening. Staring at the eerie stillness of the land unnerved Krish; he felt he was scanning the landscape for the tiniest movement, which would make him jump out of his skin. But not a thing stirred.

'I can't see anything,' said Krish.

'Yeah.' Balthrir took a deep breath and then exhaled slowly, quivering a little. 'That's the thing I was most afraid would 'appen...'

CHAPTER 15

THE IMPENETRABLE CANOPY

'What's a "mouse-rail"?' Krish asked.

'Malshrael!' Balthrir corrected him, without looking over her shoulder.

There was a long pause. Balthrir's magical grip on the flaming tumbleweed was wavering, sending smoking splinters flying onto the path. Balthrir grunted irritably and used the distraction to ignore the question.

'Balthrir…?' He thought he saw her eyes dart back over her shoulder for a moment.

'Yer'll fall,' she said flatly. 'If yer not bloody careful yer'll fall!' And then under her breath: 'Bloody idiot.'

She was right; he wasn't concentrating on the path. But it was her fault for ignoring him. If she'd just let him know what was worrying her he wouldn't be so distracted.

'What's the problem?' said Krish. 'We got the twine.'

A brief, sarcastic chuckle from Balthrir. She was shaking her head.

'What?!' Krish persisted. 'We *did* get the twine!'

Balthrir kept going, paying him no attention.

'So, you're not talking to me because…?' said Krish.

Balthrir took a few more steps before answering. 'Thinking,' was all she said.

'So, is the King sending somebody?' Krish said. 'Guards or, or… I dunno… assassins…?'

She kept walking across the snow-covered summit.

The descent would have been comparatively fast but the silence between himself and Balthrir was killing Krish. They reached the base of Ugethrid as the dawn light appeared. Balthrir hurled some mikan bread at Krish and then started summoning the odd creatures that would form a stair to the ground. She didn't stop. While Krish

117

swallowed a few hastily chewed bites Balthrir headed for the ground. Krish spied the large moss-like feature on the land ahead of them again.

'What *is* that?' Krish pointed to the covering, like a massive rug stretched out across the landscape.

Balthrir peered over her shoulder. 'The Night Ocean.'

'Doesn't look much like an ocean,' said Krish.

Balthrir didn't bother answering, leaving Krish very confused. It looked more like a forest than an ocean.

In the full light of day Oobna was glorious. Krish felt like a tiny creature on a gigantic tree. The sight of the ground far below through the gaps in the jelly-like steps protruding from the wood was less that reassuring though. The cool air was giving way to the desert heat once more. He could feel the heat rising from the sands below. But his mind was still on those dogs. Gusts of wind made him jump and then he saw them. Within the briefest of moments they were gone. Had he really seen them?

They reached the ground and Balthrir busied herself with finding the mule and loading him up to continue their journey through the approaching night. Krish continued to ask questions as they walked but Balthrir simply brushed off his enquiries. She must have been mistaken about anything leaving the Black Palace, she'd say dismissively over her shoulder as they walked. Then she'd move the conversation on to whatever else seemed to come to her mind. She'd tell him about trees and plants; their names, their tastes, their fragrances. Why smell should come into it Krish had no idea and most of them didn't smell half as sweet as she made out they would.

'What's coming? Why did Old Margary give us the twine if I lied? Why did I see those dogs? Why—?'

Balthrir went quiet again. Once more, 'thinking' was all she said.

When Krish and Balthrir reached the Great Plain the terrain was bathed in the light of Mother and Sons, Ilir's moon and her four children. The four small moons danced around their mother moon from the coming of dusk to the arrival of dawn. Dark shapes of enormous towers of rocks were spread throughout the plain. This place must look spectacular in the full light of day, Krish thought, but at sundown the rocks were ghostly shapes sprouting up out of nowhere amongst miles and miles of level ground. Sitting there. Watching. Waiting.

They found the sturdiest tree they could and tied the twine around it, unravelling the ball as they went. Balthrir seemed to be hiding some kind of fear and insisted on casting an invisibility spell on the twine that would come into effect as soon as it left the ball. They skirted around the desert and a harsh wind whipped up and grains flew into Krish's eyes. He was haunted still by visions of those terrible dogs. He'd see them, sometimes only for an instant, but they were so clear. Clearer than anything he'd ever seen. Often he'd catch a glimpse of the rocks far across the sand, way behind them, and suddenly he could see them, sniffing around the rocks, but it was as if they were very close. For a fraction of a second he could see those cruel-eyed beasts on their scent, hunting them down, and then they were gone.

'Balthrir…' he'd begin, before the wizard shrugged off any attempt to believe that they were being followed. Not that she was walking at the leisurely pace of someone who wasn't being pursued.

'Balthrir! We need to rest!' Krish cried out.

'No we don't.' Balthrir marched on.

'Balthrir, we haven't slept since—'

'Come on!'

In the following hours Balthrir stopped only to tear some discarded carrion, not yet a feast for maggots, in two, wrapping it in skins and slinging it into her bag before a squawking raptor could swoop down and claim it for itself. Looming ahead of them was a smudge of dark grey on the horizon.

An hour later they reached the edge of Betsarhldeth; the forest of the Night Ocean. Balthrir explained that the canopy of the forest was so thick that light could hardly penetrate it. And in the middle of the forest was the Night Ocean itself. A gargantuan mass of salt water littered with Gilimed trees, which grew from rocky outcrops fathoms below the surface. The Gilimed trees in the ocean itself were few and far between, but still their branches, coated with thick black leaves, stretched out to meet others, blocking the sky from sight. Gilimed trees were frightened of the light and fed on the blackness of endless night, said Balthrir.

Balthrir took out a lantern and held it up to catch the bright sunlight. She then produced the Salvean blade with its tiny wooden handle no longer than Krish's little finger, and its small, needle-like blade which was only visible when sunlight shone upon it.

'We're bloody lucky to 'ave this!' said Balthrir. 'Only meant to be a couple o' Salvean blades in existence!'

'Who has the other one?' Krish enquired.

Balthrir shrugged and proceeded to cut a line in the air between the sun and the lantern so they would have light in Betsarhldeth. As they took their first heedful steps under the impenetrable canopy, Krish felt for the first time since he was a small child that he was truly scared of the dark.

The woods were dead. Or so it seemed. Occasionally Krish would hear the rustle of leaves or the sound of some small animal scurry across the forest floor, but mostly unnerving quiet surrounded them. The kind of silence that makes you aware of how heavily you are breathing, of your heartbeat, of the pulsating veins just under your own skin. Of how the gentle breeze irritates your eyes. The dogs. He was determined to ignore them.

Krish hated the sight of the Gilimed trees. They were like huge long shadows stretching up into the cloud of black that was the canopy. Occasionally one creaked and groaned as he passed, as if it was aware of him being there, as if he was standing too close. He felt as if unseen eyes could be hidden in the gloom, watching his every move.

They rested in a clearing. Krish felt more at ease lying on his side, head leaning on a rock, than against one of the trees, no matter how uncomfortable he was. He began to realise that not all the light was coming from the edge of the forest, which was already a long way behind them. A small amount of light was filtering down from where the canopy, high above them, was thinnest. It must be this, he pondered, which was making the Gilimed trees creak. The sunlight was causing them to contract, wince almost, in pain. No sooner would these cracks in the canopy appear than they would vanish, the trees apparently conspiring to rid their realm of light.

Balthrir's lantern of sunlight, which was comparatively dim in the murk of the woods, had a similar effect on the Gilimeds, so she learned to place it far from the trees when they rested (which wasn't often as she was keen to press on) to stop them having to endure the unsettling sound of the tree they were leaning against contracting.

'Your eyes will adjust,' said Balthrir slowly over the crackling of the fire. 'A few days and you will be used to the dark.'

Krish doubted this. The idea of a few *hours* in this place was more than enough for him. He was famished. Balthrir had been reluctant to cook all of the carrion for some reason.

'You must be tired,' she continued. 'Get some rest.' Her gaze was firmly settled on him for the first time in days. Her eyes were cold and distant, but intrigued. As if he were an experiment.

'You said something was coming,' said Krish.

'I was wrong,' said Balthrir.

'But Old Margary—'

'The last of her kind,' she said patiently. 'The Sheekarla. They pledged to help any magical folk – or their friends – whose cause was motivated by genuine selflessness. She was bound to help you whatever you said. She would have given you the twine anyway. She was bound to by traditions dating back millennia. Doesn't stop her from... well...'

Krish couldn't be bothered to press Balthrir on her last, rather vague sentence. 'I didn't *mean* to lie—'

'Yes you did.' Balthrir poked the fire. 'I told you, I just wanted you to be polite and not lay into that cantankerous old bint.'

'Well... you could have been a bit clearer about—'

'You *don't* lie to the Sheekarla.' She was speaking so slowly, so quietly, it seemed to make her pronounce everything correctly and that unnerved Krish. As if something was wrong with her. 'They always know. The Sheekarla. Or they find out.'

'But that stuff, that potion... it made those dogs appear!'

'No. All it did was bind you to her for a short time. Even if you'd lied she'd feel the truth in you.'

'But that painting—'

'Is the catch.' She looked up at him again. 'She *had* to help, as the last of the Sheekarla. Didn't mean she couldn't report it to the King and let him take care of things from then on.'

'Balthrir, that paint—'

'Forget it. Get some sleep.'

'But I saw them! And I keep seeing them. Why did I see them? And what's a "mal-shral"?'

'Malshrael. And it's nothing. Get... some... sleep.' Balthrir spoke in a voice which was almost irritated by its own calmness. Krish couldn't deny that he was desperate for sleep. But every time he felt himself nodding off the dogs were there. Just on the edge of the woods. Lost. Sniffing the ground, the trees, the plants. Anything. They were trying to pick up the scent. *Their* scent. He knew it.

'Sleep...' Balthrir's staff made gentle circles in the air. Krish began to slip away from the conscious world.

In an instant, a dream swooped in and took him...

CHAPTER 16

NIGHTMARE OF THE VULREIN

*A snort... a muzzle lifts out of the dirt... looking ahead
...into the trees... eyes wide... an ecstasy of barking...
lean, muscular legs bounding through darkened woods...*

*Screaming... he was screaming
in the dark...*

Their paws beat the ground... they were close... too close...

*Screaming... she calls out... she calls
again... he doesn't understand her words...*

So close... the smell of putrid meat on their breath...

*Her desperate whispers... Where?
Which direction? He points...*

Their pace quietening... their quarry near...

*The twine thrust into his hands... the mule
neighing, running from them... her tearing the
dead creature on the ground, scattering
flesh behind them as they run...*

Some chewed the meat... others barked...
this was not their prey...

Running, running... hearts beating wild in their chests...
violent breaths... stumbling over branches... feet too close...
confused... fingers, his fingers, large as swollen branches...

They were on their scent again...

The swish of a blade... a shriek of pain across his arm,
his friend opening his vein... a faint attempt at reassurance
through stuttering breaths... her mixing his blood with
the meat... discarded on the ground...

Beasts tearing into the bloody flesh... swallowing
leaves and twigs and dirt stuck to that filthy mess...

Wading... rancid, stagnant water... her
commanding him to drench himself... her
hand on his wound...

The scent was cold...
they had had their fill...
for now...

Water so close, too close... feeling it at his
waist, seeing it up to his neck... he would drown! He was
lost! He'd die! Falling under the water, one eye above,
both below. No sense. What? What?! Help!
Deep, deep below. Drowning! Dying!
Fetid water pouring down his throat...

Her over him, shouting, shouting,
screaming, no sense.
Every mark, every scratch, every bead
of sweat on her skin so clear...

'Open yer eyes!'

He swore she was calling to him in his dream and
in the real world all at once...

'Krish! Open yer eyes! O-pen your—'
He jolted awake.
'—eyes!'
He was lying in a shallow pond, no higher than his knees. Balthrir still hovered over him but she was a little farther away than she had been in his nightmare.
'Where are they?' she asked.
He looked into her eyes, confused, and she asked again.
'I don't know,' he said.
'Look.'
He looked roughly in the direction of where the dogs had been chewing the meat in his dream. But he saw nothing.
'*Look*,' she said. 'Just for a moment...'
Then he realised. The smoke in his eyes. The grains of sand. The wind. That's when he'd seen them. Hesitantly, he allowed his eyelids to slide over his eyes.

Across the forest... a clearing... dogs stood
over the carcass... One's head shot a look in his
direction... snarling...

Krish opened his eyes with a gasp. Balthrir was looking expectantly at him.

'There!' he said. 'Over there! One looked—'

'It's fine. The water will keep them off our scent for now. At least... well, it should do. We'd better move on. And keep yer eyes open.'

Krish looked up into her eyes, which were fearful, apologetic.

'They're real, aren't they?'

She nodded.

'But why—?'

'The Vulrein,' Balthrir interrupted. 'The ones you saw at Old Margary's weren't real. It was a projection from the Malshrael. But the ones we just ran into were real.'

'The Malshrael... what the hell—?'

'Come on.'

'What happened to the mule?'

'Oh 'e'll turn up. Always does.'

They gathered up their packs, struggling with the mule's burden added to their load. After ten minutes they were forced to leave behind Balthrir's magical bandages, a blanket and the largest of their three water flasks. Balthrir's voice was weary as they walked.

'Old Margary was bound to 'elp us in one way but that didn't stop 'er 'oldin' us up in another. Been a long time since the King was allowed to set 'unting dogs on the trail of the disloyal; there was almost revolt last time 'e used 'em! But 'e gets away with using the Vulrein. 'Ounds of air and shadow. Easy to deny that 'e's ever set them on anyone when only the intended victim can see them. Never really know 'ow they find yer but they do. I mean, I've read about 'em but nobody really knows much about 'em. The King's sendin' 'em to 'unt yer down. To make sure you can never get a pearl from the Night Ocean, a feather from a FireHawk and tie a bow – sorry, *pretty bow* – round the world. Might not 'ave taken yer seriously before but 'e knows yer got Old Margary's magic on yer side now. Real old school *powerful* magic. 'E must be 'avin' second thoughts about yer. What did yer see? When yer looked into the Malshrael?'

'Horrible, *horrible* shapes! Dogs! Their eyes—'

'No, no, NO! What did you see *first*? When we'd just arrived?'

Krish tried to remember. For a moment he couldn't get rid of the image of those malevolent eyes staring at him from out of the painting. But then his mind cleared and he remembered.

'Nothing. Just… lines. Like a big grey cloud or something.'

Balthrir nodded. 'Hm. Sounds right. A Malshrael is like a link to the King. Should 'ave spotted it! Those who are loyal and stuff don't see a thing in the Malshrael, those who aren't see the Vulrein. The King then unleashes the real Vulrein and they can hunt yer down, pickin' up the scent every time yer eyes are shut, and that's the only time yer can see 'em. From what I've 'eard, readin' about it and stuff, yer vision is like, kinda… sharpened. Yer know? Yer see 'em even if they're far away. Everything's magnified. Even things right up in front of yer face.'

Suddenly so much made sense. Not just seeing the Vulrein when his eyes were closed but why they appeared so close. Why his fingers seemed so big. Why he thought he'd drown in what was little more than a puddle. Everything had been magnified.

'But I didn't see the Vulrein, not straight away, and I'm clearly not loyal to the King…'

'That's because Old Margary is a powerful sorceress. The Malshrael were all burnt, a long time ago, so they say, but she clearly kept 'old of one. She's a big fan of that crowned old bleeder but she wouldn't allow a Malshrael to do its work for that reason alone. No. What the Sheekarla 'ate is dishonesty. That lot could never lie. So she's probably enchanted the bloody thing to alert the King if, and *only* if, you're disloyal *and* dishonest. But a woman that old could never see 'ow furious the King would get at the idea that you'd be after his Myrthali. This 'as changed things. 'Is Maj knows y'er a serious threat now.'

'Me…?' Krish looked over at Balthrir. She looked back with a sigh in her eyes.

'Oh yeah… *we*.' A long sigh, her eyes appearing to deepen with sudden hopelessness. 'Bang goes my chance of a job for the old codger,' his wizard friend muttered.

'Balthrir, I just don't understand why you'd want to work for the man who has your parents impris—'

'Oh, *because* 'e 'as my parents imprisoned! It's not just that it's the only job I could actually make a decent living off of using magic. It's because yer get one wish that the King *has* to grant. As long as it's not unreasonable. Yer know, like "Can I be King instead of you?" Obviously that wouldn't fly. But 'e *does* release prisoners. Might 'ave to come up with some new law if too many ask for prisoners to be released, but 'e loves creating new laws.'

'Sounds like a pretty nasty boss.'

'Ha! There are worse. At least 'e appreciates magic.'

'You miss your parents?'

Balthrir stared at her feet, leaving one of those awful silences that Krish was coming to hate. He changed the subject.

'So... every time I shut my eyes... they'll be there?'

'Uh-huh.'

'So, they're just over there?'

'Yes. But they can't 'arm us. They can't even find you while yer eyes are open. Not that they can't keep 'eadin' in our direction. Think they've lost us at the moment. But every time they're closed, every wink, every blink, they'll see yer and pick up the scent.'

'But-but surely there's a spell you can use...?'

'Mate, I can't ward off Vulrein. I can whip up some enchantment to stop yer eyes gettin' dry but yer'll still blink. Everybody does.'

Krish felt coldness creeping over his whole body. His eyes tingled. All he wanted to do was to shut them right now. But to see those foul dogs again... He thought for a while. Only one course of action stood out to him.

'What if you made me blind?' he said.

'Then yer'd see nothing else but them.'

'But there must be something...'

'No. I'm sorry, matey boy. But sooner or later they'll catch up. And we'll 'ave to fight 'em. I can attack when yer eyes are closed but yer'll 'ave to guide me. And although they're after yer, I'm guessin' they're not gonna look too kindly on anythin' in their way. And right now, I really 'ave no idea what we'd do. A poorly aimed spell'll do more 'arm than good. Once they catch up we'll be in real trouble. And they will. In the end. No one keeps their eyes open for ever. So we'd better stay ahead of the game. Shut yer peepers for a few seconds every now and then, get a bearing on them, and then we can come up with a plan. They'll know where we are but we'll know where they are too.'

'Why didn't you tell me?' Krish was too tired to be angry, but he gave it his best shot. 'You know, about the Malshrael?'

'Yes,' admitted Balthrir. 'But...' She trailed off and for the first time since they'd met Balthrir was temporarily speechless. 'I... I dunno. I panicked, all right? I-I-I just thought, *'E'll blink! If I tell 'im 'e'll blink!* Thought they'd be on top of us in hours an-an-and... I dunno! I thought maybe yer'd blink less if yer weren't thinkin' about it!' Krish had to admit that she was right: all he wanted to do now was shut his eyes. 'S-so I thought we should get an 'ead-start. So come on. We'd better regain some of that distance before we do anything else.'

Krish didn't budge and Balthrir stared down at him with wide-eyed urgency.

'If you're gonna crack out all that *Balthrir, I'm sorry for getting you into all this* stuff then do it on the move please, before we get eaten by invisible dogs!'

'They're going to *eat* us?!'

Krish didn't think it could be possible for Balthrir's eyes to be as wide as they were.

'Eat us, tear us apart, 'owl at us till we bash our own 'eads in... Does it really matter 'ow they're gonna do us in? *Maybe* we shouldn't 'ang around and find out!'

Krish got to his feet.

'Balthrir, I'm... I'm sorry,' he said. 'I dunno how you're putting up with all this.'

As they walked off Balthrir gave him the kind of look that said that *she* didn't know how she was putting up with all this. They sped through the dark woods, edging closer and closer to the shores of the Night Ocean.

CHAPTER 17

TWO SPELLS

Night and day were now one in Betsarhldeth, forest of shadows. Krish and Balthrir hurried on through the dismal woods at an exhausting pace, until at last Krish heard the gentle sound of water lapping against the land. The trees were clearing ahead of them. Minutes later, Balthrir collapsed against a tree and Krish followed suit soon after. They had arrived.

As their laboured breathing died down, Krish turned and beheld the Night Ocean for the first time. The placid waters were eerily quiet. Only a few noiseless ripples drifted across the endless black mirror before them. The stillness of the water seemed to have infested the area with silence. The water slurped quietly, hardly disturbing the grey shingle on the slim beach, no wider than the bough of a tree. The rustling of the woods had died down.

Krish had never felt more exhausted in his life. He was enjoying the feeling of rest so much but he knew he couldn't...

'Do it.'

Krish looked over at Balthrir.

'Shut 'em for a few seconds,' she said. 'Give 'em a break and report back. Just relax and yer'll be able to focus.'

Krish closed his eyes.

> *Chewing bark... nuzzling blackened weeds...*
> *necks craned upwards... deep nasal*
> *breaths... looking in their direction...*

'They're hungry,' he said. 'They know where we are... well, which direction we're in, but none are making a move.'

'There's no much for 'em to eat in the forest. They'll rest for a while but then they'll be on our trail again. Are they far?'

'Yes. I think so. They look tiny. Must be a long way away. Give me a minute and maybe I can see—'

'Open up, kiddo!' she barked and Krish obeyed. 'Don't go the other way. They'll forget their empty stomachs once they know where to find two weary travellers to munch on. Right. Bit o' grub and we'll start trainin'.'

Balthrir tried to stew some black, bobbly fungi but they were a little plain and rubbery for Krish's liking. Not that he could afford to be that fussy but every discomfort reminded him of his aching eyes, dried out and stinging from every gust of air to brush his eyeballs.

Balthrir kept Krish distracted with a briefing, outlining her plan to capture a pearl from the bed of the Night Ocean. She had two spells to assist him. The first was to fill his lungs with air underwater. She held her staff aloft and appeared to cut a silvery wound in the air itself, no bigger than his little finger. Then she placed her staff lightly against the left and then the right of his ribcage. For one bizarre moment he saw his lungs illuminated.

'Now try lowerin' yerself into the water.' There was a sense of caution in Balthrir's voice.

Krish stripped down to his pants and T-shirt. He could barely remember what colour his clothes had been when he arrived but now they were all a mucky yellowish-brown colour. He quickly became aware of how achingly uncomfortable he'd been in these old rags. They were probably less than a year old but he felt as if he'd worn them for a hundred. He climbed into the chilly water, deeply afraid of the bottomless black pool he was lowering himself into. He felt a tinge of pain right down in the marrow of his bones as the freezing ocean enveloped his entire body. He went numb in moments, the waters so cold he could hardly feel a thing.

'Just open yer gob and breathe…' he heard his wizard friend say as the water passed over his head.

He was freezing. *Freezing!* The currents flowing gently around him were all different degrees of cold. Less than a metre under the surface he could scarcely see a thing. His mouth opened in panic. Air rushed in. It rushed in so fast he couldn't breathe. His lungs billowed. *They'd burst! They'd burst under the pressure!* His arms and legs flailed about desperately in the blackness and gripped nothing. Torrents of bubbles surged from his mouth and nose but more and more air was replacing whatever was escaping all the time. The constant stream of air was suffocating him!

Blinding white light burst across the surface above. The light dimmed a fraction and he made out Balthrir's staff coming towards him. He grabbed the staff and within moments his body was pulled through the surface of the water and he collapsed onto the shore, breathless and shivering.

'Balthr... Wha...' he could hardly get 'Balthrir, what the hell?!' out of his aching lungs and past his quivering lips.

'I know! I know! I'm sorry!' she said, pacing up and down. 'I-I-I just... Look, mate, it's a difficult spell! It is... *bloody* difficult! Yer got any idea? Rippin' a hole in the air? The air?! All this stuff—' she waved her arms around in agitation '—and keepin' it linked to some poor bugger's lungs even if 'e's miles below the water? Huh?! Any idea 'ow 'ard that is to get right?'

After some time Krish began to catch his breath and he was able to nod.

'Mate, I'm sorry,' she continued. 'But water ain't actually my forte.' He'd noticed that she stayed as far back from the shore as possible, eyeing the water reproachfully.

'How did you master all these spells anyway?' He was feeling calmer now. 'I mean, how the hell d'you find the time? You're, like, a bit older than me...? How d'you do it?'

Balthrir looked at the ground for a while, her eyes dark and reflective. He could barely make out her muttered response:

'Perseverance.'

⁘

After a few more attempts Krish began to breathe underwater with ease, although it still felt more laboured than breathing out in the open air. His breaths were deeper than normal and he really felt the weight of the air itself as it entered his lungs.

According to Balthrir, the second spell, something Krish certainly wasn't delighted to hear, was slightly more complex than the first. Krish had forgotten that lack of oxygen would not be his only challenge underwater. The deeper he got, the more water there would be pressing down on him, so to avoid being crushed under the extreme pressure, Balthrir gave him a parrel stone. She placed the parrel stone in a blue flame and enclosed both in a glass globe. Parrel, she assured him, was the hardest known rock in the world. The fire was an enchantment which would bestow the strength of the stone on the holder of the globe until the rock burnt out. The parrel stone would last three days, she said, at best. If it began to crack he must head for the surface at once. The blue flame would also light his way in the depths.

Despite this apparently being the more tricky of the two spells, Balthrir carried it off with considerable ease.

'You'll be coming too, yeah?' asked Krish.

'Wizards and spells are no different to ropes and cooking pots. All just equipment yer use on your quest, innit? But I've got a nasty feeling that if someone actually 'elps yer snatch that pearl it'll be different.'

'But how would the King know?'

Balthrir's exasperated sigh was almost violent. 'Because, laddie, the truth is pretty bloody important 'round 'ere! Thought yer'd've learnt that by now! The last king wasn't the most honest o' blokes and when the people found out how much of their money 'e was spending on banquets and stuff 'e was for the 'igh jump! Maybe the truth is pretty flexible where *you* come from but people swear by it 'ere.'

'But still, how will he—?'

'Because of Gul— Actually, yer know what, we ain't got time for this!'

Tiredness had kept fear at bay in Krish for some time now but suddenly the idea of facing the blackness alone terrified him anew. And what was worse was that every time he thought about being tired he blinked and then he would see them. Just for a moment but a moment was enough for you never to want to shut your eyes ever again.

Balthrir continued to train Krish, first without the aid of any spells, then with each cast in isolation, then finally with both, having him dive deeper each time. The wizard seemed content that finding an oyster with a pearl would be the easiest part of the quest. The seabed was rich with them, she said (or so she'd read in some book years ago), and she gave him a knife for protection (just in case) and a metal bar she'd forged from a spare stirrup belonging to the mule to prise the oyster open with.

Balthrir sent Krish down for another test dive with both spells. He was still struggling with breathing underwater. Breathing. Something you did all the time, without even thinking about it, had become a slow, heavy, painful exercise. The cold water adding weight to the slightest movement. And even with the parrel stone fighting the pressure he still felt it. That crushing feeling, just a metre or so below the surface. Down there he felt like he was living his life in slow motion. The illusion of having more time was a momentary comfort before a shiveringly cold current whipped past his face, his eyes shut and he saw them... closer...

He jerked upwards. His body went from horizontal to vertical. His head broke the surface and he breathed normally.

'Good. Yer lookin' ready,' said Balthrir, unprompted, unconvincingly.

'I don't feel ready,' he said.

'Where are they?' Balthrir asked.

Krish closed his eyes.

Heads darting about... necks craned... running...
stopping... running... stopping... sniffing... running

'I dunno,' said Krish. 'They seem lost.'

'They sense yer but I guess the water did the trick and they can't pick up our scent. Better make a move now though. Yer should be done in a couple of hours.'

'They can't find me underwater though, can they...?'

'Shouldn't be able to. Dunno. These aren't usual creatures. Don't risk it. Eyes open.'

Krish nodded. She was right. He should get going before... well, before he let fear take him over. He chewed a few more rubbery fungi and then it was time. He stripped down to his pants and T-shirt again, the parrel stone glowing blue on one side of the belt Balthrir had given him, the knife on the other. She had also gave him a bag for the oyster, which he used to hold the metal bar, and a flask of fresh water (he was not looking forward to trying to drink that underwater). Balthrir had recommended not gulping down even a little of the Night Ocean if he could help it.

One other thing he took, when Balthrir wasn't looking, was the distress stone. The little red rock Balthrir had invented would send up a flare through earth, water, wind or fire, she had said. He wasn't sure what she could do from the surface but he took the stone anyway.

'Good luck,' said Balthrir.

'Balthrir, what if—?'

'Yer can deal with it. Whatever it is. Yeah?'

Krish nodded at his friend. 'Yeah.' *I guess*, he thought. He stared into the black pool before him. He jumped.

CHAPTER 18

A DIVE INTO DARKNESS

Ripples broke the black, glass-like stillness of the water as the Night Ocean swallowed Krish whole.

At first it was difficult to adjust, even after so much practice. He found himself drawing water into his mouth but the bubbles of air he exhaled pushed the icy-cold liquid out again. This took a while to get used to. Each time he felt as if he was going to drown, that his body would fill with water, but it didn't.

Freezing currents billowed sightlessly around as he dived deeper. Icy water rushed past his eyes and a few times the sting caused him to blink. The Vulrein were preoccupied with... It was the mule. They'd torn him apart and were feasting on his carcass. A wave of guilt spread through him. They should have searched for the poor creature. Anything that would delay the Vulrein was welcome but he didn't wish this fate on such a loyal beast.

Down and down he dived, holding the blue light of the parrel stone in front of him. The pressure of the water adjusted itself around him as the stone did its work. He felt weightless, dizzy almost. He could see nothing. Just endless black tinged with blue. He was so afraid of this place. He swore he could make out his Mum's tired face in the depths.

I'm coming... I'll be there soon... You won't be tired any more... I promise...

Suddenly Krish felt so alone that he could feel the loneliness dragging him down and down... *That sinking feeling isn't fear*, he valiantly tried to tell himself. *You're just going deeper and deeper and that's how it feels...* He looked down into the blackness and convinced himself he could see her face smiling now... *That's why you're here... You're getting closer... You're getting closer...*

The seabed began to take shape. Ridges and trenches cut across the marine landscape but there were no signs of life. *This shouldn't be called the Night Ocean,* he thought. *The Dead Ocean, more like.* Surveying the ocean floor from above, he spotted white dots in the distance. He swam in their direction. He was in luck. There were scores of giant oysters laid out before him. He swam down and inspected the crusty shells. He gingerly tried to prise one open with the metal bar. To his surprise, he opened the oyster with incredible ease. The thing was dead and one half of its shell snapped clean off and floated away. But there was no pearl. He tried another. The same happened. He tried another and another and another and another. They were all dead and the pearls had deteriorated to a black fragments. It must have been a long time since they were alive for the pearls to have rotted away.

He swam around in panic. These creatures must have been dead for hundreds of years. Thousands, on this world! He swam in urgent circles, breathing hard and fast. It was a trick! The King had tricked him! There were no oysters left alive in the Night Ocean.

After several minutes his mind became calm again. He looked about and saw that the oysters were in a rough line, leading to the mouth of a trench. He swam over and looked down into the bottomless groove in the ocean floor. There could be nowhere deeper and darker and farther away from home than this, surely. But he peered into the darkness all the same. The blue flame illuminated very little but there was something… some little white shape in the unlit chasm. He was terrified of the dark now, so much more than before. What if it was some ravenous fish that had been waiting for a morsel of food for decades?

Krish was afraid but he knew that if he could just take a closer look…

He *could* take a closer look… When he'd seen the Vulrein his vision had been magnified. What if he could focus it on that white shape in the depths? He'd been able to look around a little when he'd seen them before. It was a mad plan but he knew that if he got that deep into the trench and there was something waiting down there, escape wouldn't be easy. Just a quick peek… Just for a moment…

A fraction of a second was all it took for Krish to give in to temptation…

Legs beating the water... dark shapes moving...
deeper and deeper...

Oh, God! They were in the water! Not even in the shallows! Their red eyes saw him! They corrected their course and were on their way down to him. But how could they stand the pressure? How could they breathe? They weren't *usual creatures*, that was what Balthrir had said. But Balthrir had said... She was wrong. The water hadn't really put them off. Not for long anyway.

But Krish had also seen a cave. A faint light coming from the end of a long passage in the rock face. And at its end he saw...

He had no time. He dived into the pitch-black terror, praying he'd make it out alive to see his Mum, his Dad, his sister, to see Balthrir, to see anyone ever again. He shot through the water, his eyes fixed on the spot where he had seen the oyster.

He'd lost it. The blue flame struggled to pick out any details whatsoever. His head darted from one side of the chasm to the other. Nothing. The water rushed across his tired, stinging eyeballs as he sped through the blackness. He had no choice. To alleviate the pain at least, he shut his eyes.

... a glimmer in the depths .. .a tunnel of soft light...

... the shapes... dark shapes entering the chasm...

He opened his eyes. There! Just above him to the right. He'd swum right past it.

He turned, rushed towards the mouth of the cave above him. Curious lights of green and orange, dancing, mesmerising, on the walls of the—

A shot of pain. An excruciating sensation spread through his body in an instant, originating in his Achilles' tendon. The light from the passage had blinded him and, for a moment, his eyes had been shut and a Vulrein had seized the opportunity. But all he could see now was blood pouring from the wound on his foot into the water.

Krish pulled out the knife and slashed and slashed around his foot. It had no effect. He'd have to close his eyes to attack them with any accuracy.

He closed his eyes.

Bubbles erupted from the beast's mouth. He felt the vibration from its growl and its tightening grip sent another surge of pain through his body. He could see it up close now. The horrifying creature's eyes were the red-black of magma but he saw something almost human in its stare. He was reminded of every cruel, vindictive person he'd ever encountered. Its charcoal coat clung tightly about its bones, emphasising its sharp features, and there were more of them homing in on him.

Krish slashed maniacally at the Vulrein, caring not if the blade cut himself or the creature first. The bag over his shoulder wasn't helping. It was floating all over the place, getting in the way of both his seeing and hitting the beast. The blade tore across the creature biting into his foot. Blood of shadow poured from the beast and the others barked wildly in the deep, the terrible noise low and muffled by the water. But its grip was just as strong. In seconds the whole pack would be upon him. He thrust his arm back, the parrel stone helping push the water aside, and readied himself to dive the blade straight into the neck of the beast with all his might. The knife hit rock, the blade flattened itself against the mouth of the cave, the handle parted from his fingers and his weapon drifted out of sight. The bag blocked his vision once more. He thrust one hand inside and seized the metal bar. He struck the beast but its teeth simply sank deeper into his flesh. The bar was heavy and even with the parrel stone the water was slowing him too much. He jabbed at the Vulrein's dull red eyes. Its fierce, unforgiving malevolence never dimmed as he struck the beast again and again. The others were paddling with remorseless purpose towards him. They were spread out to reduce any chance of escape. He had seconds. He struck once more and the Vulrein winced in pain, pawed at the metal bar as he retracted it for one more strike. A split second before he hit the creature it opened its mouth and bit at the bar. The relief was instant but the water stung as it moved in on his wounds. The rest of the pack were excited by the clouds of his blood which were now mixing with the water.

Then something caught his eye...

He was now lying just inside the mouth of the cave, rocks packed tightly into the ceiling above. He pulled himself backwards, until all but his feet were in the cave. The Vulrein were on his heels. Their jaws opened wide. He jammed the bar into the tightly packed rocks and a volley of stone deadened those red eyes.

All was quiet.

Krish was in pain but for a moment or two he relaxed.

He lifted a handful of rocks off his leg. His lower leg was riddled with cuts and grazes, clouds of red pouring into the water from his stinging skin. He'd seen how to cope with this on some TV programme his Mum had let him stay up and watch one night. He tore off the lower section of his T-shirt, brushed the grit from the gashes in his skin and bound strips of the length of material – roughly cut with some help from the metal bar – tightly around the most severe-looking of the wounds.

He took in the silence once more. There was certainly no Vulrein on his foot any more. But one could be in the chamber the rockfall had created. The fluctuating lights guided him as he slid backwards on his rear, searching for the knife. Once he'd found it he pressed himself against the wall, to make sure there wouldn't be one behind him, then held the blade in front of him, his arm tense, ready, staring at the pile of fallen rocks that filled the cave mouth.

He shut his eyes.

... pawing at rocks... energy dwindling
... they were still... waiting...

His lids parted and he sat calmly in the underwater cave. He had outsmarted them. For now at least. He couldn't tell if there were any fewer of them, if any had perished in the rockfall. He didn't even know if they *could* die. They had bled, he'd seen that, and Balthrir said he would have to fight them at some point.

But this did not concern him for now. He had been awake for so long. He had run, he had swum, he had fought, and his eyes ached with tiredness. The parrel stone should burn for two to three days, Balthrir had said. And right now, he could sleep without any fear that the Vulrein could get him.

Just for a few hours… a few minutes… he thought. *Must rest…*

His eyes shut. The Vulrein paid him no attention and, for now at least, he barely feared those terrible creatures that filled his dreams.

The water swirled around Krish, the lights soothed him, drifting past like a mobile hanging from the ceiling above an infant's cot. He slept in safety for the first time in so long. The only noise, which he hardly registered, was the tiniest crunch, like the sound of a light tap to crack the shell of an egg.

CHAPTER 19

THE CAVERN OF LIGHT & COLOUR

*… sniffing at fallen rocks… some searching…
no other way in… waiting…*

Krish opened his eyes and sat up. He'd rested more than slept. Visions of the Vulrein in his dreams told him they weren't any closer to finding a way in. He still feared them but he was considerably more relaxed about their presence than before. Not that he should be relaxed: he was no closer to finding a pearl.

He floated through the cave. As soon as he moved, pushing himself along with his hands against the walls, he found he was still rather weary. But he was hungry more than anything. The amplified vision, staring into the cave from above with his eyes shut, had given him a false impression of how long the cave was. It had felt a lot shorter when he was looking from the top of the trench. The water meandered past his ears, making them deaf to the sounds of the cavern. It masked another sound too. The tiniest cracking noise.

The lights became brighter. There were curious shapes up ahead. Krish could see one of them turning gently in the distance. As he came closer he was faced with two of the strangest creatures he had ever seen. The first was long and white, dotted with suckers, with a slight bulge in the middle, and its shape reminded Krish, in a bizarre way, of a white flute stuck through the middle of a tennis ball. The second was like a many-pointed star of rippling tentacles with a similar bulge to the first at its centre. A green translucent membrane separated the tentacles. The light changed seamlessly from green to orange and then blue before returning to green.

As he moved forward the star creature's tentacles extended. The tennis ball-like bulges on each creature completely detached themselves from the rest of their bodies and formed a separate, tightly packed, protective ball. The ball drifted to the rear of the rest of their bodies. The flute section of the first creature attached to the second, somehow pushed its abdomen inside the latter, which lengthened its tentacles farther. The tentacles began to rotate with increased intensity in his direction. It was as if a multicoloured fan was very slowing attacking him. Krish slipped past them quickly and the spinning stopped shortly afterwards. The two creatures soon re-formed and seemed not to be bothered by him any more.

He passed more of these creatures, who seemed keener to show they could defend themselves than to do any actual defending. Another creature looked like a rubbery blue bag that kept turning itself inside out to reveal a sucker on the end of a long stalk, before returning to its blue side. Across the floor scuttled small, semi-transparent crustaceans, the size and shape of twenty-pence pieces, their tiny organs just visible through their thin shells, protuberances from their heads scanning the floor for sustenance.

They were the most perplexing beings Krish had ever come across but at least they didn't seem too hostile. And in a bizarre way he was glad of the company. They were no substitute for Balthrir's cutting remarks though. He'd do anything for her to be there to make fun of him right now.

He ventured forward. Something was shimmering ahead of him. The cave opened out into a large spherical chamber. The walls were like metal covered in dents, a sheen of colour glimmering in the stone. Pale greens and blues and pinks. And set into the rock, all around, were hundreds and hundreds of oysters.

But this was not the most blissful sight on offer in that vibrant chamber. At the roof of the cave, in the very centre, was a wide shaft from which dim sunlight was pouring, filling the cavern with a tranquil glow that was causing the splendid walls to glisten. Krish allowed relief to overwhelm him for a moment. He had no idea how there could be sunlight when presumably he was still in the centre of the Night Ocean, but he didn't question it. Not right now anyway.

Another crack. He heard it this time. Was it the oysters? One must have moved. He looked about but each one lay there motionless. After some consideration he went for a plump-looking oyster in the lower section of the cavern. On closer inspection these oysters were rougher yet brighter than the ones he'd found on the seabed. He imagined that adjusting to a life in the caves had changed them somewhat. He carefully ran his hand along the top of the shell, just as Balthrir had taught him, and the oyster tensed up, closing its mouth. He stroked it several times and it reacted by opening and closing a number of times in a vague attempt to protect itself. Krish managed to jam its mouth open with the bar. He saw the pearl within. He pulled the pearl with both hands and it came away with little resistance. The pearl was smooth and beautiful, like mist frozen in time at the centre of the shining black globe. But it was a little too heavy to admire for too long. He lowered the pearl, which was almost the size of a football, down to the floor of the cave. He removed the bar and the oyster snapped shut, masking the sound of another crack.

Krish placed the pearl in the bag Balthrir had given him and put the bag on his back. It was going to be a long journey to the surface. He was tired. His eyes were heavy. In fact everything about him felt heavy. He straightened up, ready to make his ascent. He might not have noticed the minuscule piece of debris float down from his waist but it was sharp. It brushed past his little finger and the object caught his eye.

It was a shard of glass.

His eyes darted to the globe that contained the parrel stone. How had he not noticed? The sunlight had smothered what remained of the blue flame. It had almost gone out; a grain of dust at its centre was where the parrel stone had once been, the glass itself covered in cracks. He had minutes if he was lucky.

Krish hastened in the direction of the shaft but the weight of the pearl was pulling him down. He fought and fought against the drag, trying not to paddle with too much ferocity and waste the little energy he had left. His wounds stung as his legs beat the water. He began to make his way up the shaft. The power of the parrel stone was fading and he felt the pressure close in on him while at the same time it lessened from the ascent, a dizzying effect coursing through his body. The faint glow of the stone faded to nothing. The light from above was getting brighter. The circular shaft was narrowing.

Krish's hands gripped the side of the shaft and he was surprised not to feel stone. It was soft and dark, reddish-brown in colour. Fragments of the shaft walls floating above him looked like the shredded duck his Dad would get from the Chinese takeaway. It was wood softened by years in the water. He must be inside a hollowed-out tree.

His legs were enveloped with pain. They beat the water as he guided himself up, his hands struggling to grip the mush of wood lining the shaft above him. His hand caught hold of a solid section of wood. He heaved himself upwards and collided with the side of the tree. *Crunch.* He was dragged down with ferocious force. The bag's strap cut into his shoulder as if it contained something the weight of a cannonball. He looked to his side. The glass holding what was left of the parrel stone had been completely crushed as he'd crashed against the wood. The stone itself was gone, floated off somewhere. Everything had returned to its normal weight.

Krish clawed and clawed at the mushy wood. He was being dragged down and down, farther and farther. He was near the chamber of oysters once more. The pain in his legs, the weight tearing into his shoulder, shredded wood embedding itself under his nails. He'd never have the strength to get out. Could he reach the distress stone in his bag? Both hands were occupied with trying to prevent himself falling back into the chamber. Down and down he was dragged, his wounds stinging, his breath short and his very bones feeling heavier than ever.

Krish stretched out his right leg and pushed with his foot against the shaft of wood on one side and against the opposite side with his left hand. Both pushed through the mush to the solid wood behind. He was sliding a little but he was stable. Krish's nerves steadied. He was calm (just about). He placed his left foot on the other side of the shaft to his right. It slipped. *Calm, calm. You've already got the pearl. You can do this...* Tentatively he reached out with his left foot, prodded the wall and found a solid spot. Then he did the same with his right hand. He moved his left hand up a touch, then his right foot, followed by his left foot, then he'd start over. Slowly, *very* slowly, he inched his way up the shaft. The chamber below was gradually shrinking from view. Breathing was becoming very difficult. Every breath now was short. Was that spell waning too? *Slowly, slowly, slowly, come on, you can do it, come on, come on, come on—*

Then in an instant the water disappeared and he found himself gasping for breath as his soaking body was chilled with stale, freezing air. He took a moment to regain his breath and then he looked up in delight. The rest of the shaft was nice and dry. Not too many footholds but he'd manage a lot more easily from now on.

Krish gripped the coarse, dry wood above the water level. He crawled up through the tree. The wood was covered in holes – bite marks, he guessed. Some creature must have gnawed its way through the inside of the tree, feasting on the soft interior and hollowing it out in the process. He gritted his teeth as he climbed. The weight of the pearl pressed against his back and no matter how hard he tried to support the great bulk with the help of his feet, his outstretched arms were still bearing the brunt of his burden.

Minutes after envisioning himself climbing out of the top of the tallest tree overlooking the whole of Betsarhldeth, and contemplating jumping into the sea of branches below while hoping for the best, Krish's fingers went to grip the wood and his arm shot out of a large hole in the trunk. Krish gazed through the hole. He was maybe only ten metres off the ground and there were plenty of thick branches to climb down on. He considered for a short time carrying the pearl on his back the whole way down but he'd had enough of the stupid thing. It was solid as a rock so it would survive the fall intact and the bag would prevent it from getting scratched. He hoped, at least.

He dropped the pearl onto the forest floor and climbed out into the dark woods. In minutes he'd reached the ground – barely noticing all the scratches he was sustaining from twigs as he scraped past them – and was looking around for any sign of Balthrir.

He was in luck. The wizard had a fire going (he'd seen the light fading in the tree trunk and he could feel the cold of night settling on the woods) so he followed the plume of smoke.

'Blimey!' Balthrir sat up. 'That was quick!' Krish felt as if he'd been gone for weeks.

CHAPTER 20

MANY-RULED SPLAT

Krish felt a calming tingle spread through his body as Balthrir pressed a handful of red moss, which she assured him had an antiseptic quality, against the wounds on his leg prior to dressing them.

'You don't know a spell for this?' Krish asked, wincing a little.

'Don't know a spell for everything, mate,' said Balthrir.

'So really, how do you know so many spells?'

She shrugged. 'Just... yer know? Too much time on my hands as a kid, I guess.' Krish detected that this wasn't the only reason but he didn't press her again. 'Yer said some hollowed-out old tree leads to a chamber full of oysters?'

'Er... yeah,' he confirmed.

'Hilarious! Could 'ave saved ourselves a lot of bother!' It didn't seem that funny to Krish, who'd almost died several times down there. 'So come on then, tell us more about these creatures? Sound weird!'

'Yeah,' said Krish. 'Really weird. I... don't even know how to describe them...'

Balthrir stared at him with a playful little smile on her face. 'Krish, let's face it, mate: yer not the most articulate o' bozos at the best of times, are yer?'

Krish chuckled and found himself really enjoying looking into Balthrir's beautiful dark brown eyes. He couldn't keep looking at her – he felt somewhat awkward. He blinked.

... shaking in the cold air... droplets of water flying from their coats... muzzles to the ground... find the scent...

When he opened his eyes again Balthrir was no longer smiling.

'Where are they?' she asked.

'I... think they're out of the water,' he said.

Balthrir nodded.

'Come on.'

They began to pack. Krish lifted the enormous pearl, which had lost much of its vibrancy in the dismal light of the forest, from his pack and examined it for a moment before wringing out the sodden bag. The distress stone fell out. He looked it over for a moment. He was glad he'd never had to use it but he was even gladder he'd had it with him. With that in his pack he'd felt that Balthrir was never too far away.

Krish re-packed his bag and they prepared to move out.

Life without the mule was considerably more difficult than before. Krish and Balthrir managed to ditch a lot of the items he had been carrying but still they were overloaded with bags and flasks of water. Balthrir had no spell to make clean drinking water from the Night Ocean ('What, filter microbes and all that? Separate all that tiny little stuff from the water? Do me a favour!'). They'd had to boil the water and it showed no signs of cooling any time soon. The scalding liquid left their throats hoarse and their mouths practically dry. They drank infrequently.

Krish begged to stop and eat but Balthrir insisted that they must leave Betsarhldeth before daybreak. Krish complained that he was famished and Balthrir tossed him half an old turnip-like root vegetable as they headed towards the faint glimmer of moonlight in the distance.

They reached the edge of the woods at dawn, and shortly after, Balthrir gave in to Krish's whinging and allowed them to rest. She started a fire, igniting it with a beam of sunlight cut from the air with the Salvean blade, boiled some halfire and Krish gobbled down the steaming-hot fruit in seconds. He then ate the rest of the odd vegetable and, yawning with lethargy, one hand on his full belly, he...

'Oi!' Balthrir kicked his foot to wake him up. 'None of that, young man! Yer gettin' too used to blottin' those guys out! Where are they?'

Krish *had* seen the Vulrein. He was too tired to fear them right now. Like so much over the past few... weeks, maybe even months, he supposed. His days in Ilir were indistinguishable from each other in his current state.

'Thhhh… thhhh… a' the edge of the forest…' he mumbled as he failed to hold back an enormous yawn.

'The edge of the forest!' Balthrir was already up, smothering the fire and packing. 'Come on!'

Krish practically sleepwalked his way through the rocks that littered the road to the Pale Hunting Grounds. There they would search for a FireHawk. The world was dim as he allowed his eyes to narrow, his eyelashes darkening the sight of the rough ground ahead. He swayed absent-mindedly from side to side, Balthrir's hand on his shoulder steering him back to the path from time to time. Balthrir attempted a spell which stung his eyes, forcing them to open up wide, but the agitation this caused the exhausted Krish was too much for the young wizard to put up with.

'Stop it!' she said. 'Stop scratchin' 'em! STOP IT!'

Krish's eyes ached as he tried to blink but the spell stopped his eyelids from moving far.

'J-just let me blink!' he pleaded. 'Just quickly! Please, Balthrir!'

Her voice was softer for a moment or two. 'Just quickly.' Out of the corner of his stinging eye he could make out her staff slowly making circles in the air. 'Sorry, mate. It's not m'best spell. Not one yer get much call for.'

His eyelids felt light once more and he held them shut for a few luxurious moments…

> … *hastening forward… the scent filled their*
> *nostrils… sand in their paws…*

The sight of them hardly even made him jump any more. The Vulrein had sped up the moment he'd closed his eyes. Balthrir was right: he must try and keep them open for as long as he could, despite sand blowing into them every few minutes.

The ground was a fine powder of pale sand with a hint of metallic blue. It was surprisingly hard to pass through, almost like wading through custard. Balthrir said that the sand here had some curious electromagnetic charge that bound the grains together and would hopefully confuse the Vulrein. Krish had a nasty feeling that his continuous blinking was doing a fine job of counteracting this but after some time he noticed that those foul dogs were beginning to lag behind.

Balthrir refused to let them stop even for food now. They ate straight out of their satchels or she'd pick some dried black weeds from the ground, shake off the dust and hand Krish a few to chew on. It was dry and tasteless and minutes after swallowing it he felt like he'd never eaten it at all.

Several hours passed and Balthrir consented to let them have a rest for a few minutes. Something had captured her interest.

'Used to travel a lot as a kid.' She was digging up a dead-looking bush by the root. 'Mum and Dad wanderin' the four corners, tryin' to get work wherever they could. Yer learn the tricks o' stayin' alive out in these parts.'

'Balthrir...'

'Uh-huh?' She pulled up a large, bulbous root.

'Some of the stuff in my pack... do we need it all?'

'Like what?' She had peeled off a large section of the exterior of the root and was now cutting the interior into shreds using her knife.

'Well, there's your itching powder. I mean, do we need that?'

'I invented that – works bloody well!'

'Or-or the clock-confuser—'

'Is awesome – leave it!'

'Is it really *that* useful?'

'It's genius! There's only one of 'em and if I can sell it—'

'But it's massive! Takes up half my pack!'

'Ditch the distress stone.' She'd collected quite pile of shredded root in an open skin by now.

'But the distress stone *is* really useful! And tiny! How does it work anyway?'

'Close yer palm round the little bugger, concentrate on bein' distressed and FOOOUUUNNG!'

'What? It explodes in your face?!'

'I'll explode in yer face in a minute, yer little twerp! 'Ere, try some of this.'

Balthrir offered Krish a modest handful of moist shredded root.

'What do I...' said Krish.

'Like this...' Balthrir demonstrated; she held the shredded root in her fist above her head, opened her mouth and squeezed. Faintly yellow liquid poured out of her clenched fist and into her mouth. Krish tried it. It was earthy and rather sour but cool and refreshing nonetheless. He was surprised how much water the root had retained. Balthrir discarded the root shavings in her fist and tied up the skin which held the rest of the shredded root.

'That'll keep us goin' until we can find fresh water on the other side o' the hunting grounds,' said Balthrir. 'We can ditch one of the water jars. That should 'elp. And it doesn't explode in yer face! The flare's magical; might dazzle yer a bit but yer won't feel anything. What it produces is pure light. Flies up into the sky to let people know where you are.'

'It's genius,' said Krish.

'It's no clock-confuser. We should keep movin'.'

'What?! We only just sat down!'

Balthrir considered this for a moment. 'Where are they now?' she said.

Krish closed his eyes for a few seconds. 'They're... they're making their way through the sand. They're moving slowly. They look a little lost.'

'See,' said Balthrir. 'Told yer the electromagnetic wotsit would confuse 'em for a bit. Right! Ten minutes. Then we'll bust a groove.' She pulled out an odd-looking pack of cards. They were octagonal. Each had an identical image on its back of a thin, white-lined octagon split into eight equal-sized triangles leading to a single point in the middle, all on a red background. 'Yer know Many-Ruled Splat?'

'Er... no,' said Krish.

'Right.' She dealt eight cards to each of them. 'We play one card each, 'ighest wins. One with the most wins... well, wins.'

'Okay...' said Krish, baffled by the eclectic array of imagery now facing him on the front of the cards in his hand. Each had a picture of either a range of lean mountains, fields of something that looked like wheat, a cave or a number of boats on the sea. They also featured a compass in the corner, pointing north, east, south or west (with no apparent connection to the pictures), and between one and eight pictures of the same grey-bearded wizard, spread out across the card in rows or shapes that made them easy to count.

'Right! Bored o' waitin'! Me first!' Balthrir played a card; five wizards, lean mountains, east.

Krish played seven wizards, fields of wheat, north. Seven was higher than five so surely he'd won.

'Ah!' said Balthrir with a smile. 'No more than five northbound wizards in a field! You lose three so that's four to my five. I win!'

Krish blinked in confusion. 'What?! But you didn't mention that rule!'

'Course I didn't! It's Many-Ruled Splat! Make up the rules as yer go along, don't yer?'

'But—'

'Look, yer got a counter-rule or what?'

Krish fought to make sense of the game and lost pretty swiftly. 'I... er...'

'Time's up! I win!' Balthrir grabbed both played cards and placed them to her right. 'Go on – you go first this time.'

Krish examined his cards for a long time. He had an eight, the sea, south. An eight had to win. He played it. Balthrir played a three, cave, west.

'Eight! I win!' said Krish.

'What? You mad, mate?' said Balthrir. 'Scar flows north at this time of year! Yer wizards drowned tryin' to row the wrong way! Mine are safe in the Undertowns.'

'But-but-but—'

'Counter-rule?'

'Yes! Erm... no... wizards in caves... um...'

'Yer what?! Wizards blinkin' love caves! Everyone knows that! I win!'

'This game is stupid!'

'Nah! It's brilliant! My turn.' Balthrir played a seven, cave, west.

Krish shrugged and played a two, mountains, east.

'What?! 'Ow'd you expect to win with a two?' Balthrir nabbed both cards.

'No! You can't! Erm… eastbound wizards on mountains—'

'If I lose a couple I'm still in the lead!'

'No! B-b-because no wizards on mountains while they are wizards in caves!'

Balthrir pulled a rather disgusted-looking face. 'Yer can't counter counter-rules, mate! You off yer rocker?'

Krish threw down his cards in anger. 'Oh, this game is ridiculous! How am I supposed to win?'

'I dunno, mate, how *are* yer gonna win…?' Balthrir stared at him expectantly. Krish pondered this for a moment.

'First person to throw down his cards gets fifty points…' Krish said.

'Ah! But not if the last card played 'ad more than one eastbound wizard—'

Krish interrupted as fast as he could: 'No-counter-rules-after-a-fifty-point-lead!'

'*No* counter-counter-rules!'

'No-counter-counter-counter-rules-at-all-unless-you-touch-a-rock-with-your-tongue!'

Balthrir dived to the ground, stuck out her tongue and had almost licked a rock when she stopped and said: 'Hey! That doesn't make any—'

'Time's up!' said Krish victoriously. 'I win!'

'Mate, yer gettin' too good at this!'

Their talk descended into laughter and for several minutes they forgot the Vulrein, the quest and the danger they might have to face in the days to come.

CHAPTER 21

DAY BRIGHT AS MOONLIGHT

The laughter died down. They packed. They were on the road again in minutes. The tone became solemn once more as they headed silently onwards.

The rocks receded and Krish saw a pale, endless plain stretch out in front of them. The heat was creeping back now too, the sun beating down on a barren, featureless wasteland. He was almost blinded by how bright the landscape was. The baked ground was cracked from the heat. He barely noticed the arrival of night as the near-white landscape seemed to absorb the light and project it out again after dark. Mother and Sons danced across the horizon. The land was eerily bright. The stars almost invisible, the ground glowing white, the air awash with electric blue.

They were resting. Still standing but resting, leaning against a rock, ready to move on at a moment's notice. Krish had no idea how he felt any more. Angry? Fearful? Bored? Exhausted? Or more awake than he'd ever felt in his life? He was tired to the point of forgetting what sleep was like. Was it normal to see dark when you closed your eyes? Or did you always see such things? Foul things. The redness in those black eyes so faint you had to stare right into them to truly see it. All he knew was that he felt old beyond his years. His eyes were wide, dry and stinging. Any new piece of information inflicted pain upon his tired mind, and everything ached.

'Okay.' Balthrir had decided this was the time for a briefing. 'So, we're not far now. This one's gonna to be tough.' Krish wondered just how that would be possible after fighting off the Vulrein in the pitch black at the bottom of the Night Ocean. 'Keepin' the feather alight, no problem,' Balthrir continued. 'Most people might struggle with that bit. Got a spell for that. But capturing one...' She blew out her cheeks. 'The only people 'oo 'ave any idea 'ow to snatch a Fire-

Hawk are the Goonmallinns. If yer find a group of them round 'ere they're looking to nab one. I've 'eard a few 'ave succeeded. They get a pretty penny for the meat but I 'ear the feathers burn to dust within minutes of 'em bein' plucked. And Goonmallinns don't share nothin' with no one. No secrets, no food, no water. Nothin'. So, yer could sneak into one of their camps, we could disguise yer, yer watch, yer learn—'

'Why is it me?! Why is it *always* me?!' Krish's endless state of exhaustion had forced him to conserve energy and in a few seconds he let it all burst out.

Balthrir turned up her lip at him. 'What yer talkin' about, mate?'

'Why is it always me?! I have to... to... always be the one wh-who goes down into the ocean, the Night... stupid *bloody* Night Ocean a-and get the pearl! Put up with questions from, from that old bat, that witch! That terrifying old witch, Old Margary! A-a-and... and I have to put up with the Vulrein! Do you know what this is like?! Seeing them all the time!'

'Yer don't see 'em all the time! Yer see 'em when y'er stupid enough to close yer stupid bloody eyes! Bloody idiot!'

Krish was standing up straight now, shouting at his friend, not caring if the noise summoned a hundred guards or a thousand Vulrein. 'Yeah, b-but I *do* see them! I *do* see them all the time! When I don't see them I imagine them!'

Balthrir was on her feet too, boiling with rage. 'And sorry, what's all this stuff yer've been doin'? Eh? What about me? Givin' up my time, risking *my life*... for what?! So you can give yer Mum a bit more time to live?! Boo-hoo! My folks might die of exhaustion in the Black Palace and this is the only way to 'elp 'em! Do you understand that?! They could be DEAD! Right now! DEAD!'

Krish's mouth gaped open. He'd rarely thought about Balthrir and her family. And he'd forgotten exactly where her parents were imprisoned. Trapped in that mass of sweating bodies that made up the palace.

'But... but... I'm sorry... I...' he said.

'Yer know what? Yer think *you've* done a lot? Well, there's plenty more to be gettin' on with! We've 'ardly started! This new challenge'll be much 'arder! *Much* 'arder! Much more dangerous! And we'll be doin' it for a helluva lot longer! So sit tight, matey boy! And y'er welcome, by the way!'

'B-b-but you said you'd get something out of this! The King—'

'Oh yeah! That old codger'll *possibly* give me some work but don't bank on it! D'yer know another reason why I'm doin' this? Do yer? Well, apart from the fact there is *naff all* to do round 'ere... I saw someone in need. Someone *desperate* for 'elp and I thought... why not? Why not! Who cares if I lose an arm, a leg, a head, my republoody-tation! Who cares? I 'ave got *nowhere* in life, despite bein' bloody good at magic and stuff, so why not 'elp someone else out? Eh? Risk it all because maybe *their* life'll be worth more than mine!'

Krish tried to think of something to say but his exhausted mind was a jumble of words, none of which seemed keen on getting acquainted with one another. *Your life is worth so much too...* He couldn't say it. Was it even true? He'd been so selfish. She could have died, she could *still* die because of him.

A brief silence allowed Balthrir to sigh and begin to fasten the satchels shut as she continued talking. She spoke quietly, her tone far more subdued than before.

'The Goonmallinns are a nasty bunch. They'll tear off yer 'ead for being too miserable and then tear off someone else's 'ead for laughin' too much. When I was a kid with m'parents we ran into a group and Dad almost 'ad to sell 'is 'and to get food and water off of 'em. Always tried to avoid 'em but the Pale Hunting Grounds are infested with 'em. You do *not* mess with these guys. Yer wanna fight them on yer own then that's your bag. Fine with me. I dunno why I'm 'ere really. Yer can fight them on yer own, can't yer? Yer know yer way around. Yer know plenty of spells to 'elp out, don't yer? Yer'll be fine.'

Balthrir turned around, facing back in the direction of the Night Ocean and Ugethrid and the Black Palace beyond.

'Yer want some food or will yer be all right?' she said.

Krish suddenly realised that Balthrir was about to leave him alone in the middle of nowhere.

'Erm...' was all he could muster.

'Well...?' Balthrir waited patiently. Krish was still lost trying to formulate a sentence. 'I don't know you! Yer don't say much but yer ask a lot! Why should I care? Quite 'appy to leave yer right 'ere to fend for yerself, mate.'

Krish was sure that Balthrir wasn't going to abandon him in this hostile wilderness but he feared the possibility nonetheless. He knew that she was just waiting for him to say something, to utter a few words and they'd be on their way again but he just couldn't find them. In the end, he went for the most basic, the most obvious choice of words he could muster.

'Balthrir... I'm sorry. I... I really want you to... In fact, I think I need your help or I'll probably die out here.'

Balthrir stared at him with heavy eyes for a moment. She looked down and let out a brief, droll chuckle, apparently sneering at her own feet, before looking up at him for a moment and then walking past him.

'Yeah, probably,' she said.

Krish watched as she walked on.

'Can't we at least rest until sunrise?' asked Krish.

Balthrir's thumb pointed over her shoulder and back past Krish.

'Oh, what is that big shiny thing plonked over there on the horizon...?' she muttered sarcastically.

He looked back to see that the sun was already climbing up the sky. That moment on the edge of the Pale Hunting Grounds Krish learned that in this corner of Ilir night vanished without warning, the new day bright as moonlight.

'We're gettin' there, mate,' said Balthrir with a weak yet encouraging smile. 'We're gettin' there.'

CHAPTER 22

SIX HUNTERS & A TRAITOR

Krish's eyes smarted more than ever in the blinding whiteness of the Pale Hunting Grounds in the midday sun. The occasional blink kept the Vulrein on their trail but he felt less worried now. Balthrir was with him. Her threatened departure had actually reassured him that she would never leave. They were in this together. And they were getting on better. Or so it appeared. She seemed more relaxed but she just kept laughing to herself.

'What's so funny?' he'd ask.

'Yer face,' she'd answer. 'Yer remind me of a little dog I 'ad when I was a kid. Can't believe it took me that long to realise what it was yer reminded me of!'

Balthrir seemed to be trying to humiliate him. To cut him down to size.

As they walked Balthrir outlined her plan. They would observe the Goonmallinns from afar, wait for one to break free from the others and then she'd stun her (Goonmallinns were all women, apparently) so they could steal a hair and a shred of her clothing. With these, Balthrir said, she could conjure up a mask spell of the Goonmallinn and wrap it around Krish, just like the one she'd used earlier to fool Madam Nboosa. Then they'd find another Goonmallinn to create Balthrir's disguise. Balthrir said she had a plan to keep the feather of the FireHawk burning, so Krish should leave that bit to her once they had the feather.

The dusty yellow hue of day faded seamlessly into the pale blue of night as they hid the ball of twine in the burnt-out husk of an old tree. They scanned the plain from the shelter of the rocks, slim, jagged towers of dark brown stone. Balthrir pointed. Some dots in the distance. Five, six maybe. Krish squinted at the shapes amid the low ridges that broke up the plain. He could just make out a little movement from here. As his eyes adjusted he could see poles and a large stretch of canvas. They were setting up camp. Soon a couple of Goonmallinns split from the main group, looking for kindling or a small beast for supper perhaps. Balthrir led them silently in a slow, cautious pursuit of the shapes.

They clambered over a ridge, moving swiftly, heads down but eyes always on the Goonmallinns. Krish noted that although the hunting grounds were indeed pale, the rocks were much darker, more of a muddy brown. And there was little dirt, no plants, no trees, no weeds. In the warm sunshine with its gentle breeze this seemed curious to Krish. This place did not have the eeriness of Betsarhldeth or the deep, dark terror of the Night Ocean. So why did everything keep away? And then there was the smell. What was it? He knew it. From a very specific time and place that he couldn't quite put his finger on.

As they began their descent, he looked out on the landscape. A series of narrow ridges cut through the milky-white flats and in places sand had poured in from the surrounding desert. The shallow ranges were like gigantic teeth gradually chewing up the land over the ages. In the distance were formidable rock formations that looked like waves frozen in time, bursts of lava solidified in mid-eruption.

They crouched among the rocks and observed a Goonmallinn collecting sticks. The Goonmallinn wore a hooded cloak made of coarsely stitched-together dirty brown rags, threads dangling from every poorly executed stitch. Krish clutched his knife.

'You be careful with that thing,' warned Balthrir in hushed tones. 'Not unless it's absolutely necessary.'

'You going to stun her then?' Krish asked.

Balthrir peered over the ridge behind them. 'Well, none of the others are comin'.' She turned back to Krish, who was watching her. 'Keep yer eye on the ball, kid!'

Krish didn't like being called 'kid'. Particularly by someone only a few years older than him. He turned back to the Goonmallinn. She had gone. He stared intently at the place where she had been and then saw her re-emerge.

'Where did she go?' asked Krish.

'Dunno. Stash 'er kindlin', I guess.'

Krish tried not to let his vision stray from the Goonmallinn again.

'What if the others are just behind that ridge?' he said 'And she's not alone?'

'Dunno. Oh and there was no dog, by the way.'

Krish was transfixed by the Goonmallinn, whose lips were moving. 'Looks like she's talking to herself. I can't see anyone else unless... sorry, what did you say?'

'The dog. I made it up.'

'Oh. So...?'

'It wasn't that that was makin' me giggle.'

'Oh. Well... what was...?'

'This...'

All of a sudden, Krish could hear them.

'Let's see how yer fend for yerself. See yer, kid!'

He spun round. Coming up behind him, slowly spreading out to block any possible escape route, were five hooded figures. *Balthrir. Where had she gone?* He saw a shape disappearing over the ridge. He turned to run and a savage face greeted him. Blackened teeth, filthy skin and wild eyes. The Goonmallinn snarled gleefully at him. He turned back; they had him surrounded. He held up his dagger with all the menace he could summon. Theirs were already drawn. They could sense his fear. They were exhilarated by it. They were waiting for their prey to make its move. Cruel smiles, delighted by the despair in his eyes. They encircled him. Where was she? Would she give herself away if she called out? But he needed her! He saw a shape in the rocks. He called out.

'Ba—'

A thud from behind, then nothing.

Krish awoke to the smell of strong, spirit-infused tea. Stiff and groggy, he opened his eyes. The pain from whatever they'd knocked him out with was still echoing through the back of his skull. His mouth was so dry his tongue stuck to the roof of his mouth. He swore his vision was flickering from dim to bright.

As he attempted to sit up he felt coarse rope cut into his wrists. He looked around. He was in a large tent hung with lanterns of orange and green and blue and purple. The Goonmallinns sat about on a sea of cushions, drinking their tea. They appeared to be rather intoxicated. They clapped and laughed hysterically as one danced insanely in the middle of their little circle. He could see his pack halfway across the room from him but there was no way he could reach it. He was tied to a post holding up the centre of the tent and a few tugs told him that neither he nor the post were going anywhere anytime soon.

Krish was struck by a horrifying thought. He'd been unconscious. He'd seen the Vulrein while he slept. He shut his eyes to see how close they were. They were on the edge of the plain, sniffing around the rocks where he'd been captured by the Goonmallinns. They showed no signs of moving from their current location although they were certainly excited by him closing his eyes.

Of course! He had no idea where he was so neither did they. The stinking Goonmallinns probably unintentionally smothered his scent as well, although they'd find him eventually, if he kept his eyes shut for long enough. He opened them.

Krish felt bizarrely safe, but maybe it was just the relief of having slept for a short time. Thoughts of the traitorous Balthrir returned to him but instead of dwelling on them he turned his attentions to the Goonmallinns. They hadn't noticed he was awake so he continued with the plan. Balthrir's plan… Forget her! He'd carry on with the plan. He watched, to see what he could learn.

The Goonmallinns wore robes of black or dark green which were frayed in places but generally in good condition. Criss-crossing about their robes at various points were lengths of rope holding a number of scuffed, misshapen gold bangles in place, preventing them from jingling noisily as they stalked their prey. Their hooded headdresses similarly featured rope and gold but most now had theirs thrown back. Their skin was lighter than most on Ilir, the colour of milky coffee. They were far from old age but farther from youth. Their hair was thick, dark and tangled, flecked with dry skin. He doubted they'd ever washed it. Their faces were dirty and their teeth black.

Sadly, there was little he could tell from their conversation. He managed to pick up on their names though. The leader was called

Boona. Boona was taller and leaner than the others. Through ripped, ragged sleeves Krish saw strong muscles clinging to thin bones.

Then there was Marl, a little more hunched than the others with one unmoving, half-closed, dead-looking eye, partially concealed by crusted lids. Every time she glanced over at him it was as if she had to strain her remaining eye extra hard to take in the slightest detail.

Metta was small and rarely spoke but when she did her shrill cries were so hoarse and foul he felt they could cut through bank vaults. She had the occasional spurt of energy, usually egged on by Blas.

Blas, who was almost as small as Metta, was brimming with energy. Barely a few seconds would pass without her swirling about in a clumsy dance or making strange clucking noises or high cries of excitement.

Halfa (the one he and Bal— that stupid wizard had seen first, who apparently was from another tribe but they'd accepted her for helping to capture him) was a little darker-skinned that the others, and seemed somewhat younger. She was quiet and cautious, her clothes clearly of a different tribe, her wrist less adorned with beads and bangles. She kept her headdress on.

Molran also wore her headdress. She was old and hunched, always rubbing her gnarled old hands together, dry skin falling from her fingers. She spoke even less than Metta but was constantly interjecting with stern but agreeable 'mmm's.

Blas was dancing now and Metta was balancing a glass of tea on her nose. The others laughed and cheered.

'Where you get dis?' Marl said to Blas, examining the pot of tea with her one fully functioning eye.

'Wine merchant!' answered Blas. 'At da sout' port. 'Er want pay! I stick 'er!'

They all laughed. Foul, breathless laughter.

'Mmm, mm,' added Molran.

'I stick 'er good! I say, "No, sir. It don' work like dis. Not for I kind! Goonmallinn take what dey take!" So I stick 'er! 'Er beg for 'er life. "Please!" 'er say. "Please! I got family! Chil-dran!" "What dey got?" I say. 'Er tell I. Dey got a lot! So I go to dey house and I take! And I stick dey too!'

165

Their laughter was now out of control and every last one of them fell about in hysterics. Blas started telling another story but suddenly Boona spotted Krish.

'Aaaahhhhh! What us got 'ere? 'Im wake!'

The Goonmallinns crowded around. He was greeted by a panorama of gleeful smiles, their lips cracked, their teeth dark and mottled and their breath foul, stale.

'Look at 'im!' Marl licked her lips. ''Im good meat! Boy eez good meat!'

'Hush yer tongue, Marl!' cried Boona. 'Yer ulready eat too much!'

'No!' Blas chipped in. 'Dar eez good market for dis! Give 'im meat to a spicer and she spice and smoke 'e. Tree days and 'im taste so good yer'll be eatin' nuttin' but boy for ulways from now on!'

'Mmm!' added Molran.

'Yer no take 'e to no spicer!' said Metta.

Marl squealed with displeasure. 'Yer canna waste 'im! 'Im is fresh! *Freee range!*'

'Eez waste takin' to spicer!' continued Metta. 'Give 'e to a witch! She tear 'e up but keep each part alive! Eez best fun! *Best* fun!'

The Goonmallinns rocked back and forth with laughter.

'I take 'e 'ead nort'!'

'I take 'e neck sout'!'

'One take 'im leg one way and take arm udder way! Tickle foot, 'im cannot scratch!'

The room erupted with hysterics once more. Krish was more awake than he'd ever felt and his brain was buzzing with a thousand mad, desperate plans.

'I know where to get Myrthali!' he cried.

This was only met with more laughter.

'Boy, we ull know where to get Myrthali!' said Boona. 'But King Obsendei never gonna give it to we! And we not interested in goin' nowhere near dat Black Palace of his!'

'But please! I've made a bargain with the King—'

Krish stopped in his tracks. If he told them too much they could take the pearl and the twine, catch the feather of a FireHawk and claim the Myrthali for themselves. The Goonmallinns' wicked smiles dripped with a thirst to elongate their filthy lives. If he wasn't careful he'd find himself abandoned in the desert to die.

'Bargain, yer say?' Boona spoke quietly, creeping towards him with wide eyes.

'A-and you don't get to know any more about it until you let me go!' he added.

Boona bared her rancid teeth in a gleeful grin. She turned to the others and they giggled and clapped their hands. All of them except one, who smiled cautiously and remained relatively still. Boona didn't notice this and turned straight back to Krish.

'Mebbe we *do* take 'e to spicer! Mebbe *I* am spicer!' Boona grabbed a wooden bowl full of deep red powder. 'And I make 'e squeal and den 'im tell us!'

The Goonmallinns cheered and chanted and clapped and jumped about with a terrible joy in their every move. But still there was a dissenter amongst them. Halfa, the outsider, was shrewder than the rest.

'Aye, yer ruin 'e flavour!' said Halfa. 'Feed 'e up for a few days. Nice 'n' fat! Take 'e to a *real* spicer. I don' wanna waste no time on no boy when there is good tea spoilin'! And dancin' to be done!'

'She talk right!' cried Blas.

High-pitched rhythmic squeals from the others and in moments there was music and dancing.

'Set stones!' said Boona to Marl. 'We wake at next nightfall.'

Marl produced a bag full of small stone tablets about the size of dominoes, each one carved with a strange symbol. She carefully laid them out to one side in a circle like a clock face, far from the blur that was Blas. She placed one stone on top of one of the others and left to rejoin the festivities.

After an hour or so of furious activity they began to collapse onto the cushions one by one. Halfa was the first, Krish noticed. Her fall to the pillows seemed almost choreographed. Soon all was still. The Goonmallinns slept so solidly you'd hardly know they were alive at all. Krish felt as if he was in a gallery amongst a collection of statues.

Only then did Krish notice how piercing the quiet of the desert surrounding them was. As the wind died down and with barely a breath passing the lips of the Goonmallinns, Krish could hear complete silence for the first time in his life. He twisted his body a touch to the left to check that Marl, just in the corner of his eye, was definitely asleep, and the gentle sound the movement produced made him jump. The absolute silence had made him question for a second if he had gone deaf.

Krish tugged at the ropes tied around his wrists. As he struggled he could feel the rope getting tighter. He could see his pack but there was no way he could reach it from here. The distress stone was in the top...

A tiny sound in the endless quiet. He looked over at the circle of stones. The stone that had been placed on top of another was somehow rolling itself over and over until it sat atop the next stone. The deafening hush returned.

Minutes passed.

Then there was a stirring in the silence. A rustle of robes so loud in the noiseless tent. Halfa strode over to Krish and knelt beside him. She held up a flask and without hesitation he opened his mouth and his throat was soothed with cool water.

'So, dis bargain yer struck wid da King, tell I more...' Halfa wasn't bothering to keep her voice down. Krish glanced over to check there were no signs of movement from the others. They were as immobile as rocks.

'Aye, dey not be gettin' up any time soon,' said Halfa. 'Too much tea, too much dancin'. Dey wake in a couple o' days. Till den, we talk.'

Krish still had his doubts about telling anyone of his deal with the King. Not that he was convinced that he would honour it anyway.

'It's, um... Sorry,' he said. 'I made a mistake.'

A short sharp squeal and a shake of the head from his amused inquisitor.

'Yer'll not be goin' into no business tellin' lies! Yer'll not make a Shella! Now tell me: what eez dis bargain yer struck?'

Krish knew he wasn't going anywhere fast so he told her.

When he'd finished, a knowing, almost cunning smile greeted him. 'Mersha and ullwihr.'

'Who?'

'Aye!' Halfa gave Krish a friendly little backhanded slap on the shoulder. 'Yer be better at foolin' than lyin'! Mersha and ullwihr be spices, not peoples! We got plenty o' spices! We drop a little pinch o' mersha, little bit o' ullwihr on fedder, keep it somewhere safe and fire be burnin' long time. Looong time! Dat keep yer FireHawk fedder alight!'

'But how do we capture one?'

Another cunning smile.

'You is already talkin' like we eez partners! We can be partners but I 'as conditions. One: yer'll not be seein' h'exactly 'ow we is capturin' da FireHawk. Two: I wants tree quarters of da Myrthali—'

'No! I can't! I…' He didn't want to talk about the devil. Or his Mum. Or why he was really here. The devil had said no bargains or none of the Myrthali would return with him.

'Well yer will. You 'ave no choice.'

He didn't and there was no way he could argue.

'Last ting! What 'appen to you friend?' Halfa's hand tightened on her dagger. 'She part o' bargain?'

'She's… she's gone.'

'She gone for now… but she come back…?'

'No. She's not coming back. She's no one.'

'Ah! No one is wizard!' Krish failed to hide his shock at Halfa's perceptiveness. 'Aye, I sees 'er staff. Others, dey did not see. She come back… we taste wizard.'

'Really. She's not coming back.' Krish hated being so sure. He might never see her again.

Halfa nodded thoughtfully. 'Dere be a firestorm due in a few days.'

'How do you know?'

That knowing smile. 'We know. We catch bird and I take fedder. But you stay 'ere. Don't yer worry yerself.' She stroked his head and something about the way she was doing it reminded him of a cat toying with a mouse. 'We get yer Myrthali for sure.'

CHAPTER 23

THE FIRESTORM

Krish remained awake as Halfa slept amongst the others. He barely even blinked – he had bigger problems than the Vulrein now. If he kept his bargain with Halfa, he could leave Ilir with no Myrthali at all.

The sun had risen, setting the canvas of the tent aglow and turning his surroundings hot and clammy, alleviated occasionally by a gentle breeze through the gaps in the fastened entrance. Hours passed. The stones in their little clock-like circle continued to move into new positions every now and then. The sun sank into darkness once more. The chill of night crept into the tent. One of the stones found its way into the centre of the circle and began to glow red. It emitted a high, almost serene noise, like the sound of someone running their wetted finger around the rim of a wine glass.

The Goonmallinns began to stir grumpily. Marl stumbled across the room and kicked the stones. The stone in the centre instantly became silent and ceased to glow. They began to build a fire for their pot, and when it was ready they shared a little of their bitter broth with him. Then a sound somewhere between thunder and a low, muffled roar made them empty their bowls back into the pot, extinguish the fire and begin to pack with furious speed.

'Dis time we gonna get one!' said Boona. 'Yer mark my words!'

'I'll knock boy out.' Halfa was marching towards him. 'Don't want 'e tryin' to escape while we gone.' She leant beside him, her head by his ear, opened her mouth, but she never got to speak. He guessed she was going to fake knocking him out but Boona cut in.

'Yer'll be doin' no such ting! We need him wrigglin'! Dey like 'em wrigglin'!'

'What yer sayin', Boona?' asked Halfa.

'In your tribe mebbe dey use a different way but 'ere we find not'ing better than live bait!'

And now it was Halfa's turn to be given no choice. Blas stepped in, cut Krish's bonds and dragged him across the room. He passed his pack and thought quickly. He struggled and Blas lost her grip. He fell onto the pack, knocking it over. He could see it! The little red rock – the distress stone. Sitting on top of some parcels of shredded root. If he could just... But Blas grabbed him roughly and hauled him outside to the horses, holding both of his wrists together behind his back.

Blas retied his bonds and slung him over the back of her horse, treating him no different to any of the sacks she then flung over the backs of the other horses. Marl tied his ankles to a stirrup on one side of the saddle and his wrists to the strap on the other side. When the others weren't watching, Halfa kindly gave him a swig of water from her flask and then very unkindly tied some sacking over his head.

'No peekin'!'

The journey through the mountain pass was short but more than long enough for Krish's liking. The backbone of the horse cut into his middle and with every bump he found his head was loose enough to fly up and then bang against the horse's muscular thigh. He could see very little, although through the sacking he could just make out the glow of the lamps the Goonmallinns carried, illuminating the rough ground below them and the craggy rock face to one side. When he straightened his spine for a few moments he managed to make out the hazy void on the opposite side of the path where the light fell into nothingness. They must be high above the desert now, he thought; he could no longer feel grains of sand caught in the wind, which was much stronger up here.

That smell reached his nostrils again, the odour he'd detected when he'd first arrived in the Pale Hunting Grounds. Then he remembered... Several years ago they'd had a family barbecue. His Dad and Uncle Ravi had been in charge. They were hopeless. Everything was burnt on the outside and raw on the inside. Uncle Ravi had ended the afternoon by pouring a glass of water on the fire and the coals had sizzled noisily and spat a cloud of smoke back at him. After dark, the adults in a circle of camping chairs in the garden talking quietly and laughing about 'grown-up stuff', Krish had finally given up and headed to bed. As he passed the barbecue he saw the coals were still hot, sitting in a pool of slowly evaporating water. That was what he could smell: dampened smoke.

After some time there was relative quiet. There was the infrequent shuffle of impatient hooves and the howl of the wind, but it was clear that his captors' attention was on the silent sky. Minutes passed as if they were hours and Krish's ears tuned into a distant rumbling. Then a thunderous roar reverberated around them. Krish felt the reins tense in front of him, the horse turning slightly to the right and causing the sacking to fall away a little. He could just make out the shadowy landscape, illuminated somewhat by the light of Mother and Sons. Tall jagged rocks and narrow valleys below them. He looked ahead to see Halfa in the saddle in front of him staring back.

'Enjoy da view,' said Boona. 'You be one of der last to see it.' Before he could think much on these words he found the sacking pulled over his face by Halfa.

'Dere!' came a cry seconds later. He looked about, desperately trying to make out the something the Goonmallinns were focusing all their attention on. And then he saw it. A short line of flame shining brightly enough in the night sky to be seen through the sacking. He watched closely as the blur of light above them travelled soundlessly across the sleeping world. A high, shrill cry then reached his ears and he realised that the bird must be miles away. And it really must be bright for him to be able to see it from here. The flapping of great wings. How big was it? That great heavy flapping suggested something bigger than any bird on his world. *How on earth, no, how on Ilir would they get anywhere near a creature that size?* thought Krish.

'Now...?' said Marl.

'Wait...' answered Boona.

Krish craned his neck to see the bird now far behind them. A few seconds more and it would be gone from sight altogether.

'NOW!'

A twang. Air rushed past Krish. The heat of a flame. A speck of fire sped through the air just to his left. Moments later the one pinprick of flame hit another.

Then the sky was ablaze. A wave of flame shot out in every direction from where the beast had soared a split second before. A rippling carpet of fire spreading across the firmament. The light fantastical and the heat terrible, bearing down on the mountains and valley below. The air around Krish and his captors felt as if it were smouldering. Any longer in this wretched heat and they'd surely suffocate.

'YAR!' A cry from all the Goonmallinns. The reins whipped against the horses' coats and they rushed in the opposite direction to the flames. The speed they were moving at now was incredible. Hooves beat the rock below them so fast it felt as though the rough ground was smooth as ice. Air rushed past Krish and the sacking flew off. The relief to be in the open air was instant. In fact with his face covered in sweat he began to feel cold. He looked back at the unbelievable sight in the sky behind him.

The bird was gone. In its place, a billowing ball of flame lighting the night, filling the landscape with flickering shadows cast by the barbed towers of the gigantic rock formations towering over them. They sped down into the valley until the Goonmallinns found what they were looking for. Yelps of approval. Krish was lifted off the back of the horse and dragged to a crooked, petrified, grey-white tree. The ball of flame above them had billowed into a cloud. The cloud split into five or six pieces and spread across the sky overhead. The chill of the night melted away.

'Yer never seen no Goonmallinn catch a FireHawk before?' Boona said as she bound Krish to the tree. Krish shook his head, hoping somehow that acknowledging her might make her reconsider. 'Yer don' catch no FireHawk! Not fully grown! Too strong. But yer can kill one. Only way to start a firestorm. Firestorm where dey young come to life. This dey secret. When FireHawk grow old, one day, dey climb high in the sky and H'EXPLODE! Both male and female carry eggs and when dey h'explode da eggs in dey body come to life in da firestorm. Yer see soon dey eggs o' flame! Dey born small but fully formed and ready to hunt! And what dey young want 'fore anyting else...? Breakfast!' She tightened the last bond and began to walk away. Halfa looked from Krish to Boona and back again with narrowed eyes. 'But da young full o' energy! Unpredictable! Want to burn da place up a bit! Yer want to live, yer stay still. We save yer. No worries!' Krish was not filled with hope.

The instant Boona was back in the saddle the Goonmallinns rode halfway up the mountain and observed Krish from up on high. Krish waited for sheer panic to take him over. It took a few seconds to comprehend exactly how dire his situation was. The air was thick with heat. It was becoming too hot to breathe and the harder it became the more his lungs gasped for air and...

A shadow. A shape moving across the ridge, far from the Goonmallinns. This didn't distract Krish for long.

A burst of heat burned his skin. He must be on fire, but there were no flames. He turned, the furnace-like air stinging his eyes, just in time to see what had caused the momentary rise in heat. One cloud of pure white flame was now a perfect globe. He looked closely and saw that the globe had cracked. What had Boona said? *Eggs of flame.* And in moments a young FireHawk would be born, hungry for its first meal.

Another burst of suffocating heat, blinding white light engulfing the world. The light faded, his eyes were filled with purple spots with yellow tails. Then another burst, and another and another. The egg was covered in cracks. He looked about, desperately trying to get a fix on Halfa, but his mind only cared to see Balthrir. Where was she? He needed her! His despairing mind was not too proud to admit it. If only he'd been able to get the distress stone maybe he could have attracted her attention...

The egg pulsed through the sky, the air; everything for miles around must be able to feel the hotness of the cracking egg high above. One last burst and something shot past him. Fragments of white-hot shell landed on the ground and he looked up at the glowing shape in the sky. Wings of white, tinged with gold, cupped around the magnificent form that hung in the air above him. Then, in a single fluid motion, the wings unfolded and the golden-white Fire-Hawk, sleek and fierce and beautiful, swooped down towards Krish, its eyes bright, unblinking and hungry for the first meal of its life.

The majestic creature's body was slick and white, streamlined for speed, with pointed talons of gold, a crest of flaming orange upon its head. Even from where Krish stood he could see the fire in its eyes. A screech like a thousand notes sounding in perfect disharmony filled his ears and he looked to see the FireHawk pass him in a rush of blisteringly hot air. A trail of fire marked the trajectory of the beast's dive.

'YAR!'

The Goonmallinns were on the valley floor once more. They rode about on the ground, hurling great wire nets, which smouldered red in the heat, into the air at the FireHawk. The FireHawk ducked and dived and turned, a clear line between itself and Krish. The newly born bird of flame saw three obstacles in its way, but none was even close to hindering it. Marl's net fell, Blas was pulling hers back, ready to throw again, and Boona was too close to react in time, while the others were on the wrong side of Krish. A gust of heat and the bird had passed.

The FireHawk turned and swept through the air, its eyes only on Krish. Boona threw her net, the FireHawk passed under it, Marl's didn't even leave her hands, and Blas screamed from the ground as her hand, outstretched to grab her fallen net, flew to one side, cut from her wrist by the tip of the FireHawk's passing wing, the wound cauterised before the terrible creature could reach Krish. He twisted as best he could to one side. A blade of white heat tore across his neck. His flesh boiled then instantly sealed but the terrible bird had already started to turn once more before its wing left his skin. It caught the edge of a branch and fire blossomed on brittle branches.

The tree was ablaze in moments. Several Goonmallinns ran to the tree but Halfa was the one to cut him loose. As he was hurled onto the back of Halfa's horse he saw that Metta and Molran had the Fire-Hawk in a net. It struggled and screeched and twisted round, pulling the net tighter. Metta moved closer to Molran so as not to be pulled from her horse but Molran was not as quick and was hoisted up into the air. Molran clutched at the net, hanging precariously in the air before the FireHawk made one last jerk towards the sky, lifting Metta off her horse. Metta crashed onto the ground (followed moments later by Molran), letting go of her side of the net in the process, and the bird swooped down and out from under the net then rose high in the night sky with a shriek of terror. The FireHawk whirled violently in the air, guttural cries of warning echoing amongst the rocks, barely a second passing between each one.

Boona shouted at Blas, who was a crumpled heap of agony on the ground, slapped her across the face, and moments later both, the latter with Marl's assistance, had mounted their horses. They rushed back up the mountain pass while Krish watched the FireHawk with wide, unbelieving eyes.

In its rage the beast zig-zagged through the air, leaving trails of flame behind it, and then it turned upon the mountains themselves. How such a thing could happen Krish did not understand but he saw it with his own eyes. The FireHawk whirled round and round a lone peak, leaving trails of fire in its wake, and soon the rock glowed orange, bubbled and sank to the ground in a puddle of molten rock. The bird twisted and spun in the air and soon a whole range of mountains fell into the prehistoric-looking soup that had enveloped the landscape below them. Krish felt the rock beneath his feet shake and the path began to slide forty-five degrees to one side. The horses rushed onwards and soon they found themselves some way from the molten valley.

But they were far from safety. The firestorm still raged in the sky above and more eggs were hatching. Four more birds opened their wings for the first time and followed the example of the first. Every outcrop, every peak was torn down by the heat the birds spread; as if most of the valley was bowing in submission to them, whole mountains brought to their knees. *Five... or six...?* Krish tried to remember how many he'd seen as his eyes scanned the panorama. Then he just caught it – a white sphere fading to deep red as it plummeted to the ground.

Once-great mountains were now a soup of molten lava. A roaring, enraged landscape transformed in minutes into a stodgy lake of grey-black, fiery orange glowing in the cracks on its blackened surface. The land, now melted into a sea of molten fury, bubbled and spat. Waves of lava like great, furious hands were hurled into the air.

A prickly heat spread through the air as the clouds formed overhead. A ocean of grey above and a sea of black and orange below. Then came the rain. The ferocious downpour was heavier, more violent than Krish had ever seen. So sudden and strong. You felt the rain itself could knock you out. It blasted the molten rock as it erupted into the air. The tempestuous waves of lava, like angry, clawed hands reaching out of the lake that was once the land, were cooled and within seconds they solidified. Fierce waves of lava thrown high in the air formed terrifying-looking rock formations and the gentler waves became ridges as they froze.

Krish saw a whole new mountain range spring up out of nowhere. They were pelted with heavy, near-vertical streams of rain. The downfall ended seconds later, the heat returned and his skin and clothes were practically dry again within moments. There were still damp patches under his arms (and various other places) and even on the section of the horse's coat that his body covered. It all began to chafe unpleasantly as they galloped onwards.

Still the FireHawks raged and the clouds of fire followed by the coming of more rain assisted in the re-casting of the valley. Never could Krish have imagined such a thing; the terrain destroyed and reforged within minutes, only to be torn apart once again.

Now Krish and the Goonmallinns were running out of places to flee to. Both sides of the trail led to seas of molten rock. Blas was wailing, her face heavy with despair. She struggled to hold onto the reins with one hand.

'Quit yer whinin'!' Boona shouted over her shoulder at Blas, who was falling behind. 'Yer hurry or yer die!'

A FireHawk wheeled overhead and dived towards them, slashing the path with flame, the rock boiling red just metres ahead of them. They backed away, the path splitting into fragments floating on the glowing red sea in front of them. The FireHawk returned to set light to the other side of the path. There were only two options left to them – a ride down into a valley of molten rock or to chance it down a near-vertical drop towards the desert. They opted for the latter, but the wailing Blas turned to the valley. Krish was barely over the ridge before he heard the scream. He could just make out a FireHawk lifting a shrieking, struggling creature into the air before the others swooped in and pecked and pecked until Blas's cries were silenced.

'Dey go for 'orse next! We got minutes!' Boona cried. They headed down the side of the mountain on foot, leading the horses, whose hooves struggled to grip the steep path.

'Where are we going?' said Krish to Halfa but Boona overheard.

'Shut yer noise!' said Boona

'We're leaving?!' Krish couldn't face going back but he was hardly rushing to return to the valley.

'Dey too many! Too angry! Tonight not our night.'

'But one fell! I saw it! An egg! It fell to the ground.'

Boona pondered this for a moment but didn't slow down. Krish turned hopefully to Halfa.

'It no hatch?' she asked. Krish nodded. 'Yer know where it landed, boy?'

'We not goin' back!' cried Boona.

'If he know where is FireHawk, newly born, we *got* to turn back!'

Metta spat out a warning like the hiss of a snake combined with a cat coughing up a fur-ball. 'One dead; I don' fancy bein' next!'

'Mmm!' chipped in Molran.

Boona slowed, the others followed suit. 'We turn,' she said. 'While dey eat. Leave one 'orse for dey. Molran ride wid Marl. Quick!'

Molran dismounted, tied her protesting horse to a rock and clambered aboard Marl's horse. They turned and headed down into the valley.

There it was. Glowing red rock remoulded into a mid-splash shape as the egg had hit the ground. Steam rose from the slim, smouldering waves of rock partially obscuring the egg. Its glow was faint but it was still hot.

'It no dead,' proclaimed Molran. 'Alive!'

'Good,' said Boona. 'We drag it in net. Metta, yer stay back, watch it. Anyting yer see, yer cry, we leave it.'

No one dared touch the egg. In shape it was slightly elliptical. From farther away you could be mistaken for thinking it was a perfect circle. It was three times the size of Krish's head but he was surprised it wasn't bigger. Its glow an oddly comforting shade of red-orange.

The Goonmallinns cast their net over the egg, dragged it over to Metta's horse and fastened the net to the saddle. Boona put a hand on

Krish's shoulder just before she mounted her horse. 'Yer eyes more useful to us than yer body was as bait, boy. Mebbe yer stay alive a little longer.'

Soon they were riding as fast as they could away from the firestorm and the molten valley. Krish's eyes stayed with the egg being dragged in the dirt behind them. It never lost its glow.

CHAPTER 24

COUNTDOWN

Krish, his arms tied to the supporting pole at the centre of the tent, was listening intently to the argument which had erupted between the Goonmallinns. He strained to hear a word as they spoke in hushed tones. His eyes were drawn to the smouldering shape which had been placed in an empty space at the centre of the tent. The egg glowed gently. An orange-red haze warmed the air around them. Sweat poured down Krish's face and he could see the Goonmallinns loosening their robes with the heat. Their voices seemed to rise with the temperature.

'Yer *can't* leave it in here! It a curse! It wakes, we burn!' cried Marl.

'And if FireHawks see dat, we ull burn! For certain!' said Boona. 'It not go outside! Not till it wake!'

'What da stones say?' ventured Metta.

Marl approached the egg. She hesitated then drew a knife, stepped forward and scraped a layer of the shell off while sucking air through gritted teeth. Krish had never seen someone so savage use a knife so delicately. Marl turned the blade flat and then ran it carefully across her hand, collecting the scraping from the egg in her palm. With her other hand she took a handful of the small stones tablets she'd used before as a rudimentary alarm clock. She crushed the scraping from the eggshell into the stones then dropped them onto the ground. Marl examined the stones knowingly with her one fully functional eye as they arranged themselves into a curious formation.

While Marl considered the stones, Krish looked over at his pack. In the flurry of activity that had come with the arrival of the egg, a lot of items had been moved around the tent. His pack, which he knew contained the distress stone, had been relocated several times and it was now almost within his reach. But the Goonmallinns, although a little preoccupied with the stones, were still standing too close at the moment for him to risk stretching out to try and grab it.

'It wake in five hours,' Marl announced.

'Den we sleep,' said Boona. 'Rest for tree hours den drag it outside for it wake. Kill it. Split it and den we go our own ways. We sell and dis give more gold, more jewel dan we can carry! And I is takin' da head!'

'I want wing!' cried Marl.

'Mm. Wing! I take other wing!' added Molran.

'I take a breast! Good meat!' chipped in Metta.

'A fedder...'

They all stared at Halfa.

'Yer'll not get a fedder!' said Boona. 'Dey burn!'

'Yer'll let it eat first,' said Halfa. 'Den I can get da fedder. If not it burn when it die.'

'What it gonna eat, eh?' said Metta.

There was silence as they pondered Metta's question. Then, one by one, they turned to Krish. Boona's eyes were wide, the corners of her lips on an upward curve.

'What d'yer say, boy...? Yer want yer freedom... Yer serve us well on da mountain. Want to be free...? Or mebbe yer taste good... to FireHawk...'

Krish didn't fancy his chances in the desert but it had to be better than—

'Feed 'e to FireHawk.' Halfa spoke slowly, softly and with an immeasurable quantity of cruelness. ''Im taste good for first meal.' Everyone was looking at her. There was a change in her eyes. Krish's look begged her to reconsider but Halfa's whole face was aglow with greed for the Myrthali.

'S-she's lying!' cried Krish but it wasn't a lie. 'I m-mean it's a-a trick!' It wasn't even a trick. Not to them. Not really. What would she do with a few more miserable years? No. Halfa was just being callous for the sake of being callous. She'd waste the extra years the Myrthali would bring to her and enjoy thinking on his brief suffering before his death as a result of her betrayal.

'We had a deal!' he ventured despairingly.

'What deal?' cut in Boona. 'What 'e talkin'?'

'Nuttin'!' said Halfa. ''Im made no deal wid I!'

'Yes you did, Halfa.' Halfa almost quivered at Krish using her name. He was too tired. Too tired and too sick of this. All of this. Everything he'd gone through. He looked her straight in the eye and spoke slowly, quietly so she *had* to listen. 'We had a deal and you will honour it. If you have even a *scrap* of decency left in you, you'll cut me loose, get me a feather and take me to the Black Palace, and you won't let anyone stand in our way.'

Halfa stood there, lost for words for a moment before she pulled out her blade.

'Where dis fire in you come from, boy?' Halfa called out. 'Mebbe I cut it from you!'

'Cut it from 'e! Yes!' Metta was jumping up and down excitedly. 'We cut fire from 'e and use it to boil 'e bones! Make a stew with 'e flesh and we feast with FireHawk!' She clapped wildly and the room was filled with her shrill laughter.

But Boona's narrowing eyes were still on Halfa. She pulled a curved dagger from her belt, seized Halfa and held the knife to her throat.

'What deal?! What 'e say about Black Palace?!' screamed Boona. 'Yer be talkin' true now!'

'I ain't made no deal wid no boy!' cried Halfa.

Boona pulled Halfa close, their faces almost touching, Boona spitting out words from gritted teeth; her foul breath must be going straight into Halfa's quivering mouth.

'Yer 'tray us!'

'I no traitor!' said Halfa.

'Yer traitor for sure! And yer 'tray one Goonmallinn, yer 'tray ull Goonmallinn! I cut yer so small worms no be chokin' on yer, I assure yer dat!'

'I made no deal! I kill 'e now if dat yer wish!'

'Yer not our tribe! Mebbe I spill 'e blood,' Boona pulled out Halfa's arm and tore the sleeve to reveal bare flesh and held her knife over it. 'Mebbe I spill *your* blood as well! Put boy and you in stew!'

The others clucked and whooped and cheered as they lusted for blood to be spilt.

'Yer waste Goonmallinn… or feed boy to FireHawk…?' said Halfa desperately. 'Your choice…'

Krish watched intently as Boona and Halfa confronted one another. Boona looked into Halfa's eyes; they were steady. She didn't blink. Boona's eyes were locked onto Halfa's. Boona playfully prodded the skin on the tender underside of Halfa's forearm with the tip of her dagger a few times, so lightly that it simply bounced off again. In one brief movement she cut a short line across Halfa's skin. Boona brought the end of the blade to meet the tip of her tongue, her eyes still fixed on Halfa's, and tasted her blood. The two stared into each other a while longer.

'Yer blood no good anyhow,' said Boona. 'We not feast on yer. Yer take fedder but not a scrap o' meat from our FireHawk. Boy be it first meal. Eez best plan.'

Boona released Halfa. There was an awkward silence for some moments before Halfa dared to speak again.

'I blood taste bad… 'cause there am no tea in it!'

Cries of excitement. In seconds tea was being brewed and in minutes dancing and chaos returned to the tent. Krish could barely think over the noise.

'Stones wake us, tree hours!' Boona shouted at Marl, who placed the stones in a small circle by the egg. 'No! Make two and half!' Marl rearranged some of the stones, moving them anticlockwise around the clock-face formation. It wasn't long before the Goonmallinns wore themselves out and were fast asleep. Now Krish's mind could concentrate on the insanity of the situation he was in. But having time to think was not helping in the slightest.

Some twisted, desperate part of him had wanted Halfa to be a replacement for Balthrir. He found himself using her name in his head again. He wanted so badly for her to be here. Maybe she was coming back. Maybe she was just outside. Or hidden in the room. He clung to this thought for dear life, but if she was going to appear she would have done so by now. Surely.

But Krish knew that even if she was close by she might as well be a hundred miles away in this desert. The Goonmallinns' tent was hidden in between the ridges, that much he'd deduced when they'd returned from the molten valley. And although brightly coloured on the inside, the outer tent was the same colour as the sand. You could walk right past it and have no idea how close you were.

He had only one hope. The distress stone that Balthrir had created. The rock that sent up a flare. It was 'pure light', she'd said, so he hoped it would travel through the canvas of the tent. Surely she'd be able to see that. Right now it was just out of reach. Krish extended his right leg but the pack was still too far away. He tried to shuffle forward but the bonds were too tight. He stretched and stretched and just managed to touch the backpack with the end of his big toe. He extended his leg some more and the bag wobbled. He could see it! The little red rock tucked just inside the bag, which wasn't even properly fastened at the top. He'd just about managed to grip the canvas of the bag between his big and second toes when it started to topple...

The bag fell towards him and the tiny red stone fell out and rolled across the floor right past him, while the rest of the contents of the bag crashed onto the ground. Krish let out an exasperated sigh. His plan had failed. The distress stone was now all the way on the other side of the tent; there was no way he could reach it now.

Then his ears pricked up. There was a disturbance in the silence. The commotion hadn't stirred the Goonmallinns, who made not a sound aside from the occasional snore, but he became aware of two other noises. One was a light clanging, like someone holding up a baking tray and tapping it softly with a wooden spoon. The other sounded like pebbles being dropped from knee-height onto a shingle beach.

He looked over and saw, just in front of the open pack, a green sphere no bigger than a football, covered in removable numbered tiles. Balthrir's clock-confuser. Several of the tiles flipped over with a clang to reveal new numbers. After a few seconds this stopped and Krish turned his attention to the source of the second sound. He looked to his left and noticed Marl's stones rearranging themselves, moving clockwise to their original positions. It took Krish a few seconds and then it dawned on him. The clock-confuser was indeed working. It was changing the time of the alarm call Marl had set.

A few moments more and there was silence again.

Horror coursed through Krish's veins. Marl had set the stones to wake them in two and half hours instead of three. When she'd changed the wake-up time she'd moved them a few places anticlockwise. Now they had been moved the other way by the clock-confuser, and a lot further back than Marl had repositioned them. It could be days before the Goonmallinns awoke and by then the whole place would be burned to ground.

Krish looked about, almost hyperventilating with panic. After several minutes of hysteria he got his brain back into gear and began to assess his options. The red rock was all the way across the other side of the room, behind him. Even if he managed to find something long enough to reach it (and there really was nothing anywhere near him), he wouldn't have much luck trying to locate a tiny stone without being able to see it. The clock-confuser... he might be able to get hold of it from here but he'd never figure out how to work the stupid thing. He'd probably make things worse.

The egg was glowing brighter and brighter.

After at least an hour Krish was in a state of absolute despair. Every option was a dead end and in another hour... or how long had it been...? Maybe they'd been asleep for longer than an hour. Maybe it was two. Maybe it was almost time. He could feel the warmth of the egg. He swore he could sense it moving, ready to burst through the shell and engulf them all in flames.

He had no choice. He cried out. He screamed until his voice was hoarse and his throat trembled with pain. None of them stirred and he could do no more than croak helplessly into the silence. Krish had nothing left. He would die here in the middle of the desert, countless miles and billions of worlds away from home. He would never see Dawson or Jess or Dad or Uncle Ravi or Mum, who he'd set out so, *so* foolishly to try and save, ever again.

He screwed up his eyes in pain.

... muzzles to the ground... pawing impatiently
at sand... staring... fierce red eyes...
heads up... the scent of their prey on the wind...

How much did he fear them now? He could never fully stifle his fear of them but it was certainly waning. The Vulrein had no idea where he was and even if he kept his eyes shut from now on he'd probably be dead before—

Krish thought for a moment. He closed his eyes again. The sand... they were nuzzling the sand... They weren't far...

A shadow crept across Krish's mind. One as filled with darkness as it was with hope.

He closed his eyes again. He kept them shut.

> *... their heads rose... his scent on the air...*
> *close... their prey was close... those eyes...*
> *those eyes of deep red smouldering under*
> *coal-like blackness... their heads turning slowly*
> *... looking to him... looking into him...*

They were looking straight at him and they could feel where he was. He screwed his eyes up tight.

> *... one cruel-eyed creature barking... the others*
> *answering... their paws beating the sand...*
> *a blur of dark shapes...*

They were coming. He was calling the Vulrein towards him. They had kept him awake for days, weeks, maybe months, until his body was weak and the very act of blinking had tormented him to insanity. He'd felt as if he had great gashes in his eyeballs from trying to keep his eyes open and now at last he could keep them firmly shut as he ushered the creatures forth; they were the only hope he had left in all the worlds.

If the Vulrein arrived and created chaos this would wake the Goonmallinns. Maybe he could beg them to release him, convince them amid the uproar that he was controlling the Vulrein. It was a desperate plan that would probably make them flee and leave him to the Vulrein, but it was his only chance.

The heat. The air was thick and clammy. The baking atmosphere in the tent was suffocating him, but still not the slightest of movements from the Goonmallinns. He kept his mind on the Vulrein...

> *... paws dashing across boiling sand...*
> *... hunger in their eyes...*

A noise... a tapping sound at centre of the tent...

> *... sand caught in saliva... hungry... so hungry...*

The tapping grew louder... louder... The heat was a blanket of fire around his face...

> *... so close... so close... their prey seconds away...*

A crack...

> *... sand running thin... a shape on the plain*
> *... the smell of his blood...*

The roar of the growing heat smothered the sound...
the slightest crack in the boiling air...

> *... hearts pounding... skin tight over bones...*
> *... his blood... his blood... so close...*

Krish's heart was ready to burst, his lungs
aching... *Balthrir! Balthrir, please...*

... rip and tear and kill, kill, KILL—

The sound of tearing canvas ripped through the air. He opened his
eyes in surprise and saw a gaping hole appear in the tent. The hole
opened wide as unseen shapes advanced into the room. He blinked
and they pounced, the first knocking a table onto Metta. Metta cried
out and stood up immediately. The Vulrein turned their attentions to
her and ripped into her flesh as she screamed.

The others awoke at once. All they could see of the Vulrein was
the blood on their invisible muzzles tearing into Metta. Molran ran,
tripped and sat cowering in a corner, her eyes darting about in confusion. Halfa scurried about on the ground, trying to gather her things
to flee. Marl froze. Halfa looked from Metta, whose cries grew faint,
to Krish and back again. A Vulrein brushed past Marl and in panic she
lashed at the air with her knife and soon they descended upon her.

Boona looked furiously at Krish, drew her knife, sped over to him
and straddled him, shouting at him at the top of her voice.

'What yer do, boy?! What yer do?! Yer kill us! YER KILL GOON-
MALLINN!'

Krish couldn't breathe, he couldn't cry out, couldn't beg to be
released. His head shook, his heart pounded, every millimetre of his
body was infected with hysteria as barely a breath, let alone a coherent
word, trickled out of his gasping mouth.

Boona's eyes popped with fury, foul breath stuttering through rotten bared teeth. 'I spiker you!' She grasped him by the throat, held her
dagger aloft, murderous rage in her eyes. 'I SPIKER YOU GOOD!'

Krish closed his eyes. He saw a Vulrein behind Boona. It leapt
through the air towards him as the enraged Goonmallinn lunged at
him. The beast tore into her, blood poured into his lap, but her scream
was muffled by the explosion.

White light filled the air and a shockwave of heat shot through the tent. Fragments of smoking shell were hurled in every direction. A shrill cry, even more terrible in close quarters than those on the Pale Hunting Grounds. To Krish it felt like someone was pressing pins into his eardrums. As the light dimmed a shape shot up into the air and a flaming bird cried out as it hit the roof and flailed about. A sleek, white form flapped its majestic wings about the comparatively tiny space in pure frustration. It found no route to escape by. Its head lowered and it examined Krish and his captors below. A crest of flame sat upon its head. Its eyes were small but enraged. Its talons of gold ready to kill. In a fit of anger it whirled about the tent and set the place ablaze.

All was chaos. Marl fought off the Vulrein with her dagger while the bloodied Boona bashed at them desperately with her bare hands. Molran was a crumpled, tearful mess in the corner while Halfa was jabbing at a Vulrein with a pole of some sort, one eye on the Fire-Hawk.

Krish regained focus. He saw Boona's dagger on the ground, just by his knee. He managed to nudge it backwards towards his thigh. The FireHawk was swooping at Boona, who was fighting off a Vulrein with a wooden stool as the beast tore at her legs. Just in time she saw the FireHawk and hit it square between the eyes with the stool. The bird recoiled, shook itself, its fiery crest shaking about like a blur of fire upon its head. It shrieked and came in to attack Boona but this time it pulled up at the last moment and Boona was smothered in flame. The Vulrein jumped to one side and let her burn. A gurgling scream. Flesh, blood and bone melted away and silenced Boona's excruciating scream. Then she was no more than foul-smelling vapour hanging in the air above the boiling ground.

Krish could just about reach the dagger now. He caught it with the tip of his finger and pulled it towards him. Then a Vulrein jumped at him and bit into his leg. The sharp pain barely registered. He tried to kick the beast away. The FireHawk came in low and made straight for him. He ducked out of the way, heat ripping through the air above him. The Vulrein clawed at the bird and started barking at it, giving Krish enough time to start cutting through the bonds. There was a final cry from Marl as the Vulrein sank their teeth into her neck.

The FireHawk circled and came in to attack Krish once more but the Vulrein at his heel went for the bird again and a fight broke out between the two. Pitch-black claws tore at flaming feathers, while talons ripped at the air, trying to find the invisible attacker. Halfa's eyes were on the feathers that had fallen to the ground between Krish and herself. They were quickly going out.

Then the Vulrein was on fire, yelping in agony. Its position given away, an unseen beast ablaze, the FireHawk attacked, ripped and tore taut, black-as-night flesh from bone and left the creature to die in a thin pool of shadow-like blood. With one furious snarl, the Vulrein lashed out and cut a shining gold gash into the fearsome bird's side. The FireHawk wheeled about in the air in fury as the flames ripped the tent apart.

Molran fled into the desert while Halfa rushed towards Krish, her eyes flying from him to a flaming feather. Krish was almost through the last of the rope when the tent collapsed. He dodged being hit by the pole he was tied to as it fell but then the flaming canvas was on top of him. The last of the bonds burned away and he flailed about, pure unbridled panic taking control of him. He could see nothing. He was completely lost, stumbling about under the weight of the canvas.

A tear in the fabric! He was choking on fumes as he fumbled for this exit. A blast of cool air brushed past him as the tent billowed in the breeze. He fumbled about to find his pack beneath the fabric, located it, pulled it towards him and headed through the tear which was opening wide above him. He ran forward as the canvas came down again and knocked him to the ground, but his head was through the rip in the tent. The air was for a moment cool and refreshing. He burst out of the flaming remnants of the tent and hurled himself onto the cold ground, rolling about to extinguish the flames that had latched onto his top.

He jumped to his feet, his clothes still smoking, and looked about. Halfa had also escaped, her clothes smouldering just like his. Molran was some distance from them but then the FireHawk swooped down in front of her and set the ground aflame. That most beautiful and terrible of birds skimmed the ground, slashing the land with flames metres tall, encircling them.

Krish stood to one side, waiting, considering the wall of flame all around them. Halfa stood there, still holding the pole in her hand, staring directly at the bird. Molran looked about in utter despair.

The FireHawk flew in circles, waiting for its prey to make itself known.

Molran's eyes were wide with panic. Moments later she made her final mistake. She ran. She had nowhere to go but still she ran. The FireHawk had found its quarry. It swooped, its talons hitting Molran's chest with such force that she fell to the ground. The bird began to peck and rip and tear at her flesh.

Then Krish had a terrible thought. Where were the Vulrein? He shut his eyes and looked about but he couldn't see them anywhere. Had they burnt with the tent? Could they really burn to death?

The answer came in a terrible a scream. A bloodcurdling primal cry that cut through the very fabric of his being.

'AAAAAHHHHHH! VULREIN! VULREIN! VULREEEEEEIIII-IINNN!'

The gurgling cries from the bloodied form dying on the ground made Krish and Halfa turn to look in the direction Molran had been pointing.

Krish closed his eyes. There was nothing. Nothing at all. But Molran could see them! How could...?

It struck him. He opened his eyes. There they were. Gnarled shapes stretched out on the flaming landscape in front of him. All lined up, each one slightly obscuring another on the sloping ground from the point where he was standing. Then it became clear from the way Halfa was looking high above them both as she stumbled away in fear. They were not overlapping. They were connected. He took a step back and saw they were a pack of terrible hounds no more, but instead a single, enormous creature towering over them. Several formed long, knobbly arms, four clasped together to form a bony torso, a few more the lean legs and a couple clung together to make the shape of a horrific face with a chilling expression. Their eyes had faded and now two black-red slits looked down on him. So dark in their redness that he couldn't look away. He had to look. Had to see into the darkness, to know if in there there was any light, any shape, any hope.

There was none.

It moved towards him but it was as if it hadn't moved at all. When he looked at where it stood the distance between him and the dark shape was just the same. But it was closer. Somehow it was closer and getting nearer and nearer and closer and closer without taking a single step, without even growing in size. It was just closer. So much closer. He could feel it. He could feel it so close and he knew he was going to die.

He barely noticed Halfa fighting to pluck a feather from the Fire-Hawk as the creature that had moments before been the Vulrein bore down on him. Krish had lived through so many days of terror and darkness, the only light that he ever encountered always extinguished moments later, that now, faced with this abominable creature, he no longer cared. He felt light. He could breathe again.

'It's okay,' he whispered to himself. 'I don't care any more. I cannot even be bothered to be scared. I'm tired. I'm ready. I just don't care. I'm tired. I'm ready.'

Krish closed his eyes. He felt lighter still. He felt relieved. He waited to rest at last. He waited to die.

A shrill cry so loud that it cut into his ears, his eyes, his flesh. A thousand shrieking pins biting into his skin.

In a second it was a hollow, distant cry.

In another it was nothing more than a whistle on the breeze.

He opened his eyes and saw nothing. The diminishing circle of flame and the ashes of the tent... and nothing else. The Vulrein had gone.

Krish was confused but relieved, and then he remembered the Fire-Hawk. He turned and saw the FireHawk stripping the last of the flesh from Molran's bones. Halfa, still holding her pole to defend herself, was making valiant attempts to pluck a feather from the bird.

Krish rushed over but before he got there the bird pecked at Halfa and then flew past her, smothering her in flames. She grabbed at the bird as it flew off into the distance and plucked a flaming feather from its wing. Krish edged forward and then back again several times but there was nothing he could do. He stood back as the flames engulfed her as she whirled about.

But she didn't scream. Halfa kept turning and turning, going from one foot to the next in a line of circles. The fire travelled down her robe and went out, changing her dirty yellow rags to a robe of midnight blue. The pole turned into a staff. Halfa stopped circling and faced Krish. Her skin was darker and her eyes familiar. Balthrir held the feather, still just about alight, out in front of her face, and spoke slowly, simply:

'Tell me you got this all by yourself...'

It took the wide-eyed, open-mouthed Krish a few moments to answer.

'B... Balthrir, I—'

'Tell me you got this... all by yourself...'

'Balthrir—'

Her eyes were awash with emotion. 'Tell me I wasn't there, talkin' that lot into bringin' you along, tryin' to get this poxy feather!'

Krish was now looking at the feather as its flame grew smaller. 'Balthrir, it's—'

'Tell me I didn't have to persuade them *not* to do you in straight away! Or to do you in before the FireHawk hatched! That I didn't rush over to you when the tent was collapsing, chuckin' some gust o' wind spell over you *and* tryin' to grab a feather at the same time!'

'Balthrir, you—'

'Yer wanna know how I know Old Margary? Yer wanna know why I knew the path to Ugethrid so well? Krish! Look at me!' Krish's eyes left the feather and he looked into Balthrir's. 'When I was seven – and *yes* you *are* gonna to listen to this! – when I was seven my family was so poor but I was showin' a lot of promise as a wizard and my Dad 'ad a plan that I could get some work at a circus. Kid-wizard or summink.' Krish's eyes flicked between her and the feather for a moment as she continued to speak. 'So we journeyed to Ugethrid to get Old Margary's 'elp, see if she would train me up...' Her eyes were almost quivering but she would not let tears escape them. 'We'd visited a few times. Just like lots of poorer families with wizard blood in them often do. Mum 'ad gone up there as a kid but 'ad flunked out of trainin' to marry Dad. So we climbed there in the dead of winter... There was an avalanche. Mum got trapped under the snowfall. She was dyin'. We couldn't get 'er out. I didn't know the spell to 'elp. So I ran without a bloody scrap of food in my belly for a day and a night and a day and spoke to Old Margary. She taught me a spell to melt the snow. Dad 'ad just about kept Mum warm enough with a fire.' The light surrounding the feather grew dimmer and dimmer. 'I freed 'er with the spell Old Margary taught me but Dad banned me from practising magic from that moment onwards. Didn't care that it was magic that 'ad saved Mum, just that it was magic that'd brought us there in the first place, and that hours... minutes later probably Mum would 'ave died... But I went back to Old Margary. On my own. Learned spells, curses, incantations, all sorts. Over and over again I did that bloody climb! I wanted to 'elp people. Save lives... Prove to somebody that I could do something... FOR WHAT?! For them not to care?!' Krish could hardly make out the flame at all now. 'For them just to get imprisoned and die?!... Tell me yer did this on yer own, Krish.'

'No! Balthrir, you did! You *did* help! You did so much!' Krish shouted out but Balthrir could see that his eyes were only on the feather, which had all but gone out.

'No! Come on, Krishna!' At this Krish looked up into her eyes. 'Tell me I didn't just risk my life for this bloody thing! For what? For yer Mum? So you could spend a bit more time with her? Boo-bloody-hoo! Wish I could spend time with mine! Tell me...' Her eyes must have stung, for they never blinked and he swore they must be filled with tears but not a drop fell from them. 'Tell me... that I mean something.'

Her eyes were dark, a beautiful brown, and after looking into the Vulrein's they were so bright and full of colour and so wonderfully familiar.

'Balthrir... I don't know anyone... I have no friends...' He looked deep into her eyes. 'I just have you and... and I don't how I would have done any of this... *any* of this without you.'

Krish and Balthrir looked into each other. For endless seconds they saw nothing else but each other's eyes.

And then Balthrir pulled a jar out of her robe and placed the feather inside. She waved her staff in a circle and a gentle breeze made its way into the jar and the flame grew a little stronger. She threw in a pinch of some red powder and then put on the lid.

'There. Enough to keep it burning for some time.' She looked up at Krish. 'Were you scared?'

'Not in the end. No.'

Balthrir nodded. 'Think that's what it was. Said I didn't know 'ow they was 'untin' you. Fear. That's what it was. I guess most people are pretty terrified right up till the end, but some, like you, kinda accept it.'

'They had nothing more to hunt because... I wasn't afraid any more?'

Balthrir shrugged. 'I guess.'

'You saw it?'

Balthrir nodded. 'Yer must 'ave reached, like, the pinnacle of yer fear, and with so much to feed on it took some kinda physical form, summink everyone could see, got ready to chow down, and you... stopped being afraid. So it went. Nothin' more for it to feed on.'

'Balthrir... Thank you.'

'Oh, shut up!' She gave him a little smile. 'Come on. We'd better get going.'

The circle of fire had died down to practically nothing as they made their way warily into the dawn, but Krish couldn't help feeling lighter and infinitely happier than ever before on his journey through Ilir.

⁂

It's worth noting that a thought arrived in Krish's mind on this day. A thought that would sit neatly in his brain for some time. It was mainly ignored by all other thoughts floating around his psyche but it was there nonetheless. And it would be a long while before he chose to pay it any real attention. You won't read any more about this particular thought in this book because the day he listened to that thought, which was hiding in clear sight, at the heart of his mind, would be the day that would define Krish for ever.

CHAPTER 25

MOONSTONE & GINGER

The sun peeked over the horizon and the huge flat plain was filled with the lazy, pinkish-white sunlight of a hazy dawn. Two figures crossed the plain known as the Pale Hunting Grounds. But nobody was hunting today. Their pace was slow. They were weary but relaxed, contented. Without their even realising it the corners of their mouths remained slightly upturned throughout their conversations; as if simply being in each other's company was reason enough to feel warm and happy inside.

'When?' asked the boy.

'When that Goonmallinn disappeared behind that dune,' answered the girl. 'I told yer to keep yer eye on 'er, remember? I snuck round, conjured up another mask spell (better than the one I did on you for Nboosa, eh?) and was using a voice-thrower spell to make yer think I was still standing next to yer.'

Krish suddenly remembered something else. 'That's why it looked like Halfa was talking to herself. But, I saw…'

'Oh. Yeah. That was 'er. The other Goonmallinn. Tryin' to find 'er way back to the others. Kept chuckin' auds, kinda funny noise spells, 'er way, makin' 'er think there was some beastie after 'er so she'd leg it.'

Mersha and ullwihr (the spices Balthrir had used to keep the feather alight) had been Balthrir's plan all along and she'd decided to keep it to herself and then make it sound like Halfa's idea. They had wrapped the jar containing the feather in several layers of skins for protection, placing it in Krish's pack, just on top of the pearl, so there was very little weight pressing down on it. All Krish wanted to do every time they stopped was to get out the jar and look at the still-flaming feather but Balthrir kept telling him off each time he reached for it.

'You tried to have me killed!' said Krish.

'Nah, mate,' said Balthrir. 'They wanted yer dead there and then. That's what they were whisperin' about. Kill 'im, stew 'im. So I tried to get 'em to save yer till breakfast. For the Fire'awk. Set me own alarm to wake me in case I dropped off. Was gonna... oh I dunno. Knock 'em out while we dealt with the Fire'awk. Till someone decided summonin' up the Vulrein was a better idea!'

'I was terrified!'

'Good.'

'I could have been killed, Balthrir!'

'Nah. You were fine. Even cast a wind spell to get yer out from under that blinkin' tent as it collapsed. I 'ad yer back.'

'Even when you were asleep.'

'Ah. Yeah, erm. I did actually drop off last night. That tea of theirs is stronger than yer think! And I was tryin' not to 'ave that much of it! I mean, you were tied up! What was the worst that could 'appen? Well, yer certainly gave me a run for m'money on that one, didn't yer? My alarm was set though. You would 'ave been fine.'

'But all that talk of no one else helping! What if the King—'

'Well, that's *your* fault! There I was, planning to clear the way so yer could nab the feather—'

'Well, if *you* hadn't gone off in a huff and had actually told me what you were up to—'

'All right, all right! We both got pretty narked off and did stupid things! Obsendei won't know. At least I 'ope not.'

Krish had noticed, now he thought about it, how often Halfa had looked over to him, just checking to see that he was still there. That he was still all right. Despite her tough exterior Balthrir clearly did care for him. And, he guessed, he cared for her. Yes. He supposed he really did care for her. Quite a bit actually.

Krish retrieved the distress stone from his pocket. He'd found it in the ashes of the Goonmallinns' tent. Fat lot of use it had been. Without wanting to prove Balthrir right about it being 'rubbish', he'd slipped it into his pocket.

They had recovered the twine from the burnt-out tree and were now walking away from the Pale Hunting Grounds, the twine unravelling and disappearing from sight as they went. Balthrir still insisted no 'mortal blade' could cut through the twine but Krish was more worried about some donkey tripping over an invisible wire. Balthrir said it would serve it right for being a donkey, which didn't make a lot of sense to Krish but he knew she just liked to say stupid things to amuse herself sometimes. He knew that she was really quite fond of donkeys and horses and mules and all kinds of animals.

It seemed to Krish that they had almost completed their mission. They had a pearl from the Night Ocean, a still-flaming feather from a FireHawk, and now all they had to do was arrive back at the tree to which they'd tied the end of the ball of twine. Although Balthrir reminded him that they still had to walk almost halfway round the world before they could tie it in a pretty bow and lift the invisibility spell to show it to the King, this didn't seem too daunting to Krish, who couldn't imagine being able to walk around the whole of the Earth. Most of his world was ocean but Ilir had a single sea, which circled around the eastern hemisphere like an almighty wound cut into the landscape. Hence its name: The Scar.

They were just a few days away from The Scar now and Krish could sense they were approaching water because the landscape became filled with patches of green and there was a cool sea breeze washing across the land. Dry cracked earth become softer and more soil-like. The road was lined with palmeries, ranks of palm trees running in parallel to each other, planted thousands of years ago by ancient farmers. The palms provided both shelter from the heat and a perfect environment to grow the small brown olive-like pehsa fruits. Children ran through the palmeries, playing while their parents laughed and encouraged them to return to picking the pehsas. They were all working but there was none of the backbreaking labour and starving expressions Krish had witnessed when he had first arrived in Ilir.

The palmeries also made a cool shelter from the sun for them to rest in in the midday heat. They slept in the palmeries on more than one occasion. Krish loved being surrounded by people again. It was rather refreshing to be in the company of folk who were so down-to-earth and unthreatening after days in the company of the Goonmallinns.

They reached The Scar after a week. Balthrir informed Krish that

the western shores of The Scar were the start of the territories belonging to the city of Alvaris. This was the end of King Obsendei's domain
until they reached the farmlands of Melkur.

The dock in the town of Marraghir was a flurry of activity. Market
sellers bustled through the town, offering baskets of smoked fish or
spiced insects. He could see children placing fish on the flat roofs of
the houses, allowing them to dry out in the sun. He and Balthrir were
hassled by people selling the best oars, the best rudders, the best hulls
in town. Apparently nobody here sold boats that were already assem-
bled. The population of Marraghir, without exception it appeared,
were keen sailors, fishers and dredgers. Most houses had a boat outside
or on the roof. A child ran out of her house wielding a cracked rudder
and some coins, demanding to know who would replace it for twelve
Shellas. She had an answer and a shiny new rudder within moments.

The people wore simple robes with sandals or bare feet. A shop
owner would often take your arm to try and drag you to their stall to
sell you a net or a rowlock. This freaked Krish out a little at first as
he was used to wandering around shops with Dawson and his mates,
simply browsing, without anyone seizing your arm to show you what
was on sale, but he began to get used to it and realised it was just how
people worked in this town. They could be slightly pushy but on the
whole they were friendly people who he guessed were just trying to
make a living.

The dock itself was little more than a long stretch of sand covered
in beached dugouts and canoes with a single wooden wharf at one
end on which was moored a raft the size of a football pitch. Attached
to the raft was a length of rope leading to a winch about five times
taller than any of the single-storey shacks that made up the small settlement. The winch was the centrepiece of the town and there were
even statues of the workers who built the raft and winch protruding
from the enormous supports holding up the drum. Krish could see
that the rope, which was probably as thick as the neck of the red-
faced man who worked at the meat counter at his local supermarket, stretched the whole way across The Scar, presumably to another
winch on the other side.

Although they'd spent the night in the palmery, they stopped off at a local inn and Balthrir paid to use their washrooms. For a little extra you could wash in hot water rather than cold. The innkeeper had three large cauldrons of water that were constantly full of water, which he heated and then poured into barrels in the washrooms. Krish and Balthrir had stopped off at a couple of inns on their long journey and bathed in the same way: a barrel of water in a simple stone-walled cubicle, usually with a handful of cracked tiles on the floor amongst the mud, undressing and using the small bucket floating in the barrel to bathe in chilly water from a river or that had been collected months ago when it last rained.

The cubicles weren't too much to look at but the water was nice and warm. Krish closed his eyes and drank in the feeling of absolute serenity. He didn't care that there was no power shower, like in his bathroom at home, to do all the work. He didn't care that Ilir's idea of a bath meant standing up and ladling water onto yourself. He didn't even care that he had to balance precariously on the slippery, uneven tiles and that he'd have to struggle to get his battered old shoes back on without getting mud on his feet. He could close his eyes and not see monsters. He was washing all the sand, all the grit off his body and he felt as if all the terror of his encounter with the Goonmallinns was being swept down the plughole.

'Balthrir!' he called out to his friend in the next cubicle. 'This is the best bath I've ever had!'

'Bloody good, innit?' his friend called back.

They picked up a few supplies from the town, including a flask of ground moonstone and ginger boiled in whisky and ice-cave water.

'To steady the ol' nerves,' said Balthrir, followed by a heavy sigh and a widening of the eyes. Krish had forgotten that she'd never crossed The Scar because of her fear of water. 'You'll 'ave to 'elp me.' Balthrir's eyes were weak and hopeful, looking across at him from the small outdoor café where they were eating lunch. She was scrunching up a section of her midnight-blue robe in one hand. A tight fist, like she resented the robe itself. She had never looked so vulnerable. 'I've 'elped you a lot, mate. Your turn to 'elp me now.'

'Sure, I'll, er... hold your hand or—'

'Yer ain't 'oldin' me 'and, yer twonk!' She was back to being normal Balthrir for a moment. 'Just… yer know… be there and all that.'

Krish didn't really know, but he was determined not to let her down. He'd do whatever he could.

Balthrir managed to put off the journey across The Scar for one more night and they headed back out of the town to the palmery where they'd spent the night before. They sat in the quiet under the clear night sky, enjoying the glow of the five moons, Mother and Sons, Krish with one eye on a shooting star sweeping slowly across the stratosphere. They talked a little, looking out at the stars shining between the leaves of the palm trees, of all sorts of odd things as their minds unwound. After surviving so many life-threatening situations they were finally beginning to relax. Balthrir wanted to know if shoes were any different where Krish came from and this then somehow led to them talking about ships, which fascinated Balthrir as the sea on Ilir was comparatively small so they barely had much use for anything other than a few dugouts and the ferry-raft. So many things intrigued her, such as the fact you had to lick letters to seal them rather than using wax, and Krish couldn't believe how mundane things such as cabbages seemed to completely bewilder her as well. They spoke a little of royalty too.

'What are kings and queens like where you're from, eh?' asked Balthrir.

'Er, I dunno,' said Krish. 'They… *seem* very important but I'm not really sure what they do. I just know that when one dies it's their eldest son or daughter who takes over.'

'Well that's 'ardly fair!'

'How does it happen here?'

'Simple. Once the king or queen snuffs it, the first one to shove the crown on their fat 'ead takes over.'

'Well that doesn't seem fair either! Anyway, you'd have to be pretty strong to pick the King's crown up in the first place. It's massive!'

'The crown weighs nothing to the King, mate,' said Balthrir, her eyes shut already, and in moments they were both asleep.

CHAPTER 26

THE SANDS OF TYRAAH

The morning was fresh and bright, the sky bluer than it had been for the whole time Krish had been in Ilir, but a breeze whipped around the shacks of the port of Marraghir. This unsettled Balthrir as they queued with hundreds of people to board the ferry-raft. She was worried about the wind rocking the raft but Krish was certain that the raft, being the size it was, soon to be packed with a whole stadium's worth of people (plus the fact it was being pulled by a rope), would be pretty stable as it crossed the ocean.

The breeze died down as they crowded on board. They had to sit at the back in the corner, the water itself within spitting distance (which didn't make Balthrir very happy) just so they could run the twine off the end. Carrying the twine through the town had been a nightmare. People kept tripping over it, despite Krish's best efforts to hold it nice and low under some sacking Balthrir had acquired that morning ('legally' she'd added in hushed tones before looking around rather quickly). The queue had been the worst and they'd had to keep to one side so as not to knock anybody into the water.

Balthrir managed to tie the twine to the edge of the raft, running a length of rope through the middle so it would unwind as they went. Krish tried his best to reassure her as she lay on her front, her head and arms dangling over the edge to tie the twine in place, shaking at the sight of the water below her, but it just caused her to tell him to 'Shut up!' The way the water bobbed the raft up and down was really unnerving her.

'Balthrir,' said Krish, 'stop being such a bloody coward!'

Balthrir turned to him in shock. 'Blimey, since when did you stand up to, like, anyone?' But she knew the answer. From the moment he had demanded that Halfa (who he hadn't realised at the time was

Balthrir) untie him and take him away, Krish had begun to feel a little more self-assured.

'I'm just trying to help,' said Krish. 'Go on: sit up and look out over the water.'

'If yer wanna 'elp yer can shut yer trap!' spat out Balthrir before doing as he suggested.

Once they were underway Balthrir began to relax a little, although she looked quite apprehensive. The fact that there were no barriers around the edge of the gigantic raft didn't help. She jumped every time someone fell in (which happened quite a lot, often deliberately as a child pushed a brother or sister in, simply making them laugh as they swam back to the slow-moving raft).

The atmosphere on board was very relaxed, jovial in fact. There were no chairs. Everyone just sat on the floor or on sacks of rice or vegetables, gathered together in little circles playing cards, chatting or even cooking with fires on small metal plates that prevented them from setting the wood of the raft alight.

The air over the water was welcomely cool on such a hot day and breezed past them as the mighty rope hauled them across The Scar. Balthrir didn't look too comfortable; as if she was waiting for something to happen, for something to go wrong. But nothing did. She didn't really want to talk and answered most of Krish's enquiries with 'Yeah' or 'Probably'. But she did keep breaking away from her staring competition with the middle-distance to check that he was still there. And it seemed that that was all she wanted. To know that he was just next to her and for some time he enjoyed just sitting there beside her in silence.

The sea was calm and rather flat, gentle little waves brushing past them. A few dugouts with fishermen and women aboard passed them and the fisherfolk waved but apart from that there was very little to see on the vast expanse of water.

The sun began to sink into the water. Ahead they could see the blue of the sky fade to pink then the orange of the setting sun, filling more of the horizon than the local star in Krish's world would, and partially obscured by a row of palm trees. Land. They entered a delta rich with islands of green. There were many fishing boats here, some small, some big. Krish saw a farmer leading a cow into the water. The cow was not enthusiastic at the prospect of bath-time and mooed loudly as the farmer splashed her and rubbed the mud from her coat. In the distance a number of towers, long and pointed with globes near their pinnacles, stuck out above the palm trees. Farther back was a line of lights, suspended in the air.

Just before dusk they reached a large island clad in greenery with a winch visible through the trees. Everybody piled off and there was a flurry of activity to load people onto small boats to taxi them into the main town further along the river. A smaller, faster boat made Balthrir feel uneasy. She clutched the invisible ball of twine over the side and spent the whole journey looking like she was about to empty her insides of the lunch she'd refused to eat. Fortunately they weren't on the water long. The oarswomen and men were rowing with furious speed to get to the city before the sun was completely submerged. Instead of lighting torches they managed to row for five minutes in relative darkness, with a little illumination from the twinkling cityscape up ahead. The light emanated not just from along the banks but also from a raised area now looming over them. There was also noise, a hubbub drifting across the water from the city.

They disembarked and were loaded into large wicker baskets which were somehow being hoisted up to the raised area unsupported. Krish then noticed that a wizard with a staff stood on the higher ground, using his magic to lift them up into the air. This would never happen in Al Kara, where wizards were sideshows. Here, it seemed, magic was an accepted part of life. They rose through the canopy of palm leaves and Krish beheld the city of Alvaris clearly for the first time. Lit all around by the yellow light of floating candles was a large rock formation, like a mountain with the top half sliced off. Some houses were built into the rock face but most buildings were on top of the rock. Ornate towers and minarets. Houses entirely of glass, tinted every colour of the rainbow. Tall buildings with no windows at all, plain and soulless.

They stepped out of the basket into a swarm of people. Balthrir had to conjure up an enchantment to make them smell of rotten vegetables to keep everybody away so they'd be less likely to trip people up with the twine.

'Balthrir?' said Krish, not bothering to be quiet as he wouldn't be heard over the hubbub and no one was listening to anyone they weren't already talking to anyway. 'What if somebody here has the other Salvean blade? You said there was another one out there and, well, people seem pretty loaded here!'

'Perhaps,' answered Balthrir, also not keeping her voice down. No one around them had batted an eyelid. 'But it's a million-to-one shot, mate. And the twine is blinkin' invisible! They'd 'ave no idea what it was even if they did stumble upon it!'

'And if they have something else that could cut through the twine?'

Balthrir shook her head so hard Krish was concerned that she might do herself an injury. 'It's made o' pure sunlight. Nothin's cuttin' through that 'less they've got a Sal— oi! Watch it!' she added as a troupe of smartly dressed and arrogant-looking wizards shoved past them. 'Unless they've got their own Salvean blade,' Balthrir continued, keeping her voice down as much as she could while remaining audible, 'then nothin's cuttin' through it.'

Balthrir was becoming increasingly irritated by the crowds so she dragged them into the next guesthouse they saw. She paid up and they headed straight to bed while the housekeeper prodded the strange invisible line that had appeared along the wall and seemed to lead to the new guests' room.

The room was tidy and orderly. The walls were dark green and the bedsheets and rugs on the floor were dark red. Fresh flowers of matching red and green were presented in pots by the window. The comfortable-looking beds were big enough to fit three or four people in each.

'Blimey!' said Balthrir, eyeing the room with concern. 'This place looks expensive! Perhaps I'll crack out a bit of m'itchin' powder in the mornin' to see if we can get a discount.'

Balthrir forgot about this idea as soon as she lay down on one of the massive beds with its heavenly soft mattress and fell asleep pretty sharpish. Krish stayed up a few minutes longer. He reached out of his bed and unfastened his pack. The large, dark bowling-ball-sized pearl from the Night Ocean glinted in the meagre amount of light that had made it into the room from the crack in the curtains. Then he pulled a carefully wrapped package out of the pack, unwrapped the jar and basked in the glow of the feather of the FireHawk that was still gently burning without showing any sign of ceasing. He smiled, re-wrapped the jar and placed it back in his pack and drifted away from the waking world for the night with a broad smile upon his face.

In the morning they explored the city. The buildings here were mainly made of stone, several storeys high, and the streets were, well, actual streets, ordered and practically clean. People's clothes looked tidier and almost designed, rather than just some rags that were sewn together and passed down several generations until they fell apart. All was shiny and new (compared to the rest of Ilir, anyway).

'Alvaris,' declared Balthrir. 'Kingdom of the rich. Got this new craze round 'ere. Called busy-ness or summink. It's like bein' in charge o' stuff but not actually goin' out there and seein' how it all works. Yer just like hide in some buildin' talkin' about how yer know what yer talkin' about for so long that nobody gets a chance to realise that yer 'ave absolutely no bloody idea what the 'ell yer doin'.'

Krish remembered Uncle Ravi trying to explain what he did in the office he worked in. It had all sounded very confusing, so he could understand what Balthrir was talking about. Everybody around them seemed to be either rushing about in remarkably clean robes that looked like they'd never been worn before, paying absolutely no attention to anybody else, or they were lying about in the streets looking as if they and their clothes had never had a wash in their lives and as if they wished somebody, anybody, would notice them. The latter of these two groups held signs asking for money, played instruments or performed unimpressive magic tricks, only to be widely ignored.

A dishevelled-looking man with dark thick curly hair and a battered old suit was carrying a basket full of scrolls and making a very good job of spilling them all over the street, picking them up and then spilling them all over again seconds later. People shouted at one another as they passed but none stopped to commit to a full argument.

One shouted something like 'Ilaea!' at Balthrir as he passed. There was quiet anger in her face. Krish chose to start a conversation before she became too distracted.

'So, this is the place you were talking about?' asked Krish. 'Where there might be call for wizards?'

Balthrir's lip curled up on one side in an unpleasant way. 'Nah. This ain't the place for me. It's flippin' crackers! Nobody's talkin' to nobody! Can see why market traders never set up shop 'ere; nobody'd pay them any attention! Besides,' she said with a heavy sigh, 'millions o' miles away from the folks.'

There were no palmeries to sleep in here and the parks were guarded, so they stayed the night in another guesthouse on the opposite side of the city. Balthrir tried to get them a decent-sized room by offering the owner a free sample of her itching powder ('What d'yer mean yer'd 'ave no use for it? In't yer got long-term guests, 'angers-on yer just wanna get shot of? Perfect for the likes o' them!') but with no success. There was just one room available that they could afford and it had only one bed. That night, Krish lay awake, across the bed from Balthrir. He felt odd, yes, but as if this was the one place in the world he wanted to be more than anywhere else. Somehow, though, he just couldn't help feeling unbelievably nervous. He was so sure she was awake too, all the way over there on the other side of the bed.

They left Alvaris in the morning. A basket flew them down the eastern side of the city to the green valley of palm trees below. Rather than being a sheer cliff edge like the western rock face, the eastern side was like a gigantic wave of stone curling round, almost touching the ground.

As the days went by Krish began to realise that his relationship with Balthrir had changed since they'd escaped the Goonmallinns. They were far more comfortable with each other now. What would once have been awkward silences were now just pleasant periods of quiet where they no longer had to speak to communicate. 'Thanks,' she said to him one morning, for no apparent reason, her eyes smiling, and then the corners of her lips twitched hesitantly for a moment. Maybe 'smiled' was the wrong word, he thought. Her eyes almost glowed and she looked into him like she'd known him for a hundred years.

The city of Alvaris was far behind them now. The mountains sprang up all around, craggy, fearsome structures of rock looking down on them. Balthrir pointed to Hudaffrid, Ugethrid's twin and the second highest mountain on Ilir (although this one was firmly planted on the ground rather than stuck up a tree).

They climbed through a mountain pass and from his vantage point high above the world Krish looked ahead and saw a tiny dark dot on the horizon and realised that the Black Palace was now in front of them rather than behind. A shudder of fear crept through him. Although they had the pearl, the feather and were well on their way to tying a bow around the world, Krish still felt sure that the King would be able to refuse him the Myrthali. Balthrir banished his doubts with a dismissive wave of her hand over her shoulder.

'Yer said yer 'eard bird singin' when yer left the palace?' said Balthrir.

'Yeah,' said Krish.

'Then trust me. Yer'll be fine.'

Although Krish was really enjoying Balthrir's company, he wished she'd get out of the habit of only explaining things when she could be bothered, not when it would be handy for him to know. What did the sound of birdsong have to do with anything?

As they continued to unfurl the twine they became aware of an odd sensation. It felt as if someone was tugging on it. Had it been discovered? Had it been untied from the tree they'd attached it to back on the Great Plain? Krish and Balthrir stared at each other in puzzlement as the tugging continued for a few more moments and then stopped.

'Could it be all those people in Alvaris?' suggested Krish. 'Or... I dunno, wind on The Scar? Or a ship trying to cross over it?'

'I guess,' said Balthrir, unconvincingly. She pulled the twine hard and it didn't budge. 'It's not been cut. So if someone's found it they're not the person with the other Salvean blade.'

It troubled them both greatly but there was nothing they could do. They moved on.

They descended into the land of Tyraah, swapping Ilir's most mountainous landscape for its flattest. Balthrir stated that they were now back in the domain of King Obsendei. Tyraah was a seemingly endless plateau of dark brown stone, criss-crossed with shallow crevices, the terrain masked by the sand caught in the strong wind constantly swirling just above the ground. Balthrir pulled out long headscarves from her pack.

'Most folks go around,' shouted Balthrir above the howling wind. 'But it's miles that way!' She pointed off to the north-west. 'And we'd 'ave to risk Argyrhyr Pass.'

'Not a very safe place?'

'*Not a very safe place?!* It's the kinda place where thieves steal from assassins. It gets pretty messy up there. I 'eard there was a guy who once just *looked* at the pass and found 'is shoes 'ad been nicked! I would *not* risk takin' a priceless pearl and still-flamin' whatsitmacalled through there!'

Balthrir helped tie a headscarf into a turban for Krish and then wrapped it around his face, leaving only his eyes exposed to the elements.

'Oh, and whatever yer see,' she said, 'don't pay it any attention.'

'What?' said Krish.

'Seriously. Won't do yer no good. Eyes to the ground. Might stop yer gettin' sand in 'em.' She didn't seem keen to elaborate.

They rarely stopped. Even with his face almost completely covered Krish still found sand gathering in his eyes, the corners of his lips and even getting into his ears. He soon learned that the satisfaction he got from a sip of water was hardly worth it once a volley of grains flew into his mouth. Regardless of the noise of the ceaseless gales whipping around them, Balthrir was determined to keep talking. Not that he heard much between the wind and the headscarf muffling her voice.

'Huh-huh-huh-huh-hah. Huh. Huh-huh-hah. Huh-had? Huh! H-h-huh, bucket o' the stuff and a-huh-huh-huh-huh-worth the bother if you-huh-huh-hah 'bout the size of a-huh!'

And she kept pointing at the ground like there was something interesting to see, but all Krish saw was more and more scarred stone. After fighting the Vulrein in the deep, facing death at the savage hands of the Goonmallinns and almost being burned alive by the Fire-Hawk, he was surprised to find that this was the worst ordeal of the lot. All the other instances had lasted relatively short lengths of time and as horrifying as they were he could never complain about there being a dull moment. The trek through the Sands of Tyraah went on for hour after hour after mind-numbingly boring hour. He turned his mind towards thoughts of home. They were almost there. They had achieved everything they had set out to achieve.

The thoughts didn't hang around in his mind for long. Balthrir was his friend. A friend unlike any he had ever had before. But it wouldn't last. As soon as he touched a grain of the Myrthali she would be gone. This whole world would be gone for ever. He loved and feared Ilir but the latter was fading in his mind. He would leave this world having walked around the whole of it and somehow that placed it firmly in his brain in a way that meant it would never truly diminish. But she would be gone. One touch of that dust and he'd never see her again. This feeling weighed him to the ground like nothing he had encountered previously. A few minutes later he would have a similar sensation that was just as dark, if not more so.

When he did look up the horizon was so hazy that he felt he'd gone blind from seeing so much bland rock stretching out in front of him. It was then that the shapes began to form before his eyes. First they were just stains, blemishes upon the landscape. Dirty yellow-brown forms up ahead. Then they started to appear at his feet. They were everywhere. He was suddenly wary of tripping but they didn't appear to be solid. He walked through them like they were mist but no wisps of vapour fled to the sides as he brushed through. There were so many of them. Stretching on way in front of him.

Krish was aware that Balthrir had stopped talking and was looking back at him.

'Ignore 'em,' she said, quite clearly all of a sudden.

'What are they?' he asked.

'Nothin' yer wanna worry about.'

Krish was starting to worry because the shapes were now a lot more familiar. Each was a large, sausage-like shape aside from the way they all became somewhat narrower at one end. No more than a couple of metres long and less than half a metre or so wide, knee-height off the ground. They were wrapped in coarse sacking, bound with rope. The rope emphasising the globe-like object that would be on top of the shapes if they stood upright. And Krish knew which way up they went now. They were bodies. Hundreds and hundreds of bodies and they were wading straight through them.

'I said don't look!' Balthrir shouted over her shoulder.

'Balthrir... seriously... I can't... What are they?'

'Nothin'. Don't exist. Ignore 'em.'

'Balthrir, please! What are they?'

He couldn't tell if it was the wind or a fearful sigh before she spoke. 'The future. No! What was it Nboosa said... "Consequences. Consequences of the actions yer see yerself taking in the immediate future."'

'I... How can I... I wouldn't kill anyone!'

'Not intentionally.' She glanced over her shoulder to see a classic Krish-needs-it-spelt-out-to-him expression peering out from the small slit in his headscarf. 'Look, the consequences of yer actions are always measured by the number of people who could be affected by them. And how d'yer measure that? Yer gotta see 'ow many of 'em 'ave snuffed it, right? Look, imagine you eat a fruit. Yer leave the seed on the ground and a bird that 'appens to be passin' eats it. A bird that would never 'ave eaten those seeds if *you* 'adn't been there. Seed goes through the bird's digestion system, bird plops it back onto the ground somewhere, a tree starts to grow, few 'undred years later a man rides into the tree and dies. A man who, I dunno, saves lots of people some'ow. From a fire or summink. Bloke 'oo wouldn't've snuffed it if *you* 'adn't eaten that fruit. Or maybe that tree'll feed 'undreds of people in the future and yer'd see less bodies. Yeah?'

'So, all these are people who are going to die because of something I do?'

'Yep.'

'What if I change what I do?'

'It's not the future. It's the *consequences* of what yer plannin' to do at the moment.'

Krish had been thinking of taking the King's Myrthali. Of leaving this world. Of returning home to his Mum and saving her.

'But seriously, how can I—?'

'Look, mate! Yer go and see the King, blardy-blar, get yer Myrthali, 'e's right narked off, declares war with someone because 'e's in a bad mood. Many folks get knackered, life-wise.'

'But... I...'

'Think of another course of action.'

Krish considered this. What if he found a way to remove the King before leaving? He knew what that would mean. Balthrir had said the King had to die before another took his place. He could never do this, but he was thinking about the possibility nonetheless and he saw the world around him changing. The bodies were now laid out before him for miles.

'But... Balthrir, it got worse!'

'Keep thinkin'! Or don't. Pretty bloody awful thing to dwell on really.'

Krish thought again. He concentrated on what would happen if he took his Myrthali and then stayed. He looked hard at the bodies. Were some now semi-transparent? It was hard to tell with sand flying everywhere and with the sacking being so close to the colour of the ground. Krish looked around. Yes, they were definitely fading into nothingness. In moments most of the bodies had vanished. So this was the best course of action? To stay? He tried to refine his train of thought a little. What if he took the Myrthali, stayed and the King remained? His mind must have already been on this track as he barely noticed a body appear or disappear. And what if he stayed and the King died? A few more bodies popped up. Krish was inconsolable and his grief left his mouth gaping open, sand pouring in, and soon he was wincing and grunting in pain.

'Oh for Fumdugga's sake!' cried Balthrir. 'Come on! It in't 'elpin', Krish! 'Urry up!'

Krish felt all his confidence drain from him. Maybe he'd just imagined it? Maybe it was just a brief phase with the Goonmallinns when he'd felt able to stand up for himself. Now it was gone and he was back to the aimless wandering and tripping over his own words.

The hours dragged on and the bodies came and went, mounting to great heights and receding to smaller numbers, but they never completely vanished. Krish's mind was so sick of the sight he took to walking with his eyes shut, waiting for Balthrir's random comments to bring him back on course. He could still see them though.

CHAPTER 27

GULWIN'S TALE

As evening came they passed from the Sands of Tyraah to the pasturelands of Melkur. No tree was fair game here, so they visited a farmer who sold them some wood for their fire. Balthrir pulled out the Salvean blade and cut a beam of deep pink sunlight emanating from the setting sun, which was just strong enough to set the kindling alight. The tugging on the twine came and went every now and then but they largely ignored it. If something was going wrong somewhere between where they were now and the tree they'd tied the other end to, they were resigned to the fact that there was nothing they could do about it right now.

'Balthrir,' said Krish, his eyes stinging from the woodsmoke, still retrieving sand from the corners of his lips and behind his ears. 'I don't get it. Whatever I did—'

'I know. Yer can't go through yer 'ole life without affectin' other people's. Most of all that consequences cobblers is accidental stuff that no one can ever 'elp.'

'But when I thought about one action specifically... about the King... dying or being killed or someone else being King, it got worse.'

'That's because as soon as 'e's gone, some other ponce in the palace'll nick the crown. That's the way it goes! And they could be worse! Trust me, mate, as long as that palace stands there'll be some nasty old bugger on the throne.'

'But when I thought about staying it was... you know, better. Less people died.'

Krish looked up at Balthrir and he couldn't tell what was hidden in her expression, but the pause said a lot. Balthrir rarely showed much emotion unless something had annoyed her.

'Well, stay.' It was Balthrir's turn to read Krish's look, one that he did not intend to give. 'Or don't. Yer've got yer Mum to get back to. In fact, yer risked a lot to get that Myrthali. So yer'd better not muck it up now!'

'I'll stay. For a little while. Make sure you're reunited with your Mum and Dad.'

Balthrir nodded. There was a strange silence. Calm but strange.

'How d'you know he'll even give me the Myrthali?' asked Krish. 'I mean, you said he would but... God, I-I've just not really thought about if...'

''E will. 'E'll 'ave no choice.'

Krish was taken aback by Balthrir's absolute certainty. 'Why?'

'Because o' Gulwin.'

'Who?'

'Gulwin! 'E's a common gossy.'

'A wh—?'

'A gossy. Small bird. In't yer seen 'em in the palmeries? Beautiful plumage! Green and blue. Little red beak. Tiny beady black eyes. Small enough for a kid to 'old in the 'and. Everyone 'ere knows o' Gulwin! Fireside tale, innit?'

'Fireside tale?'

Balthrir sat back, got comfortable and rubbed the side of her head a little, as if it would help her brain work. 'Fireside tales. Stories passed on from traveller to traveller on the road. Most kids 'ere are told many fireside tales. Gimme a minute. Let me see if I can remember all the details. It's not the oldest, and was always one of m'favourites, but it's the first time I've told it to someone else. Was usually someone tellin' me the story!'

And by the light of the fire, not far from the palace where they had started out, Balthrir told Krish a tale...

Gulwin's Tale

The King and his men were resting in a glade on the road to the palace after a long day's hunting. The King demanded his men pick him the plumpest, freshest, juiciest apple they could find. His men fulfilled their duty but the King grumbled at the flavour, accustomed as he was to the finest food in the land.

Gulwin the Bird, whose Song of Truth never ends –

'There's always some poxy, goody-two-shoes little squat 'ose song lasts a million *boooooring* years in these stories, in't there?'

– flew down and perched on a tree near the King. Gulwin addressed the King and said, if he was not enjoying his apple, would he be most kind and toss it to the ground for him to feast upon. The King was dismissive of Gulwin, who was no more than a common gossy, although Gulwin's plumage of green and blue was somewhat brighter than most. The King told Gulwin that the apple was not fit for rats, let alone birds, and shooed Gulwin away.

Once the bird was gone, the King tossed what was left of the apple onto the forest floor. Gulwin, who had not flown away quite as far as the King had thought, returned and pecked at the apple lying upon the ground. 'Why this is the plumpest, freshest, juiciest apple I have ever tasted in these woods!' cried Gulwin. 'You lied to me out of pure malice rather than share food with me that you did not like and did not need! Now it is gone to waste and it is sinking into the mud!' 'Away with you!' shouted the King. He raised his hand and Gulwin flew far away before the King could strike him.

Months passed. The King found himself forced to venture out onto the balcony of his palace to address his people, who were restless with hunger. It was the coldest day of the bitterest winter in years and the people were demanding more food be brought in from neighbouring towns. 'You did not work hard enough in the fields this summer!' cried the King. 'And the crops were rotting before they found their way to the storehouse! Work harder next year and the food will be plentiful for all!'

At that moment, Gulwin the Bird, whose Song of Truth never ends, flew down to the balcony and sang the truth to the people of the town. 'The crops were harvested in good time, gathered in earlier still than usual, and were so fresh that your King could not resist! He and his wives and husbands and consorts have feasted all autumn and all winter so far, leaving little to fill your starving bellies!'

The people called out angrily at the King, who seized Gulwin by the throat. 'I'll wring your little neck, slanderer!' 'No! No!' called the people. 'This bird is a rare gift! He sings the truth! You will keep him by your side, to always remind you to speak the truth or we will tear down this palace with our bare hands!'

The King had no choice and was forced to keep Gulwin in his palace to remind him never to lie again. 'But you will not live in comfort, you feathered fiend! I will have a well dug in the throne room and you will be chained up and you will never escape until the day this palace falls to the ground!'

And Gulwin said this that was the first of many truths the King would tell from now on.

CHAPTER 28

THE FESTIVAL OF MAGIC

'So, what's the first thing yer gonna do when yer get back?'

'Er, I dunno. Maybe have a Mars Bar or something.'

'What's that?'

'A Mars Bar... erm... it's a... chocolate bar? It's like... dunno... Milk! Milk and sugar and... beans! Yeah, cocoa beans. They crush them up and, yeah, make chocolate. I guess. And there's this caramel stuff inside. That's... well, that's made of more sugar, I think.'

'Might as well have a bowl o' sugar and wash it down with some milk!'

'Yeah!' Krish chuckled. 'I guess I could.'

Krish and Balthrir were now walking past the mountain on top of which Krish had first arrived in Ilir. He was sad at how fast these last few days had gone by. They would soon be re-treading old steps to reach the Great Plain where they had tied one end of the twine, and the familiarity of the land simply made the hours fly past. They talked and joked but the whole time it was as if they were laughing about everything so they didn't have to talk seriously about what would happen once Krish had the Myrthali. Freeing Balthrir's parents was top of the agenda, that was a foregone conclusion, and the King surely wouldn't be able to refuse. They hoped, at least. Krish had told Balthrir he would simply vanish once he touched the Myrthali and his friend didn't really react to this. She just employed her usual trick of swiftly changing the subject.

Krish had largely forgotten about the visions the Sands of Tyraah had cursed his mind with. He was now filled with wonder at the sight of a terrain that had felt so strange, so fearsome some months ago. He was experiencing a curiously nostalgic sensation for a landscape he had grown to love.

They were now walking along the road, approaching the shallow trenches where Krish had seen people harvesting crops months ago. The Black Palace loomed up in front of them. They were taking turns holding the twine but swapping more than usual. The odd tugging sensation was intensifying. A force was pulling on the twine practically the whole time now.

Krish and Balthrir distracted themselves from the incessant tugging by hatching a plan to present the three items to King Obsendei. They'd buy a scroll and ink and draw up a proclamation to deliver to the gates of the palace, addressed to the King. Then they'd rush off to get to the tree on the Great Plain that they'd tied one end of the twine to and tie the two ends together, relieve the twine of its invisibility and present the King with the pearl from the Night Ocean and the still-flaming feather from the FireHawk. If he questioned anything they could say that Gulwin had heard the King promise Krish the Myrthali in exchange for completing these three challenges. Neither wanted to use the word 'foolproof' but they were nonetheless quietly confident.

'Well,' said Krish. 'Guess it's almost over. Balthrir, I just wanted to say—'

'Don't give me any of that mushy stuff, kiddo! We've not got it in the bag yet!'

She was right, of course. They might have walked around the world but until they tied that bow it wasn't over. There was still one last leg of the journey to go. They had tied the twine to a tree just past Ugethrid, on the road to the Night Ocean, so their journey would end there.

As they reached the trenches themselves, Krish was surprised to see that nobody was sowing seeds or harvesting the crops. In fact there were a number of tools discarded rather clumsily by or in the shallow trenches. He looked over at Balthrir, who seemed equally bemused.

As they entered Al Kara they were in for a bit of a shock. The town was largely abandoned. All doors to dwellings were shut tight and tent flaps fastened. Many market stalls had been half packed up, the wares still on display coated in a light covering of dust. Even food had been left out on the stalls, flies picking at the meat and maggots crawling over fruit.

The Broken Scythe had several slats of wood nailed across the door. Krish recognised innkeeper Tol's scrawl on a handwritten poster on the wall next to the door:

Looters will be

prosscutted

prossacutted

presecuted

BARRED!

Tol's spelling clearly hadn't improved since he'd been away. But Tol's words suggested that he expected to come back and that his customers would return also. What had happened here?

As Krish and Balthrir stared up at the Black Palace they took in a new addition to the tallest tower. Several of the prisoners who made up the palace stood on each other's shoulders at the very top of the tower to form a flagpole. Flapping lightly in the breeze was a black flag with the emblem of a golden crown embroidered across it.

"E ain't 'ere,' said Balthrir, staring up at the flag. 'That flag only flies when 'e's not 'ere. Just to say, yer know, "I ain't 'ere but I *am* 'ere in spirit." Or some cobblers like that.'

'So where is he?' asked Krish, beginning to worry that their whole quest had been for nothing.

Balthrir opened her mouth to answer but then spotted something in the distance. Far off, in the direction of Ugethrid, there was a cloud of dirt rising into the air. The cloud followed the road they had taken on their adventures to meet Old Margary, to the Night Ocean, the Pale Hunting Grounds and beyond. The direction they would now be heading in to finish their journey around the whole world and tie the bow to complete the third of the tasks the King had set for Krish to win the Myrthali. If there was anything going on on the Great Plain they might struggle to tie the bow undisturbed. The tugging on the twine was now ceaseless.

Krish and Balthrir reached the road. When they'd walked down it months ago there hadn't been a soul in sight on that dusty expanse. Now there were carts and wagons of all sizes. Some drawn by horse, others by mule and a few smaller ones by hand. They ducked behind a ridge to observe the chaotic caravan heading out of Al Kara. Carts were filled with men, women and children. Most looked fairly poor but they could see some closed, jewel-encrusted carriages with the odd noble fanning themselves at the small windows. But nobody seemed angry. Most appeared rather jovial. There was much laughter. Some in open carriages filled to the brim with people had even found space to brew tea and pass small glasses around for all to enjoy. Children sat happily at the back of the carts, their feet swinging playfully over the edge.

'What the blinkin' 'ell?!' said Balthrir. 'What is going on round 'ere?'

Guards marched at the side of some of the carts and carriages, all in pairs, most chatting with each other, not too concerned that anyone would make a break for it. These weren't prisoners – well, aside from the slaves in their large caged wagons, though even they seemed surprisingly relaxed. Nothing severe appeared to be going on, but still Krish and Balthrir kept their distance.

'Come on,' said Balthrir. 'We'll go through the farmlands in Tassi. It's the long way round but we might pick up some info on the way. And there's no road that way. You can only get there on foot. So we shouldn't run into any of this lot again till we reach the Great Plain.'

They journeyed for several days through farmlands which were far from rich with crops. The meagre amount growing in the fields tended to be dried out and dead-looking. Eventually they came across fertile fields. An old man was hard at work picking the leaves off a knee-high crop. He had a shock of messy hair, silver in colour, hay-like in texture, and was slim, his clothes baggy, but there were still muscles clinging to his old arms. He caught sight of Krish and Balthrir, pulled a marginally displeased expression, then returned to his work.

'If yer lookin' for the festival, it'd be quicker by the road,' the old man said with gruff indifference.

'Do what, mate?' said Balthrir. 'What festival?'

'We've been off, er, travelling,' Krish tried to explain. The old man didn't seem to care.

'What festival? Ha!' The old man continued with his work picking leaves, his breathing laboured, looking like he'd keel over at any moment. Krish and Balthrir waited on tenterhooks for the old farmer to elaborate but he said nothing.

'Yes!' barked Balthrir. 'What festiv—?'

'They can't make me go!' the old man interrupted. 'What's the point, eh? Forced fun and all that! What's the point? Old Obsendei wants to cheer up all the poor unhappy people in his kingdom by forcing 'em to have fun at his festival? Ha! Not for me! There's crops that still need harvestin'! They'll just go to waste 'less someone does summink. This old rebel'll be harvesting till 'e's more use as compost!'

'So, the King's holding a festival to keep everyone *happy*?' asked Krish.

'Ha! Makes the poor forget how poor they are for a time, eh?' said the old farmer. 'Not me! Plenty o' work still to do! All that accursed R'ghir's fault, they say!'

Krish remembered the name. R'ghir was one of the nobles: Lord of the East.

'One of 'is messengers turned up late,' the old man carried on. 'Lost a whole bag of Kalrahs. Taxes from the Lean Mountains. Said 'e'd fallen from 'is 'orse. A likely story! Took the money for 'imself, didn't 'e? R'ghir wanted to execute 'im, probably to save 'is own neck! Stop old Obsendei executin' 'im instead! Yer know what old Obsendei's like? Blames whoever's nearest! So this messenger spins some yarn. Says 'is 'orse was tripped over by some magic, invisible wall. Ha! Likely story, eh? Likely story! But old Obsendei loves the idea! Travels out there! 'E 'imself says it's real! This magic wall that nobody can see! Ha! Mad as a jagga-jagga! Now 'e's draggin' everyone, *forcin'* 'em to go to some festival! Festival o' magic with this magic wall at the middle of it. People like it! Mad as jagga-jaggas! Mad as an 'ole bunch o' jagga-jaggas! The lot of 'em! Not old Amsi! Not old Amsi, I say!'

They left 'old Amsi' to his ranting but they were now deeply concerned. This 'magic wall' that had tripped up the horse of one of R'ghir's messengers was clearly the twine, which Balthrir had made invisible and which ran straight across the Great Plain. It had become the centre of a festival that all the people of Al Kara had been forced to attend (not that it sounded like they needed much persuasion to skip work or school to be invited to a festival of magic). And it was the idea of the King himself. If he wasn't at his palace then it was very, very likely that he was at the festival. The King was in the right place, but getting his attention and making sure that he saw the twine being tied without their being stopped or arrested could prove a challenge.

Both Krish and Balthrir were lost in thought, trying to come up with a plan, as they trekked through the empty fields. They reached the woods on the edge of the land of Tassi by nightfall. There was very little twine left to unfurl as they made their way through the tall trees. A feast of faint sounds drifted through the night to the ears of the two weary travellers. Music. Great drumbeats. Applause. Cheering. The odd roar like fire exploding into the air followed by more applause. The anticipation of seeing what was happening on the Great Plain quashed any chance they had of trying to think up a plan.

The woods began to thin and a sea of flickering lights was visible up ahead. They emerged from the woods to a narrow ledge looking down on the plain below. The light of the five moons, Mother with her Sons dancing around her high in the sky above the plain, shining down on the tall towers of rock on the borders of the vast landscape, did little to illuminate the land below. Fire and torchlight were what lit up the night. A trail of torches from the carts and carriages snaking along the road led to a vast walled rectangle that practically filled all of the nearside of the Great Plain. Interior walls had been erected, splitting the enormous structure into many different areas, all of which were filled to the brim with people milling about this way and that. There were many torches to show people the way through the night. From some sections of the structure great fireballs would often burst into the sky, followed by enthusiastic applause. Spinning batons, hastily changing colour from vivid pink to neon green, then shining purple and orange and blue and red and indigo, were hurled into the air. More cheers. More fire. There were rows upon rows of stalls and a clamour of laughter and excitement all around. There was something odd about it all, though. Something not quite right in the sounds of cheering and jollity. Drumbeats and the music of strange instruments drifted up from the festival below.

As they inched forward to see the far side of the vast structure, Krish and Balthrir saw that one entire side, stretching past the end of the main festival area, almost reaching the halfway point of the plain, was a walled section, a sort of arena, empty in the middle, with tiered stalls each side full of spectators. Two figures on horseback cantered back and forth, sizing each other up from opposite sides. It was hard to tell with the large, dark-coloured splatters that were dotted about the ground here, but Krish had a nasty feeling that come daybreak, they would turn out to be blood red.

In the middle of the western side of the arena, the corner nearest them, a section of the stalls about the size of a house jutted out from the rest of the crowds. It was level rather than tiered and covered instead of open. Squinting in the darkness they could just make out the black drapes overhanging the sides of this box-like section of stalls. A golden crown was emblazoned across the drapes. Guards surrounded the box area, but from where they were seated, the front of the box faced away from them.

'Well,' said Balthrir. 'Yer've found yer King!'

'That's not all we've found.' Krish pointed and Balthrir followed his line of sight to an object not far from the royal box. A white tree, partially supporting one set of stalls. Their gaze traced their route months ago from the tree to the other side of the Great Plain. It ran directly through the middle of the arena. Krish now noticed that many of the bloodstains were one side of the invisible twine or the other. There was a sickening feeling in his stomach. Had people died because of the twine? He was filled with rage and wanted the King dead and gone more than ever. But he remembered all the bodies lining up in the Sands of Tyraah. Why was it that whatever course of action he chose, whether King Obsendei stayed or was removed by one means or another, many people would die?

One of the figures on horseback approached the centre of the arena.

It was difficult to see what was happening but the figure appeared to be holding something. A sword, he guessed. The figure brought the item crashing down on the invisible barrier at the centre of the arena. After a few seconds' delay, Krish had his arm almost yanked from its socket as there was a sharp tug on the twine.

After several minutes of indecision, they started their descent towards the festival. The line of carts and carriages became an expansive queue of humans, their modes of transport discarded haphazardly by the entrance. A whole battalion of guards were stretched out across the entry point to the festival, leaving only a small gap for people to filter through. The guard captain, sporting a majestic purple doublet over his armour, was barking at every citizen as they entered:

'You *will* attend His Most Magnificent Majesty's Festival of Magic! You *will* pay fifteen Kalrahs for the privilege! You *will* have a jolly good time!'

There was much grumbling at this.

'Fifteen Kalrahs?!'

'Extortion! That's what it is!'

'What if I don't want to have a good time?'

The guard captain stepped up to the dissenters and shouted in their faces, spittle flying from his mouth.

'YOU WILL PAY FIFTEEN KALRAHS! YOU WILL HAVE A JOLLY GOOD TIME! On pain of death or imprisonment! Those caught not smiling or only laughing infrequently *will* form part of His Most Wise and Noble Majesty's newly commissioned North Wing Extension of the Black Palace!'

The grumbling died down and those citizens in the queue practised their smiles. A pale, miserable-looking man with shaggy black hair looked almost pained when he tried to smile – like he'd never actually done it before.

'Not my idea of fun,' whispered Krish from their hiding place in the rocks.

'Nope,' said Balthrir. 'Just an excuse to wring a little bit more money out o' people. Fifteen Kalrahs!' She shook her head. 'Ridiculous!'

Beyond the line of guards they could see into the festival itself.

They climbed a little way back up the hill to get a clearer view of what was going on. There were many alleys full of stalls where children and adults alike were playing games. Throwing rocks at strange fruit to win a prize or trying to catch floating balls of water which held children's toys within. There was music and singing and a number of wizards had their own stages to perform tricks. They were busy turning parents into animals or making small children lift off the ground for a few moments, much to the amusement of the spectators. The wizards looked to Krish like someone had just given ordinary street performers a quick scrub and a half-decent outfit to wear. Their magic was okay but nothing compared to Balthrir's.

'Blimey!' said Balthrir with a smile that was both envious and amused. 'If I 'adn't sorta caused this festival malarkey I might 'ave actually got a job at it!'

'So how are we going to get in?' asked Krish. 'It looks very well guarded.'

The outer wall of the festival was a channel with guards on either side.

'They've gone to pretty extreme lengths to make sure everyone pays fifteen Kalrahs!' said Balthrir.

Krish thought for a moment and then voiced a mad idea out loud.

A great explosion ripped through the quiet in the guard channel and everyone stepped back from the blast zone.

'GET OUT THE WAY!' cried a guard. 'GET BACK!'

Two of the guards ran across to the inside of the guard channel. The rest of the guards were too busy reeling from the chaos around them to notice the hole the explosion had created in the wall or that two guards were just about to slip through into the northern end of the arena when...

'Balthrir...'

The two guards turned to see a familiar person holding a staff. The rounded face and kindly features of Balthrir's harsh but fair young teacher stared back at the two guards.

'You really have perfected those mask spells but now your perfection gives you away,' said Madam Nboosa.

CHAPTER 29

THE AMATEUR'S DEFIANCE

Madam Seesi Nboosa turned to a nearby guard captain. 'I will take these two to Madam Eshter myself.'

'Yes, Officer Nboosa!' answered the guard captain.

Nboosa escorted the pair of guards into an alley away from all the main areas. Several guards stepped forward to see what was happening and flinched as they came into contact with what felt like an invisible wire trailing behind the two guards Nboosa was escorting.

Nboosa and the two guards were now underneath the stalls of the arena. They could hear cheers from above and people stamping their feet in excitement. Nboosa waved her staff to reveal the two 'guards' as Krish and Balthrir.

'Oi!' said Balthrir, adopting a low voice in a valiant attempt at keeping up the pretence of being a guard. 'What 'ave you turned us into, lady!'

'I think you and your accomplice should drop it, Balthrir!' said Nboosa, looking not only angry but disappointed. 'They could have killed you if they'd realised you'd broken in!'

'Madam Nboosa!' said Krish, much to both Balthrir and Nboosa's surprise. 'It wasn't her fault! See, I kidnapped her and—'

'Oh, like you could kidnap me, mate!' said Balthrir.

'Your parents are fine.' Balthrir stared directly at Nboosa as her teacher said this. Balthrir suddenly looked like a child. A little relieved but desperate to know more. 'I imagine that's the question you've been wanting to ask,' Nboosa continued.

'I...' Balthrir was rarely speechless. She was totally confused.

'I knew about your parents, Balthrir,' said Nboosa quietly. 'I just hoped you'd stick around school long enough for me to teach you a little more. Then you might have been able to get a job and earn some money. Rather than trick people out of it! If it was magic you'd wanted to know I would have taught you some more if I could and—'

'Where are they?' said Balthrir impatiently. Krish had never seen his friend look so emotionally fragile as she waited to hear more about her parents.

'Still in the palace,' said Nboosa. 'The King's not removed anyone. Only added them. But don't think I didn't realise who it was you'd run off with!' She indicated Krish, who looked at his feet sheepishly. 'Some time after you'd left the King went mad. A description of a young boy very much fitting your young accomplice from the Broken Scythe here was circulated. Any information on him or anyone who was associated with him would be rewarded with three weeks' rations. Days later all went quiet. Story was, Madam Eshter had cast some spell to sort it all out and I was worried sick about you.'

'You ain't my Mum, miss!' said Balthrir. Although she'd spat the words out, Krish could see that Balthrir had a lot of respect for Nboosa. He'd always imagined her being in a lot of trouble with Nboosa if she ever returned, but it seemed that Nboosa was more concerned than anything else. 'And I ain't never seen that staff before!'

Nboosa smiled. 'I took my exams in secret long ago. But Madam Eshter was never keen on wizards in Al Kara unless they were lowly street performers. I had to keep my interest in magic a secret.'

'You're a wizard?!' said Krish.

Nboosa turned to Krish. 'Was it the staff that gave it away, by any chance?'

'I've never seen it before...' said Balthrir, in awe of Nboosa's staff, which was slim, curled round and round from top to bottom, and pearl white.

'You're not the only person from a magical family who struggled to make a living, Balthrir,' said Nboosa. Then her ears appeared to prick up. She'd heard something. All kindness disappeared from her voice and she adopted her strict teacher act once more. She spoke quickly, under her breath. 'Now whatever stupid scheme you're involved with, give it up! Go and sign up to Quaali's Freak Show and keep your head down until the festival's over! And if I—'

'WHERE ARE THEY?'

Krish, Balthrir and Nboosa turned to see a furious Madam Eshter striding in their direction, incandescent with rage. Her face as pale as porcelain, her eyes wild with fury. Her orange and blue hair flew behind her. The misty jewel twisted into the roots atop her staff glowed brightly.

'Somebody has committed magic here!' said Eshter, advancing on Nboosa. 'You! Amateur! Please don't tell me you've failed at the position we gave you.' Eshter seemed far more energetic than before. Krish was certain that her hair was falling out, and she kept running her hands through it, grabbing at clumps like she might just tear some of it out there and then.

Nboosa was trying her best to mask her contempt for Eshter. 'Just some stupid kids trying to show off!' Nboosa kicked Krish in the back so hard that he fell over. Before he could stand up and swear at her he realised why she'd done it. Nboosa had worked out who Krish was and that Eshter was on the lookout for him and his associates. Eshter didn't know what Balthrir looked like but she did know what he looked like. Everyone in Al Kara seemed to know about his confrontation with the King in the Black Palace months ago by the sound of it. Nboosa had kicked him onto his front, facing away from Eshter. 'This one has some promise though.' Nboosa was now pointing at Balthrir.

Eshter waved her staff in front of Balthrir. The crystal glowed red for a moment. 'But not a magic licence, I see. How did she get in?'

'She used a distraction to sneak through the perimeter,' said Nboosa. 'An impressive fire-cast.'

'And you of course would know what constitutes "good", wouldn't you, amateur?' Eshter's goading of Nboosa was not received well but again Balthrir's former teacher stifled her scorn. 'She should be imprisoned in the Black Tower or perhaps even executed!'

Krish almost looked up in shock but then managed to keep his face turned away from Eshter, viewing the confrontation out of the corner of his eye.

'And I thought you, Madam Eshter, would know better than to waste such talent propping up the walls of His Most Magnanimous Majesty's bloated palace,' said Nboosa.

'I don't have time for this, amateur!' said Eshter. 'The King is laughing heartily, and you know what that means?'

Krish was a little mystified. Was this really a bad thing if the King was happy?

'It means,' stated Eshter, 'that he will exhaust himself with laughter and grow weary of any entertainment thrown in front of him fairly soon. Then he will probably start executing any subjects, high-born or low, who displease him. Most likely whoever is nearest. And I do not desire some amateur such as you taking my place and enchanting my bones to dance a jig for him! So am I going to stand here and watch as you imprison them or—' Eshter raised her staff '—shall I despatch them here and now...?'

'They would do better as part of Quaali's Freak Show,' Nboosa ventured. If she was hiding her desperation in her face, from where Krish was crouching he could hear it in her voice.

'As would you.' Eshter relished the cruelness of her own words.

Nboosa considered. 'Perhaps,' she said. Krish swore there was a hint of humour in her voice. 'But if you want to keep your King amused, I think you may be missing an opportunity with this one...'

Krish turned a little more. Eshter was looking away from him, eyeing Balthrir up and down as if she was a mysterious brown lump that had just been served to her for dinner.

'Show her...' said Nboosa to Balthrir. Then she turned back to Madam Eshter. 'Her mask spells are incredible.'

Balthrir sprang into action. She stood a little way back from Eshter and Nboosa, giving herself plenty of space. She waved her staff and a giant green rabbit ran in one direction, then a pink elephant in the other and finally a purple horse with yellow spots in yet another direction. They all circled back. Eshter readied her staff for attack but was too intrigued to act. She was distracted enough for Krish to crane his head all the way round to watch. The giant green rabbit, pink elephant and purple horse with yellow spots sped past Balthrir, obscuring her from view for a moment and when they had passed, the figure standing there in her place was none other than King Obsendei.

'Don't gawp at me like that, Eshter!' said the vision of the King. 'Or we'll see just how good your ribcage is as a toast rack!'

Eshter closed her open mouth and waved her staff in front of the vision of the King and all the animals vanished, leaving Balthrir standing there, still pulling her best stern expression to impersonate Obsendei. Eshter was not willing to show how impressed she had or hadn't been.

'Very good illusionary and mask spells indeed,' said Eshter softly, narrowing her eyes and stroking the side of her face in deep thought. A sly smile was spreading across her lips. 'Perhaps... yes, perhaps this child's skills will be an effective distraction... allow me to correct myself: a temporary relief from the ongoing fights in the arena which could persuade him to consider less bloody amusements in the days to come. Yes... Well, he'll either love her or hate her. It'll keep him occupied for a while. I would advise against an impression of His Majesty himself though, young lady. I'll take her to the holding area for the performers. As for him...' Krish quickly looked away again so Eshter wouldn't see his face. 'I want him imprisoned. See to it, amateur!'

Krish heard Eshter march off with Balthrir. He braved turning to look. They were still just about visible. Eshter glanced over her shoulder and for a moment she stared directly at Krish. A stab of fear coursed through his body. Had she seen him? Was he far enough away for her not to recognise him? There was quiet. Eshter and Balthrir had stopped. Moments later the footsteps started again.

'Come on!' said Nboosa, stepping forward to help him up.

'No, please!' begged Krish. 'There's a tree. Just over there at the edge of the arena. Can you get me to it?'

'Listen, boy, if I'm caught—'

'If *I'm* caught a lot people will die,' said Krish with all the persuasion he could muster. '*A lot of people!*' Was that true? It could be. The Sands of Tyraah had been so unclear. All he knew was that he wanted to show the King just what he had in his bag. And then he wouldn't care what happened to the wicked old monarch. He only cared that Balthrir and her parents would be okay. 'If you've had it up to here with Obsendei, I strongly suggest you point me in the direction of that tree and let me go.' He looked straight at Nboosa and hoped he looked suitably commanding.

Nboosa stared back for a time and then nodded. She pointed through the shadows under the tiered seating, in the direction of the royal box. 'Be quick,' she said. 'And if you fancy knocking Madam Eshter down a peg or two in the process...' She didn't say 'good luck' in as many words but it was there in the nod she gave.

Krish darted towards the far end of the stalls, carrying the twine with him. He crouched as the tiered seating reached its lowest points. He could see people's feet through the slats. He could hear cheers and chants and smell sweat in the air. And there was the tree. Small, white and dead-looking. A few ropes had been tied around the tree to help support the stalls but as he ran his hand over the dry wood, he came to an invisible barrier. It was still there. He undid the twine. He'd waited for this moment for a very, very long time. There was still a fair bit of excess twine in the ball they'd been unfurling. He found the end and prepared to tie the two together...

No. He'd wait. Krish decided that there was a better way. Obsendei had to be watching. And pretty soon he should have a way to seize the King's attention.

CHAPTER 30

THE ARENA

The light of dawn was spreading over the bloodstained floor of the arena. Krish crouched behind the tree and looked out on the chaos taking place on the cordoned-off area of the Great Plain. The space between the two opposing rows of the audience went on for miles. It was strewn with blood, swords, spears, daggers and the corpses of men, women and horses, which were attracting far more attention from the flies than from the spectators. The audience were busy cheering a group of knights, three on each side of the invisible barrier, which Krish knew full well was the twine.

The crowd were laughing and cheering at the goings-on down in the arena and guards were posted at many points within the stalls, just making certain that everyone was enjoying themselves. Krish saw one old lady, who clearly preferred being asleep, being dragged away by the guards.

A great cry from the crowd, half sounding disappointed and the other half triumphant. One knight had relieved an opponent of his head. Another retaliated by launching her horse over the barrier and sticking her sword clean through the perpetrator. The perpetrator, knowing his days were numbered, pulled the sword even deeper into his torso with such speed that the sword's owner was pulled close to him. Krish watched the grisly scene as the two fell from their horses and rolled about on the ground, the skewered knight resorting to using the twine (the end was almost yanked out of Krish's hand) to strangle his opponent before collapsing and moving no more. The crowd went wild. Only three knights remained, two on one side and a lone knight on the other.

Krish realised that he needed to do something to stop himself dropping the two ends of the twine. He wouldn't be able to reveal the pearl and feather in his bag to the King unless he had his hands free.

He placed one end of the twine carefully under his foot and tied the other around his right-hand wrist. Then he took the end under his foot and tied it to his left-hand wrist. He just hoped that a horse didn't run straight across the path of the twine and pull one or both of his hands off. He crept a little closer to the royal box. Nobody was looking down as everything was going on in the distance. He inched closer. He could hear voices now. Familiar voices. He took a few more steps into the arena.

'Caution, sire! Caution!' said Eshter. She hadn't wasted any time in heading to the royal box. Her haste concerned Krish.

'Oh, be silent, Eshter!' That cruel, mocking voice. So arrogant, so lazy, so self-important. He hadn't heard the King's voice in months and still it made him boil with rage. 'Look! LOOK! This one's going to take the other out!'

Krish looked up at the confrontation taking place on the arena floor. One knight went to strike the other with his sword, missed and hit the invisible twine instead. The crowd were uproariously disappointed and Krish was yanked in two different directions as the twine buckled under the impact of the knight's blade. Krish quickly regained his balance and saw an opportunity while the crowd were distracted. There was a simple wooden chariot on its side next to the corpses of a knight and a horse. He ran towards them and ducked down by the chariot. He waited for some reaction to his dash. None came. He peered out into the royal box.

There he was. Those grey, chilling, indifferent eyes, sharp nose and his beard of grey and white. He slouched in his wooden throne, his bejewelled wooden crown upon his head, shouting and jeering encouragement at the crowd. Every time he became enthusiastic Eshter pointed her staff towards his throat and the King's voice was amplified for the whole stadium to hear. The audience took their cues from the monarch, cautious to cheer anyone until the King had done so first. Krish hated how the King sat back lazily in his throne, as the arena did their best to appease this selfish man. In that moment Krish just wished for the whole royal box to collapse on top of him.

Also in attendance were the King's closest advisors: R'ghir, Lord of the East, richly dressed, as tall and slim as a pole, his beard trimmed short. Elwynt, Lord of the West, plump, pale and nervous. Hesh, Lord of the South, short, slouched, cautious-looking but calm and self-assured. And then there was Vira, Lady of the North, fearsome yet beautiful. Her smile could bring any admirer to their knees, and her hands, free of rings or jewellery, her nails blood-red in colour, looked ready. For what, Krish did not want to imagine. Surrounding them were various other nobles, servants and advisors, plus a few of Obsendei's bored-looking wives and husbands, helping themselves to platters of fruit, meat and cheese.

'Sire, please!' said Eshter through gritted teeth. 'I saw someone!' Krish was panicking. She had recognised him! Did she remember from where? She was pacing up and down, rubbing her head, pulling at her hair distractedly.

'And I am seeing many people right now!' The King laughed. 'Relax, Eshter! I'll remove your head if it's bothering you...'

Eshter stopped pacing and yanking at her hair. 'A good joke, sire,' she said. 'But I'm serious. I saw someone and I knew their face! I cannot remember where I've seen it before but I tell you something's wrong!'

Krish, hidden by the chariot, was somewhat relieved that Eshter hadn't worked out where she recognised him from yet. He didn't have long. Should he reveal himself now or wait? He really needed everyone's attention or the King might be able to brush him aside. Where was Balthrir? When was this half-time show Nboosa had mentioned? Would she be allowed to perform on her own? What she see him and be able to draw everyone's attention to him?

'Will you just relax and – OOOOHHH!' The King stood up and clapped heartily. Eshter held up her staff to his throat so his voice was amplified. 'Fantastic! Fantastic!' He waved the staff away so his voice returned to normal volume. 'Did you see that?! Her own team-mate! Just pulled out a dagger and cut his throat! What style!' He flapped his hands about excitedly, signalling that Eshter should hold her staff up to his throat again. Eshter sighed and did as she was bidden. 'We have our finalists!' the King called out.

The crowd went mad.

'And now they will embark on their final challenge! The first over my magic wall will be rewarded with riches beyond their wildest dreams!'

More uproarious cheering and then the two knights stood side by side, shook hands and mounted their steeds.

'THREE! TWO!' The crowd joined in the King's cries. 'ONE!'

The knights accelerated from one side of the arena to the other. Faster and faster they went. Krish's brain raced. He had to do something or his arms would be pulled clean out of their sockets as the knights collided with the twine. The knights were getting closer and closer. Krish didn't have time to untie the twine from his wrists. He hastily wrapped the excess twine around the shaft of the chariot and braced for the impact. He hoped it would just splinter the shaft rather than pull his arms off with it. With an almighty crash both horses tripped over the wire, sending their riders hurtling through the air. The shaft burst into splinters and Krish was pulled to the ground as the twine tightened but then a moment later the twine returned to its normal level of slackness. The crowd's full attention remained on the two knights' collision. They laughed and cheered in equal measure and the King was enjoying every second of the bizarre festivities.

'My magic wall has claimed two more victims!' the King cried. 'But who was victorious…? Good Lady Knight Palseferous…?'

One rather dizzy-looking knight bowed, almost falling over in the process.

'Or good Sir Knight Althrain?'

The second knight *did* fall over as he bowed.

The King turned to an advisor. The advisor stared blankly back. Realising she should probably respond, she shrugged and then quickly bowed apologetically, apparently quite relieved to find that her head was still attached to her body as she brought it up to meet the King's gaze. He was clearly having too good a time to litter the royal box with the blood of fools.

'Our verdict is—' the King addressed the crowd '—too close to call! Maybe they will decide for themselves who the victor is!' The King pulled a gold plate from under the lump of cheese one of his larger husbands was munching on, and tossed it at the two knights, who then fought around in the dirt to claim it. The crowd found this all hilarious.

'And you wanted war, Vira, Lady of the North!' said the King, which Vira greeted with one of her coy smiles. 'Would we have made this much with the sale of arms?'

'Surely not, Your Most Gracious Majesty,' said Vira, her smile both sly and beautiful. 'And there was I thinking, so foolishly I see now, that guaranteed financial gain would benefit the kingdom so much more than a mad gamble on a brand-new festival, O Fortunate King. How wise, how fortuitous Your Most Majestic Highness and his trusted wizard Eshter are. The wisdom of your many combined years – I apologise – *centuries* certainly does not make fools of you both.' There it was again, Krish thought as he stared over at the royal box, that fire in her eyes. Vira's calm exterior hid some unparalleled ferocity beneath.

'Of course not!' continued the King. He gestured to Eshter to raise her staff again. 'MAGNIFICENT MAGNIFICENT!' He turned back to Vira. 'We are swimming in riches once more! Each one of them bought a ticket – well, was *made* to buy a ticket – and the gullible fools even seem to be enjoying themselves!' Eshter quickly woke up and stopped pointing the staff at the King's throat but the crowd were cheering too loudly to hear what the King had said. He scowled briefly at Eshter before staring daggers at Vira, who successfully hid the smugness in her smile. The King looked out to see the two knights still fighting over the gold plate. 'This has become exceedingly dull. Let's have these two executed. Yes! Let's have a mass execution! Perhaps some prisoners or...'

While the King was lost in thought, Eshter jumped in with a suggestion. 'Perhaps you should see how you feel after the half-time show, My Most Wise and Noble Majesty.'

'The half-time what?!'

Eshter held her staff aloft. Krish glanced in the direction Eshter was looking. He just caught it – a guard by one of the entrances in the stalls had nodded in response. He in turn nodded to someone unseen behind the stalls. Krish hoped more than anything that it was Balthrir. If it wasn't, should he risk trying to get the King's attention? What if the King just had him dragged off before anyone could see? No. He had to wait. He'd gone through so much to win the Myrthali off the King, to save his Mum's life, that he wouldn't squander his only chance with impatience.

As he was still pondering this thought, a wall of fire shot across the stadium. The audience shrieked. The King looked up slowly, curiously in the direction of the flaming barricade which had just sprung up at the centre of the arena.

'What new amusement is this...?' he said, toying with his grey-white beard.

Seconds passed. The wall of flame remained. Anticipation mounted. All eyes were on this baffling vision on the arena floor. Then great shapes came haring forward out of the fire. Gigantic elephants performing somersaults, tigers doing back-flips, majestic birds pirouetting through the air and cows dancing jigs. People whooped and cheered. Krish knew Balthrir was good but this was unbelievable. He turned to gauge the King's reaction. He sat in his throne, smiling and shaking his head, awestruck.

Then a figure emerged from the flames and Krish saw the familiar visage of... Elwynt. Yes, it was Elwynt, Lord of the West. The plump lord ran from side to side, being chased by an elephant.

'Your Majesty!' cried the vision of Elwynt from the arena floor.

The King burst into hysterics. He turned to the real Elwynt behind him. Elwynt looked at the vision of himself in dismay. He felt his own belly, just checking that it really was as large as it appeared out in the arena.

'Please, Your Majesty, please!' screamed the vision of Elwynt. 'I don't know how they escaped! I was just so busy eating cheese and smoked grambit and drinking lots and lots and lots of wine that I didn't have time to make sure they were secure! AAAR-RRGGGHHH!' The elephant caught up with Elwynt and squashed him. The real Elwynt winced, still holding his belly, as the King continued to laugh wildly. The crowd followed his lead.

As the elephant departed, a new vision stood up in the spot where Elwynt had been. This time it was Hesh, Lord of the South. Hesh was shorter and slimmer than Elwynt and he looked even more cowardly than usual. 'Please, My Liege!' The elephant chased him. 'Please stop the elephant! I'll do the whole harvest of Melkur myself! I'll sleep in the cowshed and you can use me as a compost heap!'

Krish didn't know quite how accurate Balthrir's impressions of the lords were but the King was lapping it up. Hesh was caught between two elephants charging towards him. They crashed into each other. Hesh and the two elephant shapes became one unfocused blob and then morphed into two new shapes: R'ghir, Lord of the East, with his rich-looking robes and short beard, and a large, snarling tiger which R'ghir clutched in his arms. The tiger kept trying to bite and scratch at R'ghir but the lord was defiant. 'I can tax a tiger!' said the vision of R'ghir. 'Look at me, Your Majesty! I can do it! I can tax a tiger! I can tax anything! A-ha-ha-ha-ha!'

Krish watched as the King rocked back and forth in his throne laughing. The crowd were also falling about the place in hysterics, much of it genuine, it seemed. Even R'ghir chuckled a little, until his own vision was swallowed by the tiger. The tiger burped then stood on its hind legs.

'Well, well, well,' said the tiger in a beautiful, seductive voice. It strode gracefully in the direction of the royal box. 'What have we got here...?'

The laughter was dying down. The crowd were curious. They all recognised the voice. Then the tiger was on fire. Engulfed in flames it continued to stroll elegantly towards the royal box. Its eyes were still visible and looking directly at the King.

'Is this a mirror your Lady of the North sees before her...?' said the voice of the tiger. Except it was no longer a tiger. The flames had died down and the form of Vira came gradually to a halt. Upon her head was a crown. The laughter had ceased. 'Yes, is this a mirror...?'

The King was frozen to the spot. He was eagerly awaiting the vision's next move. Vira looked into her own eyes. Her expression was one of hunger, a smirk on her cherry lips.

'Or a dream that will never become a reality?' said the vision of Vira. 'Oops!' The vision tripped and the crown fell from her head. The crowd let out a laugh and for the first time it was the King who followed suit. The vision of Vira stood up straight but was still looking a little wobbly. 'O Your Most Wonderful Incredible Smart-arse Clever-clogs Majesty! I was so certain it would fit me! Silly old me! I'm just so clever with all my amazing words that I thought one day you might just hand it over to me.' The vision winked at the King. 'But turns out I'm not as smart as I am beautiful and maybe I'm not as beautiful as I am smart and now I'm so confused by my own cleverness that I might just take a nap next to your bravest knight. Promise you won't chop off my pretty old head now!' The vision of Vira winked again at the King.

The King was hysterical. The crowd were roaring with laughter. It may not have been the most accurate impression but everyone loved it. Disturbingly, though, Krish saw that Vira was smiling. Her mouth closed, barely putting any effort into her grin, one hand folded tidily over the other. She was the very image of beauty, elegance and cunning. She nodded her approval to her own vision, then turned to the Lords Elwynt, Hesh and R'ghir and nodded at them also, her smile unwavering. Krish did not like the lords' hostile glances at Vira any more than he liked Vira's immovable grin. He was deeply suspicious but had quickly turned back to the vision of Vira. He had a feeling his cue was on its way. He began to untie the twine from around his wrists.

'So...' said the vision of Vira, marching towards the royal box. 'You enjoy a seeing a familiar face...?'

The King was still chuckling away uncontrollably. The vision of Vira became a haze. All the animals and the wall of fire faded to nothing. The vision of Vira turned at last into Balthrir. She marched confidently up to the royal box and stopped. She tried to stay looking calm and collected while also scanning the vicinity for signs of Krish. Krish chanced sticking his head over the top of the chariot. Balthrir caught his eye. A nod between the two of them. With one hand Krish was fumbling with the bag containing the pearl and the feather, while with the other he kept hold of the two ends of the twine. Moments later he was prepared.

'Well,' said Balthrir, raising her staff. 'One more won't do any harm then.' She turned and indicated the chariot. Krish took a deep breath and, with the eyes of thousands of citizens in the arena upon him, he emerged.

There was a murmuring of unrest among the crowd.

The sight of the King was enough to frighten the hardiest of men but Krish found himself feeling calm. He'd faced death so many times that this cruel-looking man in his crown no longer intimidated him all that much.

'Your Majesty,' Krish began in his noblest of voices, Balthrir's staff amplifying his voice for all to hear. 'I seek an audience with you.'

The King glanced around the near-silent arena. The crowd were intrigued – maybe this was all part of the show.

'Well you seem to have an audience with me whether I desire it or not,' said the King.

'THAT'S HIM! THAT'S HIM!' Eshter had stepped forward, wild with excitement, pointing an accusing finger at Krish. 'I REMEMBER HIS FACE! HE'S—'

The King raised his hand to silence his court wizard. The urgency died in her tired old eyes.

'Your Majesty,' Krish continued, 'you recall some months ago a young boy who visited you requesting your Myrthali in return for—'

The King was no longer amused. All his good humour had vanished in an instant. 'I recall making no such promise for any price! Why would I—?'

'You don't recall asking for this…?'

Nobody had ever interrupted the King in his long reign and even Balthrir was shocked for a moment. But the world forgot the incident without delay when Krish, whose hand was curled up by his shoulder, clutching something hidden by the bag placed over it, unfurled his arm. The bag dropped to the ground. The crowd shrieked once more as Krish held aloft the shining pearl from the Night Ocean. Eshter's eyes did not believe it. R'ghir, Elwynt and Hesh were entranced, greed in their faces. Vira let out a short, self-satisfied laugh.

The King considered this for a moment, his countenance stubborn. His expression cracked into a smile and a chuckle escaped his lips.

'I know you remember me,' said Krish. 'I know you thought your precious Myrthali was threatened. I know you sent the Vulrein after me. And you know what? They ran off screaming…'

The King's eyes hadn't left the pearl.

'Impossible! Absolutely impossible!' said the King.

'Ask me before Gul—'

'And even if it were from the Night Ocean, I believe I also requested…'

The pearl thudded to the ground and revealed the smaller object Krish had been concealing. A glass jar containing a golden-white feather, still aflame, in the crook of his arm. Using the thumb and forefinger of his left hand (he was trying to hide the fact he was clutching the two ends of the twine in this hand) he transferred the jar to his right hand, which moments ago had been holding the pearl. He held the object aloft. The beautiful feather sat at the centre of the jar, surrounded by flame.

'The feather of a FireHawk!' said the stunned Eshter, not realising how loudly she'd spoken (or that her own staff was now amplifying her voice). 'How can it still be aflame?!'

The effect it had on the crowd silenced the King once more. But he soon regained his composure.

'I care not for these trinkets,' he said. He gestured for the guards to approach Krish and Balthrir. Balthrir held out her staff warningly but guards were approaching on several sides. She was clearly conflicted as to whether or not attack was the best option right now.

'But Your Majesty,' said Krish, 'you said before Gul—'

'Oi! Let go!' Krish was momentarily distracted from listening to the King while Balthrir struggled with a guard who'd snuck up behind her and was trying to take her staff.

'If I had wanted a pearl from the Night Ocean,' said the King, 'or a feather from a FireHawk, I have no doubt—'

'Let go!' protested Balthrir.

'Gimme the staff, miss!' said the guard wrestling with Balthrir.

'—I could have ordered one of my bravest knights—' continued the King.

'Give it back!'

'—to obtain them for me!'

'GIVE IT BACK!'

Eshter's eyes narrowed and she gripped her staff tightly, raising it a little as she looked over at Balthrir struggling with the guard.

'Besides, as my recollection is somewhat improved,' continued the King, 'I believe there was one more task I set... And I don't see a pretty bow tied around the entirety of—'

'Blimey!' said Balthrir, glancing over the guard's shoulder. 'Is-that-a-guard-lookin'-the-wrong-way?'

'What?!'

The guard followed Balthrir's gaze and while he was distracted she snatched back her staff. In a single motion she swung the staff as far forward as she could reach and struck the twine. Eshter thrust her own staff forward, casting a spell that knocked Balthrir's staff out of her hands, but its work had already been done. A jet of light flowed through the twine and seconds later it had travelled around the entire globe of Ilir and reached the end of the thread in Krish's hands. The twine glowed in the midday sun and all the colours of the rainbow could be glimpsed as the light caught it. A gargantuan shriek from the crowd, then silence, then finally applause.

Krish brought his two hands together and—

'STOP HIM!' cried the King. 'STOP HIM!'

The guards rushed forward but it was too late. Krish's defiant eyes locked with the King's as he tied the two ends into a little bow. Balthrir pulled Krish out of the way before the guard brought down his sword. The sword hit the twine, then rebounded and flew up into the air as the guard fell to the ground. Balthrir picked up her staff and smiled smugly at Eshter.

'Sunlight twine! It's sunlight twine!' cried the King, unbelievingly. He reached for something in his pocket. 'I'll cut it!' He rushed forward. 'I'LL CUT THAT DAMN—'

'Sire...'

Gritted teeth and wild, furious eyes met Eshter's sheepish face.

'It is already done.'

The look the King gave the old wizard in return had the desired effect. Eshter gave a polite smile and a tired sigh in apology. 'I'll just...' She reached for a sword and held it up high, hoping she could lop her own head off before one of the clumsy palace guards made a mess of the task. (She'd seen the one standing closest to her trying to saw a loaf of bread in half with a rusty spoon once before so she didn't hold out much hope of her own demise at his hands being a swift affair.) But the King wasn't interested in punishing her right now.

'I have no time for fools! A SEA OF FOOLS IS LAID OUT BEFORE ME! I AM DROWNING IN THEM!' The King screamed at the crowd. Then he paced back and forth, the crowd clapping and chanting in celebration at Krish and Balthrir's achievement all the while.

'*Pretty!*' the King spat out. 'I-I-I said it must be *pretty*! A-a-a-a pretty bow to tie around the world, I said! I do not consider this monstrosity *pretty!*'

'Oh, come off it, mate!' chipped in Balthrir. "E tied it round the bloody world! What d'yer want? Flippin' great flowers on it or summink?'

'And you! YOU!' The King pointed accusingly at Balthrir. 'YOU helped him! I-I said *him*! And *him* alone!'

'*He* dived into the Night Ocean! *He* tied the bow—'

'But the feather! The feather! Did *he* take the feather or did—?'

'Sire...' Eshter clearly hadn't diced with enough death for one day. Not that anything seemed to trouble the tired old wizard that much any more.

'What?!' said the King.

'Erm. Well... Gulwin, whose songs of truth never e—'

'Yes, yes, yes! I am more than well acquainted with the feathered little jackanapes!'

'Well... the law decrees that if there is any doubt in the truth of matters then he must be called upon to determine the facts.'

The King's sigh would have been a roar if the excitable crowd were not doing an excellent job of drowning him out.

'Very well.'

CHAPTER 31

THE BIRD IN THE DEEP

The King declared Krish and Balthrir prisoners until their testament was proven true and imprisoned them in the slave carriage, which, despite the smell, was quite a relief to them, seeing as they had just travelled the world by foot. The carriage was essentially a cage on wheels, the size of a lorry, pulled by six horses. The slaves found the whole story of their adventures hysterical. Balthrir must have re-enacted it about a dozen times before they reached the Black Palace. They particularly loved her retelling of Krish's first encounter with the Vulrein.

'Oh, Balthrir! Balthrir! Help me! Those nasty dogs are coming to get me!' The high-pitched voice she added and the exaggerated feint that followed were met with guffaws and even Krish found it hilarious. Many didn't believe all the stories of the strange creatures Krish had encountered in the deep or the way the Vulrein had formed a single creature but Balthrir had a secret weapon which she used to convince them: the Salvean blade. It was so small, only the handle visible unless held up in direct sunlight, that the guards hadn't confiscated it as they had her staff. She cut a beam of sunlight out of the air and the slaves gasped in disbelief as it fell and sizzled on the ground. Balthrir loved all the attention and even gave away some of her itching powder for the slaves to use on the guards, although she spilt some of it and three slaves found themselves itching like crazy on the floor of the carriage while everyone else roared with laughter. The merriment put from their minds the fact that they'd be in trouble once the King realised it was Balthrir who'd caught the feather from the FireHawk.

The festival had been declared over (due to the King's rotten mood) and as they left the festivities Krish and Balthrir saw the stalls, the seating areas and the walls of the festival enclosure itself being taken down. The carts and carriages on the road moved aside for the King and his prisoners. A second carriage of slaves followed them, Eshter riding on a horse in front of this carriage. Krish was less than happy to see Madam Nboosa imprisoned in the large barred carriage behind them. Every now and then Eshter snarled at Balthrir's teacher. Krish had a nasty feeling they could be seeing Nboosa in the walls of the Black Palace very soon. Despite the sight of the imprisoned Nboosa leaving Krish with a sinking feeling in his stomach, he turned back to Balthrir and enjoyed the unexpectedly jolly proceedings aboard the slave carriage for the rest of the journey.

The jovial atmosphere evaporated the moment they arrived at the Black Palace. Krish and Balthrir were escorted to the throne room in silence. The King was pacing not far from the apparently bottomless well cut into the ground on the far side of the chamber. His wives and husbands, scantily clad as always, were lounging nearby on golden chaises longues and in golden bathtubs. The pearl from the Night Ocean and the jar containing the feather from the FireHawk were being passed around. Many shrieked in awe at the sight of one or the other, smiled brightly and then passed it on to their neighbour. Many nobles, including R'ghir, Hesh, Elwynt and Vira, had placed themselves exactly halfway between the King and the throne. Eshter stood next to the well.

The King turned to Krish and Balthrir.

'You!' he said to one or both of them, neither was sure. 'Here!'

The guards marched them both up to the King. His Most Royal Majesty stared into them, his brow heavy with the weight of his long years finally coming to an end.

'You...' This was definitely aimed at Krish. 'I set you three tasks. *You!* And you alone. In return for this...' The King's arm gestured towards the Myrthali in the font made of crouching prisoners and in it Krish saw his home, the park, the streets, Bob's Store on the corner. Even the hospital. And of course, his Mum, that laboured smile becoming lighter with happiness at the sight of him by her bedside. 'That was my word. That you may be entitled to this bounty should you follow my requests *to the letter...* Did *you* dive into the Night Ocean to bring me back this pearl...?' He now pointed towards the shiny object in the lap of one of the prettiest of his wives.

Krish looked at the pearl and back to the King.

'Yes,' answered Krish.

The King turned to Eshter, who looked down at the well. A few delicate notes echoed from the deep.

'O wise Gulwin,' said Eshter, 'whose song of truth—'

'Never ends, yes, yes, yes!' came the King's agitated voice.

'—says the boy speaks the truth.'

The King turned back to Krish. 'And the feather—' Krish saw the jar in the hands of a slender husband '—you plucked this from a Fire-Hawk...?'

Krish considered this. It was all about to come tumbling down. But he could not lie. Not this time.

'No,' said Krish. 'I delivered it to you but I had assistance. From Balthrir.'

A look to Eshter and a distant chirp agreed on this.

'And did this Balthrir help with anything else...? Such as acquiring the twine or helping transport it...?'

'Yes. But I tied it.'

A look, a chirp, a nod. The King looked back at Krish, somewhat calmer now.

'Then this is not your Myrthali...'

The sinking feeling in Krish was deeper than the Night Ocean, than any sea that could ever exist in any world. He just wanted to step forward and strangle the life out of the old King. What he would do now he had no idea, until a faint note from the deep sparked a little hope in him.

'Gulwin,' spoke Eshter, 'proclaims this to be a lie.' The King's eyes widened at Eshter as the bird continued his song. 'Gulwin says that His Most Noble Majesty promised the boy every last grain of his Myrthali if he brought him a pearl from the Night Ocean and a still-flaming feather from a FireHawk. Who acquired these items in the first place is immaterial. The challenge was that *he* was to *deliver them*, and this he has done. Similarly with the bow, using a wizard or indeed anyone else does *not* disqualify him. He set out to tie a bow around the world and we all witnessed him achieve it. From this day forth,

King Obsendei's Myrthali will become the legal property of the boy known as Krish.'

It was as if that sinking feeling had exploded into a joyous sensation which took over his whole body. Relief soared within him and he looked at Balthrir and both laughed with happiness.

'Very well...' The King's voice was sly, hesitant. 'So my commitment is to deliver the Myrthali to the boy? Nothing more...?'

Gulwin confirmed this.

'I see...' More pacing and pondering from the King before he eventually emptied the font of Myrthali into a leather satchel. He stared at the satchel for some moments, the realisation of his loss apparently spreading through his mind. 'Then I shall indeed deliver My Myrthali, My Sands of Time, My Protector From...' For a moment, a handful of seconds, the brutal, unforgiving King Obsendei was quiet, reflective. He stared at the ground, unmoving. A statue of his old self, frozen in a moment of realisation. '... From What Awaits Us All... eventually.' The statue that was King Obsendei returned to life. The old man looked at Krish and Balthrir, something different in his ancient eyes.

The King approached Krish with the Myrthali. He stared into Krish but was reluctant to hand over the satchel. Obsendei was considering his next move. Krish had waited so long for this moment and, just after believing himself to be victorious, he now had doubts. He glanced over at Balthrir. She glanced back, a wary look in her eyes. She looked around to see where all the guards were standing, where Eshter stood, to the King and then back to Krish, who'd been following her gaze. Was she considering making a break for it if it all went wrong? She was staring again at Eshter's staff. Eshter watched the King but her grip on her staff hadn't slackened. Everyone was eyeing the King and Krish, wondering if there was going to be a fight. The walls tensed, breathing slowly in anticipation. All around hands were on swords, ready to unsheathe them.

Krish saw one guard, not too far away, so mesmerised by the goings-on in the chamber that his hand remained by his side, not on the grip of his sword. *Could I reach it?* thought Krish. *Could I do it? Slay the King?* His fury at the King for goading him in the throne room at their first meeting had been eating away at him for so long he decided yes. He didn't care what was wrong, what was right, what he'd seen in the Sands of Tyraah. He'd do it. If he could reach that sword…

And then, the one thing nobody expected to happen occurred. Something that had never been seen within the walls of the Black Palace. King Obsendei bent one knee, lowered himself to the ground and knelt before Krish. He held the satchel of Myrthali aloft and bowed his head.

The reaction in the chamber was instantaneous. The entire palace seemed to gasp; a gust of air as every prisoner making up the walls inhaled in shock. The wives and husbands held hands to their mouths in horror. The nobles and advisors narrowed their eyes. All those who did not form part of the walls of the palace were looking down on their King for the first time.

Krish hesitated no more. He stepped forward and lifted the satchel out of the King's hands. His eyes had been only on the satchel for some moments now, and as he pulled it away from Obsendei, he, and indeed the whole room, were audibly shocked. The King was no longer a tall, imposing figure. He was diminished in stature, his beard now completely white and thinning, his arms no more than bones with crinkled skin hanging off them. His whole complexion was paler, a hint of ash about him. His eyes were ancient and misty, staring up at Krish like a lost puppy.

Some nobles began to smile, to stand tall, to move into position, closer to the King. They eyed their prey with glee.

Krish was now aware of what the consequences of his quest were about to become. Although he was still breathing, the King was, to all intents and purposes, dead. Deposed. As he rose gradually to his feet, the robe hanging loose on his shrivelled frame, Krish noticed that the crown now looked heavy upon his head. He and Balthrir had effectively dethroned the King.

A few moments more and the former fierceness in the King's eyes began to resurface. His voice was hoarse, croaky, but still strong. 'I deliver my entire stock of Myrthali unto you at once and I shall never lay hands on it again…'

The frail figure of the King shuffled back towards his throne, hunched and exhausted-looking. The nobles gingerly moved apart, allowing the King a narrow passage to the throne. He collapsed like a bag of old bones. He wheezed. His eyes opened and closed slowly, as if a moment was soon coming when they'd remain shut for ever.

Many nobles were now circling the throne like vultures. R'ghir stroked his beard, his eyes on the throne as if no one currently sat on it. Hesh approached and ran fingers along the arm of the throne, enjoying the feel of the wood. Elwynt backed away, catching the eyes of a number of guards with robes a similar look and colour to his own. They nodded in acknowledgement, their hands on the grips of their swords. Vira stayed put. A simple, confident smile on her blood-red lips. One hand remained folded neatly over the other. She waited patiently, her eyes never leaving the crown on the dying King's head.

The King's eyes opened. His breathing steadier for a moment. He stared hard at Krish, those milky old eyes narrowing. There was something else in them now. Spite. Krish and Balthrir's smiles wavered.

'I say once more… my promise was to hand the Myrthali over to the boy, to be shared between himself and his companion also, if he pleases. They shall remain in possession of the Myrthali forever-more… *but* they shall *never* leave this palace!'

'NO!'

'That is the extent of our arrangement. I shall honour it.' There was still some of the King's hateful energy in the old bag of bones collapsed on the throne.

'NO!' The guards had already seized Krish by the arms.

'You have *no right* to leave my domain for the heinous crime you have committed!'

'NO!'

'You slimy old ba—' the last word was muffled as a guard clasped a hand over Balthrir's mouth.

A line of prisoners were being ordered to lower themselves from the ceiling and soon their sweaty hands seized Krish and Balthrir. Krish and Balthrir were hauled over to the mouth of a shaft at the far side of the throne room. They were lowered into the endless dark of the dank well, a dot of light shrinking to nothing high above them.

'Live out the millennia in the dark with your precious Myrthali if you will... but you shall *never* venture out into the world again!'

CHAPTER 32

'I WILL LET BLOOD FLOW IN THE HALLS OF THE BLACK PALACE…'

All was cold and darkness. In the dank at the bottom of a narrow funnel of earth, Krish shivered in a corner. Although she was probably only a metre or so away, he was only just able to see Balthrir's outline as she paced back and forth in the gloom. Between them, at the centre of the chamber, was a small, round, waist-high podium which narrowed a little from the base to the top. A little shape, no bigger than a sparrow, sat patiently, caped in shadow, next to the perch he was chained to. Krish had not yet paid much attention to Gulwin on his podium. He stared across at his friend. Agitated breaths infused with terror and anger in equal measure flowed from her mouth. As she spoke her words themselves seemed to quiver.

'You've killed them…' she muttered and then louder: 'Yer've killed 'em! They were all I 'ad and yer've bloody killed 'em!'

'Balthrir… You-you don't know and I'm… I'm sor—'

'Don't you dare! Don't you DARE! Yer come 'ere, tryin' to save *one* person's life and look what yer've done!'

'Balthrir, please! I never wanted this to happen! I—'

'Well it bloody well 'as, mate! You just wait! If Obsendei lives long enough 'e'll execute a fair few prisoners outta pure spite! If 'e snuffs it and someone else seizes the throne then there'll be blood sacrifices to honour the late old codger! Just you wait! They are DEAD, Krish! Dead because of you!'

Her dark beautiful eyes shone in the dimness of the well, piercing him. The guilt sank any glimmer of hope he might have had and clouded his mind, preventing him from even attempting to come up with something vaguely resembling a plan. When he could no longer look into Balthrir's furious eyes he glanced inadvertently at the leather satchel on the ground. Balthrir saw what he was looking at.

'Well go on then!' she screamed at him. She picked up the satchel and hurled it at him. '*Get the hell out of here!* One touch, eh? And y'er gone? Can't wait! Can't wait, mate! Get out of my life!'

Those last five words hit Krish harder than any he'd ever heard in his life. One touch and he'd be gone. None of this would be his problem any more.

Krish didn't move. He looked back into Balthrir's eyes.

'No.' He kept Balthrir's stare and the two of them looked into each other for what seemed like hours.

Balthrir broke eye contact with Krish and looked down at her feet. She muttered under her breath.

'Bloody idiot.' Then louder, to the centre of the compact little chamber they stood in at the bottom of the well: 'What d'yer reckon? 'Im? Bloody idiot, eh?'

There was a slight pause and then for a few seconds the dank air was filled with sweet notes from the beak of the little bird covered in shadow on the small stone podium in the middle of the floor. Krish had still not really seen Gulwin. He could make out the shape of a small bird perched on the cold stone, unable to move more than a few inches from the spot where he was tethered.

'Blimey!' said Balthrir. 'Apparently y'er not that much of an idiot. Let me tell yer, if I ever met another kid who's as stu...'

Balthrir's voice trailed off. She listened for a moment and then looked up. Krish's eyes followed hers to the pinprick of light at the top of the shaft. There had been the faint sound of voices in the chamber above the whole time they had been down there but its volume had suddenly increased. Krish could just make out the voices of the nobles and advisors speaking over each.

'—sub-section forty-seven, paragraph three—' said R'ghir, Lord of the East.

'—in the case of abdication. *Not*—' said Elwynt, Lord of the West.

'—was drawn up to prevent precisely this manner of debate and—' continued R'ghir.

'—coalition of monarchs is not unheard of, if the crown—' said Hesh, Lord of the South.

Krish became aware of another sound too. A constant rasping

cough from a hoarse throat. When the accompanying voice spoke it was just as fierce as Krish had ever known it to be but its tone of authority had waned to one of desperation.

'I'm not-a-hhuh!-a-hhuh!-dead yet, you cretins!'

'Your Majesty, we are simply speculating the very worst-case scenario,' added Elwynt. 'For the good of the people, you understand. Should the unfortunate hour arrive I am sure His Majesty would want nothing more than the best for—'

'I AM YOUR-a-hhuh!-a-hhuh!-KING!-a-hhuh!-I command!-a-hhuh!-a-hhuh!'

It was barely a voice, more a noise, like dried, brown, autumnal leaves being crushed underfoot. Krish could picture the scene up above clearly. The withered old King stumbling around as the nobles and advisors discussed what would happen to the kingdom as if its ruler were already deceased.

'Your Majesty, the last thing I or indeed any of us here want—'

'Why waste your breath?' A new voice cut in. 'He is finished.' The voice was calm but heavy with threat. 'The decrepit ruler of yesterday is no more use to *anyone* than the *dust* he is about to become!' Her voice was rising. 'Fresh young blood must course through the veins of the kingdom's new sovereign!' He knew that voice. 'When the time comes there will be actions, not words!' Her voice was becoming louder and louder, fiercer and fiercer. 'And all those who do not *bow* before me and *hail me* as their queen better have bones fit to sharpen my blade with! I will let blood run in the halls of the Black Palace before I see *ANY of you* on the throne!'

It was Vira. He could picture the fire he'd seen before behind those terrible, seductive eyes. They must be ablaze now. This was her time. He could see her striding about the chamber, surveying it, making it clear to all that this was her territory now.

'Yer see?' Balthrir's voice was low and heavy. 'I told yer. I told told yer, I told yer, I told yer! There's worse than 'im. Didn't yer learn nothin' from the Sands o' Tyraah? This was never about Obsendei.'

As if he had heard his name over the hullabaloo, the King screamed in the chamber above, his voice full of terror and desperation. That crunching sound, crushed leaves, brittle branches being twisted slowly, splintering, followed every footstep.

'I AM KING! I COMMAND!-a-hhuh!-a-hhuh!-I will execute fifty-a-hhuh!-a-hhuh!-prisoners at once to sh-a-hhuh!-to show my strength to the people! You will see!-a-hhuh!-You will see! They will still fear and-a-hhuh!-ahhuh!-bow to me!'

"E must 'ave been on the brink o' death from the first time 'e took a spoonful o' that Myrthali!' said Balthrir. She looked over at Krish's guilt-ridden eyes in the darkness and offered him a sympathetic little smile for a moment. 'Yer in't killed 'im, Krish.'

Krish looked down sheepishly.

'Oooh,' said Balthrir, something dawning on her. 'Yer not annoyed about him dyin'. Yer annoyed that you in't gonna—'

'SHUT UP!' spat Krish.

Awkward silence for a few moments and then a few notes of bird-song trickled through the gloom.

'What did he say?' asked Krish.

Balthrir nodded towards Gulwin. 'Get closer.'

Krish turned. He could just about make out the shape as it hopped nearer to him in the darkness. He knelt. Gulwin was tiny. In the shadows he saw little more than a rather ordinary-looking garden bird like a sparrow or robin on his thin legs. He could see nothing of whether Gulwin was dull or bright in colour. All he could see was the slightest glimmer in a line of dim light, which was the tether, attached at one end to Gulwin's leg and at the other to a small, simple perch. The only other place he saw light was a reflection in the bird's tiny black eyes, disappearing and reappearing as he blinked.

Gulwin's turned his head to one side to look at Krish from another angle. He then straightened his head and hopped closer. He considered for a moment and then sang once more.

Balthrir translated. "E says that although yer don't want anybody to die, yer feel cheated that you can't see Obsendei snuff it.'

'No!' said Krish, uncomfortable with the truth. 'I don't—'

'Mate,' said Balthrir. 'Trust me: 'e can see the truth in yer eyes.'

Krish was quiet for a moment. He shrugged. 'I don't want anybody to die but with him… if it's going to happen, I just… Is it bad that I wanted to see it?'

'Maybe not. 'E was a nasty piece o' work anyway. But I said before, it's not about 'im. There's bigger things to worry about. One king pops 'is clogs, so what? 'Nother one comes along 'oo could be just as bad. Worse, maybe. When yer saw all those bodies at the Sands o' Tyraah? Wasn't getting rid of Obsendei that was causing the number o' bodies to go up or down. It's 'oo's next.'

Gulwin chimed in with a few notes.

'Ha!' laughed Balthrir. 'Says I'm surprisingly astute for my age. Whatever that means.'

Overhead the argument between the King and Vira was still raging.

'You are not worthy-a-hhuh!-a-hhuh!-to wear this-ahh!-crown, Vira!'

'You are not worthy to kiss my foot, Your Most *Foul* and *Pathetic* Majesty! But perhaps I shall allow it at the end, O Unfortunate King! When you *beg* for my blade to slice the life out of you at long last, *old man!*'

There was a harsh scraping noise. A sound like twigs tightening, creaking, moments from splintering. From the way the King's voice was amplified Krish guessed he had staggered to his feet, the throne hurled backwards as he stood, looming over Vira. His voice wheezing, rasping, as if he was inhaling the whole time as his hoarse cries escaped his withered throat.

'The weight of the crown will break your body and your blood will flow! None shall call you queen, Vira, Lady of the North! Not even the worms, for their mouths shall be full as they feast…'

Silence.

Life ticked on in the eerie quiet of the chamber above for all but one man.

A moment later there was an almighty crash of what sounded like a ton of wood hitting the ground, followed an instant later by the sound of what must be little more than a pile of robes landing in the dirt.

'The King is dead,' came the solemn voice of Eshter. 'Long live the first to raise the crown and be burdened with it upon their brow.'

Krish recalled what Balthrir had said a few nights ago in the palmery. *The crown weighs nothing to the King.* At the moment of death the crown on the King's head ceased to belong to him and must have regained its full weight, pulling his body down, toppling off his head and reaching the ground the instant before the late King's corpse. Now the crown belonged to the first person brave enough to make a grab for it.

If he was honest with himself, he had fantasised for weeks about seeing Obsendei die. As wrong as it was, he couldn't deny that seeing that arrogant, spiteful monarch crumple and die would have been immensely satisfying. But now he felt anything but disappointment at being robbed of this sight. In fact he was experiencing many different feelings all at once. He felt power for bringing a king to his knees. Pity to see Obsendei diminished. Anger at the late King for casting them into the well. Fear for what fate would befall Balthrir's parents and indeed all of Ilir. Temptation to touch a grain of Myrthali and leave all these problems behind for ever. And last of all shame for even considering such a course of action. A course of action he knew, as he stared over at his friend who'd done so much for him, that he'd never take. And she was right. His desire for something dreadful to befall Obsendei had festered in his mind for so long that he'd not considered what would happen if relieving the King of his Myrthali led to his death. Would the kingdom be any better under another monarch? Elwynt or R'ghir or Hesh or, worst of all, Vira?

'Yer not about to witness the best o' moments in our 'istory, mate,' Balthrir continued her train of thought. 'A lot o' people in that chamber up there may decide that that hunk o' wood looks good on their 'ead. And from what I've 'eard, on a day like this there could be a lot o' very short reigns before everyone decides they don't wanna join the big ol' pile o' bodies by the throne.'

The discussion overhead had become surprisingly civilised, as if now the moment had actually arrived nobody had the guts to reach for the crown.

''Ow long's it gonna take?' said Balthrir to Gulwin, who chirped a reply. ''E says minutes, probably. Minutes… Oh God!'

Balthrir rested her head in her hands, her eyes screwed up as if she was doing everything she possibly could to stop tears escaping. Krish knew she was thinking about her parents and how long they might have left. At this moment he understood exactly how Balthrir felt. When he'd first come to the palace and been thrown out by the King he'd felt he'd lost not only his Mum but his Dad as well. And Uncle Ravi, Aunt Nisha, Aunt Meera, Jess, Dawson and everyone. They were all still alive but he'd never see them again. With no way of getting the Myrthali he'd had no chance of getting home. Balthrir didn't really have anybody in the first place. Two imprisoned parents she could never see were all she seemed to have in the world, and in a few minutes' time they could well be dead.

'It's all over, mate,' said Balthrir, not looking up. 'Why don't yer just clear off while yer still can?'

Krish had become quite calm. His mind was scanning through a number of events of the last few months.

'Balthrir, does the next king or queen have to be one of the nobles? One of the lords or ladies?'

'Ha!' Balthrir's laugh was bitter. 'Fat chance o' anyone else takin' the crown!'

'Why?'

'Just wouldn't 'appen, would it?'

Gulwin's tuneful chirping sang in the darkness. Balthrir listened closely, becoming somewhat stoic for a moment. She translated.

''E says nobody would accept a monarch 'oo weren't o' noble birth as long as the Black Palace stands.'

More chirps from Gulwin.

''E says the palace itself is a symbol of oppression. That no common person would be allowed onto the throne without rebellion from the nobles unless somebody committed a monumental symbolic gesture to show that times were changin'.'

'A monumental symbolic gesture?' said Krish with a cunningness that unsettled Balthrir. 'Like tearing down the Black Palace?'

'H-ha!' Balthrir laughed through tears, driven momentarily insane by Krish's line of conversation. 'Yeah? You really think you can do that?'

'No.'

'Well, there you—'

'I don't think I can. I think *we* can.'

'Just us two?'

'Us three.' Krish indicated Gulwin, who blinked and watched with interest. Gulwin chirped agreeably. 'Us three and whoever else will join us.'

'Krish, mate, we are at the bottom of a well with *nothing* on us—'

'Balthrir, what have you got on you?'

'I in't got m'staff and that's all that matters! No staff, no real magic, no escape, no takin' down some big smelly palace. Next question.'

'But what *have* you got on you?'

'Nothin'! You?'

'Just the distress stone, which isn't much help right now. But what have *you* got on you? What about that itching powder? You were dishing it out to all those slaves.'

'Oh yeah! Brilliant idea! Bein' super-itchy really 'elps when y'er tryin' to escape from a well!'

'How much have you got on you?'

'Krish, mate, what the 'ell—?'

'Enough for a few people or enough for hundreds?'

Balthrir looked over at him curiously.

''Undreds. Thousands probably. Little goes a long way. Why?'

'And how does it work?'

'Tiniest amount of powder, yer start itchin', few minutes later y'er rollin' about on the ground scratchin' like…'

They looked up. The debate overhead had intensified.

'The King requested that fifty prisoners be executed,' said Vira. 'I will see that his wish is fulfilled. I will have these blessed fifty sacrificed in his name to honour his blood.'

'I will sacrifice a hundred in his name to honour his blood!' said Hesh.

'I will sacrifice two hundred in his name to honour his blood!' said Elwynt.

'I will sacrifice four hundred in his name to honour his blood!' said R'ghir.

'I will sacrifice *a thousand* in his name to honour his blood!' countered Vira.

'Mate,' said Balthrir. 'Whatever mad plan yer've got I'd spit it out sharpish or a lot of people'll become proper dead pretty bloody soon!'

'What if we spread itching powder to every prisoner in the palace?'

'Then we'd *definitely* all die! Great plan, mate!'

'But I've seen some of them climb down. They know a safe route and they're surely all just praying that they won't be sacrificed anyway right now.'

'Oh yeah, they take breaks and all that, obviously, or the 'ole place'd come tumblin' down!'

'What if we could spread the powder and spread the word at the same time that they have to get out of here? If we could do it in the right order...'

'And yer know what order that'd be, eh?'

'No. But what about...?'

Balthrir followed Krish's gaze to Gulwin, who was perched under shadow on his podium. He considered. After a few moments he sang his reply and Balthrir translated.

'Well, 'e said it's possible. If yer were to start at the top of the tower and work yer way down. That lot'll all be pretty damn tense. Waitin' for somethin' to 'appen. They're probably all ready for action o' some kind. Should work.' Gulwin chipped in. 'Long as nobody panicked, which, erm... Mate, so much could go wrong and why—?'

'What if we could bring down the whole palace *and* seize the crown? Put someone better than that bloodthirsty lot on the throne. The powder will force most of the prisoners to abandon their posts and how much do you bet the rest'll follow once the walls start coming down?'

'Dunno 'ow much I'd bet, mate, but it in't certain! So much could go wrong! And 'ow are yer goin' to go about snatchin' the crown anyway?'

'We save some powder for anyone who's fighting over the crown, drop it on them and while they're scratching like mad we rush in and—'

'Krish, mate! That is *not* a plan! That's a bloody gamble!'

'I know! But what the hell else do you suggest?!'

Balthrir was speechless for a moment. Then she thought of something. 'And 'ow exactly yer gonna spread this itchin' powder when we're stuck down 'ere?'

'The King was reaching for something. I saw him. At the arena. He was going to cut the twine. You said Old Margary made stuff for the King. What if he had some of the twine and a Salvean blade? You said there were only two. What if he had the other one?'

'Krish, mate, I've got no idea how yer gonna spread the powder and let everyone know and—'

'Do you have the Salvean blade?'

Balthrir checked her pocket. 'Yeah. But 'ow does that 'elp? The only thing it cuts is…'

Then everything slotted into place in her mind. She looked down at Gulwin. Gulwin's beady little eyes shone in the gloom. She ran her hand over the podium and her fingers found the small length of twine tied to the bird's foot at one end and the podium at the other. It felt as light as sunlight.

'Yer'd do this?' Balthrir asked of Gulwin, as if he were an old friend. Gulwin gave a long reply after very little consideration. 'Could cause a load o' deaths, 'e says. But loads'll die if we do nothing. And the destruction of the palace, which 'as been a symbol of enslavement for so long, would indeed allow people to accept radical change, 'e says. A new kinda monarch. Someone fairer. 'Ang on! Only someone who could be king or queen can do that! And yer in't stickin' around!'

'I guess it'll have to be you then.'

Krish's comment hit Balthrir with a force equivalent to the entire world having smacked her in the face.

'Me?! Be king?!'

'You couldn't be king.'

'Exactly!'

'You'd be queen.'

Balthrir was rarely speechless but at that moment she couldn't even muster a witty retort to diffuse the tension hanging in the air. Chiefly because this occurred in the instant in which she realised Krish was right.

'There's no one else,' she said. 'If we do this who else… but I can't be queen! I mean, surely… I can't!' She turned to Gulwin. 'Can I?' Gulwin chirped a brief reply. ''E believes the crown will find its rightful wearer.' She drew a deep breath. 'Well… bloody 'ell!'

CHAPTER 33

THE CROWN

A storm of voices from the chamber above echoed down to the bottom of the well. They waited in the darkness. The damp air chilling them to the bone. Balthrir had cut the twine. At first Gulwin had struggled with Balthrir's pouch of itching powder, which must have been ten times as big as him, but eventually he managed to lift off. For such a small bird his strength seemed incredible. He was hoping to pour at least half of it from the top of the tallest tower and allow it to trickle down among the prisoners. The fluttering of tiny wings had echoed down the shaft. As the bird disappeared from sight they were left with no option but to wait.

First I will use it as a threat, Gulwin had said. *I will tell them that they are all to start making their way down, as they would if they were being sent for a rest-hour, slowly, then no one will get hurt. If they do not start to move I will use the powder.*

Balthrir had given Gulwin two priorities. 'Once it's kickin' off, find my parents: Ahava and Faltura Wessra.' *Balthrir Wessra.* It seemed so odd to know her surname now, after all their time on the road together. 'Then grab m'staff and get it to me sharpish!'

Krish had a firm grip on the satchel of Myrthali over his shoulder, which was tightly fastened so none would escape. The waiting was painful. To be poised ready for action, with no idea of what they would be faced with. They were two insignificant little kids trapped in the shadows at the bottom of a well, waiting for their work to tear the palace above them apart.

'I don't want anyone to die, Balthrir,' Krish had said in the minutes after Gulwin had flown up into the light.

'People are gonna die. Whatever you do,' said Balthrir. 'But less of 'em will die. In the future. If we do this. Just to 'ave anyone. Anyone

other than one o' that lot on the throne. Got to be better than doin'
nothin'!'

Krish didn't like the way she was speaking. All those pauses. She
wasn't certain. But Krish knew it was their only option.

'This is why I hate stories, you know?' he said. 'Books and that?
Always have a happy ending o-or they save *everyone*. Not just a few
people. *Everyone*. And they all lived happily ever after and all that.'

'Well life's not that simple, is it? That's just stories. Things can never
be perfect. Guess yer just try and make it as good as it can be for as
many people as yer can.'

These words stayed with Krish for a long time. He and Balthrir
stood there in silence, much as they'd done in the last few days of their
journey. Understanding each other without the need for words.

They stared up the shaft. All was darkness with a tiny circle of light
at the top. There was noise. A general hubbub. Had the sound of the
chamber above changed in any way? The waiting was killing Krish.
What was happening? Had Gulwin been successful? Was the palace
starting to come down? Or had he failed? Minutes ticked by and then
the noise overhead did indeed change. Calm for a moment and then
the unmistakable tone of raised voices.

Panic.

Shouting and screaming as Krish tried to focus his eyes on the speck
of light above them.

'It is,' said Balthrir. Krish looked over at her to affirm that the same
question had been on her mind. 'It's getting brighter.'

The light of dawn shone down the shaft of the well for the first time
in centuries. It hit the shaft at an angle, so Krish and Balthrir were
spared being blinded after hours in the murk. The walls of the Black
Palace were coming down.

Then Krish noticed tiny shapes descending the shaft. Was it just the
fizz of the dark playing tricks with his eyes? No. A whole line of prisoners were lowering themselves down the shaft at great speed. Krish
and Balthrir jumped to one side as the line almost crashed onto the
floor of the well, the prisoner hanging at the end of the line just stopping himself from hitting the ground with his hands. The prisoners,
both men and women, were stripped down to their undergarments

and hanging upside down. They panted heavily. All were sweating profusely, glistening a little in the light now shining down the shaft. They looked alarmed but ready for action. Krish wondered if the prisoners had dreamed of a time such as this during their endless days forming the walls of the Black Palace. The prisoner at the end of the line stretched out his arms, barked at Balthrir and then at him.

'You! Climb one up,' he indicated the prisoner above. 'And hold him by the waist! You! Arms around my waist and hold your friend's legs! I'll hold yours!'

Balthrir stepped forward and the lead prisoner cupped his hands together to form a step. Balthrir stepped into the cupped hands and the next prisoner up held on to her legs. Balthrir put her arms around the prisoner's waist. 'Where's my staff?!' cried Balthrir.

'They are searching for it! Quickly!' answered the lead prisoner.

Krish swung the satchel of Myrthali behind his back and approached the lead prisoner. 'What is happening up there?' asked Krish, a commanding tone in his voice that seemed as unfamiliar to himself as it was to Balthrir. He had passed beyond panic. He could leave any time he wanted. But he wouldn't leave yet. He would not abandon Balthrir and he would not allow this land to be ruled by a figure as malicious as Obsendei ever again. He was ready to fight.

'Everything!' said the prisoner. 'It's chaos! COME ON!'

Krish took a step forward and then hesitated. A dark powder covered the prisoner's skin. It covered all of them.

'It is not the powder the bird Gulwin spreads!' said the prisoner in answer to the question in Krish's eyes. 'We have to wear it to grip one another. The eastern wall was covered in the powder Gulwin is spreading. The wall began to fall. Most escaped although some fell to their deaths.'

A dull, sinking sensation in Krish's stomach. This was his scheme and some had already perished thanks to his actions.

'COME ON!' said the lead prisoner.

Krish hugged the waist of the prisoner, the mix of sweat and powder cutting into his face. How did they put up with this all day long? The lead prisoner gripped his legs firmly. He barked a command and this was echoed by others up the glistening line of captives dangling down the shaft.

'The powder hit some of us,' continued the lead prisoner as they rose through the shaft. 'But everyone started to climb down rather than risk falling. The palace! It is vanishing!'

Krish could see some of the prisoners above flinching. The powder was starting take effect but none had a free hand to scratch with. They didn't have long. The prisoners gripped tightly to each other but he could tell that their strength was waning. They were used to being part of whole walls, not holding a long line of inmates.

Krish kept his eyes fixed on the mouth of the well as it grew larger and larger. His determination kept his lips shut tightly over his teeth as he breathed steadily through his nose, his eyes unblinking as the air rushed over them. There was a hammering in his chest and in the chest of the prisoner he clung to as their hearts beat almost in time with each other with fear and anticipation.

'You ready for this?' said Balthrir over the shouts and screams from the chamber above that they were about to burst into.

Krish had no idea. He could never be ready for this and in truth he hadn't a clue what they would have to face in the throne room. He didn't get a chance to consider this any further as he heard a voice close to the mouth of the well crying out...

'CUT THEM DOWN! CUT THEM DOWN!'

The prisoners started shouting at those farther up to heave faster but no one could hear over the cacophony of screaming that followed. A mighty thud. Krish felt it. It carried through the line of prisoners and shook the body of the man he held on to. His mind was wild with panic. *THUD. THUD. THUD.* He felt every terrible stroke shake him and the sound of screaming felt as if it would rip him in two – *he felt it* – he felt the sound collide with him, the shrieking – desperate, primal screams pummelling his eardrums as if they would break, as if they would physically break – and then the blood, the warm blood pouring down the body he gripped, the man's breath racing through his hyperventilating form the ribs expanding and contracting and the fury of everything around him assaulting all his senses and then he was practically deaf with the cries of dying men and women blood across the man's body he couldn't grip – he couldn't grip! – and then they were falling – falling into blackness!

Krish clawed and clawed at dank air. His nails dug into sodden earth. He gripped tightly, somehow, holding on with both hands. A shape fell towards him. A prisoner had lost his grip. As the inmate fell past him he grabbed at the satchel, the seams of the strap tore a little, and Krish's hands were ripped from the wall, clods of earth still in his grasp as he fell. He plummeted, light from the mouth of the shaft filling his vision as he fell backwards. The prisoner holding on to his satchel came to a sudden halt and Krish shot past him. Krish jolted to a stop. He looked up and saw that the prisoner had grabbed hold of the earthen wall. Krish hung from the strap of the satchel. He dug into the earth of the shaft with his free hand just as the strap gave way. He placed the strap in his mouth to keep hold of the satchel. For a moment he feared the Myrthali would spill down to the bottom of the well. For a moment he was tempted just to dive a hand into the bag of sand and disappear...

No. He looked up. A circle of light filled his vision. They were near the top. A number of prisoners had survived the attempt to cut the whole line of inmates down.

'BAL-FEAR!' he cried, the bag strap in his mouth muffling his voice.

'KRISH!' He saw her: she was right at the top, her hands gripping the floor of the throne room. 'We're almost there!'

Krish looked up at the mouth of the shaft. Dazzling daylight poured through. Dust was flying in the low light. He could see silhouettes. Figures with swords fighting furiously. He also saw one wall of the palace still standing but wobbling precariously.

'BALTHRIR!'

Balthrir was struck dumb with shock, almost wonder. Her staff was being lowered to her. She smiled, grabbed hold of it and was pulled up. Krish knew the voice – it was Nboosa. Balthrir turned and lowered her staff towards Krish. He grabbed hold and Balthrir hoisted him up. Krish bit into the strap of the satchel, determined not to let it drop. He could reach the mouth of the shaft. He hauled himself up and into the light.

All about him on this patch of ground where the palace once stood was chaos. One wall remained but it was wavering badly. Freed prisoners were shouting encouragement for the inmates in the wall to lower themselves down. Guards pointed spears at the wall threateningly. Those in the wall itself were crying out in frustration – they appeared torn. Should they rebel or obey the guards? Krish looked around and saw similar scenarios everywhere but on a smaller scale. The circle of the outer wall of the palace was still just about discernible from the small number of prisoners who hadn't been brave enough to lower themselves to the ground yet.

Prisoners and nobles and guards abandoning their posts ran in every direction. The late King's wives and husbands were fleeing, carrying as much gold and jewels as they could carry. On the far side of what was left of the chamber, just next to the throne, Krish saw a twist of bodies engaged in the biggest brawl he'd ever witnessed. Several hundred figures, mostly nobles although a few were prisoners or common citizens, were fighting it out. Fists and swords and spears hit flesh. Cries of pain. Bodies fell but still the conflict continued. Krish could see two groups of guards advancing on the fight and he also saw Eshter swiping her staff left and right just above the ground several metres away from the action. Each swipe coincided with a number of guards or participants in the fight being knocked off their feet.

Krish also noticed that he and Balthrir were completely exposed on the flat plain that had made a perfect ground floor for the palace. But no one was looking their way across the patch of dirt that had once been the throne room. He could see the town and the mountains beyond in the low light of the early day, but all those engaged in the fight weren't even looking in their direction.

Krish hastily tore a small hole in one side of satchel, just below where the strap had been broken, pulled the end of the broken strap through, tied it in a knot and threw the bag over his shoulder.

'Where are they?!' Balthrir was crying out. 'Nboosa! Where are they?!' Balthrir was helping a number of prisoners climbing up the shaft to reach the surface. She gritted her teeth as she pointed the staff at their midriffs, using her powers to drag them a little way further up until someone could reach down and pull them up. She groaned, clearly in considerable pain. She could not simply drag someone out of the well using magic alone – she had to employ as much of her own strength as possible for the spell to work.

Nboosa ran up to Balthrir and helped pull one of the prisoners up. And Krish saw another familiar face accompanying her. Tol – the innkeeper at the Broken Scythe with his large, knobbly, ginger-root-shaped nose and grey whiskers. He held a large plank of wood, which Krish couldn't help noticing had the odd bloodstain on it.

'We can't find them!' said Nboosa to Balthrir.

'What?!' said Balthrir, standing up straight. 'We have to find them! We have—'

'Balthrir!' barked Krish. He could do it. He could keep calm and get this whole mess sorted out. He'd come this far and he could see it to the end. Balthrir turned and looked at him. 'They'll be dead for sure if we don't get the crown before anyone else!'

Tol turned to look at Krish and raised his eyebrows in his usual understated manner.

'Oh, it's you!' said Tol. 'My young friend whose handwritin's better than 'is dustin' and sweepin' skills! Gonna 'ave to charge extra for the room belonging to the boy 'oo made a king bow before 'im after this! If there is an "after this", of course.'

'Er, yeah,' said Krish. 'Sure.'

'As for the crown – ha!' said Tol. 'We get the 'ell out of 'ere – that's the only plan there is!'

Krish turned to Nboosa hopefully. 'What is happening over there?' He indicated the fight. 'Do you know?'

'A battle for the crown. What did you expect?' Nboosa continued, sensing that Krish needed to know more. 'R'ghir killed Hesh and is using both their guard regiments to clear the nobles and any other citizen who's trying to claim the crown. Vira is using both her own guards and Eshter to clear the way. R'ghir's watching Elwynt closely. Elwynt is waiting. Biding his time.'

''Opin' the others'll wipe 'emselves out so 'e can stroll in and nab the crown, no doubt!' Tol chipped in, scratching his nose with the less bloody end of the plank.

'Well, we need to get to the crown.' Nboosa and Tol were taken aback by Krish's bold statement.

'Yer weren't no good at sweepin' the floors!' said Tol. 'What makes yer think yer'll be any good at bein' in charge o' thousands o' people?'

'Not me...' Instead of finishing his sentence, Krish looked over at Balthrir.

'You?!' said Nboosa, her face a combination of horror and awe. 'You don't even turn up to class and you want to be queen?'

'Yeah, whatever,' said Balthrir impatiently. 'Can we just get on with this nabbin' the crown malarkey and find my parents?!'

Shouting and screams from the other side of the throne room. They turned to see the two guard squads closing in on one another. Bodies were being flung aside from the main scrum of the fight. They fell bloodied, crumpled and inanimate. Soon there would be very few people left to fight over the crown. And above the scrum, Krish saw the solitary wall teetering. The screaming, desperate faces of women and men in the wall as it arched towards the ground. It was too late for them to climb down now. They had minutes left.

'Where's Gulwin?' said Krish to Balthrir, Tol and Nboosa. 'Does he have any itching powder left?' Nboosa and Tol looked blank. Krish turned to some of the prisoners lying near the mouth of the well who had been too exhausted to run. 'The bird Gulwin, where is he?' Nobody responded. 'We need to find him! He needs to drop the last of the itching powder on the fight – we may be able to seize the crown while everyone is scratching themselves silly!' Krish was greeted with blank looks. He stared back at the gradually collapsing wall and made a quick decision. 'Balthrir...'

'What?!' said Balthrir, agitated to the point of hysteria. 'I don't 'ave some 'andy bird-summonin' spell if that's what y'er after!'

'You go to the left of the fight,' he pointed at the conflict. 'And Tol, Nboosa, IN FACT ANYONE WHO FANCIES STOPPING SOME OTHER MANIAC SITTING ON THE THRONE!' He shouted the last bit as loud as he could to the prisoners nearby. 'Spread out between myself and Balthrir and you get anyone between Balthrir and the crown out of the way! I'll clear the way to the right.'

Krish remembered all those times at the campsite in Battle when he'd made friends and assumed command. Where nobody knew him or was familiar with how shy and softly spoken he was normally. He could play at being someone confident, someone in command, and right now he had every reason in all the world to take charge. He'd thought he wanted to see a heartless, vindictive king wither and die before his very eyes prior to departing Ilir with the Myrthali. But he realised now that Balthrir and Tol and Nboosa and all the people of this land would be left with another ruler who was just as cruel and bloodthirsty. No. Krish was taking charge to leave this land a different and better place altogether. It might be a mad, desperate gamble, but he would not leave without doing everything he could to prevent another vindictive tyrant being crowned queen or king.

A few of the prisoners rose to their feet. Some picked up discarded swords or spears. Tol seemed pretty happy with his plank of wood. Nboosa found both a sword and a shield.

'If I'd found it I'd rather have had my staff,' said Nboosa. 'Like my worst pupil over here. She'd better be as good at ruling as she is at magic! And it's the magic, the way she won that crowd over in the arena, the fact she was there when you brought Obsendei to his knee—'

'Yeah, yeah, yeah!' Balthrir was boiling with impatience. 'COME ON!'

Krish himself picked up a sword from under a shield. He was surprised at how heavy it was. How could you fight with this? He struggled at first just to pick it up. There was blood on the blade. He wiped some of it off with his sleeve then looked at the bloodstain on his top and wondered why the hell he'd just done that. He looked at Balthrir. There were no more words they could say to one another. He knew that she would do anything to save her parents. He knew she trusted him. And he could see that look in her eyes as she glanced at the blood on his sleeve. Her eyes acknowledged that he didn't want anyone else to die, but he knew that this day would not end well for this world if he didn't do what was necessary to save as many lives in the long run as he could.

A nod of understanding and then the two friends separated. Balthrir headed to the left of the fearsome conflict, Tol, Nboosa and a number of the prisoners fanning out to her right, ready to take on whoever they could. They looked like a desperate band up against two squads of fully armed, highly trained guards. Krish held back, feeling cowardly not to dive in straight away, but he kept his eye on the furious scrum by the throne. The sun was slowly rising, shining in his eyes, he was struggling to see—

A shape out of the corner of his eye heading straight for him. Krish dodged to one side and a blade swung right past his ear. He saw eyes wild with bloodlust. Vira. Her smile still small, coy but powerful on those dark red lips. She brought her sword up again and swung for Krish. He was ready this time. With all his strength he lifted his sword. His blade met hers.

'Is that really you, little boy?' Her manic eyes were locked with his. Krish wouldn't let his fear show. She thrust her blade forward but he pushed back. His muscles ached as he pushed against Vira, their blades still crossed. 'The same quiet, *pathetic* child who begged for his mother's life?' Krish pulled his sword away from Vira and swung for her leg. Vira parried. 'You may have brought that old man to his knees but not me! Do you know what plans I have for my new queendom?!' Vira went to strike Krish and the two parried back and forth for a few seconds. Over Vira's shoulder Krish spotted a glorious sight. A tiny bird, a blur of green and blue, swooped over the fight and a cloud of white dropped from the bag he was holding.

While Krish was preoccupied by the sight of Gulwin, Vira saw her chance. Her eyes open as wide as they would go, almost as if they were going to pop out, she swung at Krish's heels and he had to jump backwards to avoid having his feet severed. He fell to the ground and Vira held her sword to his throat. A sly, victorious smile spread across her face.

'You may have brought down the Black Palace but I shall build myself a Red Palace! It shall be sturdier, taller and more terrifying a spectacle for all my foes to behold! I SHALL SLAUGHTER ALL THOSE I PLEASE, RELIEVE THEM OF THEIR SKINS, PRE-SERVE THEM IN SALT, FORCE ESHTER TO ENCHANT THEM SO THEY GLISTEN AND SHINE AND BUILD A

TOWER FROM THEIR CORPSES TALLER THAN THIS WORLD HAS EVER SEEN!'

'You really are flippin' crackers, aren't you?' said Krish. He could see those who had been embroiled in the fight now lying about scratching themselves all over. Nboosa, Tol and the prisoners were battling their way through those left standing. Tol was doing a particularly excellent job of knocking down as many people as he could with his bloodied plank. Krish, unseen by Vira, reached into his pocket. 'No palace will ever stand on this spot again and neither you, nor anybody remotely like you, will ever wear that crown upon your head!'

Krish pulled out the distress stone, held it under Vira's torso and pressed hard. He shut his eyes. Even through his closed eyelids he saw the flash of red. A shrill scream from Vira and her body shot to one side. He opened his eyes and saw the blinking Vira, partially blinded by the flare, staggering to her feet. But now she was aware of what was happening behind her. Balthrir was rushing towards the centre of a heap of scratching bodies lying on the ground by the throne. Vira wasted not a second more. With incredible speed she shot across what remained of the throne room. Krish stood and made chase. He sprinted across the chamber, his legs clumsily beating the ground, his heart pounding furiously in his chest. He was gaining on Vira. His breath was short, his heart beating. He could see it! The crown! Balthrir was close…

Eshter ran towards Balthrir. Balthrir saw and struck out with her staff. Eshter raised her staff too and although the two wizards were some metres apart, their staffs appeared to magically make contact with each other through the air. The two began to fight, parrying back and forth, their staffs never making physical contact, striking at each other magically across the ether. Krish was only a metre or so behind Vira now. Balthrir swung her staff and struck Eshter directly across the back, actually making contact this time. Eshter had grabbed the staff as it struck her and pulled Balthrir to the ground with her. Then Eshter reached out… she was so close to the crown… Krish had no way of getting there first and Balthrir lay on the ground, winded. Suddenly a spell sped through the air and hit Eshter in the face. She was knocked to one side. Krish turned to see Nboosa, her arm out-stretched, mouthing a rather rude word in Eshter's direction before turning back to the guard she was fighting.

Vira sprinted past the two fallen wizards. Her eyes saw nothing but the crown. Krish was just behind her. He pushed himself and his body reacted. He was beyond pain, beyond exhaustion. He rushed forward. He raised his sword and swung at Vira. She struck clumsily back at him with her blade, her eyes still on the crown. Krish hit out again, catching the side of Vira's wrist. She cried out, dropped her sword and lashed out at him. Red, claw-like nails tore across his face as Vira knocked him to the ground. She bent down to lift the crown.

'Oi!' came Balthrir's voice. She was on her feet, just ahead of Eshter. She pointed her staff down at Vira, who froze as the tip of her middle finger made contact with the crown.

All noise evaporated in the hot air. Dim sunlight danced in the dust. The fight had ground to a halt in a single moment.

'It is mine...' Vira spoke in a low soft voice so that everyone had to be near-silent to hear her. 'It is mine, wizard. Step aside.'

'I don't think so, matey.' Balthrir was her casual, confident self again.

Vira's finger didn't abandon its loose, shaky grip on the rim of the crown but her eyes glanced up at Balthrir.

'You're leaning all the way forward, wizard,' said Vira. 'You can't put all your strength behind striking me from there.' She was right. Krish could see that Balthrir was leaning so far forward that she'd fall at any second. She certainly wouldn't be able to reel back and strike with any real speed. 'You'll fall before you can even utter a spell. Bend your knees... move your body into a bow... to your new queen!' Vira's smile was small but powerful. Her delicate, beautiful tones seemed to command the room's complete attention without her raising her voice. Then, her eyes lusting for a life extended, she added, just so the very nearest could make it out: 'And have your companion pass his satchel to me...' Her smile held the kind of simple confidence that said it was all over.

'Let's see 'ow long the crown stays on yer 'ead... *dear*...' Balthrir's eyes were narrow and she barely opened her mouth to speak.

Krish looked from Balthrir to Vira and back again. There must be something he could do.

'Hand the crown over to me, wizard!' came the voice of Elwynt. 'And we will spare you!'

'I don't think s—' Balthrir began.

'And him...' finished Elwynt.

Balthrir turned her head slowly upwards, away from Vira. Krish looked too and his eyes were almost as horrified as hers. Elwynt held a knife to the throat of a tall man with a round, hairless face and large, bulbous eyes. R'ghir held a dagger to the throat of a woman. She had long, flowing hair and a deceptively youthful face. A face that was familiar.

'No!' said R'ghir. 'Give it to me!'

Balthrir hesitated. That, combined with the fearful look in her eyes, confirmed Krish's guess. These were Balthrir's parents. Krish felt helpless. What could he do? He saw the fear creeping through his friend's mind.

'I... I don't know them...' said Balthrir weakly.

'They are your kin!' spoke R'ghir. 'I see your face in hers! Your eyes are his eyes! I will spill her blood! Your blood! So give me the crown!'

'No! You will give it to *me*!' interjected Elwynt. 'I will spare him!'

Balthrir's eyes were darting all over the place. She was determined to keep one eye on Vira. Her father's large, round eyes stared lovingly at his daughter. Her mother watched her child with a look of horror and pride. Her teeth were gritted and defiant. Krish's mind was racing with a million different solutions but none that he could formulate into a realistic plan.

'You see,' said Vira simply to Balthrir. 'A lot of people may fight me for the crown... but not you. Stand aside. And there will be no further bloodshed.'

I don't want anybody else to die, thought Krish.

He watched Balthrir closely; her whole body was vibrating with panic.

I DON'T want anybody else to die. He'd had enough. This had to stop.

Balthrir was losing control of her lungs; her breath spilled out of her.

I don't want anybody else to die, thought Krish, *but I've seen it. More will die. If I don't do this.* Krish had a handful of words on the tip of his tongue. Words that would save Balthrir. Save her parents. Save more people than would be killed if he didn't utter them. *I don't want anyone else to die. Even someone as evil as her. But this is the only way.*

Krish knew that nobody deserved to die. But the visions of the bodies piling up in the Sands of Tyraah were now all he could see. And he had three words that were the best weapons he had.

'She's not armed.' He directed it at Vira and then looked straight at Elwynt and R'ghir. The Lords of the East and West stared back and followed Krish's gaze to the sword Vira had dropped. Krish locked eyes with Vira once more before meeting Balthrir's gaze. She nodded back in sudden realisation.

'All yours, boys...' Balthrir stood up straight, releasing Vira, who snatched up the crown and placed it delicately upon her head. Her eyes were ablaze with awe. With fury. With fire. With a lust for blood and power.

'All hail Quee-AARRRGGGHH!' Vira's scream tore through the air above the flat of land that was once the throne room. Her blood poured onto the ground as Elwynt and R'ghir, who had rushed over, abandoning Balthrir's parents, withdrew their blades from Vira's chest. The weight of the crown returned as the life left Vira's body and she crumpled into the dirt. Elwynt, R'ghir and Krish all sped towards it but Eshter hurled them aside. Balthrir raised her staff to Eshter's. Their staffs locked in mid-air.

Krish ran for the crown again but the ground vanished beneath a flurry of feet rushing in the other direction. Krish looked up to see why they were running. The wall that had been wavering was now collapsing. They would all be crushed.

'BALTHRIR!' Krish cried.

Balthrir saw. She unlocked her staff from Eshter's and pointed it up. The wall came to a halt in mid-collapse. She held it there, grunting in pain, hardly able to halt its descent. The wall was slowly advancing towards the ground. It wouldn't be long until it was low enough for everyone to fall in an undignified heap with most surviving, but Balthrir was going to lose her grip any second now.

'ESHTER!' Balthrir called out to the old wizard who was reaching for the crown. 'ESHTER! HELP ME!' They would both be crushed if Eshter didn't help.

Eshter held up her staff, pointed it at the wall of screaming prisoners and began to lower it. Krish ran forward, looking again for the crown, but all he could see was dust. Then he saw it. He sprinted forward but R'ghir was crawling towards it, laughing insanely. Krish accelerated but R'ghir's hand was outstretched, inches from the crown...

A bloody wooden plank appeared out of nowhere and struck R'ghir across the face, knocking him out cold. Krish looked up to see Tol nodding to himself, looking quite satisfied. Tol then looked up in terror and ran as fast as he could. The wall was moments from collapsing. Screams from the prisoners assaulted Krish's ears and their horrified faces filled his vision.

'OUT!' cried Balthrir. 'KRISH, GET OUT!'

'Not without y—'

'I'm bloody comin', mate!' Balthrir turned as she began to lose her grip. They ran. The wall of prisoners hurtled towards the ground. Eshter was close behind them. They ran and ran, their legs sore, breathing madly, their hearts aching in their heaving chests. Krish gripped the satchel close. And then there was an almighty crash and the screams faded to silence.

They ran a few more metres, to be sure, hardly able to stop themselves, and then they turned and looked.

The Black Palace was gone. Dust twisted up into the air above the spot where the palace once stood. A sea of bodies, most groaning but some quiet, lay in the dirt.

As the dust settled Krish became aware of a beam of light shining towards them. He looked up to see a jewel-encrusted circle, held up high, partially obscuring the sun as it arched towards the highest point in the sky. He could just make out the shape of tiny wings beating with ease just above the crown and he realised that this was the first time he had really seen Gulwin. His tiny sparrow-like body, his feathers of emerald green, his wings of deep ocean blue, his little red beak and his beady black eyes. He forgot for a moment how the crown worked as the sight of such a small creature clutching a comparatively large object just looked so odd. But as he turned to Balthrir his eyes clearly echoed the question on his mind.

'The crown weighs nothing to the King,' she answered.

CHAPTER 34

PALACE OF THE SKIES

Before returning to Krish and Balthrir's story, it's worth talking, for a short while at least, about what happened in Ilir after their adventure came to an end.

The days that followed saw much change in Ilir. The reign of King Obsendei was over and the reign of King Gulwin had begun. Many of the nobles and the late King's husbands and wives feared execution for trying to seize the throne but Gulwin was not interested in shedding more blood. Instead he put them to work in the fields for the rest of their days, allowing the long-serving families to retire immediately as the treacherous nobles took their place.

Those nobles remaining didn't seem to care too much about what would happen to the people but more about the rebuilding of the palace and how much that would cost. Gulwin had other ideas. Many riches were recovered from the palace and Gulwin decided to use these to build houses and to better equip the doctors and surgeons to help care for the sick. The nobles were horrified at such a suggestion as clearly the palace was needed if the King was to retain his authority.

Gulwin disagreed. Good judgement, fairness and justice were what was needed for him to retain his authority, he said. And besides, the skies would be his palace. From there he could see all of his kingdom. He would get to know his people, rather than hide behind walls and the deception a world of finery brought you.

The people hoped there would be no more working in fields and mines and perhaps even the abolition of prisons altogether but Gulwin said that this would not be fair either. Those who were cruel and unfair would be punished by being made to perform the most undesirable jobs. (This included R'ghir, who was charged with the murders of both Vira and Hesh. Elwynt had perished when the palace had collapsed. Eshter, who had only ever done as she was told, aside from a brief bout of rebellious behaviour during the fall of the Black Palace, continued to serve the crown. Her treacherous behaviour did however lead to a demotion. She became a senior wizard serving in an advisory capacity rather than retaining her role as official court wizard as before.)

It would be a careful balancing act as Gulwin did not want to invent crimes (as previous monarchs had done) to keep the important work in the mines and the fields going. So instead he shared out the jobs widely so most able-bodied people had to spend at least a short time working these undesirable occupations, though prisoners took on the vast majority of this burden.

Gulwin also refused to wear the crown. He had Eshter bury the bejewelled band of wood in the ground where the Black Palace had once stood and enchant it to grow into a silver tree. The enchantment did not allow the tree to bear any fruit unless King Gulwin died. Then from the tree would grow a single golden apple. Only a fair, worthy and truthful individual would be able to pick the apple and taste the divine fruit. They would immediately become the queen or king.

Gulwin ruled from his Palace of the Skies for a century and although by the end of that time some people doubted him, missing the firm hand of the queens and kings of old, Gulwin could see, taking in the land from a great height one day, that the world was in general a happier place. Every corner of his heart filled with contentment and that very same day he disappeared into the skies, never to return.

✮

And this all would come to pass (primarily, at least) because of the actions of two people, whose story we return to now, the morning of the day after the palace had fallen.

Balthrir's mother, Ahava, stepped forward.

'My little Thrir.' Dark, unreadable eyes, her brow heavy with weariness and resolve. The wind toyed with her long, tattered hair, making her appear girlish for her age. She placed a hand on Balthrir's shoulder. Daughter looked into her mother's eyes expectantly. Ahava kissed her child on the forehead and whispered in her ear. Whatever she said made mother and daughter clutch each other tight enough, it seemed, to break one another.

Faltura, Balthrir's father, joined them. He was tall and slim and had large round eyes to match his large round face.

Krish watched as Balthrir hugged her parents in the glow of dawn. Their embrace looked tight enough to crush rock but on closer inspection it was gentle, relaxed. Their heads were hidden by their embrace as if they were a single figure. They almost swayed with the breeze, their tired forms contented at the end of one of the hardest days of their lives. Krish had never seen a family look so happy doing so little.

They broke apart and Faltura took his daughter's staff.

'I thought I told you to burn this?' he said.

'I, er…' said Balthrir.

Faltura smiled. 'If you had we'd all be dead.' He put his arm round his daughter, held her staff high above his head and called out to the crowds around them. 'My daughter saved you! My daughter saved you all!' The people around them still hadn't processed what was going on; a few cheered but many were exhausted, some preoccupied with mourning those who had perished in the chaos. Many former prisoners, thanks to Balthrir's itching powder, were also rather preoccupied with scratching themselves. But it didn't matter because there was a bright smile on Balthrir's face that said she was truly proud to be her parents' child for the first time in a long while.

Krish sat in the dust amid the makeshift refugee camp of ex-convicts and nobles, none of whom had anywhere to live. Gulwin was flying around desperately trying to arrange places for them to stay and to sort the criminals into those who had committed what he was calling 'trivial crimes' or 'non-crimes' like eating cheese on a Thursday (a law the old King had passed to maintain his palace) and those who had committed serious crimes and would have to face further imprisonment. Most were committers of 'trivial crimes', so his job became fairly straightforward. Few feared Gulwin and even fewer fled. Most seemed happy to accept his judgement. Gulwin had spoken briefly to Balthrir, although Krish hadn't had a chance to ask what they had discussed yet.

Tol had ripped the boards off the Broken Scythe and allowed many of the homeless to stay there for free until they could find somewhere to live. Krish had also seen Madam Nboosa out in front of the Scythe with her staff, using it to treat wounds and start fires for the refugees to cook with. He got the distinct impression that she'd been waiting a long time for the opportunity to use her staff again for a reason other than policing the Festival of Magic.

After some time Balthrir broke away from her family and floated over to Krish.

'You, er, wanna go for a walk, mate?' she asked.

'Sure,' said Krish. 'Sounds good.'

⁂

The river was flowing. Spurts of green were poking out of the banks of the shallow waters as life returned the desolate lands of Ilir. Balthrir led Krish along the river, in truth no more than a brook, to the gardens that lined its western bank. When they'd left Al Kara they had been dry and dead-looking, but the revived river had brought the gardens back to life and now they were green and lush and teeming with life. They walked around the winding paths of the empty gardens, under boughs of trees and trellises entwined with vines. There were flowers of yellow and white and purple and orange and a feast of sweet scents wafting through the air.

Balthrir brought Krish to a stop at the edge of the gardens, where the path led down to the water, next to drifts of fragrant little flowers of white and purple. Balthrir sat on the bank and pulled off her boots. She tentatively lowered her filthy, hardened soles into the cool water and let out an involuntary yelp of pleasure as the river soothed her feet after their long journey. Krish joined her. He had never felt so relaxed. The soft light of the sun meandering through the leaves as it climbed to full strength in the late-morning sky set his eyes aglow with delicate orange and yellow under his closed lids. His body was warm from the heat of the star above him, his hot feet cooled by the running water. He placed a wetted palm on the scratches Vira had left upon his cheek, and the teethmarks from the Vulrein on his right leg tingled in the stream.

'Might go back to The Scar,' said Balthrir.

'Yeah? Sounds good,' answered Krish. 'Not scared of water any more?'

'Dunno. Don't think so. Scarier things out there, yer know!'

'Yeah!' Krish let a little laugh escape. 'What did Gulwin say? You gonna be court wizard?'

'Nope. Don't wanna be, anyway.'

'Oh.'

'Asked if there was anything else I'd like to do.'

'Sure you could do loads. Your powers are just...incredible.'

'Yeah. You said that before.' Krish loved how relaxed she sounded. She spoke more slowly than before. Taking to time to enjoy each word she spoke. 'You said I was powerful and I never thought about it but... maybe I can use it for something more than just... yer know? Impressing kings and all that? So I said maybe I could... build stuff, help people... I dunno. Loads I could do with my magic.'

'That's great, Balthrir. Really great. Bet you've always wanted to do something like that.'

'Yeah.'

Balthrir opened her eyes and looked over at Krish.

'You could come with us for a bit. Travel the lands,' she said. 'I mean, I guess you should get back...'

Balthrir looked at the satchel full of Myrthali. Krish did the same. He picked up the bag and placed it in his lap. He opened it up and looked at all the tiny grains glistening in the sunlight. All he had to do was touch them and he'd be gone. He'd never see Balthrir again. And the sinking feeling inside him was so overpowering that all he wanted to do was think of something else. Anything else.

'I guess I could,' he said, trying hard to stifle the emotion in his voice. 'For a little while. One last journey together.'

They were both looking into the satchel at the grains of Myrthali. Balthrir took a pinch of it and let the grains fall until she had a single grain held between her thumb and index finger.

'All that palaver for this stuff, eh?' said Balthrir. Her smile weakened and her eyes darkened. 'Wouldn't want to lose that on the road. Not after all we've been through.'

'No.' Krish thought of how happy Balthrir had looked with her family. How much he wanted to see his family. 'Balthrir...'

'What?'

'If I stayed... what would happen to us...?'

Balthrir looked rather odd, with an awkward, almost shy expression on her face. She turned away for a second and then turned back. 'Well... I dunno. What do you want to happen to us...?'

'We'd always be... friends, wouldn't we...?'

Balthrir answered slowly. 'Yeah. O' course. Course we'd be friends. O-or something like friends. Whatever you want, mate. I mean... Krish.' She sounded like there was more she wanted to say. 'All we've been through I doubt we could never *not* be friends or... something. I wouldn't bloody let you not be my friend!' They laughed.

They looked into each other's eyes and said more to each other in a few seconds than all the words in this book ever could. Krish still wanted to articulate it in some way. He wanted, just for a moment at least, to say something.

'Y'er a bit of a wally, Krish,' said Balthrir, resuming her normal pace of speaking. 'But bloody 'ell did yer keep fightin'. Didn't stop. Wouldn't say boo to a bloomin' goose at the start of our little quest and a few hours back yer were mouthin' off to a king! Yer made him kneel before you!'

Krish smiled. He paused for a moment to think.

'Balthrir...' he said. 'If I did leave... well... every time anybody called me a "bloody idiot" they'd probably wonder why the hell it would make me smile. I'd tell them it was because it made me think of the best wizard in the world, in all the worlds, and they'd just walk off, shaking their head thinking, "Yeah, he is a bit of an idiot!" But I wouldn't care. I'd be smiling like I'm totally bonkers and I wouldn't care.'

Balthrir gave him a warm little smile. 'Yeah. And I'd think of yer every time *I* ran into a bloody idiot! And I'd be like, "Nah! Y'er an idiot, mate, but I've known better!"'

Krish chuckled again and looked straight at Balthrir, who was toying with the grain between her finger and thumb.

'*If* yer went, o' course,' she added.

'Balthrir,' Krish began, one hand outstretched a little, slightly cupped as if it was helping him gather his feelings. 'Thank you. I want you to know that you're the best. The best—'

'Oh, shut yer face!' And Balthrir dropped the grain of Myrthali into the palm of Krish's outstretched hand and the light of those dark, beautiful eyes vanished into the dull grey of his own sky.

CHAPTER 35

THE EMPTY HAND

He'd rarely seen a cloud in months and now he was faced with the dull, heavy sky of grey belonging to his own world, framed in his bedroom window. It was a few moments before he tuned back into the real world and noticed that there wasn't a grain of Myrthali in his still-outstretched hand. There was no satchel of Myrthali by his feet either. He knew the satchel wouldn't return with him but there should be a pile of Myrthali on the floor in front of him. There was none.

Krish stood on the floor of his bedroom, looking out of the window at the iron-grey sky of his dreary world. Everything he'd done. Everything he'd been through, that he and Balthrir, who he'd never see again, had been through, was wasted. He missed her already. Seconds ago he had been pondering spending his entire life with her in Ilir. Now he just felt confusion and frustration and he didn't want that picture of her beautiful eyes ever to fade.

He looked about the room. He searched everywhere. He pulled the covers off his bed, searched his hockey kit bag and threw all his dirty clothes in the laundry basket across the floor. Nothing. It was gone.

What now? He could hear footsteps hurrying up the stairs. Krish didn't have time to think before his Dad burst into the room.

'Krishna, what the hell are you doing up here?'

Krish stared at him for a moment. He'd almost forgotten what his Dad looked like.

'Dad…' He was so happy to see him, even though he was angry. His father looked back at him, puzzled. He looked at his clothes.

'What have you done to your new jeans?'

Krish looked down at his clothes. They were filthy. Much of the dust of Ilir had gone although some of it still stained his clothes.

'And have you cut yourself?' his Dad asked.

There were bloody holes on his right trouser leg thanks to the Vulrein. Then Krish realised that his father was looking at the bloodstain on his T-shirt, where he'd tried to wipe the bloody sword.

'I, er...' Krish was struggling. 'Had a nosebleed.' He didn't sound very convincing. 'I'll put everything in the wash,' was the best thing he could think of saying.

'Has somebody scratched you?' His father was now looking at the marks Vira's nails had made. 'And what have you done to your neck?' He indicated the burn the FireHawk had left. 'A-a-and your hair! I thought you were meant to get it cut the other day! You know your mother'll nag me for not nagging you!'

Krish tried to remember. Yes, he'd had it cut just before he'd left for Ilir.

'Er... yeah... sorry,' was all he could muster.

Krish's Dad didn't look impressed but he clearly didn't know how to react at all.

'Get changed,' he said. 'We're going to the hospital.'

All was quiet. The sky was still grey outside the windows of the ward and the world (most of which was at school or work while Krish and his Dad had the day off to see Mum) was just too quiet for Krish.

The nurses said his Mum had been awake all night so now she was sleeping. They didn't say why she'd been up all night but he guessed that he would have too much on his mind to sleep if he were her. He hated seeing her asleep. It was the last thing he wanted to see right now. To his father Krish couldn't have missed her that much as he'd only seen her the day before but for Krish it had been months. That was what the devil had said. One touch of the Myrthali and he'd return to his bedroom at the exact moment he'd left.

She just lay there. Her arms folded across her chest, her hands holding her bare elbows, keeping them warm, he guessed. She barely moved. Her chest rose and fell, but not much. He hated seeing her like this. He had gone to Ilir to collect the Myrthali, to see her walk and smile – or at least sit up in bed. He didn't want to see her with her eyes closed, lying on her back. Hardly moving.

Krish's Dad had taken a seat by the bed. He looked exhausted. He probably hadn't slept much either. He laid his hand on his wife's arm and in a few minutes his eyes started blinking heavily with tiredness until they closed completely. His head tilted back, his mouth opened wide and he let out a snore so loud that Krish wondered if the whole hospital could hear. He'd always thought his Dad's snores sounded like a chainsaw getting stuck while trying to cut down a particularly thick tree trunk and the idea of this, to his surprise, made him giggle. For a few seconds all his fears vanished and he just enjoyed laughing at the bizarre sound of his silly old Dad, who he loved so much, making the most hilariously awful noises.

Krish's eyes left his Dad for a moment and he saw something that made his entire being feel lighter. His Mum was sitting up in bed, looking over at his Dad, a firm, warm smile on her face, a glow in her eyes. She looked over at Krish for a second or two, before her eyes returned to her husband snoring in the chair.

'Your father could wake the dead with his snoring,' she said. 'Listen to him! It's like a bloody chainsaw or something!'

Krish giggled hysterically for a few seconds. 'Yeah, I've always thought that!'

Unlike most people, who swear when things are going wrong, his Mum had a habit of swearing when things were going well. And she preferred to do it when his Dad was out of the room, under her breath, as if it was their little secret.

She turned to Krish. 'Only just got some peace and quiet in this place! He doesn't bring me grapes but he brings his bloody snoring!'

Krish chuckled for a moment. Then there was a second or too when Krish wanted to stay something, to keep the conversation going, but he couldn't think of what to say. His Mum seemed to detect this so she reached for the pack of cards on the table by her bed.

'You going to play some cards with your old Mum or what? And what's happened to your face? Been in the wars?'

He felt the scratch marks left by Vira and the burn from the Fire-Hawk on his neck. 'Er, yeah.'

She rolled her eyes. 'Huh! Typical!' She seemed almost back to normal. Not weak as she had looked the day before. For her it had been a single night since they'd seen one another last. To Krish it had been months. He could see she was tired but that a certain energy had returned to her.

They played his mother's favourite card game: Rummy. Krish had three sevens, the eight and nine of clubs, the two of diamonds and the jack of clubs. All he needed was the seven or ten of clubs to win, and each go he simply picked up a card, saw it wasn't what he needed and replaced it. His Mum was doing the same thing.

'Are you all right, Mum?' Krish said quite suddenly, not entirely certain of why he had asked.

His Mum's eyes looked up into his, an unwavering smile on her face. 'I will be if you put the bloody seven of diamonds down soon!'

Krish laughed again.

Minutes later he walked off to the toilet. He had almost forgotten about Ilir. About the devil. About Myrthali. About the empty hand. His face ached from smiling. His Mum had been smiling too but there had been something hidden in her face when she looked at him. Something he couldn't quite put his finger on.

⁎⁎

The sparse, immaculately clean white and blue toilets smelled strongly of chemicals, although he preferred the smell of this place to the odd, clinical odour of the hospital. Weariness was catching up with him again. He splashed water on his face. His mind flooded with all-too-recent memories, which also seemed curiously distant.

To Krish it was still the same day as the one when the palace had fallen. He hadn't slept since the day before they had returned to the Black Palace. He couldn't believe it was still the same day when they'd fought Vira and Eshter and seen hordes of people scrabbling over the crown. The same day when he'd sat on the banks of the river with Balthrir, staring into her eyes. His feet in the cooling water. The water on his scratched face now stung. The same day when he'd had the satchel of Myrthali sitting in his lap. The same day she'd dropped that single grain into his hand...

Two realisations hit Krish in a matter of seconds. The first was that he was not alone.

'You're here...'

A sly, low giggle echoed from one of the cubicles as the second realisation slithered across his mind.

'WHERE IS IT?!' Krish flung the door of the cubicle open and saw the devil crouching on the ground between the toilet bowl and the false wall. 'WHERE?!'

'Hush, little 'un!' He hated that cruel little voice. That hunched creature with her skin like charred wood, gnarled and twisted, wearing her tattered robe. She sat there, a sinister grin on her lips. 'Yer'll not be gettin' far with that attitude!'

Krish didn't care. He seized the devil by the scruff of her neck, her skin like coarse, cold, paper-thin leather. He banged her small frame against the false wall.

'Tell me where it is!' Krish screamed. All of his relaxation from playing cards minutes before had disintegrated. 'DO YOU KNOW WHAT I WENT THROUGH—?'

The devil pushed him away with surprising strength.

'Yer can't threaten me, boy!' Her eyes were angry but her voice was steady. 'I knows things tha's worst than the unmovin' terror of death!'

Krish allowed himself a second to calm down a little.

'You promised—'

'When we's done!' The devil clutched the golden vessel around her neck. 'Then we shares!'

Krish stared at the vessel in open-mouthed disbelief. 'You might have told me the Myrthali'd come straight back to you!'

A flicker of a smile from the devil.

'Thank you, Krish!' Krish said to himself sarcastically. 'Thank you for risking your neck against Goonmallinns and some totally bonkers nobles fighting over a crown and invisible flippin' dogs!'

The devil simply continued to smile.

'How much more Myrthali is out there then?' asked Krish.

The devil's brow furrowed. 'Enough,' she said.

'What does "enough" mean?'

The devil toyed with the vessel for a few moments before answering. 'There is three more worlds—'

'Three?!' Krish felt exasperated at the very idea of going to one more world, let alone three. 'I can't do this again! Not three more

times! I–I–I'll die! Do you know many times I–I almost drowned! O–
or got chopped in half or burned alive…' He ran his hand over the
scar on his neck he'd been given as the wing of the FireHawk had
brushed past him. 'Maybe I'll just do myself in now!' he added sarcastically. 'Save somebody else the job!'

'No more o' your foolin', boy! We had a bargain…' came the creature's low growl through gritted teeth as she clutched the vessel. 'All
of it…'

'What do you want it for?' Krish was shouting now and he didn't
care who heard.

'Tha's my business!' the devil spat out. 'Half for me, half for not you!
For I! You'll go! Three more worlds then we's done!'

Krish was pacing about angrily. He stopped and stared back at that
disgusting little creature in its torn old robe cowering in the corner, a
fist clutching the golden vessel.

Krish exhaled heavily. 'What are these other worlds like then?'

'One at a time, boy,' the devil answered. 'One at a time.' She slanted
her head to one side, viewing Krish from a slightly different angle.
Her voice softened slightly as she spoke. 'I should've told you what
would happen to the Myrthali. From now on… no more lies.'

And Krish was surprised to see her extend a bony hand towards
him; open and inviting.

'I speak true now,' said the creature. 'I can't tell you all but what I
won't say is lies.'

After some hesitation, Krish took the devil's cold, leathery hand, no
more than a bunch of bones held together by her paper-like skin, and
shook it.

'I want some,' he said. 'Just a little. Please! My Mum, she—'

'No time will pass,' interrupted the devil. 'If we is quick us'll be
done in no time!'

'Please!' Krish pleaded with his eyes but the creature was unmoving.
He was beginning to see something different in her, though. There
was kindness in those eyes. But why wouldn't she give him at least a
handful?

The devil moved the conversation on.

'Yer did well, boy. Almost messed up yer little song on Brandhurst Hill.'

Krish eyed her curiously. 'You were watching?'

She gave a little smile.

'Just to be certain yer got on yer way okay. Peaceful up there. Likes the view.'

Krish didn't much really care for a view of the Lion's Hospice and the parade of shops on Singlewell Road.

'So, what's this new world I'm going to then?' he asked.

'Oooh! See, boy!' That mad glint had returned to her eye. 'Yer keen now! Keeeeeen!'

'Where?'

'Different world. Very different! A world under the light of the gas-stars.'

A crooked smile appeared on Krish's face, accompanied by a brief chuckle.

'All stars are made of gas,' he said, pleased for once that he'd paid attention in science.

That sly smile he was getting to know so well grinned back at him.

'Yer does not understand! Let me tell yer...'

CHAPTER 36

STORIES

Krish sank into bed that night. There's nothing quite like your own bed after a long time away from home. The mattress felt so soft against his back after months of sleeping on the hard ground, the root of a tree jutting into his spine, strange birds wheeling in strange skies as he tried to sleep while it was daylight all around.

Things in his life were not perfect right now but in this moment he felt strangely content. His Mum wasn't cured but she seemed so much better. Seeing her smile (and indeed hearing her swear) made him smile.

He'd made a friend. Such a good friend, and even if he never saw her again he was so glad that he'd ever met someone as amazing as Balthrir in the first place. He could never forget her. 'Stupid and boring', that's what he'd called wizards before. Wizards and jungles and spies and all those ridiculous things in stories.

Krish looked over to the book Jess had lent him months ago (which almost felt like years, now). He'd never even opened it. He browsed the pages. The book seemed to be all about wizards and kings and knights and all sorts making big speeches on mountains and rescuing princesses and stuff. He still wasn't too keen on books but he understood the appeal a little more now. The stories didn't make him feel the dirt on his face or the sting in his eyes or the feelings... all those dark fears and soaring sensations of joy. Nothing could compare to getting out there and experiencing it all for real. It was like watching a hockey match on the TV. It would just never compare to what it felt like actually being out on the pitch. But maybe if your imagination was strong enough you could picture it, some far-off place, and then maybe, even if the setting for the book wasn't real, you might find yourself inspired to get out and explore. Yes, maybe stories were okay if they got you up off the sofa and out of the house to see what real wonders were out there.

But he wasn't sure if the next place he would be visiting was going to be that full of 'wonders'. The devil's words, her description of the new world, echoed in his ears...

All stars made of gas, yes, but these stars... these stars POWERED by gas! Huge globes of glass, glowing yellow, covered in pipes! Billowin' gas! Floatin' around a world of steel! No skies! No clouds! All world in one huge, huge, HUGE metal box! All walls, no skies! Stars float around not far above the ground, watchin' over all, makin' everythin' stink from the fumes! No, boy... these stars different... And this time, the one you seek, the one what knows how you is gettin' the Myrthali, knows yer comin'...

He'd been afraid of leaving again but now he felt different. Krish had never been the confident type but now he knew what he was capable of. He smiled at the idea that nobody would know, as he sat there quietly in class, other kids making fun of him for being rubbish at maths or something, that he had dived into a pitch-black ocean, torn down a palace, had a king bow before him and fought fear itself.

His Mum's face kept coming back to him. The way she'd looked at him in the hospital. A warm but small, almost weak smile. She seemed afraid to blink, as if he might not be there any more by the time she opened her eyes again.

Mulling over his Mum's face made Krish feel happy and sad all at once. He tried to think of other things and his mind began to unwind and then, at last, he fell into the deepest sleep he'd had in a long time. The last thought to flicker through his brain as consciousness ebbed away from him was that he was ready. Ready to face the world of KnockThrice.

Acknowledgements

My Mum Jacqui Knighton for proofreading the very first and the very last draft as well as for support and encouragement throughout. Jake Martin for pulling out all the stops to shoot a great video for the Unbound promo. My brother Jack Bowsher for all his encouragement (he was the one to pledge a second time and get the book over the 100% line) and his wife / my sister-in-law Alex Bowsher, also for encouragement and telling me what the underside of an NHS hospital bed looked like.

Sam Melling, Sue Pagram and Alison Barron for proofreading the first full draft when the book was still called *The Time Thieves*. I have to single out Alan Mandel Butler and Samantha Neill-Paton for their in-depth feedback, which really helped me reshape some parts of the story. Hugh David, Sophia Chrisafis and Tim Berry also did a fair bit of proofreading for me early on which I really appreciate.

Helen McVittie who kept me going throughout the writing process. Much of her fire, her no-nonsense attitude and her determination went into Balthrir, the scene with the feather in chapter 24 in particular.

Lyall McCarthy for his amazing artwork and Mark Ecob for his adaptation of Lyall's work for the final cover.

My structural editor Craig (C M Taylor) whose feedback made me go a little mad and come up with four more chapters (it wasn't quite what he'd expected but we were both pretty pleased with the results!). Copy editor Helen Pisano, who was a real joy to work with, despite how brief it ended up being! Typesetter Andrew Chapman and proofreader Helen Angove.

Thanks for support throughout from Unbounders Georgia Odd, Phil Connor and Xander Cansell. But out of everyone at the Unbound camp I really must thank both Mathew Clayton and Kwaku Osei-Afrifa the most, for the simple reason that this book would not have been published without them. I pitched by tweet, Mathew responded and made sure that the book was considered. Kwaku was the man who sent me this email which made a dream come true:

Mark,

Been reading Time this afternoon. I'm a fan. Let's move with it?

K

I'd love to name all the Unbound authors who gave me so much advice, social media support and generally cheered me on... so I will. In no particular order: Karen Attwood, Stevyn Colgan, Michael Smith, Jessica Martin, Julie Warren, Maximilian Hawker, Virginia Moffatt, Alice Jolly, Lucy Sullivan, Sarah Marr, Owen Michael Johnson, Elaine Chambers, John Michael, Roman Krznaric, Abda Khan, Sabeena Akhtar, Nasrin Parvaz, Lucy Crehan, Adam Roberts, Gautam Malkani, Amy Kean, Ronnie Le Drew, Sheila Parry, Nii Ayikwei Parkes, Philip Womack, Wayne Garvie, Jillian Edelstein, Keith Tutt, Charles Fernyhough, Jane Hayward, Patrick Kincaid, Raz Shaw, Martin Cohen, Aidan McQuade, Beth McColl, Lev Parikian, Kerensa Jennings, Mary Horlock, Dave Dawson, Tom Cox, Damon Wakes, Tamsen Courtenay, Eli Allison, Ste Sharp, Wallis Eates, Andy Bush, Imola Unger, Patrick Wildgust, Judy Pascoe, Lucien Young, Ben Cameron, Happy BirthTime!, Hannah Wroblewski, Lily Dunn and Sarah Lee.

And finally, all the friends, family, colleagues, clients, random people I met on trains, in bookshops or on the intersplat who supported and encouraged me in so ways. You kept me going. Thank you!

If I've forgotten anyone it's because I'm an absent-minded, unappreciative berk.

Pronunciation

Ahava
Ahava-(like 'have' with the word 'a' at the beginning and end)
A-have-a

Althrain
Al-(like 'all')-thrain-(like 'pain')
All-thrain

Alvaris
Al-(like 'pal')-varis-(like 'paris')
Al-varis

Argyrhyr
Ar-(like 'far')-gyr-(like 'gear')-hyr-(like 'here')
Ar-gear-here

Baa-la
Baa-(like 'bar')-la
Bar-la

Bahrtakrit
Bahr-(like 'bar' but you can make the 'h' sound like you're about to spit it out)-tak-(like 'tack')-rit-(like 'bit')
Bahhhr-tack-rit

Balthrir
Bal-(like 'pal')-thrir-(like the start of 'through' with 'ear' added at the end)
Bal-threar

Benhu'in
Ben-(like the name)-hu-(like 'who')-in
Ben-who-in

Betsarhldeth
Bet-sarhl-(like 'snarl')-deth-(like 'Beth')
Bet-sarl-deth

Calcara
Cal-(like 'pal')-cara-(like 'para')
Cal-cara

Elwynt
El-(like 'smell')-wynt-(like the end of 'squint')
El-wint

Eshter
Eshter-(like the name 'Ester' with a 'sh' in the middle)
Esh-ter

Evia
Ev-(like the start of 'ever')-i-(like 'bee')-a
Ev-ee-a

Falkesh
Fal-(like 'pal')-kesh-(like 'mesh')
Fal-kesh

Faltura
Fal-(like 'pal')-tur-(like 'pure')-a
Fal-ture-a

Gilimed
Gil-(like a fish's 'gills')-i-(like 'bee')-med
Gil-ee-med

Goonmallinn
Goon-(like 'spoon')-mall-(like 'snarl')-inn
Goon-marl-in

Gulwin
Gul-(like the end of 'seagull')-win
Gull-win

Hri
Hri-(like 'free')
Hree

Ilir
Il-(like 'spill')-ir-(like 'ear')
Ill-ear

Jarhi
Jar-(like 'far')-hi-(like 'bee')
Jar-hee

Jashir
Jash-(like 'bash')-ir-(like 'ear')
Jash-ear

Kalrah
Kal-(like 'pal')-rah-(like a lion's 'raa!')
Kal-raa

Kalrika Mavalrh
Kal-(like 'pal')-rik-(like 'reek')-a Mav-(like 'have')-al-(like 'full')-rh-(like a lion's 'raa!')
Kal-reek-a Mav-ull-raa

Lal'Fryaill
Lal'-Fryaill-(like 'frail')
Lal-frail

Maiylyr
Maiyl-(like 'male')-yr-(like 'ear')
Male-ear

Malshrael
Mal-(like 'pal')-shrael-(like 'pale')
Mal-shrale

Marraghir
Marra-(like 'para')-ghir-(like 'gear')
Marra-gear

Mersha
Mer-(like 'fear')-sha
Mear-sha

Meslahir
Mes-(like 'mess')-la-hir-(like 'here')
Mess-la-here

Mikan
Mik-(like 'Mike')-an
Mike-an

Myrthali
Myr-(like 'fear')-thal-(like 'snarl')-i-(like 'bee')
Mear-tharl-ee

Nahbrin
Nah-(like 'bar')-brin
Nar-brin

Nboosa
N-(like the French number 'un' said from the back of the mouth, almost through closed lips)-boo-(like 'boo')-sa
Un-boo-sa

Obsendei
Ob-send-ei-(like 'eye')
Ob-send-eye

Oorarka
Oo-(like 'boo')-rark-(like 'dark')-a
Oo-rark-a

Palseferous
Pal-(like 'pull')-sef-(like 'deaf')-er-ous
Pull-seaf-er-ous

R'ghir
R'gh-(like 'rug' – roll the 'R')-ir-(like 'ear')
Rug-ear

Salvean
Sal-(like the start of 'Sally')-ve-(like 'bee')-an
Sal-vee-an

Sia
Si-(like 'sea')-a
Sea-a

Tyraah
Tyr-(like a 'tear' that you cry)-aah-(like relaxing in a nice warm bath)
Tear-aah

Ugethrid
U-(like 'you')-geth-(like 'Beth')-rid
You-geth-rid

Ullwihr
Ull-(like 'dull')-wihr-(like 'wire')
Ull-wire

Viona
Viona-(like the musical instrument 'viola' with an 'N' instead of an 'L')
Viona

Vira
Vi-(like the start of 'virus')-ra
Vi-ra

Vra'hool
Vra–(like 'spa')–hool–(like 'fool')
Vra-hool

Vulrein
Vul–(like 'dull')–rein–(like 'rain')
Vul-rain

Patrons

Jane & Roger Adams
Sarah Agha
Sabeena Akhtar
Wendy Aldiss
Lucy Anderson Jones
Tamsin Andrews
Karen Attwood
Florence Ayisi
James Aylett
Alexander Baines
Paul Bains
Janet Baldwin
Anthony Barnett
Alison Barron
James Benmore
Chloë Berry
Tim Berry
Sarah Bikhit
Mart Bira
Happy Birthtime!
Tim Blanchard
Darren Bloxham
Mark Bolsover
Julia Booth
Jeannie Borsch
Michael Botten
Sabrina Bowsher
Henry Bowsher
Jenson Bowsher
Hannah Brackstone-Brown
Sarah-Beth Bradley
Stuart Brian Mather

Lauren Brown
Alex Buckingham
Sophie Bulcraig
Ali Burns
Helen Busby
Marta Cabot Codina
John Carr
Benita Carter
Elaine Chambers
Jane Chappell
Georgia Clark
Jenny Clarke
Martin Cohen
James Cook
Heather Coombs
Ben Coombs
Gareth Corcoran
John Crawford
Lucy Crehan
Oriana Curls
Ella Daley
Edward Davey
Carl Davidson
Mitch Davison
Dave Dawson
Shakella Dedi
Victoria Denard
Emma Dickman
Philip Doyle
James Duffy
Wallis Eates
Jillian Edelstein
Georgina Edwards
Carolyn Edwins
Angela Ekaette Michaels
Amy Elizabeth

Sara Escriva
Gayle Evans
Gillie Fairbrother
Charles Fernyhough
Alice Field
James Flint
Bryony Forde
Adam Fransella
Stein Fussel
Megan Gragg
Elliot Grove
Mandi Harkett
Phil Harvey
Jane Harvey
Maximilian Hawker
Jane Hayward
Daniel Hitch
Callum Holmes
Sian Hoolahan
Mary Horlock
Marigold Hughes
Jacinta Hunter
Theo Ip
Jodie Jackson
Andrew James
Lisa Jenkins
Annie Jones
Amy Kean
Jamie Kennerley
Rory Kenny
Grace Ker
Abda Khan
Patrick Kincaid
Mark Kinsella
William Klarenbeek
Maik Kleinschmidt

Elysse Knighton-Holland
Roman Krznaric
Mit Lahiri
Emma Lane
Ronnie Le Drew
Marc Lebailly
Sarah Lebrecht
Sarah Lee
Darren Lee Sherry
Kit Leonard
Kim Lewis
Suyi Liangga
Filip Lipiecki
Elena Lopez-Brea Sanchez
Anya Lukover
Dan Mackey
Olivia Maiden
Alan Mandel Butler
Sarah K. Marr
Sheelagh Marshall
Eleanor May Clarke
Priscilla McBean
Lisa McGeoch
Kristina Micakova
Kaz Mills
Christopher Mills
Virginia Moffatt
Kyle Monk
Helen Mullane
Marc Munro Scott
Sandy Nairne
Manuel Nashi
Carlo Navato
Victoria Nixon
Xander Nolan
Joe Nutt

Rosie Owen
Amy Page
Gemma Paget
Sue Pagram
Nii Ayikwei Parkes
Isobel Payne
Jonathan Petherbridge
Johanna Pettersson
Théo Pierre Buchaillard-Davies
Hannah Plant
Iris Pokorny
Mary-Anne Pontikis
Louise Reid
Judy Reith
Laura, Rich & Rosie Rhee
Glenn Rice
Claire Richardson
Ian Ridley
Liam Riley
Adam Roberts
Kate Roberts
Jennifer Robins
Brandon Robshaw
Carina Roots
Rachel Rourke
Marta Rubio
Jo Sally
Jenny Schwarz
Yvonne Servante
Seema Shah
Mike Shanahan
Raz Shaw
Chris Sheryn
Burak Simsek
Rosemary Smith
Shaun Smith

Matt Smith
Shayna Soong
Anne Southgate
Sophie Sparham
Kirsty Stanley
Jean Stanton
Peter Stark
Sarah Steel
Andrew Stern
Nigel Strickland
Lucy Sullivan
Leila Talmadge
Lauren Tansey
Sarah Tattersall
Melanie Tebb
Andrew Tees
Laura Thompson
Helen Thompson
Annie Tremlett
Jackie Turley
Luca Uggias
Imola Unger
Cara Usher
Emma Walker
Thomas Walton
Katherine Ward
Hayley Whitehouse
Wolfgang Wild
Patrick Wildgust
James Wilkins
Jan Willem Dees
Derek Wilson
Philip Womack
Justin Woolhouse
Hannah Wroblewski
Catherine Wycherley

Lucien Young
Mathew Young
Victoria Zeißler